CHARLIE'S PROMISE

By

George Donald

For my friend - Gerry McGoldrick

Chapter 1 — Saturday night

The darkness of the alleyway hid the shame that sat frozen on Mary's face. Her left hand pressed back against the rough brick wall and her right hand straining, pushing against the chest of the man who stood over her. His cheap aftershave and the stale smell of whisky and cigarettes on his breath caused her to feel giddy and nauseous.

"Come on sweetheart, there's no need to be scared," he leered, his face just inches from her while he tried to force his lips against hers. Mary gagged and turned her head away, the man's bristle scraping against her soft cheek and he grew irritated. "We've got a deal here, love," he angrily reminded her, running his left hand down her side, his fingers grasping at the cheap material of her skirt and trying to drag it up. She tried to protest, tell him she'd made a mistake, but the words died in her throat. Fear overcame her resistance and she knew she was weakening as he continued to push harder against her, his aroused state now urging him on, pulling at her to come with him deeper into the darkened lane. He pushed hard against her, both hands now tugging at her skirt, the weight of his body forcing her backwards and pinning the slightly built Mary against the brick wall. The short skirt rode up and was now round her waist. She wanted to cry out, but no sound came, just a murmured plea for him to stop, that he ignored. She could taste her tears as they flowed down her cheek.

"See there now, nice and easy," the man attempted a smile, his eyes glazed as lust overcame him. She felt him pushing his groin against her, one hand reaching down, trying to undo his trouser zip as he continued to force her tightly against the wall with the other, his breath now coming in short, excited gasps. Suddenly he snarled, angry at her resistance and she saw him raise a hand to slap her. Mary panicked. A reckless instinct overcame her terror and she jerked hard with her knee, striking the man in the balls and pushing hard with both her hands at the same time. His eyes widened with surprise and then he gave a startled cough, slumped back, and then fell heavily to the wet cobblestones.

"Bitch!" he screamed, both hands now wrapped around his groin, but Mary was off, running as though the devil himself was after her. She slipped on and uneven cobblestone and cannoned off a wall, her left shoulder taking the brunt of the strike but her momentum carried her on and finally, gasping for air, she emerged into St Vincent Street, almost knocking down an elderly couple walking by. The old man was startled and the woman surprised, both turning their heads to see who was pursuing the young girl. But no one had followed Mary.

"Sorry," Mary wheezed, "so sorry," and spun away, running to her hiding place, her refuge, the only place she knew she would be safe.

*

Bobby Turner switched off the car lights and sat for a while, watching the end of his fag glisten in the dark. He thought about what he was to do. His attempt to coax a few extra drags from the cigarette betrayed his nervousness, an excuse to delay him getting out of the hired vehicle and heading for the place. He watched the people passing by his parked car, noisily excited and intent on enjoying their Saturday night partying in Glasgow city centre. The local Mecca for the young and brain dead, he sneered from the safety of his vehicle. He imagined himself in their place, having a few drinks and pulling some wee skirt, inwardly grinning that it wouldn't be hard, now that he had a couple of quid in his pocket. With a sigh, he checked his watch and exhaled, conscious that he was postponing the inevitable. He'd already accepted half the money and knew he was committed. He had done this kind of work before, but usually to some place that was nearly down, on its way out, but never to a working, viable business. His brow creased at the enormity of what he was about to do and reflected that this was serious stuff. Heavy time, if he got himself caught. Checking his rear view mirror, he adjusted his dark blue coloured baseball cap and with a quick glance about the vehicle, made sure nobody in the street looked like they were cops before he got out of the car. Locking the door he went to the boot and retrieved his old rucksack, now weighted down with the two-litre milk carton and his equipment. Shouldering the rucksack, he took a deep breath and quickly sauntered away to begin the five-minute walk. Head down and bag bouncing against his back, the container made quiet slopping noises as his training shoes beat a steady path towards Hope Street.

*

Mary, still shaking from her encounter with the man, slowed to a brisk walk and again looked behind her, relieved the drunk hadn't come after her. With a sob, she turned from Hope Street into the dark cobbled service lane, gingerly stepping between the cardboard boxes and rubbish discarded by the companies whose rear doors and garages backed into the dark of the narrow, common lane that run between the rear of the adjoining old, Victorian buildings. She stopped, held her breath and listened, but couldn't hear anything other than the traffic noises and muffled laughter from the well-lit street, thirty yards away. With a final glance around her, she crouched down and using both hands, carefully tore at a sheet of ragged corrugated tin that to any casual passer-by, would appear to be nailed to the brick wall. With a quiet squeak, one side came away, revealing the top of a rounded archway, just knee high and two foot wide. Turning, she crawled backwards into the space, pausing when her legs dropped, then feeling her feet touch the top of the wooden crate. Pulling at the tin, she dragged it back into place across the gap. The claustrophobic darkness caused her to gasp in panic, but she took a deep breath and forced herself to remain calm. With shaking hands, she reached forward to the makeshift shelf, groping gently with her fingers till she felt the waxy touch of the candle. With a start, she thought she'd missed the matches then found them, inches from her fingers. Hands still shaking, she struck a match and slightly gasped with relief when the fiery glow instantly lit up the darkness, bringing sanity to her terror. She held the candle close till her breathing returned to normal. She saw from the dim light that the small cellar like room seemed to be as she had left it and nothing had been disturbed. Carefully, she stepped from the wooden crate and bent low, lighting the other stubs of candles scattered about the room, then turned and pulled the dark sheet across the archway to prevent the pitiful light from casting its glow into the lane. She sat down wearily on the child size, brightly coloured sleeping bag, a present from the charity shop. Admittedly, the assistants were unaware they had donated it for the sleeping bag had left the shop under Mary's coat when the women weren't looking. Yet another sin to confess, she sighed. She glanced about her at her hiding place. Though she was unaware, her room had once been a storage cellar for one of the majestic homes above, but industrialisation and business ventures through the years had converted the tenement building from homes to offices and cellars to store rooms. Mary's small cellar had been of little use to the company currently occupying the offices above, for the access door to the corridor had long ago been bricked up and the archway to the lane sealed by a stout plywood door. The passage of time and neglect had rotted the wood that was replaced many years later by the sheet of corrugated tin that in turn through neglect, had rusted. But luckily for Mary, no one had thought to replace the tin and the rusting bolts holding the tin, providing the opportunely that now allowed her access to her hideaway, her sanctuary, her home. Still shivering with fear from her encounter, she huddled on top of the sleeping bag, grateful that though cold, the cellar was at least dry. Her shoulder ached from where she had banged it against the wall and she rubbed it hard, knowing there would be a bruise. She'd always bruised easily her mother was always telling her. Thoughts of home brought on the reality of her situation. Her lips quivered and tears escaped her eyes and rolled unchecked down her cheeks. Sitting upright, she wrapped her arms about her legs and rocked back and forward, silently weeping. Then she remembered. Reaching into the pocket of her cheap anorak, she pulled out the two ten-pound notes, crushed and grubby. The memory of her shame, the horror of what she had agreed to do with the man causing her to weep even more. A scraping noise reached her ears and instantly she was alert. With bated breath she listened, conscious that there was no way out of the cellar other than through the rusty tin that covered the entrance and into the lane. On previous evenings she had heard courting couples using the lane, their giggles and amorous words embarrassing her or drunks spilling out from the nearby pubs and urinating in the darkness. She held her breath and listened carefully, but heard no further sound. Rats, she thought with horror, her worst nightmare. She knew they were about. She had often seen them scurrying off with discarded food that lay about the streets, the weekend debris from the adjacent take-away restaurant, but thankfully had yet to see one near the cellar. Her breathing slowed and she relaxed, desperately tired and needing to sleep. She curled up on her side. Exhaustion and belated shock took their toll and soon her eyes drooped. Unconsciously tugging the sleeping bag about her shoulders Mary Cavendish drifted into a deep and much needed slumber.

*

Bobby Turner grasped the windowsill and silently swore as his rucksack scraped the wall. Left hand and left foot on the drainpipe and the right foot resting on a protruding piece of brickwork, he knew that any slip would result in him plummeting twenty foot to the cobbled lane below and no way could he avoid injuring himself. Desperately, fighting a sudden panic, he used his free hand to push at the bottom of the window frame. The sash window quietly slid upwards. Bobby pursed his lips and exhaled, sighing with relief. The bastard had told the truth and left the window unlocked, as he'd promised. Taking a deep breath, he pushed the window up further, creating enough space to enable him to fully grab hold of the ledge and scramble in through the window, his rucksack falling over his head and thumping heavily onto the linoleum floor. Finding himself in a narrow toilet with a WC and washbasin, he quickly reached into his jacket pocket and fetched a small but powerful torch, the lens covered with tape to cut the beam down to a pinprick. He picked up the rucksack from the floor and pulling on a pair of rubber kitchen gloves, carefully made his way into the main office. Acting on the man's instructions, Bobby made his way to the computer room that he had been told was situated off the main office to the left. Finding the room, he smiled with relief and breathed easier. So far, so good he grinned, a forced confidence to overcome his nervousness. The room wasn't large, the walls drawn in with wall-to-wall shelving on three sides of the room, each shelf loaded with cardboard files. In the centre stood two desks, standing slightly apart; one with a computer and monitor and upon the other desk was a commercial scanner and state of the art printing machine. Cables running between the two desks seemed to indicate the machines were linked. Networked, Bobby knew it was called. Several boxes of CD discs surrounded the desks and by the small beam of light he could see some with labels attached while others were stacked, awaiting data. Placing his rucksack on the floor, Bobby bent down and got to work. Putting the torch between his teeth like he'd seen the movie star Clint Eastwood do in a movie, he gagged and realised maybe that wasn't such a good idea. He placed the torch on the computer table, using a file to hold it steady. The small narrow beam lit the room with a ghostly hue, but gave off enough light to work by. Opening his rucksack, he extracted the plastic milk carton containing the petrol and a tin biscuit box with his equipment. The petrol carton was placed in a corner. No point in taking chances at this stage, he thought. The tin box produced a box of large, kitchen matches bound in PVC tape, with a six inch wax candle taped to the box. The bottom of the candles taper was pressed hard against the phosphorus heads of the matches in the box. The last item he retrieved was a condom. He smirked and thought I should have got extra large for this job. Carefully, he placed the matchbox on the floor beneath the computer desk and stacked two files on either side, ensuring that the matchbox would remain supported with the candle uppermost. With the condom in his hand, he unscrewed the top from the carton and manoeuvred the pliable condom over the top of the spout and then carefully tipped the carton sideways, allowing the condom to bulge as it half filled with petrol. Once satisfied, Bobby tied the neck of the condom in a knot and, using a drawing pin through the knot, pressed the pin to the underside of the computer desk, suspending the petrol filled condom two feet from the floor and directly above the candle. The remainder of the petrol Bobby splashed about the floor and nearby files, taking care to avoid splashing himself. Securing his rucksack, he checked about the room and ensured he hadn't missed anything, ignoring the now empty milk carton that lay upon the floor. From his pocket he brought out a cheap, plastic cigarette lighter. Bending down, one hand on the desk top to support himself he took a deep breath and flicked the lighter, the glow illuminating his face, now glistening with sweat. Anxiously holding his breath, he reached out and lit the candle, surprised to see that his hand shook ever so slightly. With a relieved sigh, he extinguished the lighter and returned it to his pocket, then quickly made his way back to the toilet. Bobby had tested the candle and condom method, but at that time filled with water only two days previously and figured he had between forty and sixty minutes before the rising heat melted the condom and dropped the petrol it contained onto the naked light. But Bobby was no fool. He was a professional, for he had devised a backup plan. If for any reason the ballooning condom didn't melt, the dwindling flame of the candle taper, attached to the match heads, would ignite them when the candle burned to a stub and create a surge of heat that must certainly explode the petrol filled condom hanging above it. And when the condom did melt, he knew the fireball that it created would in turn ignite the scattered petrol. No matter how it ignited, he grimly smiled, he'd be long gone and out if it. Listening for any sound and looking for movement in the lane below to ensure that no one was about, he slid his body over the windowsill and placed his feet onto the drainpipe, aware that getting down would be a hell of a lot easier than climbing up. His last act before descending was to pull the window closed after him. It wouldn't do, he thought, to have some nosey copper finding the window open. At least, not within the next hour or so, he grinned to himself. Gently, he lowered himself to the cobble stoned lane then, checking his watch, strolled swiftly to his car. Whistling to himself, he licked his lips in anticipation of the half dozen cans of lager in his fridge back at the flat.

In the cellar below the office from which Bobby Turner had just descended, Mary Cavendish slept soundly, a soft cough interrupting the gentle snore from her lips. The stubby candles around her stuttered as the wicks continued to give off their feeble light.

*

Constable Annie Vaughan looked at her watch for the umpteenth time, annoyed that the Sergeant had put her on the 2am refreshment break. Meandering slowly northwards on Hope Street, she ignored the wolf whistles from the drunken slobs exiting the club across the road. As she prepared to cross Hope Street towards the Central Railway station and a much needed cuppa with the British Transport cops, a sudden bang then the sound of breaking glass alerted her to a problem in the lane behind her. Hurrying back, Vaughan turned the corner into the lane and was taken aback to see flames billowing from a first floor window, shards of broken glass lying in the lane beneath. Shocked, she reached for her transmitter and gasped out the message.

"Alpha six seven, I have a fire in a first floor office block. Rear lane at Hope Street," then turned her head to identify a coordinating location, "near to St Vincent Street, over!"

The controller at her office had a direct line to the Fire Brigade and was soon informing her that both police and fire assistance was en-route.

"Can you pinpoint the premises to enable me to contact a key holder Annie, over?"

Vaughan hurriedly pushed past the rapidly assembling crowd of late evening revellers, some of whom cheered noisily, excited at the prospect of some action to round off their night.

"The premises are at 663 Hope Street, but there are about eight companies in the building," she reported, reading the brass plate directory at the door, "and nothing to identify whose office is on the first floor, over."

Within minutes, the sound of a two-tone horn and a flashing blue light heralded the arrival of a marked police car. Sergeant's Eddie Johnston and Pete McClure got out of their vehicle and immediately began to push the unruly crowd back from the entrance to the lane.

"Got a live one here then, Annie," smiled McClure as he stood illuminated with his back to the fire lit lane.

Vaughan, all thought of refreshment now gone from her head, sighed with quiet relief. Things were getting a bit out of hand before the arrival of her supervisors and she had even contemplated drawing her baton to keep the noisy bastards from getting into the lane, where the fire was now swirling out massive amounts of black smoke. Glass and debris continued to fall from the three, first floor windows. More sirens heralded the arrival of a further two marked police vehicles and the officers began cordoning off Hope Street and the adjacent junction with St Vincent Street. The noisy appearance of two fire engines produced loud applause from the crowd. Quickly, the station officer identified himself to Pete McClure, as his fire crews unrolled snake like hoses and began aiming jets of water into the blazing windows.

"'We're going to have to force the main door to get inside," the station officer shouted, trying to make himself heard above the noise of the diesel engines and catcalls of the crowd. "If you guys," he began, pointing at the police, "can deal with these bampots," indicating the crowd, "then we'll get on with our job."

McClure nodded his understanding. Relations between the police and fire brigade had been strained in the recent past, since two of the local fire personnel had been arrested after lifting some souvenirs from a jewellers shop. McClure knew a lot of ground would have to be covered before the two services would get back to the working relationship they had previously enjoyed. Christ knows, he thought sadly, we've got a few shifty characters in our mob without having to worry about the firemen.

The main door to the building that gave access to the stairs and premises was no match for the fire fighters axes and was soon crashed open. An automatic intruder alarm immediately sounded as the fire personnel, now wearing breathing apparatus and carrying hoses, warily entered the building. McClure turned and found his Inspector, Jimmy Morrison standing behind him.

"The one night I thought I was going to have time to do the two reports I'm behind with, then this," Morrison complained.

McClure smiled, reaching into his pocket for his cigarettes. Offering them to Morrison, he pointed to his young officer.

"Annie came across the fire about ten minutes ago. We haven't established whose company offices are ablaze, but the Brigade is in there now. It shouldn't be too long before they get the place damped down."

"CID?" queried Morrison, dragging the smoke deep into his lungs.

"Nothing yet to suggest it's criminal, boss. Besides, I heard earlier on that the nightshift CID is away to the casualty department at the Royal about an assault. If they're needed, I'll have them attend here.

The station officer approached and McClure introduced him to Morrison. Formally, the pair shook hands.

"Just got a call on my set," the station officer indicated the radio strapped to his jacket, "seems the seat of the fire is a law office and the place is reeking of petrol."

McClure looked at Morrison, anticipating his response.

"Right Inspector, a couple of detectives coming up," he grinned, pleased that any report would now be the province of the CID rather than the uniform.

*

The Glasgow Royal Infirmary located at the top of High Street is one of the busiest Accident and Emergency Wards in Scotland and as such, deals with a large variety of injuries. Saturday night, however, invariably finds the Ward dealing primarily with the victims of assault, ranging from domestic beatings to wounds inflicted by a range of weapons. The medical and nursing staff members who attend to these victims are themselves often subjected to abuse and violence and, through the years and circumstance, developed a working and trusting rapport with their local police. Detective Constables Jimmy Rae and Nicky Mullen were in the staff room having a well-deserved cup of tea when the Dragon Lady, or more formally the Casualty Ward Receptionist called through that Jimmy was wanted on the phone. Mullen smiled his condolence as Rae sighed and went through to the front desk, carefully avoiding the stares of the dozen or so walking wounded sitting in the foyer, all eagerly anticipating their name to be called and complaining amongst themselves about the time they'd spent awaiting treatment. He reached over the Dragon Lady's desk and grabbed the receiver, ignoring her lustful leer and tactfully avoiding the thrust of her thigh against his hip. She leaned against him and pushed a button on the consul, her halitosis breath whispering in his ear, "Here, lover boy, let me turn you on."

Rae smiled at her through gritted teeth while thinking, not in my wildest nightmare. That the Dragon Lady fancied him was plainly obvious, but a woman in her late fifties, caked with make-up and wearing ill-fitting dentures that gleamed yellowy against the slash of bright, red lipstick was definitely not what the thirty-year old detective wanted. No sir. Besides, it was common knowledge that the Dragon Lady had no distinct preference in me. The only requisite she had was that the man had a pulse.

"DC Rae," he wearily said into the phone.

"Jimmy? It's Alex at the control room here. Have you finished with that serious assault at the Royal, yet?"

Rae turned his eyes upwards. He and Mullen hadn't had a break since they started nightshift and this was undoubtedly another job coming their way. '"There will be no police action on that call, Alex," he reported formally, aware the Dragon Lady was all ears. "Stupid bugger," said Rae unkindly of the victim, "spent his wages at the pub and the bookies then went home to his loving wife, empty-handed. She's taken umbrage and smacked him on the back of the head with a frying pan. Opened up his skull, but he still loves her and won't make a complaint. And Nicky Mullen wonders why I'm still single," he laughed, then realised admitting his bachelorhood was a big mistake as the Dragon Lady's hand seemingly by accident stroked his thigh, a huge smile revealing her false teeth with a smudge of lipstick smeared on the upper set.

Rae gulped hard, then moving away from the desk as far as the telephone cable allowed, hurriedly telling Alex at the control room that he and Mullen would be down to the office in ten minutes.

"Don't bother calling in," Alex suggested, "just get yourselves over to Hope Street and meet with Pete McClure. There's a report of a wilful fire-raising and the Brigade are in attendance, have you got that?"

Rae acknowledged the call and backed off out of reach of the Dragon Lady. Hurriedly he fetched Mullen and the two made their past the assorted Saturday night wounded and out into the small car park to their unmarked vehicle.

*

Sergeant McClure greeted Rae and Mullen's arrival at the scene of the fire with relief. In short bursts, he summarised the situation and informed the detectives the

Fire Brigade had already damped down the scene and isolated the damaged area. The building was now declared safe and free from further combustion. With sinking heart, both Rae and Mullen knew that if they were to leave a full note of circumstances for the dayshift inquiry officers they would have to inspect the seat of the fire, first hand. Glumly, they looked at each other, knowing their tailored suits and leather shoes weren't designed for this kind of enquiry. As the detectives entered the darkened, smoke fumed building, they saw scenes of crime officers, distinguishable in their white overalls, already present and sifting through the watered down debris while fire officers rolled their hoses into neat bundles. Emergency lamps were being propped into place, the light producing a smoke laden, and ghostly aura. The station officer greeted the detectives and pointed to a room off the main office.

"That's where the seat of fire was set," he began. "You can still smell the petrol. Our forensic boys will take a closer look in the morning along with your guys, no doubt, but if you want my opinion?" He stopped and looked at the detectives, challenging them to disagree.

"You're the professional, sir," Rae said, knowing that a small deference to the man's rank wouldn't go amiss. The station officer nodded his head, eager to demonstrate his expertise.

"It's my opinion," he loftily began, "that the culprit has come in through that window," his arm indicating the hole in the wall where the window was once located "and poured the petrol around the floor. His problem was how to ignite the petrol without getting himself caught in the ensuing blaze."

Mullen reached for a notebook, hoping the pompous sod wouldn't make it too complicated.

"The culprit has probably used a makeshift timing device... ...."

"Like what?" asked Rae, his eyes betraying his curiosity and already smelling the smoke that permeated through the material of his suit.

The station officer obviously wasn't used to being interrupted and irritably continued, "a candle or matches. Anything that burned slowly to allow him time to scarper." Bending down, the fireman used a pencil to push at what seemed to be a blob of plastic. "This, I reckon, is what he used to carry the petrol in. Like most of these types, he probably believed the fire would consume the petrol but, as we know," grinning now and in full swing, determined to demonstrate his knowledge on the subject, "the smell lingers even though the fuel doesn't. And that, gentlemen, is the case for the prosecution," he boastfully concluded.

Rae smiled blandly at the station officer, ignoring the grins of the fire personnel standing behind their boss and formed the opinion that the stations officer's men didn't think much of their boss.

"Thanks for your input, sir and if you don't mind, I'll have my colleague note some details for our report," he said as the station officer turned away. "Nicky?" he grinned as he turned to Mullen who, caught with his notebook in hand, quietly hissed at Rae, "You bastard, Jimmy, leaving me with this clown. That's a definite pint you owe me."

At the other side of the room the station officer listened to a whispered report from one of his men, then put his hand out to stop Rae walking past him.
"I've just had word. There's something in a cellar below us, off the lane at the rear of the building that I think you should see.

Chapter 2 – Sunday morning

The noise of an early morning truck delivering goods to the shop below his flat filtered through the open window and woke Charlie Miller seconds before his alarm noisily burst into life with Clyde Radio belting out a Status Quo hit. Charlie groaned and reached with his left hand, groping for the off switch. His head hurt, but what's new he thought, and then accidentally sent the clock radio crashing to the floor. At least it's off, he sighed and, turning over onto his back, knew right away he'd made a big mistake. The bile rose in his throat. Breathing deeply, he clenched his teeth and relaxed his body, waiting for the habitual morning nausea to subside. Slowly, he twisted his body, then stretched his legs and placed his feet on the floor. Odd, he thought as he stared at his feet, I've still got one sock on. Pushing up from the mattress, he got unsteadily to his feet and stepped naked over his discarded clothes, then made his way to the bathroom and flicked on the shower, turning the water to tepid. Balancing against the window ledge, he peed what seemed to be a deep yellow stream of pure alcohol and was nauseated by the stink of his urine. Taking a deep breath, he stepped into the bath, allowing the water to run over him then realised he was still wearing the one sock. Lifting one foot, he tried to pull off the now soggy item and nearly toppled out of the bath. Sod it, he decided. Needed washed anyway. He stood for a few minutes under the running shower, allowing the water to ease the tension in his head. Holding onto the bar that held the hose, he upped the thermostat and used the sliver of soap that was remaining to lather his chin. Delicately, with great care and gritted teeth, he run the razor round his face, instinctively aware that his shaving was crap, that he'd nicked himself at least twice and making the daily promise to purchase new blades that wouldn't tear his sodden face open. That done he rinsed off and stepped out of the bath to the sink. He looked in the mirror and examined the angular face that stared back at him, now bleeding slightly from the chin and a small cut on the cheek under the left ear. His unruly thick hair, though still mostly dark brown, was greying at the temples and showed slivers of silver peeping through the pile. Bags under his watery brown eyes testified to both his irregular sleep pattern and recent fondness for the golden nectar. Pulling back his lips Charlie grinned. At least I've still got my own teeth and not a lot of forty year olds can boast that, he mused. Rapidly, he brushed his teeth and, for good measure, his furry tongue. Splashing aftershave on his face, he winced at the stinging pain as it seeped into his cuts. Finally, he drew a comb through his hair, unconsciously thinking it was time he had it cut. Satisfied with his ablutions, or as best he could be given the bloody state he was in, Charlie again stared into the mirror. He realised that though now groomed, the face that returned his smile was unable to mask the hung-dog look of sadness that lay beneath. Returning to his bedroom, he began dressing and searching in his wardrobe for a clean shirt, but discovered none there. Now wide-awake, albeit with a splitting headache, he lifted the dark blue shirt from the floor, smelled the armpit and decided it was better than nothing. From the sparse wardrobe, he grabbed a red tie from the floor, still loosely knotted with its half-nelson slipknot. Slipping the tie on over his head, he turned to inspect his six-foot frame in the full-length mirror. Admittedly, his trousers could do with an iron, but glancing at his watch he realised time was passing and made for the kitchen, grabbing his scuffed shoes from the bedside floor as he went. Charlie's kitchen wasn't so much a mess as a disaster zone. Dirty dishes, discarded grocery tins and empty packs littered the sink and worktop. With a sigh, he filled the kettle, mindful that if he didn't make the eight o'clock train, he'd be late again. Spooning coffee into a dirty mug, he ladled in three spoonfuls of sugar and two day old milk and squatting down instead of sitting at the small kitchen stool and risk toppling over, tied his shoes while the kettle boiled. His eyes were drawn to the whisky bottle, now lying on its side on the floor, a dribble of its contents remaining within. Charlie licked his lips. Maybe just a taste, to get the day started. With shaking hands he reached for the bottle and upended it, savouring the few drops that trickled onto his tongue. The kettle screamed its warning. Charlie filled the mug and tossed back three aspirin. Hell of a way to start the day, he thought. Checking his watch yet again, he sipped at his coffee, and then grabbed his jacket from the living room couch. Pulling closed and locking his front door behind him, Detective Sergeant Charlie Miller headed for work.

*

Chief Superintendent Chris Deacon sat behind his desk, waiting for the storm that he knew was about to descend on his office. The rap of knuckles on his door heralded the arrival of that storm. He took a deep breath.
"Come," he shouted. The door burst open and in strode, or rather waddled, the grim faced Detective Chief Inspector Nancy Rogers.
"Sir," she began "I must protest!"
"Good morning, Nancy. How was your evening?"
Without invite, Rogers sat down, her ample backside smothering the wooden chair that creaked as it took her weight.
"Cards on the table?" she asked.
Deacon sighed and shook his head.
"Not this time, Nancy. I've made my decision. And it stands. You know that he has the experience and ..."
"But he's a fucking drunk!" she cried. "For Gods sake, sir, think of the damage he'll cause if he's not supervised."
Deacon shuffled papers on his desk, regretting his decision to come in and tidy up his paperwork this fine and bright Sunday morning.
"Nancy, let me explain," he patiently began. "The division, must I remind you, is just getting back on it's feet after a protracted a murder enquiry that had you, as

the Senior Investigating Officer, out of general duties for almost two months. The Detective Inspector who assisted you is now detached to help the Procurator Fiscal compile the murder case and is re-interviewing witnesses, so he'll be gone for at least four weeks. Your other DI is laid up with a back complaint and your Detective Sergeant, who is acting up as temporary DI, is collating the violent, indecent assaults that have occurred with increasing regularity in the city centre for the last two years and now, due to a breakthrough with DNA evidence, seem likely to have been perpetrated by the same man. The Serious Crime Squad are mostly tied up with protection duties for the EURO Summit conference at Troon so," his face reddening and his voice rising to a crescendo as he stood up, hands slapping the top of the desk, "*WHO THE FUCK ELSE DO I HAVE TO DEAL WITH THIS, EH? TELL ME!*"

Her thin lips pressed tight together, Rogers shook her head, contrition on her face. "Sorry, boss, I wasn't thinking," then defiance overtook her again, "but you must realise that this will attract media attention. And we're going to have the homeless charities and the rest of the left wing namby-pamby crowd biting at our arses for a result."

Deacon fleetingly couldn't imagine anyone wishing to bit at the voluminous arse of Nancy Rogers and, calm now, replied "I've had a word with the Assistant Chief Constable (Crime) and he is well aware of the lack of resource situation we currently find ourselves in. It is his authority, Nancy, that is the final word and whether you or I like it or not, the decision stands. Now, I want you to conduct the briefing and also to make it clear that this matter is to be cleared up with the minimum of fuss. If there isn't any detection, so be it. But I want it settled without any problem. I'll not tolerate a fuck-up. Do I make myself clear on this issue, Detective Chief Inspector?"

"Crystal, sir."

*

Charlie Miller pushed through the back door of the Central police station at Cowcaddens. Made it, he inwardly gasped glancing at the old-fashioned wall clock in the CID general office, knowing his timekeeping would be the ideal opportunity for the bosses to sideline him into uniform. Privately he wondered how he had made it this far in CID since…since that time, was beyond his understanding. Shrugging off his coat, he draped it across his desk and walked to the tea tray that stood on the corner table, calling out "Good morning" to the only other occupant in the general office.

His colleague uncrossed her long legs and nodded her greeting to him. DC Carol McFarlane stared at Charlie's back and quietly shook her head. God he's a mess, she thought, suspecting he was wearing the same shirt as yesterday. And, her face contorted as she stared at him, is that bits of paper he has sticking to his face? "Coffee, Carol?" Charlie asked over his shoulder.

McFarlane shook her head. "No thanks, Charlie I've had my caffeine quota for this morning. Good night last night?"

Charlie shrugged his shoulders. "Quiet, as usual. Just the TV and me," he mumbled over his shoulder.

I'll bet, she thought, guessing that a bottle of whisky would make up the threesome in the Miller flat. It was then she remembered the message.

"The DCI is in and she wants to see you when you arrive."

Puzzled why Rogers would be spending her Sunday at the office, Charlie turned to face his colleague.

"Any idea why or didn't she say?"

"No idea," she replied, but knowing fine well it had to do with the fire through the night in Hope Street. Like everyone else in the CID office, Christ, probably the whole bloody Force, she knew that Charlie Miller wasn't given general enquiries any more. Not trusted to deal directly with the public, due to his drink problem. Why he remained in the CID was anybody's guess. Rumours abounded that hinted he had some boss by the short and curlies or that Charlie knew where literally, the bodies were buried. Others opined he had been a favourite of the Chief at one time. But the truth was that nobody really knew. McFarlane had once heard Charlie described as a hell of a detective, but in the two years she had been with the Central Division's CID, she hadn't any reason to believe that one. Now, if her guess was correct, Charlie Miller was going to catch himself an enquiry. And about bloody time too, she thought as she glanced at the heaped paperwork on her desk.

Setting his mug down on his desk, Charlie wearily climbed the stairs to the first floor and knocked on Nancy Rogers's door.

"Come in," was the curt command.

"Looking for me, ma'am?"

Scowling and still smarting from her meeting with Deacon, Rogers couldn't look at Charlie, but nodded for him to sit down.

"Last night," she began "a law office located within the building at 663 Hope Street was entered via a drainpipe at the rear and through a first floor window. Petrol and what seems to be a rather amateurish ignition device was used to set fire to a room within the office. By whom and why are not yet known. The resulting fire and smoke spread and regretfully a young female, who had apparently been living rough in a cellar below the office premises, was discovered to have succumbed to smoke inhalation and subsequently perished. At this time there is no evidence to suggest that she was the target for this crime. In short, it seems she was in the wrong place at the wrong time."

Pausing for breath, Rogers sat back and stared at the drunk in front of her. Unless she was mistaken, even from where she sat, she could smell whisky on his breath or sodden into his dishevelled clothing. Either way, Miller was a mess. A fucking disgrace, she inwardly bristled, not only to the CID, but to the police service as a whole. Taking a deep breath, she continued.

"Resources, as I'm sure you will be aware, are tight at the moment and after some deliberation it has been decided," but not by me, she sullenly thought, "that you will conduct the investigation. This is not a murder investigation, Detective Sergeant At best it is culpable homicide," and leaned forward to pass him a cardboard file. "In there you will find statements of the attending officers, both CID and uniform and also one from the Fire Brigade station officer. Scenes of crime are rushing the photographs through as a priority and forensic will result their findings as soon as possible. The key-holder for the premises did attend, but was too upset to provide more than cursory personal details that are also included in the file. The body has been removed to the mortuary and from the library card discovered on her, the deceased's address was confirmed and the next of kin is being informed, as we speak. Your remit is to establish in the shortest time possible, the identity of the culprit and report those circumstances to the Procurator Fiscal. The PF will then decide if a charge of culpable homicide will be libelled. In my opinion, this is a wilful fire-raising and the culprit probably didn't realise anyone was living under the office when he torched the place. Right then, any questions?"

Charlie blinked and then blinked again, not sure if the machine-gun summary was entirely understood by him. This was a joke, surely? Did he have any questions? Too fucking right he had questions!

"With respect ma'am, I would have thought this type of inquiry would best be served by a Detective Inspector as SIO. Plus, if the fire-raising has resulted in death, shouldn't we be talking a team effort, what with the number of inquiries that will have to be followed up?"

Rogers didn't respond right away, but stood and walked to the window. Turning, she stared at Charlie.

"Cards on the table?" she softly asked him.

Charlie slowly nodded, guessing this didn't sound promising.

"Personally, I wouldn't let you near this type of inquiry. Christ, Miller I don't even want you in my divisional CID," she spat at him, the vehemence in her voice startling him, "but I've been ordered to let you handle this inquiry and against my better judgement, that is what's going to happen." Rogers sat down and then leaned forward to emphasis her condemnation, her massive bosom almost covering her desk pad. "I think you are a drunk and incapable of doing your job. I heard you were good, once. At least, before personal problems took over your life. Well hear me out, Miller," she hissed at him, "I really don't give a shit about your personal problems and neither does the Force."

Folding her arms, but with difficulty due to her massive upper arms, she continued, her beady eyes boring into him. "You have got yourself an inquiry now and if you fuck this up, I will personally recommend your dismissal on anything that I can make stick. You draw a good wage and do little for it. You're a joke amongst your colleagues," then almost viciously, while staring at the stain on his tie. "Shit," she sneered "you can't even keep yourself tidy."

Charlie, white faced, was aghast. His leg shook beneath the desk. Not trusting himself to speak he stood, holding the chair for support. Drawing breath he lifted the file from the table and turned to the door then stopped. Slowly, he turned to face Rogers. An anecdote he'd once heard about the wartime Prime Minister, Winston Churchill, sprang to his mind.

"Cards on the table," he reminded Rogers, nodding his head, his breath coming in quick gasps. "Yes, you're right. I am a drunk and I might be a useless bastard as you so succinctly put it. But I can get sober, but you?" Charlie smiled without humour, "You'll always be a vicious, horrible cow."

*

Carol McFarlane watched a white faced Charlie return to the general office and walk to his desk. She knew he had one of the few desks in the office with a locking drawer and it was an open secret what Charlie kept in that drawer. Ignoring her, he flung the cardboard file on his desk and noisily wrestled the drawer open and removed a brown paper bag. He strode away towards the Gents toilet in the corridor adjacent to the rear office door that led to the outside yard. Carol exhaled noisily, praying Charlie wouldn't get so pissed she'd have to find an excuse to leave the office. Recalling the last time he had got drunk, she had to persuade a uniform mobile crew to get him home before the duty Inspector wandered through, as was his custom.

In the toilet, his hands shaking, Charlie snatched the stained tie from round his neck and flung it into a corner then tore the wrapper from the half bottle of Bells whisky and broke the seal on the top. With a sigh, he raised the bottle to his lips then stopped. The DCI's voice echoed in his head. A drunk, she had called him, a joke amongst his colleagues, she had sneered. He lowered the bottle to his side. A few droplets spilled over his trouser leg. Charlie faced his image in the cracked mirror and leaned forward, his forehead resting on the cool, white tiled wall. His body shook with anger and his throat felt tight as an outraged tear escaped his eye. He didn't realise that he was nodding his head, unconsciously agreeing with her, that she was right. So damn horribly correct. Charlie Miller is a drunk. He rested his hands on the enamel bowl of the sink and bowed his head. What had happened to him? Why had he become like this? His anger grew and his body shuddered with the tension of the last ten minutes. Almost three years since it happened and it seemed like yesterday. But that was no excuse; he should be over it by now. He stared again at the face in the mirror then took a deep breath. With an angry curse, he turned and hurled the bottle at the tiled wall behind him and watched it smash, the glass scattering like shrapnel and the whisky splashing about the floor. He gaped at the mess he had made, surprised and astonished that he had reacted so. A banging at the door made him turn as Carol McFarlane burst through.

"Are you alright, Charlie?" she asked, concern etched on her face. "I thought I heard…" then stopped, staring at the broken glass and spilled whisky.

"Have you had a wee accident, then?" she smiled, unsure what had gotten into him.

"No Carol," he replied "just a wee burst of common sense."

*

Constables Sadie Forrest and Javid Anwar both hated these calls. Delivering death messages to a nearest and dearest was the ultimate low in this job, they agreed. People reacted so differently when they were told. Most accepted the news quietly and painfully, retaining a modicum of dignity in their bereavement while others, as Javid recalled in one instance that had astonished the young cop, received the message with celebration.

"Have you got the name right?" Sadie inquired as she jabbed at the button to summon the lift.

Javid checked the information on the paper he'd torn from the printer. "Mary Cavendish, Flat 196, 67 Stevenson Street," Javid read, then looked at his neighbour with a frown on his face. "Sadie, the lassie was only fourteen," he gulped.

"And do you know what's worse than that, Javid?" Forrest asked, turning her head to look up through the little window in the sliding door.

He shook his head, puzzled.

"The lifts out of order and the house is on the nineteenth floor."

Almost fifteen minutes later, gasping and wheezing, the officers arrived at the nineteenth floor, cursing their equipment belt with its accessories and the bulky stab proof vests they were obliged to wear, but caused them to sweat buckets. Taking a few minutes to regain their composure, they made their way to flat 196 and saw a thin woman wearing a long black coat, about to lock the door. Startled, she turned at the approach of the uniformed police.

"Mrs Cavendish?" Sadie asked. The woman nodded in response, her face suddenly pale, one hand reaching for her throat and the other, Sadie saw, holding a black bound bible. "I'm Constable Forrest and this," she indicated towards Javid, "is Constable Anwar. Might we come in and have a wee word, do you think?" Gently now, Sadie thought, don't be rushing her.

Her eyes widened and her mouth gaped, but still the woman hadn't spoken. Her hands shaking, she stared speechlessly at the officers and replaced the key in the lock. As she made to step over the door, she faltered. Javid put a hand out to steady the woman, but she primly shrugged him off and shook herself, then led them into the lounge. Sadie glanced about her, noting the neat and orderly tidiness of the flat. A large framed print of Jesus Christ, His hands spread and His heart, surrounded by a glowing light shining in His chest, dominated the wall above the fireplace. Candles in red coloured glass candle-holders, burned on either side of the hearth and rosary beads hung suspended from cheap hooks screwed into the wall. A statuette of the Virgin Mary stood on a low table, atop a bleached white cloth. A heavy, bound bible lay on a low coffee table, its pages open and displaying a picture of angels assisting the body of Christ to ascend to heaven. Javid frowned and thought the religious artefacts were strangely at odds with the Irish republican mural on the opposite wall that displayed a gunman wearing a balaclava mask and brandishing an automatic rifle.

Bloody hell, thought Sadie, apart from the IRA poster, it's like being in the Glasgow Cathedral. Her thoughts were interrupted. The woman didn't ask them to sit, but pointedly looked at the wall clock and said, "I was just going to Mass. This will be about Mary?"

"You are Mrs Cavendish, Mary Cavendish's mother," Javid asked, wanting to get this right.

"I am," hand again unconsciously moving to her throat, her greying hair tied severely back in a bun and a silver crucifix hanging from a thin chain around her neck. Javid looked at Sadie, silently pleading for her to break the news and she inwardly sighed.

Men!

"I'm afraid I have very bad news to give you about your daughter Mary," Sadie slowly began, her mouth suddenly dry.

"You found her then, the little madam?" The words snapped out of Mrs Cavendish's mouth.

"I beg your pardon?" Sadie replied, confused at the woman's hostile attitude.

"What has she done to warrant you people coming to my home," she snapped at Sadie, "What trouble has she landed herself in?'" her pale face, devoid of make-up, head thrown back, chin jutting out and her eyes blazing, apparently anticipating that her daughter had been arrested.

Sadie looked at Javid. "I think there might have been a misunderstanding, Mrs Cavendish, you see ..."

"No!" she snapped, "no misunderstanding. She disappears for over a week and now you come to my door. I have never had this kind of problem. Never had you," standing now, "type of people come to my door" she spat the words out. "Well, if you have her, you can keep her!"

"Mrs Cavendish!" Sadie stood almost nose to nose with the angry woman, her hands in front of her, palms uppermost, her authoritive voice demanding calm. The woman stopped talking, her mouth gaped open, a sudden dawning in her eyes. She sat heavily down on the couch, afraid to speak further. Sadie remained standing and stared at the woman. "Mrs Cavendish," she repeated, softer now, "the news we have is the worst kind."

*

Later, as they left the flat and started their winding journey down the long flights of stairs, Sadie was mystified. Mrs Cavendish had taken the news more calmly than she'd expected, refusing their offer to summon a relative and ignoring the obligatory card they offered that provided bereavement contact numbers. Their instruction, scant though it was, had merely been to inform the mother of the death, advise her of the name of the contact officer in the case, a DS Miller working out of the Cowcaddens office and finally making a tentative arrangement for her to attend and identify the body at the mortuary. Curiously, Mrs Cavendish had laboriously noted all these details, making some comment about telling her brother. Ah well, Sadie thought. It takes all kinds. Still, she decided, might be worth giving the Detective Sergeant a phone call, just to warn him that the mother was a religious nut.

"Seems to be a good Catholic woman," commented Javid, thumping down the stairs.

"Aye, maybe," agreed Sadie, hat in hand, her lengthy fair hair woven into a plait and bouncing as she tried to keep pace with the younger officer, "but not, I suspect, a good Christian woman."

Charlie Miller drew keys for an unmarked car and as usual, disappeared again into the Gents. Making sure the stalls were empty, he fetched an old, outdated breathalyser kit from his coat pocket and tested himself. The result indicated he was just within the legal limit to drive. With a sigh, he got rid of the disposable tube and returned the kit to his pocket. Satisfied he wasn't going to get caught or at least not today, he drove the car through the deserted city to Hope Street and parked on the main road. With the file in his hand, he nodded to the young uniformed Constable on duty and ducked under the blue and white police tape. The brightness of the Sunday morning had just begun to penetrate the gloom of the lane, now filled with the debris from the fire in the office above and a fine ash, like a winter snow, covering everything that lay there. But first things first, he decided. Using a powerful torch, he climbed down the aluminium ladder left by the scenes of crime staff and into the cellar area. With a shudder, he tried to envisage the choking death of Mary Cavendish, aged fourteen years. A lump formed in his throat. Poor wee soul, he thought. According to the preliminary report he had read in the file, the note from the attending casualty doctor indicated the girl likely died in her sleep from smoke inhalation and had been completely unaware of the smoke filling this cramped, death trap. Taking a pad from the file, he quickly sketched a drawing of the cellar, counting off his footsteps to roughly measure the dimensions, knowing that his shoe size was the approximate equivalent of one foot in length.

Christ, he thought, I could use a drink, and then stopped, aghast at what he had considered. Standing there, in the room where a wee lassie had died, all he worried about was where his next drink was coming from. The snarling comment from Rogers, a joke amongst your colleagues, hit him again like a thunderbolt. Staring at where the wee girl died, Charlie's brow creased and he swallowed hard, making the decision that on this inquiry, he'd try not to be a joke.

He recalled the DCI's statement about the amateurish ignition device. Not so amateurish that it didn't work, he decided. Whoever set this fire knew what they were about and he guessed it probably wasn't the first time they had done so. Climbing out of the cellar, he examined the drainpipe the nightshift detectives, Rae and Mullen, had suggested was the route to the point of entry. Athletic bugger, he presumed the culprit to be and idly wondered why Rogers had decided the culprit was male? Pushing at the debris around him with his foot, he knew there was nothing to see and if the charred wooden frame and broken glass had offered any clues or hint of such then the forensic boys, he was certain, would have picked up on them.

Making his way to the front of the building and into the ornate Victorian entrance, he examined the front door and concluded the damage was, as he had read, consistent with the battering the Fire Brigade had inflicted when they entered the building. So far so good, he wryly thought. Continuing up the wide, Greco-marble stairway, he entered through a second set of broken doors into the offices of Taylor, Taylor, Frobisher and Partners (Solicitors) and saw before him a scene of utter devastation. The air reeked of smoke and dust mites danced visibly in the daylight, filtering through the gaping holes in the windowless walls. Two men wearing dust masks and with their backs to Charlie, were sifting through a number of charred box files, but stopped when he entered the room. The older man, in his late fifties Charlie guessed, with cropped grey hair, morning stubble and dressed in a casual sweater, grey flannel trousers and with a stoop from spending too many hours bent over a desk, slipped his mask down as he approached Charlie.

"May I help you?" he asked, attempting to rub the dirt from his hands.

"Detective Sergeant Miller," replied Charlie, producing his warrant card. "And you are?"

"Oh, I'm Steven Taylor, the senior partner," he announced in a quiet, cultured voice. Turning, he pointed to the second man, "and this is Thomas Frobisher, my associate and the other senior partner."

Frobisher came forward, pulling off his mask and a bright yellow, rubber glove from his right hand that he offered to Charlie. Charlie judged him to be about forty, hair slicked back with a pencil thin, military style moustache, a few inches shorter than Charlie and wearing a tight, blue boiler suit that revealed the start of a mid-life paunch. Charlie thought Frobisher had the look of a ladies man. When they shook hands, his grip was firm and strong.

"Nasty business this," said Taylor with a wave of his hand. "Can't think why this was done. I mean there's nothing here to steal. We don't keep cash on the premises and apart from the equipment there is nothing of any value. And as for that poor girl, oh dear," he ran a bony hand across his face, the knuckles large and symptomatic of the onslaught of arthritis. He sighed heavily. "And here I am worried about the office."

"I assume that you are the officer in charge of our arson inquiry so, do you have any clues, chum?" Frobisher's clipped voice interrupted Charlie's thoughts, his chin jutting forward and his posture smacking of authority, making it very clear he believed he was dealing with a subordinate.

Charlie had an inexplicable and inane desire to scream at Frobisher to 'Fuck off!' that if the police had any fucking idea they wouldn't have put a drunken halfwit like him on the case, but he bit his lip and, amazed at his own composure, calmly replied, "We're working on it, but regretfully haven't any real idea at this time who might be responsible."

With a tut, tut and a shake of his head, Frobisher drew him a look of contempt and returned to sorting out the box files, clearly dismissing Charlie's presence as nothing more than an inconvenience.

Taylor, appearing to be embarrassed by his partner's attitude, noisily cleared his throat and again asked how he could assist Charlie?

"Maybe you could walk me round the office, sir. You know, sort of orientate me as to the layout, where items were stored, that sort of thing. As I can see, the Brigade has moved everything in their effort to dampen down the blaze. Could we start at the seat of the fire, perhaps?"

"Of course," he replied, leading Charlie into the office that backed into lane, the hole in the wall where the window had been now streaming fresh air and sunlight into the room. Charlie saw blackened walls, pools of water from the Brigade hoses and the rectangles of tiles on the floor where the desks had been located and the fire had swept around them. The molten remains of computer and scanner equipment lay twisted and melted into ugly shapes. Nothing of value had survived; everything having been scorched or destroyed as a result of the intense heat.

"I presume we are standing above the cellar area?"

"That's right, the cellar where the poor girl was apparently staying. Of course, we had no idea. No idea at all she was there," Taylor said, his head nodding in sadness.

Tight-lipped, Charlie resisted the urge to smirk and thought typical bloody lawyer, the likelihood of litigation always in his mind.

"What was the function of the staff in this room?"

Taylor sighed, remembering he had resisted the change for as long and as best he could, but all to no avail.

"We, I should say that is Mr Frobisher, the partners and I, had recently discussed updating our filing system and it was finally agreed that all paper file would be transferred to, what do you call them, the round silver things? Sorry, I'm not at all computer minded," he lamely added, then smiled, "I find I get very confused if I don't use anything other than a pencil or pen."

With a straight face, Charlie suggested "CD discs?"

"Yes, yes, of course. That's right. Silver coloured… thingies. Anyway, we as a company were established some fifty years ago, by my father in fact," he said with a touch of pride, "so you may imagine that there was a large number of files that required to be transferred to the… thingies. In order to facilitate this, we recruited two girls who were, what do you call it, computer literate I think is the term, to carry out this work. I can provide their details, if you wish?"

"That would be useful, sir and all the other employee details, if you can."

"What, you need to speak with everyone? Dear me. Is that truly necessary?"

Charlie nodded his head, "Yes sir, everyone. But of course I won't keep them off their duties longer than necessary." He glanced about him. "How will you fare until this lot," waving his hand at the mess, "is sorted out? Do you have other premises to relocate to in the meantime?"

"We have a sub office in Paisley where we can transfer the day-to-day running of the business. But as you can see, the files that were stored in this room are completely destroyed."

"What sort of legal business do you conduct at this office?"

"The main thrust of our business is financial investment, ensuring our client's interests are legally protected and apprising them of tax and investment opportunities. Of course," he continued with a hint of snobbery, "most of our custom is obtained by word of mouth. We have a distinguished clientele and discretion is guaranteed at this firm."

"The files that were stored in this room were I assume being scanned by your staff and thereafter awaiting transfer to disc?"

"That's correct, Sergeant," said Frobisher from behind him, having entered the room while Charlie's back was turned. "Steven isn't yet comfortable with our approach to modern filing systems," he continued with a half smile, "but we are trying to bring the firm into the twenty-first century, isn't that right, Steven?" Taylor reluctantly nodded his head and Charlie harboured a notion that the real power in the firm now lay with Frobisher.

"Just a few more questions, sir," Charlie addressed Frobisher. "What were the files that were currently stored in this room, the ones that have been destroyed?"

"Historical stuff," Frobisher replied, his disinterest plainly obvious, "So why an arsonist would bother breaking in and setting fire to that lot is anyone's guess. There was nothing relevant to our day-to-day business, was there Steven?" Taylor shook his head, confirming Frobisher's statement.

Charlie thoughtfully stroked his chin. "So neither of you two gentlemen can offer any idea as to why this office was set on fire?"

Both shook their heads, Frobisher clearly bored and Taylor seemingly anxious to get on with the clear up. Charlie turned to leave then stopped and turned. "And of course this office doesn't deal with criminal work," he looked at Frobisher, who turned with a look of surprise.

"No, we don't touch criminal court work," he replied. "How did you know?" Charlie smiled, pleased to have caught the smug bastard out. "It's just that in Scotland we don't have such a crime as Arson. The crime is Wilful Fire Raising," and nodded his goodbyes before going down the stairs, mentally licking a finger and striking one up to him.

*

Irene Cavendish stood silently in the doorway of Mary's room and stared. The carefully made single bed with the print of Jesus Christ and His Apostles at the Last Supper pinned to the wall, above the headboard. The desk with the portable CD player and the rack of neatly arrayed CDs, the titles that Mary loved, Adele, Boyzone, Girls Aloud and others. None out of place, all tidily sorted in their respective plastic covers. The framed photograph of Irene with Mary, dressed in the white dress, hands together as though in prayer at the celebration of her First Communion. Wall posters that proclaimed her teenage adulation of the Irish pop group Westlife and Ronan Keating in particular. A Celtic Football Club scarf hung neatly over the back of the single wooden chair. With a sob, Irene turned and softly closed the door. Crying now, she stumbled to the lounge and threw herself onto the couch, the tears falling unchecked down her cheeks. Her body convulsed as she wept. A sudden thought struck her. Frank, her brother, he would know what to do. I must phone Frank. She reached out clumsily for the phone that rested on the table at the side of the couch, then drew a deep breath and dialled the number.

*

Seated at the dining table in his first floor flat, a tumbler with three fingers of Jamieson's at his elbow, the sudden ringing of the telephone startled Frank Brogan, who was trying desperately to concentrate on the figures he had written in the small ledger in front of him. With a scowl, he snatched at the receiver and shouted "What!" No one answered him. "Hello?" his eyes narrowed, suspicious of the silence. A sob burst through the earpiece. Stunned, he pressed the phone against his ear, uncertain of what he heard. "Hello?" he again asked.

"Frank?" the sound of crying. "It's me, Irene. You have to come up. Come quick. Something's happened," she cried with further cries and heaving sobs.

"Calm down Irene, calm down now. What's wrong? Are you all right?"
Bewildered, he tried to coax something from his distraught sister, some reason as to why she was in such a state.

"It's Mary, the police have been," she sobbed. "Mary's dead, Frank. Mary's dead."

*

Charlie Miller was about to drive off from Hope Street when the young cop on duty, lifting the police tape to allow him passage, raised his hand to flag him down.

"I've just had a radio message, Sarge. You've to phone a Constable Forrest at," consulting his notebook, "the Eastern Division. Sorry," he blushed "I didn't take the number."

Charlie smiled tolerantly at the Constable, aware there was no need to rebuke him and that he was embarrassed and unlikely to make that mistake again. "Thanks," he grinned then, as an afterthought, "when Mr Taylor, the older of the two men in there comes out," he flipped a thumb backwards over his shoulder to the building, "please remind him I'll need a staff contact list. Maybe you could collect it for me and leave it on my desk?" he suggested.

Eager to make up for his mistake, the officer willingly agreed and thought that the Sergeant seemed a decent type after all and nothing like the useless drunk whose name he had heard bandied about the muster room.

Charlie nodded his dismissal of the cop, switched off his engine and fetching a mobile phone from his jacket pocket, punched in the number of the Eastern police office, then asked for the extension of a Constable Forrest.

"PC Sadie Forrest, can I help you?" answered the polite voice.

"Hello, Charlie Miller here. Got a message to phone you?"

"Oh, thanks for calling back, Sergeant...."

"Please, Charlie," he interrupted.

"Right, well, it's about a death message my neighbour and I delivered earlier this morning to," there was a slight pause and he guessed she was searching through her notebook. "Ah yes, here it is. A Missus Irene Cavendish, about her daughter, Mary. To be honest Sarge, I mean Charlie. I feel a wee bit foolish, now that I've thought about it..."

"Go on," he encouraged her.

"Well," he heard her take a deep breath, "the thing is the mother was very calm and at first she thought her daughter was in trouble with us. Seems the lassie took off just over a week ago and hadn't been in touch since. The mother," said Sadie, suddenly acutely conscious of the Forces discrimination policies, "and please don't think I'm prejudiced or anything, but the mother is very Catholic. By that I mean…"

Charlie could hear her swallowing hard and interrupted her again. "Look Sadie, something has niggled at you so come right out with it. You won't be offending me, of that I can assure you," he smiled to himself.

"It's only my opinion, of course but I think the mother's religious convictions might have something to do with the girl leaving home. The house is decorated like the Sistine Chapel. There are pictures all over the walls, crucifixes and bibles and, believe it or not, an IRA poster on the wall in the front room as well. Don't ask me to explain that one," he heard her exhale, "and when I had a wee peek into the girl's bedroom it was just like most teenager's rooms. I think from what I saw she just seemed to be a normal wee lassie, but living under that kind of religious fervour," she didn't finish the sentence, preferring to leave the rest to Charlie's imagination.

"The only thing that I'd add is that I've had a chat with the divisional collator here and nothing is known about Mary Cavendish. She's never been recorded by us locally and you might be interested to know that curiously, she wasn't reported by her mother to be missing either. I'm not suggesting that the wee girl has been a total innocent, but nobody here's heard of her, unlike some of the kids in this area. I could go to the school tomorrow, if you like and make some discreet inquiry?"

Charlie thought about it and agreed, requesting that anything she turned up, friends, boyfriend, anything that seemed out of the ordinary to give him a call. His mind raced at the news that her mother hadn't reported her fourteen year old daughter as a missing person. Now that was very curious indeed.

"Did you make any arrangements about the mother viewing the body?" he asked.

"Aye, she took some notes. That, I definitely found odd. And she said she would have her brother accompany her. I didn't fix a time, I'm afraid, but kind of suggested if it was suitable, tomorrow morning might be appropriate? I figured you might want time to make some preliminary enquiries," she hazarded a guess. Charlie dug out his notebook and privately considered Sadie Forrest to be a smart cop.

"Didn't happen to get the mothers phone number?"

On the other end of the line, Sadie smiled to herself, pleased that she had remembered, and passed the details to Charlie.

"Excellent," he complimented her and then almost as an afterthought, added, "take my mobile number in case anything else comes to mind." Reading the digit's to her, he thanked her again.

"Oh, and one more thing," she recalled. "If you're going to visit Mrs Cavendish today, I don't think the council will have had their repair crew out, so take some climbing boots," then hung up, with a smile.

*

Frank Brogan sucked at the stub of the cigar as Liam McPhee drove the dark blue coloured Vauxhall Vectra into the car park at the bottom of the flats. Brogan looked around him at the devastation wreaked upon the landscape by the idle local youth. The shell of a burned out Ford Escort lay on its side. Glass littered the ground and the walls were covered in graffiti, sprayed with paint that proclaimed the locals allegiance to the IRA, Celtic and various teenage gangs that nightly roamed the Gallowgate housing estate. Brogan glanced upwards at high-rise flats were his sister lived, shuddering at the idea that anyone could reside in such a hellhole. Turning to McPhee, he said, "I don't know how long I'll be, Liam. Maybe you'll want to get off home for a bit. I'll give you a call when I need you." McPhee nodded then replied in his strong, Belfast brogue, "Give my condolences to Irene, won't you? Tell her, well, you'll know what to say," trusting Brogan to deliver the right sentiment.

Brogan nodded and opened the door, using the handle above the doorframe to pull his bulky body from the car. Standing upright, in his tight fitting dark blue suit, with white shirt and bottle green tie, Frank Brogan looked every inch the businessman. His perfectly groomed black, wavy hair, just over his ears, neatly trimmed dark beard and gold-rimmed glasses added to his appearance, a look that he cultivated to impress his subordinates and customers, as he liked to term them. Turning, he waved to McPhee then walked to the entrance door. The building concierge saw him approach and rushed to open the door. Neither of them took any notice of the dark green van that drove slowly past the entrance.

"Morning Frank," the old man almost bowed as he pulled the door open, his respect for Brogan evident. "Bad business," he added.

The word was out then, thought Brogan and quickly changed his smile to a grim face, in keeping with the sombre mood he believed was now appropriate. Apologetically, the concierge admitted the lift was out of order again and that Brogan would have to use the stairs. With an angry grunt, Brogan entered the stairwell and, with several rest breaks, slowly made his way to the nineteenth floor. Chest thumping and heart racing, he made his way to sister's door and found it slightly ajar. From within, he heard voices and his brow furrowed, wondering who would be visiting Irene at this time on a Sunday. As Brogan entered the hallway, his sister came rushing to meet him and threw her arms around his shoulders, sobbing into his chest. With a frown, he gently pushed her back, seeing with distaste that her tears had stained his lapel. A priest stood in the front room, his hands crossed in front of him. Brogan nodded his greeting over Irene's head. The priest acknowledged the greeting, but didn't speak.

Irene broke free from her brother. "You know Father Flynn?" she asked.

Again Brogan nodded and staring at the elderly, gray haired man recognised the old bastard who had downright rudely refused his offer of a donation to the parish funds.

"Good morning Father," he said, his voice quietly respectful. He knew it would be pointless offering his hand. The older man again nodded his head in acknowledgement, but without a smile and turning to Irene, said, "I'll leave you with your brother, my dear. No doubt there will be a lot of arrangements to make. You know where I will be if you need me for anything. Anything at all," he reiterated, while reaching out for her hands.

Clasping the priests hands to her breast, Irene attempted a smile. "Thanks for coming, Father. I'll see you to the door."

"No need," said the priest, manoeuvring his way past Brogan and completely ignoring him as he went to the front door.

"And sorry about the lift," Irene called after him as he waved over his shoulder. Brogan sat down on the armchair by the fireside.

"So tell me, Irene. What happened?"

Irene Cavendish sat on her couch and, twisting a handkerchief in her hands, slowly related what little she so far knew. The story of how her daughter Mary, aged just fourteen years, who had run away from home and died, alone and in the darkness of a dank cellar, beneath a building in Glasgow city centre.

*

In the car park at the bottom of the flats, the man in the dark green van picked at his teeth with a used matchstick, and then looked at his watch. He noticed the grey haired man leave the building, but his interest died when he saw the dog collar. With a sigh, he fetched a pencil from his jacket pocket and recorded the time in a notepad that lay on the passenger's seat.

*

Father Jim Flynn sat in the presbytery office, his hand shaking slightly as he nursed the heavy crystal cut glass. He thought about the girl, Mary Cavendish and their last meeting, her confession, tearful and repentant. He looked at the whisky and sighed. As a priest, he had often encountered the evil that drink revealed in men and, partial though he was to the odd glass now and then, didn't make a habit of it and particularly not on a Sunday afternoon when he had an evening Mass to celebrate. Irene Cavendish had taken the news badly, her guilt burdening her like a millstone round her neck. The old priest sipped at the strong liquid, a gift from a grateful parishioner whose husband had no further use for whisky in this life. His thoughts returned to Irene and her loss. Before long, she'd be wearing her grief like a badge of honour, receiving the comfort and sympathy from her fellow widows, those women who turned to the Church as a substitute husband, cleaning and polishing the brass and marble, trying to outdo each other in their attendance at Mass and their piety. He shook his head, aware that the effect of the whisky was slowly addling his senses. Frank Brogan's presence in the flat had infuriated the old priest. The smart suit and polished manner couldn't hide Brogan's true nature. As far as Jim Flynn was concerned, Frank Brogan was more than just a malevolent sinner, he was, he stopped, startled that he had almost come close to saying it. Gripping the glass tightly in his left hand, he instinctively made the Sign of the Cross with his right hand, unable to prevent the curse escaping his lips. Bastard!

*

Irene Cavendish replaced the receiver and turned to her brother.

"That was the detective. He's coming to see me at four o'clock, this afternoon. Will you wait?"

"Of course I will. I'll not be letting you face the police yourself. Remember, you've nothing to be ashamed of. It was Mary that ran away. God knows, you've done a grand job raising that girl and this is the thanks you get. Away and put the kettle on, now. I'll be giving Liam a phone, just to let him know when he can get me."

Irene beamed. Frank was her strength, her pillar at this dreadful time. With a nod, she got up and went into the kitchen to make her little brother a cup of tea. Yes, she thought as she busied herself with the cups, it was the Lord's blessing that she had Frank here with her, to sort things out.

In the lounge, Brogan dialled the number. "Liam? It's me. Listen, I'm going to be tied up for a while. There's a copper coming in to interview Irene. Yes, yes, I know. I want you to get your arse down to Flaherty's pub and collect the tins. There should be five and don't take any crap from him. He was down two tins last week. No, you listen to me," he hissed into the phone, "I'll tell you when I'm ready to be picked up," and slammed the phone down into its cradle. With a start, he realised Irene was standing at the kitchen door.

"Sorry about that love, but that Liam can be an old woman a time, eh?"

Irene nodded, puzzled. Wasn't Liam the best man that Frank had? And hadn't Liam been sent by them, God bless and keep them safe, to help Frank in his work? Oh well, she decided. If Frank sometimes gets annoyed, it will be because of the pressure he is under. After all, he makes a lot of money for them and didn't people round here know that? That Frank Brogan was the man trusted to do the job for them?

The doorbell chimed.

"I'll get it," said Brogan, pulling at the armrest to raise him from the seat.

Irene glanced in the wall mirror, stroking a loose hair into place and composed herself in expectation of her visitor.

Brogan returned a moment later, indicating with his hand for the tall man with dark hair and greying temples to follow him into the room. Irene saw the detective was wearing a shabby overcoat and no tie and his eyes betrayed his weakness for drink, something that Irene instantly recognised, for hadn't her Pat had the same fondness for the devils water?

"Good afternoon, Mrs Cavendish, I'm Detective Sergeant Miller. You were expecting me?"

Irene nodded and indicated the couch. "Please sit down, Sergeant. Would you like a cup of tea?"

She watched as the detective sat down and sat herself on the edge of the armchair, her knees primly pressed together under her long black skirt. Frank Brogan sat on the arm of the chair, a hand protectively resting on his sister's shoulder.

"No, thanks," Charlie responded to the offer of tea, "but first, let me offer my condolence on your loss...."

"Maybe you could explain exactly how the loss occurred?" Brogans voice dripped with sarcasm as he interrupted.

But Charlie wasn't going to be bullied by the likes of this twat, he decided, taking an instant dislike to the heavyset man. "I'm sorry sir, you are?"

"Frank's my brother," Irene hastily introduced him. "Frank Brogan, Mary's uncle. And of course he's very upset as I'm sure you will understand."

Ignoring Brogan, Charlie turned back to Irene and continued, "As I was saying, Mrs Cavendish, I'm very sorry for your loss. I know that at this time it must be painful speaking about this but, if you wish, I can give you what details I have at the moment?"

Irene nodded her consent, her hands working overtime trying to tear her handkerchief to pieces. Brogan sat brooding, content to let this copper bastard rattle on and curious at his dishevelled appearance.

"So far what has been established is that Mary had been living rough in a cellar, which was situated beneath a law office in a lane at the rear of Hope Street in the city centre. I understand from my colleagues who attended and spoke to you this morning that Mary had," carefully now, he thought, "been out of touch for over one week, is that correct?"

Irene looked down at the floor, and then slowly raised her head. She wasn't going to discuss her families business with this man. After all, her grief stricken anger overcame her, was it not her daughter that was dead? What right did this man have to come and pile the agony on her further?

"Mary took off without a word. After all the years I struggled and strived to bring her up decently, she left me without so much as a by your leave. Without a word," she spat out, her voice brittle. She stood with arms folded, then walked to the window and stared out from the great height, looking across at a city that seemed almost at peace, unlike her.

Charlie continued, recounting the theory that a person or persons unknown had broken into the law office and set it alight, the smoke seeping down into the cellar that hid Mary. He related that the doctor had said her death would have been mercifully quick, that Mary would probably have been asleep. Charlie didn't add that there was a strong likelihood she had awakened and slowly choked to death from both smoke inhalation and ingesting her own vomit.

Irene listened as he spoke, then turned and stared at him.

"Do you have children, Sergeant?"

Charlie swallowed hard and stared back into her eyes.

"A son, I had a son."

"Had? Where is he now then, with his mother?"

Charlie smiled softly, and then nodded. "Yes, he's with his mother."

"Then you will know how difficult children can be? How selfish and…" she almost said it, how cruel they can be, but the words faded and she choked back a sob, her hand reaching out for support from the armchair. Charlie and Brogan stood together, catching Irene before she fell. Gently, supporting an arm each, they helped her sit back into the chair. Brogan went into the kitchen to fetch a glass of water. Charlie sat back down, knowing there was nothing further that he could learn in this house. Mary Cavendish wasn't the target of the fire raiser, of that he was sure. There remained one final, awkward request.

"You will wish to see Mary and the question of identification has to be resolved, Mrs Cavendish. Do you think you would be able to meet me, say tomorrow morning at the city mortuary?"

Irene sipped at the water. "Can I bring my priest, Father Flynn? There are certain rites I would like to have conducted."

"Of course," agreed Charlie, standing now and eager to leave. "Would ten tomorrow morning be sufficient time for you to make the arrangements?"

"What about the undertaker," Brogan asked, his voice formal and without any hint of affability. "Can we go ahead and make those arrangements?"

Charlie shook his head, knowing he was about to inflict further distress. To Brogan, he said, "Perhaps you and I might discuss that further," he hinted, nodding slightly towards the door that led to the narrow hallway.

Brogan seemed puzzled, and then realisation dawned. "Of course," he replied, "I'll show you out."

Charlie nodded to Irene and followed Brogan out and into the corridor outside the front door. It was evident the man didn't like the police, Charlie guessed, but that wasn't unusual in this part of the city.

"You're going to cut her up, then?" Brogan asked.

Charlie took a deep breath. "That's not quite how I'd put it, but yes, there will be a post mortem examination. It's obligatory on the Procurator Fiscal in a case like this," then almost apologetically, "we have to prove how the lassie died."

Brogan nodded, but Charlie was confused. The man didn't seem particularly upset at the wee girl's death. Much later, when he thought about it, he was surprised to discover that he thought Brogan seemed almost relieved and gave rise to the question, had Mary Cavendish been such a burden on her mother?

"You'll accompany your sister then, to the mortuary?"

"Aye, I'll get her down there for tomorrow morning. Will there be anything else, then Sergeant?"

Charlie shook his head, as anxious to be gone from this man as he undoubtedly was for Charlie to leave. Without another word, Brogan turned and re-entered the flat. Charlie stared at the retreating back, then turned and began the long descent to his car.

Outside in the car park, the man in the dark green van saw Charlie exit from the front entrance of the high-rise flats and enter his unmarked police car. Curious, he decided to log the incident and noted the vehicle registration number. Someone on the dayshift tomorrow, he thought, can follow up this one up.

Chapter 3

Bobby Turner scanned the Sunday morning newspapers, eager for news of the fire and hoping it might feature in the stop press, but nothing. Disappointed, he threw the papers onto the kitchen table and switched on the kettle. Reaching over, he turned on the radio in time to catch the midday news bulletin. The local news began with a report of the fire in Hope Street in the city centre and Bobby smiled, then the smile froze on his face as the announcer continued that a young girl, whose name had not been released, had been a victim, a casualty of the fire. Victim, he thought. Does that mean she's dead?

Bobby was stunned. Young girl, the newscaster had said. What young girl, what the fuck did that mean? A sudden thought struck him. Had there been two fires, one set by him and another by someone else? No, he dismissed the thought. It couldn't be. They must be talking about his fire. But the place had been empty, that's what he had said. He had told Bobby the place would be empty, that it was Saturday night and had even scoffed when Bobby had asked, sneered even that nobody worked in a law office on a Saturday night! Jesus Christ, Bobby suddenly thought. I've killed someone. He sat down hard, his hands shaking. He swallowed frantically as the bile rose in his throat. I'm a fucking murderer!

*

Charlie drove from the high-rise flats to Police Headquarters. Parking the car on double yellow lines in Holland Street outside the side door that was the only entrance used during the weekend, he greeted the duty commissioners and headed to the fourth floor. The Scenes of Crime office was manned by an old friend, Jim Allan, whose lit cigarette hung from of the corner of his mouth in complete and flagrant disregard of the non-smoking ban enforced throughout the building.

"See you're still adhering to the regulations then," smiled Charlie.

Allan grinned, then stood and offered his nicotine-stained hand. At just over five foot tall and almost as wide, with more hair on his bushy eyebrows than his head, Allan had almost twenty years experience attending crime scenes and produced work that rated him highly by the investigating detectives, but caused defence lawyers untold grief, or more correctly, their unfortunate clients.

"Have the powers that be decided to let you out to play again then, you old duffer? I thought that you were permanently grounded?"

Charlie shook his head, acutely aware that his reputation as a drunk must be common knowledge among the headquarters staff. "Let's just say that they're scraping the barrel and found me under it."

"I hear that you've been handed the fire in Hope Street?"

Charlie nodded and asked, hopefully, "Was it yourself that did the photos?"

Allan turned and reached behind him for a brown envelope, sealed and imprinted with his department's confidential stamp.

"I was going to deliver these to your office," he began, and then with an embarrassed smile, "I didn't think you'd be driving, if you know what I mean."

Charlie did know what Allan meant. He had come close a few times in the recent past to losing his licence. Thank God for breath kit's, he thought, breathing a silent prayer. Tearing open the flap, he emptied the envelopes contents onto a glass-topped desk to examine the photographs within. The graphic details in the book of snapshots began with night time views of the building and lane, harshly outlined in the brightness of the emergency lighting that pushed back the ghostly hue of the smoke. As Charlie sifted through the images, he saw they followed a line of continuity, beginning with Allan's descent into the cellar and finally to the small, crumpled bundle of clothing that was Mary Cavendish. Allan stood behind him, quietly respectful of Charlie's concentration. One photograph showed the girl, now turned over and lying on her back, her eyes half open, mouth slightly ajar and small pink tongue protruding. A discoloured line of vomit trailed across her chin and down the front of her jacket. Charlie swallowed hard. He would never get used to seeing death in any form. He placed the photograph to one side and continued to sift through the others, stopping now and again to examine some detail through the powerful, desk magnifying glass. But they told him nothing. With a sigh, he turned and sat on the corner of the desk as he faced Allan. "What's the chance of a cup of tea, then?"

*

Liam McPhee pushed through the double swing doors of Flaherty's pub and nodded to the bouncer standing just within the entrance. The strains of an Irish republican song drifted through from the lounge as men stepped aside to allow McPhee to walk unhindered to the bar. An Irish Tri-colour flag hung limply above the gantry, surrounded by portrait's of republican Volunteers, killed in action or murdered by the Brit's, who criminally occupied the six counties. McPhee smiled to himself, thinking that this pub, safe in the haven of the predominantly Catholic Gallowgate area of Glasgow, was no different to the pubs he knew in the Ardoyne, the Falls or the Crumlin Road areas of Belfast. Without turning, he knew that people were staring and nudging each other, mindful of his presence. He revelled in their adoration, each desperate to get alongside and be seen in the company of this veteran of the IRA's war against the Brit's.
The young blonde haired barmaid, her milky white tit's bursting from the top of the low cut blouse, greeted him with a smile. "Anything I can do for you, Liam," she coyly asked, anxious for people to see that she was on familiar terms with McPhee.
"Is Hughie in?"
The barmaid nodded and flounced away towards the lounge, aware McPhee was watching her wiggling arse and returning with a small, balding man, his shirtsleeves rolled up, a permanent frown creasing his brow. "Good evening, Liam, you'll have a pint," while nodding at to the barmaid to go ahead and pull one. The barmaid bent low over the tap, grabbing at the old fashioned handle, confidant that McPhee would lean closer to watch her draw his pint and look down her cleavage.
McPhee licked his lips, excited by the young woman's obvious attempt to charm him. He dragged his eyes from her breasts and smiled at Hughie Mullen.
"Can we have a wee word in private Hughie?"
Mullen raised the hinged lid on the bar and with pint in hand, McPhee followed him through to a small, private room stacked with boxes of crisps and crates of bottled beer, at the rear of the bar.

"You'll have come about the tins?" Mullen began.

"Are they ready and I have to tell you, Frank's not a happy man, Hughie."

Mullen's face turned pale. "I don't know what his complaint is, I really don't," he whined. "I've contributed more to the Cause than any other publican in this fucking area. For nearly the whole of the fourteen years I've been running Flaherty's, I've donated four or five tins a week as well as my bar contribution. Does he think I'm fucking made of money?"

McPhee carefully placed his pint on the lid of a box then licked his lips and turning swiftly, seized the smaller man by the throat and slammed him against the wall, knocking over boxes of crisps as he did. Mullen grabbed at McPhee's hands, trying to ease the pressure of his throat, but to no avail.

"You forget Hughie that it's not Frank that's benefiting from the money you collect. It's the men behind the wire. It's their wives and children, you little shit," he hissed, spraying spittle onto Mullen's reddening face, his breath smelling of the beer he had just consumed. "You sit here in the safety of your pub, singing your fucking rebel songs and crying into your beer every time one of our Volunteers gets hit or caged, but you have no idea what it's like going up against those Brit bastards."

Mullen continued to wriggle in his grasp, now gasping for air.

"Please Liam, I didn't mean any offence," he bleated, his voice gurgling as he fought for breath, "it's just that…"

"Don't give me any of your excuses," interrupted McPhee. "When you took the oath, you joined for life. You swore that you'd help the Movement, that the Cause of uniting Ireland was our one, true goal. Well, Hughie me lad, there's no retiring from the Movement and peace fucking initiative or not, the fight goes on. And if that means you donating money so that some other poor fucker has to go out and do the business, then so be it. But rest assured, Hughie, you will continue to donate and regularly, do you understand?"

Hughie, now thoroughly terrified of this big bastard, nodded and slid to the floor as McPhee released his grip. The barmaid stood behind them.

"Everything all right here, Hughie?" she asked, flustered yet curiously a little breathless at the sight of McPhee standing over the smaller man.

McPhee leered at her. "Everything's fine my darling. Now, I've just a wee thing to collect from Hughie here, then how's about you and I stepping out for some lunch? That is," he stared at Mullen, "if Hughie here doesn't mind?"

Mullen, now thoroughly intimidated, stared at the large hulk that stood over him. "No, of course not," he stammered "I'll just get you those tins."

*

Bobby Turner pressed the buttons on the remote control, switched the television screen to text and sought the local area news headline. His mouth was dry from the vomit he had expelled and now he suddenly found himself in a waking nightmare from which he couldn't awaken. Please, please, please, he begged over and over. Let it be a mistake. But it was no mistake. There it was, in as much detail as the police were prepared to impart, at this time. He read as it scrolled at the bottom of the screen that a fourteen-year-old girl, whose name was not yet released, was overcome by smoke and died at the scene. Police were not providing anything other than scant detail, that the fire was deliberately started and that enquiry is continuing. Enquiry is continuing? What the fuck does that mean, he wondered? What do they know?

Suddenly, Bobby felt very vulnerable. Vulnerable because he was aware that one other person knew he was responsible for setting the fire, for killing the wee girl. And that also meant that the man was now Bobby's accomplice to a murder. Now, he thought, if the man was prepared to burn the place, what more would he do to protect himself against a murder charge? What would he do to protect himself, to ensure that Bobby kept his mouth shut? Christ! Bobby suddenly realised with a start, he knows where I live!

*

Frank Brogan, breathless from descending nineteen flights of stairs, nodded again to the concierge, but stopped for a patronising word. He knew that a short discussion with the old man would be repeated a hundred fold, exaggerated by him to enhance the old mans standing with his cronies and adding again to Brogan's reputation as a man of the people. Stepping into the bright sunshine of the November day, he punched the button of Liam's number on his mobile phone, only to be answered by the automatic messaging service. With an angry snort, he punched in the number of a local taxi service and lit a cigar, as he waited.

The man in the dark green van was puzzled. Brogan didn't seem to be a happy man, after his phone call. Not like McPhee to be late either, he mused. The man glanced at his watch. Once he'd seen Brogan off he was finished for the day. He didn't fancy a one-car tail in this heap of shite and besides, he had a report to type up when he got back to the office. A few minutes later, a local private hire taxi arrived and Brogan got in. When the taxi drove off, the man switched on the van's radio and, whistling off tune to the song being played, cheerfully drove out of the car park and back to his office.

*

Carefully, Charlie Miller inspected the items spread out on a long wooden table that Jim Allan had thought worthy of further examination and brought back to the scenes of crime laboratory. Two crumpled ten pound notes, stapled together in a clear plastic bag, according to the label, had been found in the dead girl's hand. Other items, including the library card that had identified Mary Cavendish, were individually itemised with the location of their discovery described on the attached labels and matched the numbered photographs taken at the scene. Unquestionably, the young girl had been a runaway. But why, he asked himself. He knew that the answer to that question was not central to his investigation, but for his own peace of mind, he'd dearly like to find out. Had life with her puritanical mother been so awful? Or had there been another reason, he wondered. With a sigh, he finished his tea and went looking for Allen. Finding the little man in the act of lighting up yet another illicit cigarette, he made arrangements for the items to be lodged at the Cowcaddens police station and requested the photographs of the fire scene be delivered, in book form, to him personally.

"Do you mind if I take this one with me?" he asked, holding up the print of Mary Cavendish lying on her back.

Allen was puzzled. He suspected that some detective officers were closet ghouls who enjoyed shocking their colleagues with ghastly photographs of cadavers and suchlike, but not Charlie Miller. It just wasn't his style. Charlie looked sheepish and slightly embarrassed, as he explained.

"I know it sounds crazy, Jim, but I need something to focus me on this inquiry. We both know that things haven't been right with me since, well, you know what I mean."

Allen did know. Hell, hadn't he been the one dispatched to take the photos? Patting him on the arm, he replied, "There's no need to explain, Charlie. Anything an old bugger like me can do, just call, okay?"

Charlie nodded and made his way back through the almost deserted building to the exit.

*

The man stopped the green van outside the garage roller shutter door and stared curiously at the unmarked police vehicle parked on the double yellow lines. Hurriedly, he checked his notes. Yes, he was right. The car was the same vehicle he had seen outside the high-rise flats. Now what the buggering hell is that doing here, he wondered? Getting out of the van, he walked to the entrance, just in time to open the door for the tall man in the shabby coat and no tie, who thanked him with a smile as he walked out of the building. And he saw that the tall man was wearing a police badge on a plastic chain, round his neck. Now, he thought, that's an interesting wee tit-bit to add to my report.

*

Charlie made one stop at an all-day grocer in Sauchiehall Street before driving back to the Cowcaddens station, arriving just as DC Carol McFarlane was coming out of the back door. She smiled at him, her feminine intuition sensing something different about Charlie, yet not quite able to put her finger on it.

"I gather from the rumour doing the rounds that you and the DCI had a bit of a set-to? You're the talk of the steamie," she grinned then added, her mouth downcast, "and ma'am wants to see you pronto."

Charlie grinned back and quipped, "Think it's my body she wants?"

Carol didn't reply, but secretly thought it couldn't be any worse than the one that DCI Rogers inhabited at the moment. As Charlie disappeared through the door, Carol got into her car and inserted the key in the ignition then stopped. That's what it is, she suddenly realised, smiling again. Charlie Miller. He's got a spring in his step.

*

Brown paper bag in hand, Charlie ignored the instruction to attend immediately at the DCI's office and headed for the divisional CCTV room. Like all the local coppers and most of the local criminal fraternity, knew that CCTV cameras, both fixed and roving were located at vantage points throughout the city centre, usually high on lampposts and on the sides of tall buildings. In common with most major cities throughout the land, the cameras monitored the main junctions and roads that bisected the square mile encompassing the commercial and social centre of Glasgow and operated by trained civilian personnel, working within the divisional control room.

The CCTV room was a cramped, cupboard like office, one wall stacked with DVD recording machines and the other wall hidden by metal shelving that bore hundreds of hand-written, labelled DVD's. The one small window was blacked out to protect the DVD's from direct sunlight. At the over laden desk sat a friendly and familiar face, the civilian supervisor Mickey Hughes, a former Traffic Department motorcyclist who retired prematurely when he left part of his lower right leg beneath the rear wheels of a heavy goods lorry. Mickey turned from the screen in front of him and greeted Charlie warmly. "How goes it Charlie? Still sinking a few down at the Ship Inn?"

Charlie inclined his head and smiled gently. Give a dog a bad name, he sighed. "I was wondering if you could do me a favour, Mickey. I've landed the fire in Hope Street, last night and need some help with pedestrian movement that was going about the street during the approximate time of the fire," he said, casually dropping the brown bag on Mickey's desk, that threatened to collapse under the extra weight of sugar coated doughnuts.

Mickey grinned. "Bribery, what else would I expect from the CID. Right," he shrugged his shoulders as he sat upright in the swivel chair, "so how can I help you?"

"I know it's a difficult task, but the estimated time the fire was set is between 11pm and 1am, this morning. How difficult would it be to trawl through the video footage of an area, say one block square, round about the junction of Hope Street and St Vincent Street, covering the entrances to the back lane at either end?"

Charlie held his breath, realising he was making a huge demand on Mickey's time. Mickey stood awkwardly and limped to stand in front of a large, coloured map that was pinned to the wall above the desk. Charlie could see the topography of the city centre and the area that was covered by the CCTV cameras, the cameras numbered in red ink, with a coded legend at the side of the map indicating the aspect each camera was capable of monitoring. He watched as Mickey traced his right forefinger on the map to the junction of Hope Street and St Vincent Street, and then jabbed at the red numbered cameras.

"I think were looking at probably three, maybe four cameras with an angle on the entrances to the lane. Of course," he sighed, "the recorded material is only as good as the operator that is on duty at the time. Let me see," Mickey turned towards a working shift chart, pinned to the back of the door. "We're in luck," he announced, "Gracie Fields was on the nightshift, so the material should be okay." It was common knowledge that John Fields enjoyed the familiarity of his nickname Gracie, bestowed partly due to his surname, but rather more because he was one of the more overtly gay civilian operators that worked in the control room. Charlie knew of the jokes that were bandied about Gracie, who accepted them with good humour. But nobody joked about Gracie's professionalism or commitment. An excellent CCTV operator, Gracie was recently commended at court when the evidence he recorded on camera was predominant in awarding lengthy sentences to a vicious team of right wing thugs that had been targeting the rent boys who nightly plied their twilight trade in the St Vincent Place area of the city centre.

Mickey returned to his desk and stiffly sat down, smiling as he did.

"The old leg acts up, now and again. Or, rather, where it used to be," he joked. "Now, about you request. At the moment I'm tasked to work on footage for Acting Detective Inspector Brown, who's dealing with the indecency inquiries so, how soon do you need your material? Oh, and bear in mind that I've no overtime budget just now."

Charlie grimaced. He knew he was putting Mickey on a spot. Time researching Charlie's footage would mean a bollocking for Mickey, if Brown discovered that Charlie had diverted the CCTV supervisor from the acting DI's enquiry.

"Yesterday would have been nice, but I'll leave it to your judgement.

Dismissing Charlie with a wave of his hand, Mickey turned to his screen. "Bugger off then and leave me to get on with this, but don't," he cautioned Charlie "even hint to Brown that I'm doing this or he'll have my arse in a sling. I'll give you a bell if I turn anything up."

With a nod of thanks, Charlie braced himself and decided it was about time he got upstairs and faced the wrath of ma'am.

Mickey knew the situation that Charlie was in. He liked the scruffy detective, not stuck up like some of them CID tosser's that waltzed in here, thinking every inquiry they investigated had primacy over the rest of Mickey's work. He sniffed and glanced down at the bag of doughnuts. As for that cheeky bugger of a DI, well, Brown didn't bring Mickey doughnuts, now did he? And curiously, he thought to himself, it had been a long time since Mickey had seen Charlie so animated about any enquiry.

*

Bobby Turner held onto the toilet bowl with both hands as his body heaved with the exertion of again vomiting into the bowl. The yellow mucous was all that remained in his stomach. With a shudder, he sat on the floor, his feet curled under him and his back against the bath, wiping his brow with the damp clot he held in his hand. He wasn't a killer. How the fuck, he wondered, did he get himself into this mess? With an effort he used the side of the bath to pull himself to his feet and stood holding the wash hand basin and then run the cold tap, splashing water onto his face. He looked at himself in the mirror. The pale and drawn face stared back. Bobby was frightened, frightened enough to realise that there was only one thing he could do. Get the fuck out of Glasgow before the man sent someone after him, someone like Bobby, who had torched the office for him, someone to do his dirty work for him. He swallowed hard and inwardly admitted what really scared him. Someone who would silence Bobby, permanently.

Charlie knocked on Rogers door, quietly determined that she would not provoke him.

"Come in," she called. Pushing open the door, he saw her sat whale like behind her desk with her hands clasped together, a thin smile betraying her confidence as she awaited the expected confrontation. Charlie saw that John Brown his fellow Detective Sergeant, but now assuming the role of Acting Detective Inspector, was seated in the corner, lips tightly pressed together and arms folded, his white knuckles revealing his tension. Brown, his face deadpan, slowly nodded a greeting to Charlie.

"Ma'am, you wished to see me?" then returned Browns nod.

Charlie didn't like John Brown and thought the slightly built, balding man a weasel, prepared to sell his soul at any opportunity for advancement in the police.

"Sit down Sergeant Miller. I'd like you to apprise me of your enquiry, so far," Rogers purred.

It's a set-up, Charlie realised, a chill running down his spine. In his quest for promotion, a half promise or inference of a good word and Brown would happily corroborate any charge of insubordination she might like to concoct against me, he guessed. But not today, he promised. Not today.

Reaching into his jacket pocket, Charlie brought out his notebook and dramatically licked the tip of his pencil. Puzzled, Rogers stared at him. "What are you doing?" she asked him.

"Simply preparing to take notes, ma'am," he innocently replied. "We both know that our last meeting was a tad fractious, so I thought I'd record all details of future meetings to ensure that there will be no doubt of what is discussed and said," he smiled at her.

Her face reddened, and then blazing with fury, she clenched her fists and snapped, "Just get on with your report, Sergeant. What developments have occurred in your inquiry?"

In short, concise sentences, Charlie related his day and, conscious of Brown's presence, prudently decided to omit his conversation with Mickey Hughes. He concluded his report with his intention to meet with the deceased girl's mother the following morning at the city mortuary.

Rogers lowered her head and seemingly took an interest in a sheet of paper on her desk. Without looking at Charlie, she barked "Get out."

Sliding his chair backwards, Charlie stood and turned towards the door, inwardly cursing himself for what he was about to say, just knowing he was really pushing it a tad too far. Adopting a look of naive innocence, he asked, "Will you require daily reports, ma'am?"

Rogers lifted her head and stared at him.

"You're pushing too far, Sergeant," she growled through clenched teeth.

Charlie smiled and almost said that's what went through his mind, but closed the door behind him. As he walked down the stairs to his office, he unconsciously tapped his fingers on the banister, pleased and relieved the bastard hadn't riled him as she so obviously had planned.

Irene Cavendish had given the matter lengthy thought. The bible lay open at the page she had sought, her fingers tracing the words she had read, over and over. Yes, it was clear. There in black and white, in the words of the Holy Book. There was, therefore, no question of the righteousness of what she intended, for hadn't God decreed it? She had never in her life harmed another living soul, but God knew the number of times she had felt the back of Patrick Cavendish's hand across her own face, his fist in her ribs and his boot on her when she lay on the floor.

As for her smacking Mary, well, that was different. A child had to learn and besides, she reasoned, a parent's chastisement was necessary to teach the child the road to righteousness, a warning against the evils that a corrupt society would tempt her with. After all, didn't the bible instruct that the parent was the first teacher? But no, she had never knowingly hurt Mary. The smacks on her child's behind that had become slaps on her teenage cheek served only to warn her daughter of the dangers of sin. Mary would have understood, as she grew older. Irene gulped hard, her throat tightening. If Mary had grown older, she corrected herself. She remembered Mary's anxious pleas to be permitted to wear make-up like her school friends and her strict forbiddance to such an idea. After all, she constantly had to remind Mary, she was only fourteen. Then followed the arguments, the weeping tantrums and, for peace sake, finally conceding that she might experiment with lipstick, but only in the privacy of her bedroom. Men were the threat, she had warned Mary, the cause of all women's heartache.

Almost overnight, she had seen her daughter grow from a small girl into a lovely and developed young woman with breasts and a woman's hips, becoming a visible temptation for wickedness.

Her shoulders hunched, Irene again read the passage.

Eye for an eye, tooth for a tooth.

She closed the bible and returned it with reverence to its place of honour on the coffee table, between the two small white, lit candles. Lips tight together, her face devoid of emotion, she dialled her brothers phone number. At the third ring, Frank Brogan answered, his gruff voice curt and sharp. She was surprised to find her own voice calm.

"Frank? It's me. No, no, I'm all right, honestly, I'm okay. Frank," she interrupted him "I want you to do something for me. I want you to find the man who set fire to the office that killed my Mary. Yes, yes I'm sure. I want the man found because," she paused and closed her eyes as the words from the bible seemed to fill her with resolve, "I want revenge."

Chapter 4 – Monday morning

The alarm kicked in loudly, at seven am. Charlie woke with a start, realising immediately something was wrong, something different. Confused, he sat up in bed. His mouth was dryer than a Welshman's humour, but no real early morning headache. At least nothing to worry about and certainly not as bad as anything he'd experienced these last couple of years. And, oddly, he was hungry. Rubbing his hands through his tousled hair, he reminded himself he needed it cut then swung his legs over the side of the bed. Almost in surprise, he saw the unholy mess that was his bedroom. Must get round to doing something about this place, he decided. But not today, today he had too much to do.

*

Bobby Turner hadn't slept well, hardly a wink at all in fact. He left his second floor flat early and called at the newsagents down the road in time for the early morning newspaper deliveries. The local tabloids headlines screamed at him. 'Runaway Girl Burned to Death' and 'Fire Claims Life of Missing Girl'. He stood in the shop and leaned with his back against the wall, his eyes tightly shut.
"Are you buying those, young Bobby? This isn't a public library, you know."
He opened his eyes. Mr Singh, his starched white turban reflected in the glass case behind him was standing at the counter, watching his youngest son serving three customers. It was common knowledge that Mr Singh didn't serve in the shop, merely stood and watched his family attend to the sales. That way, Mr Singh truthfully told the Employment Agency that he was unemployed and could lawfully and with a clear conscience draw his benefit every fortnight.
"Sorry, Mr Singh," Bobby replied, "I'm just not feeling myself today," handing over the coins for the newspaper.
Mr Singh smiled. He had known Bobby for most of his life and liked the lad. Never had trouble from Bobby, not like some of the toe-rags round the estate that delighted in shouting their filthy insults and painting their obscenities on the shop roller shutter door and the walls. He stepped away from the counter and placed his arm about Bobby's shoulders, his paternal instinct nagging him that something was troubling the younger man.
"Is there anything that I can do, my young friend? Or do you wish to come through and have a cup of tea and a wee chat?"
Bobby was startled at the sudden kindness and, for a brief second, almost took the old man up on his offer. He had to speak to someone, but to whom? Who could he trust with this desperate secret? With a sigh he shook his head. "No thanks, Mr Singh it's a personal matter. But if I do need to speak to someone, I might take you up on that offer later, if that's alright?"
Mr Singh continued to smile and squeezed Bobby's shoulder gently.
"Of course it is, my young friend, anytime."
Bobby left the shop and hurriedly strode back to the flat. A man across the street, dressed in jeans and a short, dark jacket, caught his eye. Bobby looked away, a sudden fear gripping him. Is that someone he has sent after me, he thought? With a shiver he realised he was being stupid, the onset of paranoia setting in. Still, it didn't do to take chances. With a backward glance, he was relieved to see the man across the street jump onto a bus. Bobby turned into the entrance to his building and stopped, just inside the dark and graffiti painted corridor. He listened intently, shivering slightly in the chilled atmosphere, but heard nothing. Sniggering at his

foolishness, he shook himself and whistled noisily as he made his way up the stairs, more with bravado than any attempt at music. Outside his front door, he heard his phone ringing. Scrambling in a pocket for his key and puzzled at receiving a call so early in the morning, he stopped and stood still. The phone continued to ring. With shaking fingers, he unlocked the front door and rushed to the kitchen. The wall phone suddenly stopped ringing. He reached for the receiver as it again burst into life. He stopped, his hand inches from grabbing it and stood motionless, listening as it rung for a few moments, and again stopped. His mouth dry, he licked his lips and quickly dialled the four recall digit's. The tinny voice of the recorded message declared the previous call details had been withheld. Bobby made to replace the receiver then decided that if he did so, the phone would continue to ring. But if he didn't replace the receiver, the caller would know from the engaged tone that Bobby was at home and where to find him. A sudden panic seized him and he ripped the cord from the wall, disconnecting the set. He stood back, holding the trailing wire, his breath rapid and his heart racing. Now the line could ring forever, but Bobby wouldn't hear it.

I'm losing it, he suddenly thought, a fine sheen of sweat glistening on his forehead.

In the front room, he drew back the curtain a few inches from the front window that overlooked the street. Using his sleeve, he rubbed a moist, streaked circle in the condensation of the window and peered down to the pavement below. He couldn't see anyone other than the usual few individuals in the estate who were fortunate enough to be employed and scurrying to their work. Bobby let the curtain fall and pulled them both fully closed. The darkened room seemed suddenly claustrophobic. He sat down and stared at the headlines again. He had been to prison, but never for anything like this. His past crimes had mostly been thievery and never violence. But this was more than just violence. This was murder.

Lowering his head into his shaking hands, he groaned loudly, the noise echoing in the cold and damp room. He couldn't remember ever being so alone, so helpless and unsure. His earlier decision to leave Glasgow had seemed easy and ever so simple. But that meant money and he still hadn't received full payment for, he hesitated as he thought about it, the job. But the man now had Bobby over a barrel, knowing what he had done. Would he still be willing to settle the final payment?

Lips compressed into a tight smile, Bobby had a sudden inspiration sparking a light at the end of his dark tunnel. Sure, he realised, the man knew what Bobby had done, but it was a two-way street, for he also had the man over a barrel. A thought swiftly struck him. He licked his lips, anticipating the man's reaction. This, he knew, could mean more money.

*

Martin Cairney's mother often boasted of her sons academic and sporting achievements, but even she had to accept he was not a handsome man. This was likely due to the fact that when the ex-rugby playing six foot five inch beast of a man had fallen from the ugly tree, he had hit every branch at least twice, on the way down, then rebounded on the ground and returned upwards for a second go. His broad nose, almost flat against his face, had once drawn comment from an admiring and, some unkindly said, extremely drunk female pursuer who had asked how he had come by such an injury? His response was now legend, having politely informed her that he had been breast fed till he was thirty.

However, Cairney's lack of physical attraction was more than compensated by his keen and analytic mind, an attribute that was quickly acknowledged by his senior officers and rewarded by promotion through the ranks in the Force's Counter Terrorism Unit.

This fine, dry Monday morning had begun as usual for Cairney with the crushing underground train ride into the city centre from his home on the outskirts of Glasgow. Now approaching his fortieth birthday, the Detective Chief Inspector had given in to his arthritic knees and settled for life behind a desk in command of the CT intelligence and operational teams that worked out of Police Headquarters. Arriving at his office, he hung his coat and unlocked his secure cabinet, retrieving the folder marked SECRET that contained the weekend reports. With a sigh, he switched on the electric kettle and sitting down, emptied the paperwork onto the top of his desk. Drawing the papers to him, he sifted through the sparse reports that represented the weekend work of his depleted staff, the bulk of whom were on seconded duty to the EURO Summit conference at the coastal town of Troon. The kettle whistled and he stood to fill his mug, spooning in a generous amount of decaf coffee. Balking at the taste and quietly cursing his cholesterol level, he chose a report from the only surveillance officer he had left within his skeleton staff. Scanning the text, he read the report again and sat back, puzzled. The author had suggested a possible link between Frank Brogan and an unidentified police officer seen arriving and departing the Stevenson Street high-rise flats, about the material time Brogan was visiting his sister at the same flats. Cairney knew the surveillance man well, that he was not given to flights of fancy.

It'll do no harm to have it checked it, he decided. He reached for his phone and pressed an internal number.

"Cathy? Can you step into my office, please? I've a wee job for you."

*

Charlie Miller, dark suit ironed that morning, shoes polished, clean light blue shirt and navy blue tie, arrived at Cowcaddens police office thirty minutes before the start of his shift. As he entered the CID general office, the conversations of the dozen or so detectives died to a whisper as they turned and stared at Charlie. Conscious of their stares, Charlie strode to his desk, ignoring eye contact and wondering if his trouser flies were open.

Alan Boyle, one of the senior Detective Constables stood by the tea tray and called out, "Coffee, Charlie?"

"Please and two sugar," he replied.

"And will you want vicious, horrible cow milk with that?" Boyle asked, his face a picture of innocence.

The office erupted in laughter as his colleagues crowded round Charlie, some slapping his back and others edging closer, anxious for a recount of his meeting with DCI Rogers.

Charlie grinned at their sudden burst of camaraderie and put his hands up.

"Back off, ladies and gentlemen, nothing to tell," he smiled and wondered who the hell had been listening, then realising that anyone within fifty yards must have heard him and Rogers having a go at each other. Nobody like the polis could gossip, he knew. The crowd drifted back to their desks as Charlie opened an orange, internal envelope and found the young beat cop from the fire scene, good as his word, had delivered the typed list of employees of Taylor, Taylor, Frobisher and Partners (Solicitors). He scanned the twenty or so names, but none of them meant anything to him. The corridor door opened and acting DI John Brown entered the room.

The detectives shuffled paperwork at their desks and the cheery conversations lulled to an uncomfortable silence. It was common knowledge that Brown fed his colleagues chit-chat and slander directly to Rogers.

Charlie saw the detectives, almost as one, turn their backs and noted their downcast eyes. He hadn't previously appreciated how disliked the man was and likely, he wryly admitted, because the drink had kept him in a befuddled cuckoo land half the time.

"Morning Charlie," greeted Brown, "any chance of a quiet word?"

Charlie nodded to the gent's toilet at the back door, jokingly referred to as the Truth Room.

Once inside the toilet, Brown closed the door behind him and made a cursory check of the cubicles. It was on the tip of Charlie's tongue to suggest Brown had a look for microphones, but knew that he was such a crawling bastard that the sarcasm likely wouldn't penetrate his thick skin.

"I just want to make it clear," Brown began "that I wanted no part of that meeting yesterday."

"Then why did you agree to be there?"

"You know how she is, Charlie," he complained, the whine in his voice grating on Charlie, "I'm not in a position to refuse a direct order. Besides, this acting rank might be made substantive, if I clear up the indecency inquiry."

Charlie shook his head, looked Brown in the eye and took a deep breath.

"Let me make this quite clear to you in syllables you will understand," he began. "I think you are a whingeing, backstabbing prick. I wouldn't trust you as far as I could throw you. In fact, if you told me today was Monday I'd check the fucking calendar. Now, if you have nothing else to tell me, get the fuck out of my face."

Brown stared at him, taken aback and shocked at Charlie's outburst.

"You can't speak to me like that, Sergeant Miller," Brown eventually hissed through clenched teeth, malevolence now clearly etched on his chalk white face.

Charlie smiled. "It's Detective Sergeant," he emphasised the words, "something you'll never really be, will you John?" then strode from the room.

Carol McFarlane was standing by his desk.

"Mickey Hughes is looking for you, says it's urgent," her curiosity as strong as the perfume she liberally sprayed about her neck. Or is it I can smell better this morning, he wondered?

"Thanks Carol. And do me a favour will you," he held out the law company's employees list to her. "Have these names checked out on the computer in the control room and see if any come up for anything, anything at all."

McFarlane flushed with embarrassment, her hands dropping by her side.

"DCI Rogers was in early this morning," she hastily whispered, "Told us that you had the fire raising and that we had our own work to do. She made it very clear, without actually saying so, that you were on your own with this one, Charlie. Sorry."

Charlie nodded, too angry to speak.

The office waited, ear wigging McFarlane's explanation and anticipating an explosion of rage, but Charlie just smiled and dropped the list onto his desk.

"Forget it Carol. It's not your fault."

A hand came from behind him and lifted the list. He turned to find Alan Boyle standing behind him, coffee mug in hand and specs perched jauntily on the end of nose, staring at the list.

"I've a wee trip to take to headquarters later about an inquiry in the indecency case."

He looked up and smiled at Charlie, a new respect in his face. "Think I'll drop this in to a pal of mine at the records office and have the names checked against sex offenders. Oh, look," he pretended shock. "Some of these names are birds! Well, I never. Won't do any harm to find out if the police know any of them, eh Charlie? What do you think?"

Charlie smiled. "Just don't get into bother with Rogers," he warned, pleased that Boyle was taking a stance against the DCI's unreasonable and vindictive instruction.

"Charlie," Boyle replied "no matter what I do, I'll never get into as much trouble with the bastard as you are in," he replied, shaking his head as he walked away and chuckling to himself, "Horrible, ugly cow."

*

Cathy Mulgrew, affectionately known to her colleagues as Mucky Mulgrew, belied her nickname. At almost five foot ten inches tall, she was sleek, slender and the fantasy of more than a few of her male colleagues. With her long copper-red hair, now tied back in a business like pony-tail, face devoid of but the barest touch of make-up and wearing a pinstripe bottle green trouser suit, she could easily be mistaken for an executive of one of Glasgow's city centre companies, rather than her true profession, a Detective Sergeant in the Intelligence Department of Counter Terrorism Unit. Six of Cathy's fourteen years in the police had been with the CTU. Smart and ambitious, but now nearing her thirty five birthday, she had recently considered that a return to uniform would enhance her career development and ultimately lead to further promotion. But, like many officers in police specialised departments, Cathy had become a victim of her own success. Her bosses rated her highly and considered her to be almost indispensable. In charge of the small group of officers, or Desk in police parlance, that monitored support for the outlawed Provisional IRA in the west of Scotland, Cathy knew that she was well regarded by her bosses. Nevertheless, she realised that continuous service with the CTU might preclude her from immediate future promotion and her annual assessments had already indicated their reluctance to permit such a tenacious and knowledgeable officers return to uniform beat duties. Today, she grimly decided, Cathy intended forcing the issue with Martin Cairney and was surprised when he pre-empted her by calling her into his office.

"Sit down, Cathy. Coffee?" he asked.

Cathy recalled with a shudder the particular brand Cairney used.

"No thanks, boss. How was your weekend?"

"Same old, same old," Cairney sighed. "Janice is back from University for the winter break, so her mother took the opportunity to drag us both about the shops in town to buy her good, sensible shoes. I ask you," he complained, "Do you know the cost of shoes today? And you should have seen the ones she chose. My God, the heels must have been eight inches high! Sensible shoes indeed," he moaned, to Cathy's soft laughter. "Anyway, that's not why I've called you in. Here, read that," he instructed, handing her the surveillance officers report.

She quickly read through the report and looked up, knowing that Cairney would be awaiting her reaction.

He sat alternating between drumming his thick fingers on the desk and sipping at his scalding coffee. Seeing Cathy had finished reading, he lifted a notepad and read his scrawled notes.

"A discreet check has revealed that as indeed suspected, the vehicle is a police fleet car and used by the Cowcaddens CID. I've spoken to the DCI there, Nancy Rogers," and was surprised to see Cathy flinch at the name, then asked, "You know her?"

Cathy nodded, the memory of a lazy, foul-mouthed training instructor flashing into her mind.

"She was a Sergeant instructor on the CID course at the police college. I have to admit I wasn't impressed by her," she confided then stopped, remembering she was discussing a senior officer with a fellow DCI.

Cairney nodded his head in apparent understanding.

"I only had a brief phone call with her," he admitted "but she came across as a real strange one. Anyway, to continue," he settled back in his chair. "It seems that Frank Brogan's niece was the wee lassie that the papers are describing as a runaway, the girl that died in the weekend fire in the city?"

Cathy nodded her head, having read the story on the train while travelling into work.

Cairney leaned forward, resting his elbows on his desk.

"The investigating officer, according to your friend DCI Rogers," he wickedly grinned, "is a Detective Sergeant Miller. By all accounts and if Rogers is to be believed, Miller is a hopeless case, drunk half the time and a total incompetent. He's landed the inquiry simply because the divisional CID, like us, is stretched to the limit with this EURO Summit and there was no other suitable rank to deal with it."

Cathy grimaced, half-guessing where this was going.

"The thing is Cathy that any police related inquiry that concerns friend Brogan must involve us. Normally I wouldn't dream of having a desk bound officer deal with an operational matter, but," he placed his hands out, palms upwards, "the lack of resources means I have no other option."

"So what exactly do you have in mind, boss?" she asked, resigned to the fact there was no getting out of this assignment.

Cairney smiled, pleased Cathy wasn't going to be difficult about this.

"I intend having you, shall we call it, temporarily seconded to the Cowcaddens CID to work with this guy Miller. Stick close to him. We must presume that there is a real likelihood he will be dealing directly with Brogan and anything we can glean in the way of intelligence will be of value. You might also be interested to know that our cousins in London," he used the nickname that referred to the Security Service, immortalised in the public mind as MI5, "have already been in touch. It seems they are aware of Miller's interest in Brogan."

He raised his hands to stifle Cathy's question.

"Don't ask me how they know. I haven't a clue and the buggers aren't telling, either."

Cathy didn't interrupt, but could see Cairney was clearly puzzled and slightly miffed by the Security Service's advanced knowledge of the situation. She listened intently as he continued.

"Miller, we must presume has no knowledge of Brogan's Provisional IRA connections. However, it may become clear to him, through the course of his investigation that something about friend Brogan is amiss. Your remit Cathy is to neighbour Miller, shadow him as it were, learn what you can about Brogan and any associates and," he leaned forward in a conspiratorial manner, "I'd be very interested to know just how the Security Service have such up to the minute information about what is going on in *my* area."

Cathy contemplated her task, all thought of seeking a transfer gone from her head. Miller, she decided has to be the fly in the ointment. Yet, she admitted, she was strangely excited by the prospect of getting out from behind her desk. Getting a little of the action, as her colleagues would say. It had been some time since she had had the opportunity to practise her detective skills.

"How much do I tell Miller?" she asked.

"As little as possible and just enough to get him on board," Cairney thoughtfully decided.

She stood and returned the report to Cairney.

"Right, I'll get on with it. You realise that with me gone, your staff shortage will be even more pronounced. I won't be able to cover the Desk and deal with this task."

"That won't be a problem. We'll manage somehow," he smiled. "I've spoken with the city centre divisional commander, Mr Deacon and he has granted permission for you to be involved, however, Mr Deacon has made it plainly clear that primacy in this fire investigation rests squarely with Miller. You are simply there as an observer."

He stubbed his fingers against the desk and started at her. "There's just one further thing, Cathy. I have to warn you, a heads up as it were, that DCI Rogers isn't keen on the idea," shrewdly deciding that it wouldn't be wise to tell Cathy just how vehemently Rogers opposed the plan, "so watch yourself, where she is concerned. As for reporting back to me, I was thinking perhaps an evening call to my home number?" he suggested.

"Okay, that will be fine, sir," she agreed. "I'd prefer as little contact with the office as possible. It's probably best that the less people who know why I'm at the Cowcaddens CID the better."

She stood to leave, but Cairney raised his finger, as if in warning.

"One last thing, Cathy, you know better than most the violence that Brogan and his head case of a minder, Liam McPhee are capable of. Your safety in this operation is paramount so," he cautioned her, "no taking unnecessary risks, eh? Remember, these guys play by big boys rules."

Chapter 5

Mickey Hughes sat in the CCTV coffin that passed for a room and sipped at his early morning brew. A sigh of contentment escaped his lips. The station janitor, Jimmy Donnelly, spooned another sugar into his tea and offered Mickey the plate, the toast now crisp and hard as balsa wood, the butter congealing in the air-conditioned atmosphere of the room.

Shaking his head at the offer, Mickey enquired, "How was you weekend, Jimmy?"

"Not too bad, Mickey," the old janitor rasped, "the granddaughter was up with her new boyfriend on Saturday night. Seemed a nice guy," then added with a laugh, "for a Protestant!"

Mickey grinned tolerantly at Jimmy, knowing that in today's politically correct police service, jokes about race, religion and sex were taboo. Dinosaurs like Jimmy he thought, were too old to change and just didn't realise that even minor innuendos were unacceptable. He sighed because he knew Jimmy felt safe speaking to Mickey and even if he tried, Mickey knew that any advice he gave the old guy on the subject of political correctness would be lost on him.

"So," Mickey discreetly changed the subject "did you manage a couple of pints, then?"

"Aye, I sank a couple down at my local. There was a wee singsong going on. I would have asked the granddaughter and her boyfriend down, but I don't think he would have fitted in," Jimmy continued to laugh,

The door knocked and Charlie Miller strode in, unwittingly saving Mickey from further indiscreet dialogue and Jimmy's religious bias.

"Hello Charlie," greeted the old janitor, and then to Hughes, "I'd better be going anyway, Mickey. That bugger Rogers kicks up a fair stink if her office isn't cleaned properly and I've got one of them asylum seekers working up on that floor the now. Be a lot easier if she spoke fucking English," he added as he left, whistling tunelessly while he walked along the corridor.

Mickey exhaled noisily. "Thanks, Charlie. Jimmy's a decent old guy and always good for a cuppa and toast in the morning," nodding his head to the plate and its cardboard contents, "but he's definitely out of touch with the Equal Opportunities programme and if the bosses heard him going on," Mickey left the rest unsaid.

Charlie knew what Jimmy was like. Didn't the whole station? But the old janitor had been working at the Cowcaddens office since the foundations were laid and nobody, including the bosses had the heart to retire him. He glanced at the wall clock.

"Nine fifteen. I've the mortuary to attend, Mickey. You got anything for me?"

Mickey stared curiously at Charlie. Aye, he wasn't mistaken. There was definitely something different about him today, he decided and it wasn't the clean shirt and suit. He exhaled softly, creating a whistling noise through his false upper dentures.

"I've trawled through the tapes, like you asked and edited something that might be of interest to you into the one recording," as replied, handing Charlie a black plastic case containing a DVD. "There's quite a bit of footage on there and I'm sure most of it will be irrelevant to your investigation, but you'll be the best judge. I've kept all the tapes aside, in case you come across anything that you need. Just note the time that features in the bottom right hand corner and I'll be able to identify the relevant tape."

Charlie was pleased.

"You're a star, Mickey," and patted his shoulder. "I haven't time to view the tape just now, but I'll get back to you."

Charlie left the small, confined room and met John Brown in the corridor outside. Still smarting from their encounter in the toilets, Brown coldly snapped, "The boss wants you, pronto," while indicating with his thumb over his shoulder. Charlie glanced at his wristwatch.

"Sorry, no time now," he smiled pleasantly. "Things to do, people to meet," and before Brown could protest, rudely shouldered his way past the stunned, acting DI.

*

Frank Brogan used his mobile phone to let his sister know that he was waiting for her in the car park and telling her not to rush, to take her time. He hit the end button on the mobile phone and glanced at his watch. No way was he going to climb those stairs again, he'd already decided. The bright, November day streamed through the windscreen, dazzling him and Liam McPhee, who sat behind the wheel, and creating a rainbow of colour on the glass. McPhee reached down and inserted a cassette tape into the slot. The strains of an Irish republican flute band filled the car as McPhee whistled in accompaniment.

"For fucks sake, Liam," groaned Brogan, his fingers impatiently tapping on his knee, "give it a rest."

McPhee sighed. Frank was in his usual, cantankerous early morning mood and McPhee was getting pretty pissed off with it, running the bastard back and forwards like a fucking chauffeur. That wasn't why he had been sent over, not to be a messenger boy for this wanker. Wisely, he kept his cool and stared wordlessly ahead through the windscreen.

A few minutes later, Irene Cavendish emerged into the sunlight from the main door of the flats. Wearing her customary black coat, black skirt and with a black shawl on her head and knotted under her chin, she looked exactly as she portrayed herself, the grieving widow and childless parent. An elderly man stopped Irene, removed his cap and placed his hands in hers. Brogan watched their heads, nodding in unison, realising the similarity between the two of them and a pair of those cheap spring-necked ornaments so popular and found in working class houses. He assumed that word of Mary's death must now be widespread. He suspected that Irene would secretly be revelling in the attention she was bound to receive from her church going cronies, but a subject he dare not broach with her. Brogan climbed out of the car, opened the rear door for his sister and ushered her inside.

"Morning, Irene," he greeted her as he pecked a kiss at her pale cheek. "Are you certain you are ready for this?"

Irene manoeuvred herself into the car and glared at him.

"Who else is there to identify the body of my Mary?" she snapped, "you?"

In the driver's seat, McPhee thought it best to keep his mouth shut and wait for Irene to acknowledge him. As fast as a switch turns on a light, a smile crossed Irene's face when she saw the big Irishman.

"Good morning, Liam. Have you heard from your wife and children?" she enquired.

McPhee startled. No, he decided, she wasn't being malicious.

"I phoned them last night, Irene love. All fine, hale and hearty. Turning in his seat, he faced her. "Irene," he began "I was truly sorry to hear…"

She waved her hand at him. "It's the Lords decision, Liam and who are we to question His way?"

McPhee nodded and turned to start the engine.

"Besides," she added, leaning forward and placing her hand on Brogan's shoulder, "my dear wee brother has the matter in hand, don't you Frank?"

*

Cathy Mulgrew enjoyed the brisk, twenty-minute walk from Police Headquarters to Cowcaddens police station. She had decided there was no need to check in with DCI Rogers, that Martin Cairney had covered the courtesy of introduction. Both Cairney and she had agreed that any questions from the CID staff would simply be explained that due to the lack of Cowcaddens resources, she had been sent to assist Miller, nothing else. End of story and full stop. She knew that there was bound to be a certain amount of suspicion at her presence, but that didn't concern her.

While she walked, she thought about Rogers description of Miller and decided to make her own assessment of her new partner. The last time Cathy had been in her company had been the end of course piss-up. Rogers had made a drunken pass at Cathy's partner, provoking a tipsy Cathy to threaten the fat bastard with a hammering. Cathy bristled at the memory. For all her size, Rogers had proven to be a cowardly bully who, on that occasion resorted to pulling rank to extricate herself from physical damage at the hands of the enraged detective.

Cathy pushed open the public doors of Cowcaddens police station and flashed her warrant card at the civilian bar officer, who buzzed her through into the security door and stared lustfully after the good looking woman as she walked down the CID corridor. If she remembered correctly from her previous visits, Cathy knew the CID general office was down the passage to her left. Striding down the dimly lit corridor, her heels clicking on the well-worn tiled floor, she opened the door into the general office and was quietly relieved to see a friendly face.

"Alan Boyle," she smiled as she approached him, her hand extended in greeting, "long time no see."

Boyle turned at his name and a broad grin spread across his face when he saw Cathy.

"Well, well. Mucky Mulgrew! What threat to national security brings the Counter Terrorism Unit into this pit of an office?" he asked.

The only other occupant in the room stared curiously at the two old friends. Boyle shook hands then indicated Carol McFarlane and introduced her to Cathy.

"Mucky Mulgrew?" she asked. "So, how did you come by that name?"

Boyle cast Cathy a sharp glance and then forced a snigger.

"During physical training at the police college," he explained, "Cathy was the only one on our probationary Constable course that couldn't get over the eight foot wall. Every time she tried, she landed on her arse in the mud pool at the bottom," he told her, laughing at the memory.

Both women smiled tolerantly at each other, privately wondering at the sad humour of men and Alan Boyle in particular.

"So," he calmed down, glad to have got so easily out of that situation, "just visiting or what?"

"Actually, I'm on temporary secondment. There's nothing much doing in our department because most of the staff are away on this Summit thing, so some of us have been drafted in by the city divisions to assist the CID in general enquires. After all," she grinned, "we are detectives, too."

Boyle smiled and nodded, privately thinking that was the biggest load of bullshit he had heard all week. However, what Cathy was doing here wasn't his business

"So, are you looking for work or have you to report to the DCI first?" McFarlane inquired.

"Oh, I've already been assigned to help out a DS Miller. Don't suppose he's here, is he?"

Boyle and McFarlane looked at each other as an awkward silence fell between them. Boyle shrugged his shoulders.

"First thing, Mucky," he replied as he gently took her by the elbow, "how's about you and I having a cup of coffee? Then you and I should have a wee chat."

*

The Glasgow City Mortuary, that lies adjacent to the High Court of Justiciary, is a red-bricked morgue and is situated on the north banks of the River Clyde, facing the large expanse of parkland that is called Glasgow Green. The Mortuary clientele as a rule arrive in unmarked and closed vehicles and usually via the back door access. Its visitors attend at the ornate Victorian entrance and, through the passage of time, the Mortuary portals have welcomed not only the innocent and the good, but also many of the worst of the citizens of Glasgow.

Charlie Miller parked the CID car on the street opposite the red bricked building and, glancing at his watch, awaited the arrival of Irene Cavendish. A small silver coloured Volkswagen pulled up behind him. Glancing in his rear view mirror, he saw the elderly driver had a head of grey hair and had a small square of white in the front of his black collar. Guessing this would be the priest for Irene's parish he left the vehicle and introduced himself. Shaking hands, the elderly man spoke in a soft, lilting Irish brogue.

"And I'm Father Flynn. Bad business this is, Sergeant Miller, a bad business. Are you getting anywhere with your enquiry son, or can't you tell me?"

Charlie smiled. It had been a long time since anyone had called him son. They talked as they walked, weaving their way through the traffic, across the busy road, ignoring the hostile glares and angry horn blasts from passing drivers.

"Early days yet, Father. But I can tell you that I don't suspect it was a deliberate attempt to harm the wee lassie. Simply put, she was in the wrong place at the wrong time."

"Her mother will take it bad," the old priest shook his head, "but she's a church going woman and she'll have her parish about her. Tell me, Sergeant Miller, or can I call you Charlie?" the old man asked.

Charlie smiled and nodded.

"Then Charlie it is. Tell me, Charlie. Do you know what made poor wee Mary run off from her home, do you have any idea at all?"

Charlie didn't realise the priest was staring at him, inwardly dreading the detective's response.

"Why do teenagers do anything, Father?" he sighed. "It's an awkward time for me to intervene with questions, during a family's grief and I don't really know the nature of the relationship between the mother and daughter. It's also early days in the enquiry, so hopefully I might turn something up as I go along. My main concern, right now is to identify the person responsible for setting the fire. To be perfectly frank," he stopped and turned to the old priest, "I think there is every likelihood Mary's death will be treated by the Procurator Fiscal as culpable homicide, but even if I do discover the culprit and libel a charge, I can't see a court awarding a sentence that will be appropriate for the death of the young girl."

They'd reached safety and now stood on the marble steps, before the great oak doors. The priest shook his head, shoving his hands viciously into his coat pockets.

"I'd known Mary Cavendish all her short life," he began. "A smart wee girl she was and helpful too. She was never one to mix easily with others, though. Always seemed to be on the fringe of the crowd, do you know what I mean? A regular churchgoer," then he chuckled humourlessly. "Not that she had any choice in the matter with a mother like Irene." The old priest took a deep breath and Charlie suspected he was wrestling with his conscious. A man used to keeping confidences and secrets. "I'm sure I can rely on your discretion, son, but if I'm honest with you Charlie, I don't think Mary had much of a life, always at her mother's beck and call. Always around Irene's coat tails. No real friends that I knew of."

He groaned, a painful memory flashing through his mind. Mary Cavendish behind the confessional curtain, her shameful dark secret, blurted out through tears and sobs. But it was the confessional and, may God forgive me, nobody must ever know.

The short burst of a car horn sounding interrupted the old priest's thoughts and signalled the arrival of Irene Cavendish. Charlie saw a large man in the driver's seat who stared insolently at him, childishly daring the detective to look away first. Charlie's attention was distracted from the driver to Frank Brogan, who climbed out from the passenger side and helped his sister from the vehicle.

"Good morning, Father," Irene Cavendish greeted the old priest and, to Charlie's surprise, almost genuflected in the middle of the street.

Brogan nodded to the detective, but ignored Flynn, an obvious snub that Charlie saw and puzzled him.

The driver remained with the car, fixedly looking ahead and apparently content to remain with the vehicle that was now parked on double yellow lines.

Unconsciously he reckoned any passing warden would likely have his hands full, dealing with the acne-scarred brute behind the wheel.

Charlie stood slightly to one side, allowing Mrs Cavendish to compose herself as she spoke softly with the priest, preparing herself for the ordeal that lay ahead of her. Finally, almost apologetically, he approached her.

"Do you think you're ready to go in?" he asked, nodding towards the large, wooden double doors.

Silently, one hand resting on the Father Flynn's arm and the other carrying a set of dark, wooden rosary beads, she nodded her head and slowly began to climb the steps to the entrance. Charlie and Brogan moved forward to each pull open a heavy oak door and the four entered a brightly lit corridor, the polished floor reflecting the sunlight that streamed in through the glass cupola roof and echoing their footsteps.

An elderly attendant wearing a starched white overall rose from behind a desk to greet them. Charlie strode forward to explain the purpose of their visit and they were shown into a small anteroom. Quietly, they sat and waited. A few minutes later, a smartly dressed woman about sixty, her greying hair tied in a neat bun and wearing a skirted black business suit with a small, white porcelain brooch in the shape of a lily in her lapel, entered the anteroom carrying a metal clipboard in her hand. The woman stood in front of Irene, smiled gently and introduced herself.

"Mrs Cavendish, I'm Julia Cosgrove, the assistant deputy director. I have one or two small questions, if you're up to them?"

Charlie saw Irene nod, then watched as Brogan rose from his chair.

"Is this really necessary," he pompously demanded, "my sister's been through enough questions and this is a very trying time for her, for us all," he added sourly.

Cosgrove smiled tolerantly, anticipating some form of protest.

"We do try to make this as painless as possible, Mr, eh ..?"

"I'm Mary's uncle and..."

But he got no further as Irene pulled at his coat tail and hissed, "Sit down, Frank. The lady is only doing her job. Now, what is it that you wish to know?"

While Irene formally provided details of her relationship to the deceased, Charlie pondered the little scene that had played out before him. He was a little surprised to find that Irene Cavendish, far from being the distraught parent that he had imagined, seemed to be revelling in her role as the grieving mother and, it seemed to him, she wasn't the wilting flower she was trying to portray. Father Flynn's comment from a few minutes previously sprung to mind. 'What made poor wee Mary run off,' not why? And the old priest had also said 'always at her mother's beck and call'. Was the old priest inferring Mary Cavendish had been more of an accessory than a loved child? He cast a sidelong glance at the old priest, wondering to himself, what about Father Flynn? He suspected the priest knew much more than his vows permitted him to disclose and had seen the loathing in Flynn's eyes, when Brogan had got to his feet. No love lost there, he privately assessed, curious at the cause of such a strong dislike.

The formal paperwork was soon completed and Cosgrove invited Irene, Father Flynn and Charlie, as the inquiry officer, to the viewing room.

Brogan, still standing, made to follow, but Cosgrove raised her hand and stopped him.

"I'm so sorry, sir, but immediate family only," she told him, her voice calm and pleasant, but with a steely edge that was unmistakable.

Charlie suspected that following Brogan's rude and unnecessary outburst, Cosgrove was relishing enforcing a rule that she'd likely relax for other visitors. Brogan, his face like thunder, knew that any argument would be lost with this determined woman and turned to Irene.

"I'll wait at the car with Liam, Irene. If you need me you know where I'll be," then with a hostile stare at Cosgrove, strode from the room and into the corridor towards the front doors.

With a small sigh of relief that there was to be no argument, Irene again took her priests arm and was led by Cosgrove to a small, dimly lit room with one wall hidden by a thick, black velvet curtain.

"Are you ready?" asked Cosgrove to Irene and then at her replying nod, pushed at a small switch on the wall. The curtain glided back on silent runners and revealed a glass partition with a room beyond, richly decorated in velvet and mauve curtains, brightly lit and in where lay an open coffin.

Irene gasped and slouched. Charlie moved forward to catch her, but she regained her balance. A slight sob escaped her lips.

A young girl, her eyes closed, lay in the coffin with a white silken sheet covering her body, to just below her chin. For all intents and purpose, the girl seemed to be sleeping peacefully. Charlie choked back a sob. Memories rushed at him and he closed his eyes tightly, and blinked them rapidly open to see Irene nodding her head, confirming the girl that lay before them was indeed her daughter, Mary Cavendish.

"Do you mind if I say a wee prayer?" asked the old priest.

Cosgrove smiled in understanding.

"Of course not, Father," she replied, while raising her eyebrows at Charlie and indicating the door.

Charlie followed Cosgrove into the corridor and watching her gently closing the door behind him, was surprised when she then she extended her hand.

"Mr Miller," she began, "I know you probably won't remember me?"

Taken aback, Charlie took her hand and shook his head. "I'm sorry, no."

Slightly embarrassed at his failure to recognise her, he followed Cosgrove as she led the way to her nearby office where a coffee pot simmered on the window ledge. Without asking, she poured two cups and asked "Milk, sugar? They might be a little while," she indicated with her head back towards the viewing room.

"Yes and two," he requested, still puzzled.

Cosgrove could see he was confused. Handing him a cup, she sat behind her desk. "It was a difficult time for you, just about three years ago. I was on duty the night that your wife and son were… brought in," she began.

He sipped at the strong coffee. That night was etched in his mind as clearly as was today. But he didn't remember this woman.

"How have you been, since the tragedy?" she enquired.

A tight little smile crossed Charlie's lips.

"Drunk for most of the time, I took their deaths very badly," he continued, bemused at his own candour and also surprised that he was even discussing the affair. He couldn't recall the last time he'd spoken about that night or indeed if he ever had.

Cosgrove sighed, a half smile on her lips. "I lost my husband four years ago, in a similar way," she confessed. "He was driving home from work and some woman in a large off-road vehicle rushing to collect her kids from school, took a chance and run a red light. Hit him side on. The collision wasn't that bad," the police told me, "but the impact caused him to bang the side of his head against the drivers door post and fractured his skull. Just one of those stupid accidents," they said. "I'm grateful he didn't suffer or linger with his injury. He wouldn't have wanted that."

She smiled. "At least we had a lot of good years together and he left me with many happy memories. Plus my children and grandchildren are constant reminders of him."

Charlie put the cup down on the desk, a lump in his throat. He hadn't discussed Louise and young Charlie with anyone for a very, very long time. Cosgrove rolled a pencil between her fingers.

"There are groups that can help, you know," she suggested, her instinct telling her this man was still grieving.

Charlie was about to reply when a sharp knock at the door interrupted him.

"Hello there, Julia. Open for business?"

Professor Henry Martin stood staring at the couple. Now almost seventy years old, the small man retained a mop of thick, white hair curling over his ears. Gold-rimmed spectacles lay perched on his nose with a thin gold chain attached to the legs and draped around his neck. Wearing a navy blue three piece pin broad, striped suit with a fresh, red carnation in the buttonhole and thumbs hooked in the pockets of his waistcoat, he looked every inch the medical man and was well known in the city CID ranks, not only for his professionalism at the autopsy table, but also for his humour and wit as an after dinner speaker. It was widely known he affected this manner of dress, the better to impress his students, he would boast.

"Ah," he continued in his deep, booming voice, "I see you have the redoubtable Sergeant Miller with you," he approached Charlie, his hand outstretched, A huge smile lighting up his face. Still working for the lovely Ms Rogers, I hear?"

Charlie stood and grinned in response. How the Professor got his information was anyone's guess. There had been sarcasm in the old guy's voice and it seemed he had the same low opinion of Rogers, as probably did most of the Force.

"Nice to see you again, Prof," he replied, surprised at the strength of the old guys grip.

"Here about the young girl in the fire?" asked Martin.

"Aye, Mary Cavendish, aged fourteen years. Her mother and the priest are with her saying a few prayers. Shouldn't be to long, I expect."

"Bad business, bad business, still, no rush, my boy," replied Martin, drawing a chair up and sitting alongside Charlie.

"And you, Sergeant, how are you?"

Charlie recalled Martin had been the pathologist who had attended to Louise and young Charlie. His kindness on that dreadful night had not been lost on the distraught detective.

"Just telling Mrs Cosgrove…"

"Julia, please," she interrupted with a smile.

"Julia," he returned her smile, "that I haven't been doing too well. But strangely enough," he unconsciously fingered the folded photograph in his pocket, "the last two days have been…difficult to describe," he admitted, nodding his head in time with his statement, "but somehow different."

Martin looked at Cosgrove and they both smiled.

"If you ever need to talk," the older man began, "Well, you know where I'm usually found," as he waved his hands at the walls around him.

A second knock at the door announced the arrival of Father Flynn, who after introduction, informed Charlie that Mrs Cavendish was about to depart. Charlie followed Flynn to the front door where the Irene Cavendish stood at the top of the entrance alone.

"Mrs Cavendish," he began, "this is a bad time for you. The best I can offer just now is to promise that I'll be in touch as regularly as I can and keep you informed of my progress."

She nodded, dabbing at her eyes with her handkerchief. Somehow, when he thought about it later, Charlie had the instinctive feeling that her manner was planned, that she was performing a necessary function, that her grief was contrived. In short, he realised with a start, he didn't believe her sorrow to be genuine.

Brogan mounted the stairs and, without a backward glance at the detective or the priest, helped his sister to the waiting car. The bruiser that held open the door scowled at Charlie.

A face only a mother could love, Charlie thought, but not one that he would forget in a hurry.

As the car drove off, Flynn turned to Charlie and shook his hand. "I understand there will be…certain formalities," the old man hesitantly began, "before Mary can be released to her mother. Of course, it will be a burial so there's no fear of…" The priest stopped. Both he and Charlie knew that if a murder charge was ever to be libelled, the worst-case scenario might mean an exhumation for a defence autopsy. With cremation this obviously caused difficulties.

"As soon as I can arrange it with the PF, I'll have the wee girl released to her mother. I wouldn't want to prolong her agony any further, Father."

The priest nodded and began to walk to his car and then stopped. He turned as if to say something, Charlie thought, but then simply waved and strode across the road.

*

Cathy Mulgrew sat at Charlie Miller's desk in the empty office, that days edition of the 'Glasgow News' lying unread in front of her. A coffee sat cooling by her hand as she contemplated the hygiene risk by exposing her mouth to the chipped and stained mug. She glanced at her watch, wondering how long she'd wait, before he returned. Cathy reasoned the control room would have Miller's mobile number and considered phoning him, but decided it was better to formally introduce herself at the office rather than track him down and explain her purpose at some roadside or, worse still, the mortuary. Her problem was that he might resent being dogged by her and simply ignore the instruction from Rogers. If indeed, she pondered, he's been informed yet. She thought about what Alan Boyle had told her, urging her not to broach the subject unless Miller himself raised it, telling her in the same breath that Miller had never spoken of the accident, since it occurred. Cathy learned Miller had been an above average, popular and ambitious detective, but gone completely off the rails three years ago when his family, his wife and son, Boyle told her, were killed on a pedestrian crossing by a van driver, too drunk to see the flashing lights. She gave an involuntary shudder, vaguely recalling the incident. How anyone could cope after a loss like that was beyond her. Since that time, Charlie Miller had taken to the bottle and was delegated all the office bound tasks to keep him from the public view, slowly but surely taking less and less work on, his workload subtly looked after and managed by some of the older and more experienced detectives who, not without some difficulty, steered Miller clear of the bosses.

Then, Boyle sighed, Rogers had arrived in the division.

Cathy didn't need any further explanation at that news. Idly, she flicked through the desk diary in front of her, and then her attention was drawn to the top drawer on her left that lay slightly ajar. A quick glance about her confirmed she was still alone as she noisily drew the drawer open, flinching at the scraping of the creaking wood, and then slowly pulling at it again. The corner of a framed photograph peeked out from beneath an untidy bundle of cardboard files. Cathy withdraw the picture and saw a pretty woman about thirty, short curly auburn hair and brilliant white teeth, smiling at the camera. On her knee sat a toddler, aged about three, the same auburn hair cut short, grinning at the camera and showing a space where his two front teeth used to be. The strong resemblance declared them to be mother and son, probably Miller's family she decided.

"Pretty, weren't they?"

She jumped at the sound of the voice behind her and stood up, the photograph falling from her fingers back onto the files. She could feel the blush rise from her neck to her face. A tall, rugged looking man stood behind her, coat slung over the shoulder of a suit that badly needed ironed, his face grim.

He must have come through the rear door, she thought, angry at being caught out and aware she'd no excuse.

"May I ask what you are doing in my desk?" the man snapped at her, his voice politely venomous.

"I'm DS Cathy Mulgrew," she stuttered, her face now crimson and increasingly annoyed at herself for her stupidity. Limply, she sighed and pointed at the open desk and photograph within.

"I'm sorry, you must be DS Miller?"

Charlie nodded, not speaking and wondering who this copper-headed, nosey bastard was.

"Look," she repeated, feeling suddenly as if that she was back in the fifth form, "I'm really sorry about that," Cathy pointed to the photograph.

"So you've said, but are you sorry about going through my drawer, sorry about getting caught or sorry about my dead family?"

She swallowed hard, her embarrassment obvious and words for once failing her. She decided the best thing was just to keep her mouth shut, say nothing further that might provoke an argument.

Charlie sighed. It wasn't in his nature to be vindictive, and then curiosity got the better of him.

"So, who exactly are you, again, and what do you want?" as he placed his coat on the desk and pulled a chair over from an adjoining desk and indicating that Cathy should resume sitting in his desk chair.

"I'm DS Cathy Mulgrew, Counter Terrorism Unit. I assume that DCI Rogers has yet to inform you of my assignment, my being tasked to assist you?"

Charlie was puzzled. Assist him? What the fuck did he need a secretary for?

"Look," he hesitated briefly, "Sergeant Mulgrew. The janitor in this office receives more updates than I do, particularly if they come from on high," as he pointed upwards. Sitting back in his chair, his brow knitted in puzzlement as he stared at Cathy. "Please continue," he drolly added.

Cathy drew a deep breath and spoke at length, giving him her prepared speech that related to her instruction to shadow Miller in his inquiry, to glean anything she could about the activities of one, Frank Brogan.

"One further thing that I'd request of you," she asked him, knowing she was on thin ground and hopeful he'd got over his initial umbrage, "for the purpose of confidentiality, you, the DCI and Mr Deacon your divisional commander, are the only ones that will know my true purpose. No matter what the rest of the office suspect, I'm simply here on secondment."

Charlie nodded in acceptance, for Mulgrew's request wasn't unreasonable and he understood the police gossip machine, guessing his own drunken escapades must have been the subject of many a juicy titbit, true or otherwise. He leaned slightly forward to emphasise his response, speaking quietly as if fearing he might be overheard.

"Well, let me make one thing clear to you, Sergeant Mulgrew. I have no choice in the issue of you shadowing me. However, I decide what inquiry is to be made, I decide to whom we speak and I decide the direction the inquiry takes. I will brook no argument from you regarding any decisions I make nor do I expect you to be reporting any of my decisions you happen to disagree with, back to Rogers. Is that clearly understood?"

Cathy returned an almost imperceptible nod, her lips set tightly together, eyes blazing. She wasn't about to be bullied by this clown, regardless of what sympathy he expected because of his past troubles. Who the hell does this guy think he is, she bristled, fucking dictating to me?

Pressing her hands together in her lap, she composed herself and replied in the same, low voice. "For one thing, I'm not here to oversee your inquiry and whether or not you detect your culprit is irrelevant to me. For another, my loyalty lies with the CTU and I will report back to my own boss, but only in the issue of Brogan. As for Rogers," Cathy scoffed, "I can't stand the cow and wouldn't piss on her if she was on fire!"

White-faced, she sat back in her chair, watching him for his reaction and was taken aback when he smiled.

"Well, that's two of us, then. Look," he said more affably, "we've gotten off to a bad start. How about I let you buy me a coffee at a wee cafe round the corner then

I'll update you on how far I've got and we'll come to some sort of an agreement."
Charlie raised his hands, palms outward. "Pact?" he suggested.

Cathy slowly nodded her head, feminine instinct telling her to mistrust this sudden change in Miller's attitude, yet something….something that she couldn't quite put her manicured finger on. "Deal," she decided, "and I am sorry about going into your desk. I'm just a nosey bugger," she admitted.

"No problem," Charlie smiled as he lifted his coat from the desk. "After all," he added, now grinning at her as with gentlemanly courtesy, held open the rear door, "isn't that why the police pay us?"

*

Jimmy Donnelly, the Central police station's janitor, sat in the bar, nursing his drink. His local served a cracking pint of Guinness and why shouldn't it? For after all and smiled to himself, Flaherty's is an Irish pub. Jimmy, who had never been further west than the coastal town of Ayr, hummed along to the republican tune playing on the old, worn cassette player on the bar and patriotically imagined himself up there with the boys, standing fearlessly in 1916 at Dublin Post Office, when the Brit's came calling with their tanks and guns. "Those must have been the days," he softly sighed. He studied the photographs above the bar of the young men who had fallen, the Volunteers, murdered by the British army and their pawns, the Protestant police. Sadly, Jimmy shook his head, the second pint now making him maudlin and sentimental. With a shrug he thought about his days work, mentally reminding himself to have another word with that lazy cow of an asylum seeker, bleating at him that her bad back meant she couldn't cope with a bit of mopping.

Jimmy liked his job. Yes, he decided, liked it well enough to have done it for that last thirty odd years, he smiled. The early start meant not having to worry about city centre parking and the early afternoon finish suited his life style. Sunlight streamed through the pub window and danced on the polished surface of the wooden table. With more than a hint of pleasure, he smacked his lips and wiped his tongue round them, to clear the froth as he set the pint down on the beer mat. He thought about his conversation with Mickey Hughes in the CCTV room. Mickey wasn't a bad lad, but took his job too seriously and was like an old woman with this, what was it called again? Oh aye, politically correct nonsense. He knew he had niggled Mickey with that crack about his granddaughter's boyfriend being a Proddy, but so what? After working for all these years, he wasn't about to change now. Not at his age. Besides, Mickey knew that he never really meant any harm. A shadow loomed over the table and he looked up.

"Good afternoon, Jimmy me lad and how's about you? Guinness is it?" inquired Frank Brogan in his best imitation Belfast accent.

Chapter 6

Professor Henry Martin whistled tunelessly as he scrubbed his hands under the running faucet, meticulously working the liquid, biological soap between his fingers. He glanced over his shoulder and saw his assistant, preparing with needle and surgical thread, to begin the painstaking work of putting the wee girl together. In his mind, Martin had already begun the text of the report that he would later submit to Sergeant Miller. Nice chap that, he thought to himself. Shame about his family; took it hard, by all accounts. Martin brought to mind a recent conversation with a golf club colleague that knew Miller and had heard the officer described as a drunkard. Admittedly, his suit looked a bit of a shambles and he certainly needed a haircut, but still, there seemed to be a buzz about the policeman today, something has obviously caused a spark if his eyes are anything to go by, he reflected.

Rinsing his hands, he turned and snatched at the wide roll of paper towel hanging from the dispenser. The wee girl had looked a poor soul as he had begun his post mortem investigation. Miller had stayed for the examination as he was duty bound but Martin, sensing the Sergeant was uncomfortable, had sent him away with a preliminary verbal report, confirming death by smoke inhalation. No untoward bruises to suggest anything other than that, Martin had decided. He stood silently at the autopsy table, staring at the body that once housed the life of Mary Cavendish. He was too old and too experienced to allow himself to be anything other than dispassionate about his work. A father and grandfather himself, he knew when the day arrived that he didn't feel any emotion for the people on whom he worked, well, that would be the day he would hang up his gown. Surprising though, he admitted to himself, to find that. The Forensic Medicine laboratory at the University would do the blood works and determine if he was correct, but he didn't often make mistakes as basic as that. He would have to telephone the Sergeant. Might add a touch of intrigue to his inquiry, he wryly thought.

*

Jimmy Donnelly sat frozen, his Guinness lukewarm, the condensation of the glass forming a small pool of water on the table. Unconsciously, he sensed that the patrons who sat and stood around him were now speaking in hushed tones. Brogan had been very clear in his instruction. The old janitor clutched the scrap of paper with the scrawled telephone number and shoved it into his jacket pocket. His granddaughter's face flashed before him. Knees trembling, he reached with shaking hands for the pint and, spilling some of the liquid on the table, used both hands to lift it to his lips.

"Find out anything you can, anything at all, on what Sergeant Miller is working on. Who he speaks to, who he works with, anything at all and Jimmy," Brogan had hissed his warning, "don't be leaving anything out. Let me be the judge of what is important."

Jimmy gulped, the strong ale tasted vile in his throat. With shaking hands, he put the glass back down on the table.

Liam McPhee, Brogan's constant companion, had placed his clenched fist on top of Jimmy's fingers, squeezed tightly then leaned close enough for Jimmy to smell his bad breath and whispered, "I hear you've got a good looking wee granddaughter, Jimmy. You'll have heard Jimmy, that there's a lot of wee girls round here getting assaulted these days. Aye, a real shame it is with some of them poor wee girls losing their good looks too."

Jimmy was too old to fight them, too old to protest and wise enough to recognise a veiled but promised threat. Brogan had assured Jimmy that he needed the information for the Cause, but Jimmy knew he was lying. It was common knowledge that his niece had been killed in a fire. What he wanted, Jimmy suspected, was revenge. He wanted Sergeant Miller's information. Brogan wanted the man who had set the fire before Miller got to him.

Christ, Jimmy realised. Brogan was using Jimmy to find the man, to hurt him. Maybe even, God forbid, kill him!

*

Charlie Miller led Cathy Mulgrew the short walk across Buchanan Street to the corner of Bath Street where she saw Charlie's cafe. It was, she wryly observed, not a coffee shop but a licensed espresso bar. Inside at the counter, however, she raised her eyebrows in surprise when Charlie ordered two coffees.

Grinning, he asked her, "What did you expect, two White and McKay's with sugar and cream?"

The shapely waitress, she observed, greeted Miller with a ready smile, but he seemed oblivious to the cautious invitation Cathy suspected lay behind the smile. Curiosity aroused, she wondered as she glanced at the rumpled detective what the hell any woman would see in this wreck?

Carrying the tray, he gingerly led the way to a small table in a corner, out of earshot of the midday office trade that formed the bulk of the patrons. A sigh of relief escaped his lips as he arrived at the table without spilling the coffee; grateful the slight but habitual shake of his hands had momentarily ceased, yet inwardly his body ached for a dram, for some relief from the cramps that were pestering his stomach.

During their walk to the café, their small talk had turned to the inquiry and he had briefly outlined his limited progress so far. Patting his coat pocket, he reminded himself that he had still to view Mickey Hughes compilation DVD and they both agreed that should be their next task.

"So, tell me about Frank Brogan," Charlie requested.

Sitting with her back to the wall and with a clear view of those about her, Cathy stirred into lecture mode.

"Frank Brogan first came to prominence during the early eighties, initially as a teenage Irish republican flute band member, then graduated through their ranks to organising and coordinating the flute bands in the west of Scotland. He's strictly a hand's off type of guy, content to let others do the running about and, usually at his command, getting others to mete out physical retribution when dues don't get paid or administering punishment beatings for some perceived violation of their internal code. You'll have guessed," she wryly added, "we don't get a lot of complaints from the injured parties. Though Glasgow born, he has an Irish parental background and is a committed member of the Provisional wing of the

IRA. Fundamentally, he is the leading figure of the PIRA in this part of Scotland. He passes through the airport and seaports on a regular basis, reporting to his masters in Belfast what's happening locally, here."

Cathy paused for breath and took a mouthful of coffee.

"He's unmarried and lives alone in a well-appointed flat in the east end of Glasgow. He's the younger of two children, parents both deceased and his sister Irene Cavendish being a widowed woman whose husband was a unemployed drunkard and who, according to local gossip, put her in hospital on a few occasions after some particularly savage beatings. Rumour has it she is also a closet Irish republican supporter, but never previously came to our attention for anything other than being Brogan's sister." She paused to sip at her coffee.

"Brogan doesn't work, well, not legitimately anyway and signs on weekly at the local employment agency and regular as clockwork," she sighed, "his GIRO cheque courtesy of the British Government and taxpayer he so detests, pops through his door. He has less than one hundred pounds in a bank savings account, the only one we know of I should say," her mouth twisted in concentration, "that we find rather odd, because his flat is owned by him. He has furniture that I can't afford and his car, a Vauxhall Vectra as I recall, is only two years old, bought and paid for."

"Haven't the tax people had a look at his lifestyle?"

"Nothing they can do and besides," she countered, "he boasts he can produce receipts for everything he has got. His favourite explanation for his money is, 'Won it at the bookies' unquote," Cathy grimaced, then added, "and you'll know from your own experience this is a difficult one to disprove, particularly if you have a couple of tame bookies in your pocket who can provide you with winners receipts. We strongly suspect that Brogan is the main man who orchestrates the fund raising that is collected in the Irish theme pubs, various functions and other sources, such as from the sale of republican literature and items made by prisoners that are raffled at these events. It's highly probable that as a employee of the IRA, as it were, he's on their books and draws a salary that is commensurate with the large amount of donated money he sends over the water. Needless to say, the money he earns," Cathy made an abbreviated gesture with the fingers of both hands, "will never be disclosed."

"How much donated money are you talking about, that he sends over to Northern Ireland, I mean?"

"I can only give you an estimate," Cathy said, "but we are talking literally between five and eight thousand pounds every month."

Charlie blew through his pursed lips.

"So where does this money go?"

"Ostensibly, it is collected on behalf of the so-called Republican Prisoners of War, or as they like to call them, the men behind the wire. In reality, though there is supposed to be a ceasefire in play at the moment," she grimaced, making it clear what she thought of that political initiative, "the bulk of the money is used to re-arm and re-train volunteers of Active Service Unit's or ASU's, as they are called, that usually operate on the mainland, primarily in England," she added. Charlie rubbed his chin. "I appreciate that three to five thousand pounds is a lot of money, even over the course of a year, but is that enough to equip and train an organisation like the IRA?"

Cathy smiled. "Charlie, don't forget, we're not just talking about Glasgow here, but Edinburgh, Birmingham, Manchester, Liverpool. Anywhere there is an Irish community, there will be a Frank Brogan tasked with collecting funds and collectively the donated money more than quadruples when you also add London to the equation. And let's not forget the American sympathisers. It's anyone's guess how much money flows in from cities such as New York, Boston and Chicago, where through the years the Irish immigrants settled and flourished."

"So, in short, Brogan is the kingpin for the IRA in our part of the world?"

"That's it in a nutshell," she smiled. "He's a thoroughly nasty piece of work. Publicans that don't actively encourage the collection can being passed round at night find their customers taking their business elsewhere. If that still doesn't do the trick, pressure is put on the delivery men and if the publican still doesn't take the hint, then finally, Liam McPhee comes into play."

"And he is?"

"McPhee's a big, ugly guy who acts as both a minder and a heavy for Brogan."

A recent memory jumped into Charlie's head.

"Wouldn't be about six there or four, dark brown hair, bad skin, small scar across the lower chin?" he ventured.

"You know him?"

"No, but that fits the description of the guy who drove Brogan and his sister to the mortuary. He waited in the car, a Vectra it was so I didn't get the opportunity to meet him. Gave me the evil eye," he grinned at her.

"Sounds like McPhee, right enough," Cathy agreed. "He's driving for Brogan at the moment, since Brogan lost his licence for a year," pointing to an empty pint glass on a table nearby. "Mind you," she added thoughtfully, "the ban must be up, soon," then returned to her narrative.

"Liam Aloysius McPhee, aged thirty-eight years, Belfast born and bred and until earlier this year, he was recorded by the Police Service of Northern Ireland as an active ASU member. Fell foul of his local brigade commander when he shagged another Volunteer's wife and was ordered out of Northern Ireland before the cuckolded colleague put a nine millimetre into the back of Liam's head." Cathy took a sip of her coffee while she drew breath. "Now, where was I?" She sighed, "McPhee. Left behind a wife and, at the last count, five kids who are likely being provided for by the very funds he is assisting Brogan to raise."

A half smile played about her mouth; her teeth white and even and lips that Charlie couldn't help but notice were warm and inviting. Unconsciously, he shook his head, shocked at the fleeting thought that had invaded his mind.

Seemingly unaware of her colleague's embarrassment, Cathy continued.

"Fancies himself as a bit of a ladies man, does our Liam. By all account, usually likes them young and tender," she scowled, "and isn't too upset if they refuse his attentions, just takes them anyway. Again, just like the beatings, never any complaint, though," foregoing Charlie's question. "His reputation forestalls that. Not one to underestimate is Liam. He is documented for having a propensity for violent behaviour and the last known count, by our colleagues in the Province, lays suspicion at his complicity in at least six murders, as well as an unknown number of kneecappings and brutal assaults. As far as we can assess his role is simple. Chauffeur Brogan about until such time his years drink driving ban expires and he gets his licence returned, and deal with any complaint that Brogan might incur from the local sympathisers, usually with his fists and feet."

Charlie supped his coffee and posed the obvious question.

"The funds raised by friend Brogan and his unaccountable lifestyle. Not pilfering, is he, I mean, creaming off the top?"

"Ah, the thousand dollar question. We've considered that and suspect that is partly why McPhee has been sent to mind him. If Brogan is scamming the funds, then it has to be with McPhee's consent. Question is, if that is indeed the case then how would we be able to turn that kind of information to our advantage?"

They sat in companionable silence for a few minutes as Charlie absorbed her information.

"So what access does the CTU have?" Charlie eventually asked, referring to informants and knowing full well he was trampling on sacred territory.

"I'll be perfectly frank. None, zilch, bugger all."

With a resigned shrug of her shoulders, Cathy finished her coffee and turned to stare at Charlie.

"We can't get anyone close simply because, between them, Brogan and McPhee run the Gallowgate and south side of Glasgow by fear. Even the local Loyalist supporters that boast and brag about their affiliation with the UDA and the UVF dare not cross swords with these two. We figure that McPhee's Belfast contacts remain in place, so there's plenty of back-up for those two if it came to a shooting war, God forbid," she added fervently.

Cathy stopped for breath, conscious of the waitress now clearing a table beside them. The waitress moved away and Charlie smiled. The CTU personnel were well known for their discretion and adherence to secrecy and Cathy was demonstrating the paranoid obsession that came with the job.

"We did have one," she admitted, under her breath.

"Do you recall Sean Fearon?"

Charlie did remember Fearon, an unsolved murder a few years previously.

"He was the guy found floating in the River Clyde, hands tied behind his back?"

Cathy nodded. "I was the co-handler in the case. My partner at the time was an older guy, an experienced detective who liked Sean. The two of them," she smiled at the memory, "used to scheme to meet at the pokiest pubs you've ever had the misfortune to enter and usually to see what kind of reaction they could drag from a wet behind the ears CTU girl. Talk about having to dress down for the occasion!" She sat back and sighed. "Sean was a good man, believed in a united Ireland, but detested the things the IRA were doing to make it so. The things they did to him…"

Charlie suspected that Cathy must have been heavily involved in the inquiry and thought it prudent not to drag up too many painful memories.

She brushed an imaginary thread from her trouser leg.

"My job is simply to learn anything that might be of value, when you deal with Brogan, then," recalling his earlier warning about interference in his inquiry, quickly added, "I mean, if you have cause to deal with Brogan."

Charlie nodded his understanding of her predicament. There wasn't any real need to re-interview Mrs Cavendish or her brother, on a regular basis. The likelihood was that his dealings would be telephone updates. But he could always pop in, he reckoned. Let Cathy have a look at her target.

They stood to leave and his mobile phone burst into life.

Cathy watched Charlie listen to the call, seeing his face change from pleasant greeting to surprise and watched his eyes narrow, shoulders slump and his mouth turn down. He folded the small phone and returned it to his pocket.

"That was Professor Martin, the pathologist that examined Mary Cavendish," he softly explained. "Wee bit of a shock there," she saw him bite at his lower lip. "It appears that fourteen-year-old Mary had her own secret. The Prof is still to have it confirmed, but it seems she was in an early stage of pregnancy."

*

The man sat in the driver's seat of the car and waited patiently, absentmindedly drumming his fingers on the steering wheel. Every thirty seconds, the wiper scraped the slight fall of misty rain from the smeared screen. He glanced in his rear view mirror, smiling at himself wearing the stupid tweed cap. He had arrived too early for the meeting, but that had been planned. He wanted the opportunity to examine the fields around the dirt road to ensure that there was no surveillance. After all these years, he didn't intend to be compromised when things were going so well. Idly, he fiddled with the radio and listened as the weather forecaster predicted a relatively, bright and dry November. Yeah, he thought and Scotsmen don't drink.

The sound of a labouring diesel engine filtered through the gap in his window as it strained and laboured to drive the small white coloured van up the track on the approach to the man's car. He tensed, and then saw the driver appeared to be alone. Good, business as usual. The van drew alongside the car and stopped with the driver's windows only a few inches apart and both vehicles blocking the narrow road. But they didn't expect passing traffic, the main reason why this desolate place had been chosen.

"Good afternoon," greeted the man's handler cheerfully, as he wound the window down, "and how are we today?" he enquired.

His plummy English voice grated on the man's nerves, but he couldn't afford to piss this bastard off. Not while the Brit bastard had his balls resting securely and squarely in his hands.

"So, dear friend, what have we to report today?" the handler smiled at the man, consciously distracting him from the two camouflaged surveillance officers, former special forces operatives who were dug in less than thirty yards away and meticulously recording the meeting with their state of the art, digital zoom camera.

*

While the clandestine meeting took place on the dirt road, halfway between Glasgow and Ayrshire on the desolate Eaglesham Moor, Bobby Turner was intent on arranging his own meeting. The last two days hadn't been kind to Bobby. The news of the girl's death had taken its toll on his nerves and he hadn't slept well, hardly at all in fact. The telephone kiosk he stood within smelled of urine and decay, its glass panels long since broken and swept away. The information board was scarred and vandalised, but nonetheless sported a phone number whose author promised sexual gratification of a type usually found only in the mind of a degenerate.

With a wry grin at the bawdy humour, he searched in his pocket for the slip of paper with the contact number and inserted a fifty pence piece into the slot, then carefully dialled, silently mouthing the digit's as he read them from the paper. The engaged tone beeped in his ear.

Slamming the phone down, he cursed then decided to try again. Taking a deep breath, he counted to ten, re-dialled the number and heard the burring as the line connected.

"Hello? It's me," Bobby replied "so do not fucking hang up! We need to talk, so just listen. Get my money together and add another..." Bobby screwed his eyes tightly. Fuck it, he decided, "...another five thousand. And no argument! I'll call you tomorrow with details of where we will meet, okay?"

He slammed the phone into its cradle before the expected protest came rattling down the line. With a smile, he exhaled noisily, running his tongue round his parched lips. He was pleased with his last minute decision to ask for the extra five grand, rather than the two he had considered. A sudden rattling knock on the kiosk window caused him to jump. Turning, he saw an old woman, trolley-bag beside her, her face grim and indicating her impatience to use the phone. Pushing the door open, he leered at her and roughly shoved past, ignoring her annoyed protestations.

Yes! He thought. Screw the bastard for another five grand and that would set him up with a chance to start afresh, maybe the southwest of England. He knew there was always seasonal work to be had in the coastal towns.

Confident in his ability to handle the situation, Bobby strode cockily back to the flat. For once, he decided, life was on the up.

*

Breathing heavily and with some difficulty, Charlie regretted letting physical training routine lapse over the last few years as he pushed and manoeuvred the trolley bearing the television and video recorder into the small interview room, each of the castor wheels simultaneously deciding to go their four separate ways. Cathy stood to assist him, then thought it wiser to stay clear and instead noisily pushed the wooden table from his path. With relief, he plugged the sets in, switched off the light and tried to control his wheezing breath as they settled back to watch the DVD.

The screen lit up, showing a street scene at night, vehicles speeding by as pedestrians walked on the pavement. Cathy was surprised at the clarity of the picture, which suddenly changed to show a different scene, an adjoining street, the name and camera number again emblazoned on the top right hand side of the picture.

"So, exactly what are we looking for?" she asked.

"Anything that seems out of the ordinary," sighed Charlie, discreetly mopping his brow in the darkened room, his mouth dry and throat parched, desperate for a drink to ease his thirst.

"Mary Cavendish was wearing a dark coloured nylon coat and looked exactly what she was, a wee slim, young girl. Might not seem too out of place in Glasgow on Saturday night, I suppose."

They watched for a few minutes then both started at the fleeting glimpse.

"Wait," Cathy turned to him, rewind that bit.

Fumbling with some confusion at the remote control, Charlie got the tape rewound and replayed the previous scene.

"Can you slow it up a bit?" Charlie looked blankly at her. Technical things weren't his game.

"Hang on, I'll be back," he said, speaking over his shoulder as he left the room. He returned in less than two minutes with a casually dressed man who limped badly.

"This is Mickey Hughes, our CCTV supervisor. Mickey's ex-job," he explained. "Meet Cathy Mulgrew, down from the CTU to give me a hand."

They nodded to each other as Charlie proceeded to tell Mickey what they had both seen and what he wanted played. Expertly, Mickey rewound the tape and slowed it to half speed.

"There!" cried Cathy, surprising herself at her excitement. "Isn't that a young girl running from that lane?"

Charlie peered at the screen. "That's her," he exclaimed, eyes wide as the tape suddenly jumped to a different street scene.

"Fuck!" the three of them cried in harmony, then laughed together at their mutual outburst. The tape continued and returned to the scene where they had last seen Mary running.

"Who's that?" Mickey said, pausing the tape. A vivid white line obscured the lower part of the screen, but left enough of the upper part to show a male figure furtively exiting from the lane, according to the timed clock on the screen, seconds after Mary had ran from the same spot. Charlie and Cathy moved closer to stare at the screen.

"Mickey," Charlie pointed to the figure. "What's the chances of having this photo of the guy blown up for identification purposes?"

"I've marked the tape at the point where your man exit's the lane. I can only give you a snapshot of what you see on the screen, but the technical support boys at headquarters should be able to do something with it. Want me to give them a call, tell them to expect the tape?"

"Yes, please and I'll take the tape up to them myself. I've another guy to see when I'm there."

Twenty minutes of street scene revealed nothing further. A disappointed Charlie thanked Mickey and walked with Cathy to the general office.

"You two seem very cosy together."

They both stopped and turned to find DCI Nancy Rogers standing behind them, confrontation on her podgy face, her hands resting on her massive hips, the bell tent flowered dress in sharp contrast to the sleek and shapely Cathy.

"Isn't it protocol to report to the senior CID officer upon arrival at an office?" her voice dripped with sarcasm, her comment directed to Cathy.

"It is indeed, ma'am," Cathy coolly responded and staring into Rogers eyes, added with a shake of her head, "but I just couldn't be fucking bothered." Charlie gaped at her as his jaw fell open, taken aback at her blatant impudence and grateful there was no one in the corridor to witness the incident. Rogers choked back her reply and apparently deciding she wouldn't win any argument with the determined Cathy, turned on her heel and waddled off, mustering what dignity she could.

A pale-faced Cathy saw Charlie an open mouthed staring at her with a newfound respect.

"So, Detective Sergeant Miller, what's next?"

*

Irene Cavendish knelt at the foot of St Jude's statue, her rosary beads entwined in her fingers. Head bowed, she mumbled a prayer to herself, unaware of the soft-footed approach of the black clad man.

"Hello, Irene. I'm not disturbing you, am I?"

"Father Flynn," she stiffly raised herself from the step, "of course not. I was just saying a prayer for my Mary. I haven't had the opportunity to thank you for this morning…."

"No need, Irene, no need at all," he interrupted her. "Mary was also my parishioner."

They stood in awkward silence. Irene knew that some of the women in the church tending the flowers and cleaning between the aisles were subtly watching them and she experienced a small flush of pleasure, aware their curiosity would be killing them. Her daughter's death was now public knowledge and she'd humbly and graciously been accepting the parishioner's condolence, acutely aware that many were eager to be seen to sympathise with Frank Brogan's sister.

"You shouldn't be here, Irene," he said sympathetically, "you should be at home, resting."

"No Father, this is where I'm most comfortable, doing the Lords work," she piously replied.

He sighed, rightly suspecting that in some perverse way, she was enjoying the attention of her peers.

"Do the police have any further information?" Flynn enquired.

"Nothing yet, Father. But the detective said he would be in touch."
She wrestled with the beads in her hands and added, "Early days yet, I expect."
He nodded his head in agreement, privately wondering how he might approach
the subject. But in good and true faith, how could he? Better let things take their
natural course, he decided. Patting her on the arm, he reminded her once again,
"Remember, Irene. Anything the parish can do," the rest unsaid as he strolled
back to his sacristy.
Irene stared at his back. Lovely man, Father Flynn she thought, then guilt filled
her with the memory of her request to Frank. Reflexively, she used her right hand
to quickly make the Sign of the Cross. After the man was found and it was done,
she decided, she would make a full and frank confession. God would forgive her
sin.
For after all, didn't He always?

*

Alan Boyle was just leaving when he met Charlie and Cathy as they arrived at
Police Headquarters.
"Got that information for you, Charlie," he said, waving a sheet of paper at him.
"Apart from the odd fixed penalty for parking, speeding, etcetera, which I don't
think you'll be interested in," he smirked, "as far as my mate can determine, the
only person on the list that has any vague connection with the police is… wait for
it," he teased, "Ronnie McPherson," staring at Charlie with a smile, challenging
him to recognise the name.
Charlie furrowed his brow. Ronnie McPherson? The name was familiar, yet
eluded him.
"Okay, smart arse," he grinned at the smiling Boyle, "so who is Ronnie
McPherson?"
Cathy interrupted. "Didn't he used to work for the Procurator Fiscals Department,
a Depute Fiscal?" she asked Boyle.
"Dead on, Mucky," Boyle nodded, "nice to see one of you pair is wearing the
thinking cap today. Right," as he handed Charlie the list, "I'm off back to the
grind. Catch you guys later."
Charlie briefly looked at the list and considered it a dead end. He pushed open the
front door of headquarters and smiled inquisitively at Cathy, "Mucky?"
"Long boring story, so don't ask," while pressing for the lift and ignoring his
lopsided grin. At the fifth floor, Charlie led the way to the technical support
department and spoke to a young and pretty receptionist, whose badge identified
her as Katie. After explaining his purpose, Katie led them into a room containing
long, narrow desks, each desk crammed with all manner of technical and
electrical equipment. Sitting hunched over a desk sat a small, wizened man, thick
rimmed glasses perched on his nose with adhesive tape binding the centre, his
skin the colour of old leather, completely bald and wearing a dirty, torn once-
white dustcoat. Cathy was almost positive she could see egg stain on the front of
the coat at the buttons, or rather, where the buttons used to be.
Katie raised her eyebrows and screwed her pretty mouth up at Charlie as she

tapped the old man on the shoulder. As he slowly turned towards them, Cathy saw that he had the palest shade of blue eyes she had ever seen. Charlie produced the DVD and told the technician what he wanted

"Oh, aye," he acknowledged their request. "Mickey Hughes phoned me. Come back in an hour," the old man grumpily instructed and without another word, turned back to his desk.

Katie led them back to the reception area and issued a receipt for the DVD.

"Excuse me," said Charlie, heading into a nearby Men's Room. The young girl smiled at Cathy.

"Bit of all right, isn't he," she blushingly nodded towards the closed door.

"Eh, yes. I suppose he is," Cathy stammered, aware she hadn't given Charlie's looks a second thought.

Cathy and the girl stood in embarrassed silence till a few minutes later Charlie re-appeared.

"Okay?" he asked, oblivious to their smiling glance.

Together, Charlie and Cathy made their way to the canteen to sit and kill time.

"So, you know my story," as he looked at her bare third finger on her left hand, "is it Miss, Ms or Mrs Mulgrew?"

"I have a partner," Cathy admitted, "but not in the police thankfully. I don't think two of us working at this job would be good for our sanity. There'd never be a day off, it would be shop talk non-stop," she smiled. A very attractive smile, Charlie suddenly realised.

"So, what made you join the CTU?"

"I didn't volunteer," she shrugged her shoulders, "I was recruited. Got a good degree at Glasgow University and then discovered the police paid a probationary cop more than a student teacher, so opted for the money. A spell with Divisional CID followed uniform service and then I was sent for interview here, at headquarters. I thought it was a training post. Next thing I knew I was being security vetted and leaning how to open combination cabinets and sit with my back to a wall," she smiled, while idly stirring her coffee. "To be honest, I can't say I've regretted the decision. The police have offered me a good a good life and I've enjoyed a standard of living in excess of what a teaching post would have brought. My time at the CTU has been beneficial, but recently I've felt that perhaps I should be pursuing promotion." She laughed. "Up till this morning, I was submitting a transfer request, but then my boss told me to sling my hook and get myself down to Cowcaddens and assist some drunken bum of a Detective Sergeant."

Charlie grinned self-consciously. Cathy couldn't possibly know, he thought, but the overwhelming need for a drink right now - right here - as they were speaking - was tearing him up inside. His stomach was churning at the sudden absence of his regular intake of alcohol. But he wasn't going to let it beat him. By God he wasn't! Forcing his voice to remain calm, he returned to the subject of the inquiry.

"That information about Mary Cavendish being pregnant, Professor Martin was adamant that forensics would have to confirm his findings, but I believe he's experienced enough to be correct. I'm not keen on being the one to break the news to the mother, but it will give you the opportunity to give Brogan the once-over, if I can inveigle him to be present. Suit you?"

Cathy agreed. Her brow furrowed in concentration.

"There's something been bothering me, Charlie. The girl was gone what, about a week? How much money did she take with her? How did she feed herself and, more importantly, how did she manage to find that hell-hole that she died in? By all accounts, she wasn't a particularly street wise kid. So, how did she survive living on the street?"

Charlie sat forward. Cathy's questions had matched his thoughts on the same issue. Then he remembered the two, dirty and folded ten-pound notes in her clenched fist. A sudden realisation struck him.

"Tricks," he snapped out, "she was turning tricks. That's how she got her cash. My God," he ran both hands through his already dishevelled hair, the shock evident in his voice. "That's why she ran from that lane. That's who the guy is. He's a customer. The wee lassie was prostituting herself."

*

DCI Martin Cairney didn't like surprises, so when the commissionaire at the front door of headquarters phoned and announced the presence downstairs of Barry Ashford, Cairney swore, then sent the CTU clerk down to fetch him. The clerk politely knocked on Cairney's door. Ashford stood behind, his smile broad and wide and deep enough to hide a thousand lies.

"Come in, Barry," Cairney invited, hating himself for his false bonhomie. Ashford's hand pushed out from the starched white shirt cuff, the gold coloured Rolex prominent on his bony wrist. His clipped, English university educated voice was as smooth as silk. The smell of French tobacco clung to his clothes like a distasteful, strong cologne.

"Martin. Good to see you again, what's it been? Three months?"

Wish it were three fucking years, Cairney darkly thought.

"Yes, about that. So, what can I do for you?" he tautly replied, privately wondering why the bastard was in town and without the courtesy of due notice to his department.

Ashford sat down, taking care to pinch his trousers up slightly to avoid creasing the immaculate wool of the Saville Row suit. Slowly and deliberately, he smoothed back his salt and pepper hair while brushing an imaginary thread from his trouser leg.

"Little problem that my Lord and Masters believe you might be able to assist us with. Concerns one of your local worthies, Frank Brogan, whom I've no doubt you chaps are right on top of, eh?"

Cairney sat back, his eyes narrowed in concentration. This can't be coincidental, he thought. I send Cathy Mulgrew fishing for information and this prick shows up from London, wanting assistance?

"Please, continue," he invited, his face expressionless.

"Ahem, well the problem is that Mr Brogan is sending far too little cash over to his chums across the water and we've had a whisper that they are most dissatisfied with his contribution, so to speak. Wouldn't do for us to lose this contact, if you see what I mean," while staring directly into Cairney's eyes.

Shite, Cairney realised at once. The bastards at the Security Service have turned Brogan! Angrily he leaned forward, his massive frame building itself into a rage.

"Are you telling me, Barry that you are running an agent in my area without my knowledge? That your agent is pocketing his terrorist pal's cash and now that his arse is about to be fried, you want my assistance to bail this fucker out!"

Ashford, his face flushing at the obscenities, licked his lips and twirled his military style moustache.

"Ahem, not in so many words, but yes, afraid so, old chap."

"Don't fucking old chap me, you conniving bastard," raged Cairney, his manners lost in the red mist of anger.

"Really, Martin, it's the oldest game in town. We both know that I don't make the decision as to who is told what," he theatrically splayed his arms wide. "My hands are tied. I've rules to play by, as have you. I'm simply following my masters instructions and those instructions are," he pointedly sat forward, his voice losing his pretentious, cultured speech, "to secure without prejudice the assistance of the Counter Terrorism Unit of the police area in any matter or issue that concerns national security in that area and, if necessary, reveal only that information which is pertinent to securing such assistance."

Cairney breathed deeply, with an effort bringing under control the rage that threatened to consume his good sense and tear this sanctimonious little shit from his seat. He swallowed hard, his voice now controlled and even.

"I must confess Barry, my disappointment that your service hasn't had the courtesy to apprise me of your interest in Brogan sooner."

"It's nothing personal, Martin. Brogan is too good a catch to share and frankly," he paused for effect, "there is the matter of confidentiality."

Cairney bristled. The bastard was going too far, suggesting that his department might compromise an operation. But still, he admitted, security was vital in all agent-handling operations.

"So," he offered through gritted teeth, "what assistance do you require from me?"

*

Charlie collected the photograph and DVD from the coyly smiling young Katie at technical support and met Cathy in the car. Handing her a brown, A4 size manila envelope, she reached in and drew out a black and white glossy picture that showed a man aged about thirty with short dark hair and wearing a dark, windcheater jacket, exiting the lane that featured in the video shot. As Cathy peered closely at the photo, she was taken aback to see the man seemed to be holding his genitals.

"The quality is excellent," she admitted, then added "we shouldn't have too much trouble identifying this character, if he's known to the police."

"The problem is," countered Charlie "that it's unlikely that this guy is our fire raiser. He's probably the punter that she scored the twenty quid from and even if we do find him, it won't take us any closer to our culprit. The thing that puzzles me is why she seems to have run in panic and as you can see," he pointed to the figure, "he looks like he's holding his balls. It's occurred to me she might be escaping from him, but," he admitted with a frown, "that's purely speculation on my part and you don't get full marks for guessing in this game."

"So Charlie, what's our next move then?"

Charlie looked at his watch. "I'll set up a meeting for tomorrow morning with the mother and suggest her brother be with her, tell her I might have some news. Right now, though, I want to look in at the Fraud Squad office and check if they have any knowledge of the lawyers firm. You can come with me or do you have something to do?"

Cathy shook her head. "In for a penny, in for a pound," she replied, replacing the photo in the envelope and wondering if Charlie had noticed the name Katie and the mobile phone number scribbled in pencil on the back. Katie must like a bit of rough she thought, glancing sideways at him.

"One other thing has come to mind, Cathy. I'm thinking of the dates. Mary Cavendish was gone from the house, give or take a day for just over a week. If Professor Martin's correct about her pregnancy," he turned to look at her, "then the wee girl was likely pregnant before she skipped the house."

*

The hushed silence of the expansive Fraud Squad office at Police Headquarters reminded Charlie of a library, the detectives within all working industriously at their desks, a background noise of hammer tapping as clumsy fingers danced across computer keyboards. The subdued lighting in the room struggled against the November rays that streamed through the double glazed windows, nourishing the potted plants that lined the ledge like regimented, camouflaged soldiers. A female clerk smiled a greeting at them and in a low voice inquired as to their business? Charlie's request led to he and Cathy being directed to a stout, bespectacled detective, flowery bright red braces and shirts sleeves rolled up, his patterned tie undone, the top button loose and a pencil wedged behind his right ear, sitting at a desk that was stacked with ledgers. The clerk tapped the detective on the shoulder and, as he turned, smiled in recognition at Charlie.

Charlie thought he looked well. It had been a long time since he had spoken with Fraser McManus.

"Well I never! Charlie Miller. How are you, you old bastard? Oh, pardon me, miss," said the elderly Detective Inspector as he spied Cathy standing behind Charlie.

Cathy reached forward, her hand extended.

"Always a pleasure to hear a gentleman apologise," she smiled.

Charlie made the introductions as McManus noisily dragged forward two chairs to his desk, ignoring the furrowed brows that turned to glare at him.

"So, what can I do for you?"

Pleasantries over, Charlie related the circumstances of the fire at the solicitors office and his increasing suspicion that the culprit had been acting on behalf of someone within the firm. McManus listened, then sat back and chewed the end of his pencil.

"I know the firm, had dealings with them about two years ago when one of their paralegals dipped into the petty cash. Should have been dealt with as a straightforward theft by the local division," he scowled and squinted accusingly under his thick, bushy eyebrows at Charlie, "but your mob exaggerated the problem and called us in. Waste of our talent, really," he suddenly grinned, his even teeth a sparkling brilliant white, causing Cathy to suspect their origin lay in some dental laboratory.

"Now," McManus groped amongst a pile of diaries, "let me see. Ah, yes." Opening a book he flicked through several pages, then finding the one he was looking for screwed up his face as he read the contents.

"As I've noted here, it was a Steven Taylor, the senior partner that I dealt with." Hooking his thumbs into his braces, he sat back and recalled, "The firm dealt mainly with financial investments, most of their clientele being old money. You know, long term clients, established family businesses, that sort of thing. Anyway, we soon had the thief by the short and curlies and that was our involvement ended."

McManus scratched his chin with the chewed end of his pencil.

"About eight of the staff were lawyers, I believe, split between a couple of offices. One in Glasgow and one in, let me think now, I believe it was in Paisley. Apart from that," he sighed "there's not much I can add. Sorry."

Charlie was disappointed, but not surprised. If there was a large scale irregularity at the law firm, he didn't believe it would be obvious and thought it unlikely that any firm, particularly one that dealt in other people's money, would report the matter and risk publicly revealing the company's shortcomings to its investors. The issue of the petty cash, he assumed was more internal and unlikely to cause the clients any concern about the firm's image. It's likely, he surmised, the fire raisers primary task was to torch any evidence. Nodding his head, he stood and thanked McManus. As he and Cathy made to leave, Charlie stopped and turned back.

"Fraser," he asked, "do you happen to know an ex-Fiscal depute by the name of Ronnie McPherson?"

McManus' brow furrowed and the bushy eyebrows knitted to produce a grey fur ball.

"I do. Why do you ask?"

"According to the staff list I have, he's working for the firm now."

McManus frowned and then beckoned for Charlie and Cathy to sit down again.

"Right you two," he began in a low voice, "what I'm about to reveal can't be discussed with anyone else and definitely can't be used in any court proceedings, understand?"

Their curiosity aroused, both Charlie and Cathy nodded their heads in understanding.

"About eighteen months ago," McManus recounted, "the Police Standards Unit was requested by the Procurator Fiscal to step away from their normal role of pursuing allegations against cops and make a discreet and confidential inquiry into one of their Deputes, who was suspected of fiddling money in the Fines Department."

"Ronnie McPherson?" asked Cathy.

"Ronnie McPherson," nodded McManus. "Anyway, the rubber heels obtained the necessary permission from the PF and elicited my assistance, using me to check the paperwork and so on. I'm rather good at that sort of thing," he boasted with a wicked smile. "To continue, the bugger was in charge of the fines money that was collected from the various courts in Glasgow, a tidy sum if you add up the weeks takings from our offending citizenry," he grinned. "Added to that McPherson also dealt with authorising expense monies to witnesses, you know, travelling expenses, lunch money and so on. And of course, being a Depute, he was never questioned when he produced the paperwork for what later proved to be an inordinate number of fictitious persons."

"Isn't that just so much petty cash?" interrupted Cathy.

"Agreed, my dear, but you know the old saying, look after the pennies and the pounds will roll on in. The petty cash worked out at hundreds of pounds every week. Multiply that over a year and we're talking thousands. All money, as far as McPherson was concerned, that was untraceable."

McManus waved away an approaching detective and continued. "It turned out McPherson was changing the paperwork and altering figures, making sure that the names of those staff entering the amounts differed so that there was no continuity. Clever little bastard he was. By the time we had cottoned on to his game, we reckon he had scammed several thousands over the year he had been in the department, though he covered his trail so well that even I," he smilingly shook his head, "couldn't determine how much was involved. Needless to say, the system has been totally re-vamped since then."

"I don't recall reading or hearing anything about his arrest," Cathy interrupted, "after all, a Depute Fiscal getting the jail would have made the news."

McManus grimaced. "Said it was a discreet inquiry, didn't I? The PF didn't want the matter brought into the public domain, reckoned it would have tarnished the good name and credibility of his department, so he said. Against strong police advice, the PF made McPherson aware that if he quietly resigned no prosecution would take place. Then some weeks after the deal was struck," McManus added with a sigh, "he turned the tables on the PF. Told the fool that if he didn't provide McPherson with a glowing reference, he'd sue for wrongful dismissal on the grounds that he'd been made a scapegoat because of alleged irregularities in his department. Such irregularities that he was of course in his words totally innocent."

Charlie and Cathy stared in disbelief.

"So a deal was done?" Charlie guessed.

"Correct. By that time, you'll have guessed, all reference to and documentation about the thefts had been destroyed, so even if the PF had decided to re-instate proceedings against McPherson, he had nothing on paper with which to do so. Mr. McPherson walked free without a blemish on his fucking character. Beg your pardon, Cathy," McManus once again apologised.

"Granted," smiled Cathy, instinctively liking this bluff and shrewd man.

Charlie shook McManus by the hand. "Fraser, if nothing else you've given me a line of inquiry. And that," he confessed, "is better than what I came in here with."

*

DCI Martin Cairney was not a happy man. Still fuming, he considered at length his meeting with the scurrilous and manipulative Barry Ashford and reluctantly accepted that the Security Service man had Cairney over a barrel. Try as he might, he could think of no reason for refusing to assist Ashford and reluctantly accepted he had no option but to support him with his devious scheme. Resignedly shaking his head at what he was about to do, he reached for his phone and dialled Cathy Mulgrew's mobile number.

*

Cathy replaced her phone in her jacket pocket.

"Sorry, Charlie, I've to report to my boss. Something's cropped up. How about we call it a day here and I'll meet you tomorrow morning at your office?" she suggested.

Charlie agreed. "I'll fix a meeting with Mrs. Cavendish and then perhaps we'll track down McPherson and have a wee word with the slippery sod. Suit you?"

"It's a deal," nodded Cathy.

Charlie delivered the CID car back to the office and strode through the city streets towards the Underground train network that ringed the city, turning his collar up against the darkening skies that was threatening to unleash their rain filled clouds on the crowded mass of humanity below. With seconds to spare, he made it to the glass domed cover that sheltered the entrance to Buchanan Street subway station, then stopped, his eyes lighting upon the pub whose bright lights and smoky atmosphere beckoned him from across the pedestrian precinct. He licked his lips in anticipation, aware the dryness of his throat could be soothed by just one whisky. But then, chance intervened in his plans. A woman, her head down against the sudden driving rain and dragging two protesting children with her hurried into the entrance and cannoned off him. One of the children fell to the ground. Instinctively, Charlie reached down for the bawling child, but the mother beat him to it and seized the child by the arm. Hauling him to his feet and ignoring the cries, she screamed at the toddler, "Move your feet you, ya wee shite!" before again dragging both the crying children towards the stairs that led to the lower platforms. Bemused, Charlie watched the trio descend the stairs and shook his head. Treat a child like a nuisance, he thought and the child will grow to become a nuisance. Wincing at the woman's treatment of her children and blissfully unaware that the unexpected distraction had cancelled all thought of drink, he made his way downstairs in time to catch the southbound train.

*

Cathy Mulgrew was initially stunned, and then blew through pursed lips. DCI Martin Cairney's brief, but concise account of his meeting with Barry Ashford had been a bombshell, right enough. She had previously met Ashford and, like her boss, wouldn't trust him to tell her the time of day, unless it suited the Security Service needs.

"So what does this mean, as far as my assisting Sergeant Miller in anticipating learning something about Brogan and his associates?"

"It changes nothing, Cathy. Your assignment remains the same. Brogan might be working for Ashford, but he is still conducting activities on behalf of the Irish republican movement in our area and that is of interest to us, at a local level. Besides," he sighed "other than your newfound knowledge of Brogan, we mustn't let any inkling of his status with Ashford be known, outside this room. Too many of our department either knows of or has guessed why you're on assignment with Miller. If I was to pull you off now, it might lead to questions and that," he bitterly admitted "could inevitably lead to the compromise of what has to be a major source of intelligence for the Security Service. We know from his movements through both the seaport at Stranraer and Prestwick airport that Brogan is a regular traveller to Belfast when attending meetings with his republican masters. It's likely, therefore, that Brogan is bringing back some quality stuff so I won't have that bastard Ashford settling blame on this department if his operation should go belly-up. No way," angrily slapping his hand down hard on his desk.

Cathy sat in silence, but her mind was whirling. Her burgeoning relationship with Miller was now threatened by her need to keep from him her knowledge of Brogan's treachery to his organization. Cathy knew it wouldn't be difficult deceiving Miller, yet she couldn't understand why a part of her felt strangely guilty at that deceit. With a sigh, she nodded her head at Cairney.

"Anything else, any more little tit-bits boss?" her voice dripped with sarcasm.

Cairney smiled, aware that his revelation would hang heavy with Cathy. He'd long ago realised that though the very nature of her profession relied on discretion and secrecy, Cathy Mulgrew was one of the most honest people he knew.

"Nothing more at this time, Cathy, but just remember what I've told you previously," he wagged a forefinger at Cathy. "When you're around Brogan, be careful of his minder, McPhee. We both know that is one, vicious bastard."

*

Charlie arrived home soaked and bedraggled, having walked the short distance from the underground to his flat in what proved to be a torrential downpour. Opening the door, the smell of unwashed clothes, accentuated by the humid heat of the central heating, assailed his nostrils. With a shrug, Charlie knew it was time to get to work.

Some three hours, two washing machine loads, four CD changes and several bin bags later, the flat had regained some modicum of order. Despite the pouring rain, he'd thrown open the windows and the combination of fresh air and a long forgotten can of gents deodorant spray had dispelled the musty atmosphere.

Turning down the volume on his music deck, Charlie sat down with a mug of coffee in his fist. With a grin, he looked round the lounge and was satisfied with his efforts. Then, as an afterthought, placed the mug on the low table and fetched the photograph from his coat. Folded and crushed in his pocket, the print had fared badly, but the subject remained vividly clear. He stared at the photograph and took a deep breath. Mary, Mary, quite contrary, he inwardly repeated. What else can you tell me? What more can I do to help you? The phone rang. Surprised, for he seldom received social phone calls anymore, Charlie lifted the receiver.

"Charlie? Sorry to call you at home," apologised DC Alan Boyle, "but I'm finishing today for two week's annual leave and didn't want to leave a message at the office in case you didn't get it. Guess what I've got in my sweaty mitt?"

"Sorry, Alan but I'm not really in to obscene calls."

The chortle at the other end made him smile.

"It's me that's talking here," responded Boyle, "I'd need two hands. Anyway, my mate at the criminal records office has been on to me regarding that check on your list?"

"Yeah, go on," invited Charlie, unconsciously nodding at the phone.

"Well, I'd been chatting to him about the fire at the law office and he said he would try for a modus operandi check on their database. He's just phoned me and offered up a name."

Charlie raised his eyebrows in anticipation.

"Guy called Robert Turner whose last known address from two years ago was a flat over in Castlemilk. I'll leave the details in your dookit at the office."

"Thanks, Alan. That's a…" Charlie hesitated at the word, "…drink I owe you." Now why, he briefly wondered, did I flinch at that?

"No problem," replied Boyle, "and by the way, tell Mucky I send my regards, but not my love," he laughingly added as he hung up.

Bemused, Charlie replaced the receiver and thought about the name that Boyle had provided. Robert Turner. Well, Mr. Turner he decided, tomorrow you might just be getting a wee visit.

Chapter 7 -Tuesday morning

The following morning dawned clear and bright. A faint steam rose from the pavements as they dried and warmed in the intense sunshine.

Jimmy Donnelly usually enjoyed this time of the morning, getting to work before most of the city had even risen from their beds. But today was different. Today was the first day to the start of his mission. The first day of betraying the confidence the police had previously enjoyed in Jimmy Donnelly.

Pushing open the public door of the station, he was greeted by the nightshift desk officer, who smiled as he handed Jimmy the morning's papers for delivery to the various offices of the senior police officers within the building, mystified why the normally genial old man hadn't stopped for a chat. Jimmy knew from past experience there would be hell to pay from the bosses if the morning papers weren't sitting awaiting them when they arrived at their desks and delivered them before making his way to the boiler-room, where he kept a small office. His staff of six cleaners were laughing and smiling at some tale told by one of them. Irritably, he snapped at them and ushered them to their duties. With downcast eyes and some curiosity, the women left Jimmy and departed for their areas of responsibility. Out of earshot of the old janitor, they whispered and wondered at his attitude, for clearly this wasn't the Jimmy they knew and respected, the Jimmy that shared a fag before sending them on their way with one of his little jokes. Annoyed and cursing at himself, Jimmy followed the women from the boiler-room and made his way to the CCTV room where he knew he'd share a cup of tea with Mickey Hughes.

"Morning, Jimmy. So how's you today?" inquired Mickey as he catalogued the previous days DVDs.

"Not bad, Mickey, not too bad thanks."

Jimmy's mouth was dry. He hadn't a clue how to open the conversation about Sergeant Miller.

"Cup of tea?" offered Mickey.

He nodded, afraid to met Mickey's eye. His heart felt as though it were about to burst through his chest.

"Sure you're okay, Jimmy? You look a bit downcast, if you don't mind me saying so." "Oh, I'm all right. Just a touch of arthritis because of the damp weather," he volunteered and then taking a deep breath, asked, "So, Mickey. Who's the new detective I saw yesterday, the good-looking redheaded woman?"

Mickey's smile turned to a leer. "Trust you to notice the pretty ones, you old dog. I suppose the Viagra kicked in when you got a look at her, eh?"

Jimmy returned Mickey's smile, too tense to even reply.

"She's down from headquarters. Cathy Mulgrew, a Detective Sergeant in the Counter Terrorism Unit. One of those sent out into the real world to do a bit of policing for a change, rather than sit up there at Cowards Castle reading the bloody papers all day," Mickey laughed a his own joke.

Jimmy's throat tightened. Counter Terrorism Unit! Dear God! What was he getting himself into?

"Have to say, though," continued Mickey "she seems to be okay. Not stuck up like some of they headquarters wankers. Know what I mean, Jimmy? Jimmy! You feeling okay?" asked Mickey, concern on his face as he turned and stared at the elderly janitor. "You're as white as a sheet. Here, let me get you a cup of water." Hughes left the CCTV room to fetch water and Jimmy took deep breaths, afraid the warnings from his doctor about the onset of the asthma were true, that he was about to hyperventilate. Cathy Mulgrew. A Detective Sergeant from the Counter Terrorism Unit! He didn't know why a CTU detective would be helping out Charlie Miller, but at least it was something he could tell Brogan, something that just might keep his wee granddaughter safe from being hurt by that bastard McPhee.

*

Bobby Turner woke early, eager to be out and phoning the man. This was the day that Bobby would collect his money. With a smile, he bounced from the bed and made his way into the bathroom. Ablutions completed, he dressed and squeezed his shaving kit into the already bulging holdall. The bag contained all that he would need for a new start. He looked around the council flat. The cheap furniture, what little there was, had no value. Nothing that would remain in the flat was of any worth to him. Not even happy memories.

Glancing through the window, he was pleased to see the rain was off and the sun streamed through the dirty net curtains. A good sign, decided Bobby, smiling at the though of a bright start to a new life. Donning his dark baseball cap and dark jacket, he left the holdall in the flat and strolled to the corner shop. Mr Singh stood in his usual spot.

"Good morning, Bobby my friend," he smiled.

Bobby returned the smile.

"You seem much happy today, young Bobby."

"Happier, Mr Singh," Bobby corrected, "Happier. And you're right. Life's on the up and up."

"Up and up?" repeated the old man. "This I not understand."

"Let's just say I think that today will be my lucky day, Mr Singh," Bobby grinned as he purchased the 'Glasgow News', then added to the young girl serving him, "Can you include some change for the phone, love?"

The girl smiled shyly and replaced the three pound coins with fifty and twenty pence pieces.

That'll do nicely," joked Bobby, blowing her a farewell kiss.

*

Once again, Charlie Miller had wakened without a headache, unusually surprised at the hunger pangs that caused his stomach to rumble. The alarm clock kicked in while he was in the shower and he returned to the bedroom to hear the announcer predict the weather would remain fine for most of the day. After last night's heavy rainfall, he thought, the drains could probably do with a break.

Using what remained of his deodorant, he strode into the now tidy kitchen, pleased with his efforts of the previous evening. While the kettle boiled, Charlie planned his day. He'd given it some thought and Alan Boyle's information last night had dissuaded him from directly approaching the ex-Depute Ronnie McPherson. No, he thought, better to work round him. The tale told by Fraser McManus of how McPherson had duped the PF had been a stark warning to Charlie, a pointed reminder not to underestimate the former Depute.

Stirring his coffee, he thought of Cathy Mulgrew and smiled. Foolish of him to even consider her in any romantic context, he thought. Still, she wasn't a bad looking woman, he decided. But he knew from experience that working relationships in the job had a tendency to go arse up. Better keep it professional, at least for now. He glanced at the clock. Time he was gone. Grabbing his coat he hesitated then, almost as an afterthought, lifted the crumpled photograph, folded and replaced it in his pocket.

While Charlie was grabbing his first coffee of the morning, Cathy Mulgrew was already seated at her desk in the Counter Terrorism Unit office, busy researching a buff coloured folder that lay open before her. The photograph she was examining had been covertly taken almost a year previously and showed two men deep in conversation. Frank Brogan seemed to be listening intently as Liam McPhee whispered in his ear. An Irish republican flute band marched in the background, passing them by with banners waving, the flutists wearing what looked like toy town uniforms, but the expressions on their faces was of pure loathing and directed at the watching, uniformed cops. Cathy re-read the recent information the file contained, idly noting that most of it seemed to be the result of surveillance observations. Sighing, she came to the conclusion that there was nothing within the file that she didn't already know. She turned the pages back against the spine, making it easier to close the thick file. The entry concerning Brogan's sole conviction, for drunk driving, imposed almost twelve months earlier caught her eye. The ban would be completed in a couple of days and that's when McPhee's role might be worth reassessing, when he finishes the job of chauffeuring Brogan, she thought. As for Brogan's life style, well, that had worried at her for some time, but with Barry Ashford's confession to her boss, Cathy now knew the answer to that one. Frank Brogan was undoubtedly receiving *ex gratis* payments from the Security Service. She shook her head in disbelief, the irony of it being that the Irish republican sympathiser Frank Brogan was, in fact, a Government paid employee.

*

Across town, Bobby Turner pulled open the heavy, squeaking door of the telephone kiosk and fumbled in his pocket for the man's number. His mouth silently wording the digits as he read them, Bobby took a deep breath to compose himself and then dialled the number. His call was answered at the third ring. "Right, listen, I won't be repeating this," he said, so listen carefully, "eleven o'clock this morning, down behind the old hotel on Castlemilk Road, the one that's all shuttered up." Bobby closed his eyes tightly, listening as the man began to protest and then unconsciously raised his hand. "Well, you better fucking well find it, won't you?" he shouted down the line. "Be there, with the money or the filth will be getting an anonymous phone call, okay?"
Bobby slammed down the receiver, cutting off any protest. Pleased with the way he had prevented the man making excuses or arguing against the instruction, Bobby pushed open the door and checked his watch. There was time to kill he thought, before the meeting.
Whistling, he strolled back to the flat for breakfast and a read of his newspaper.

*

Frank Brogan replaced the receiver in its cradle and thought about what the hushed voice of Jimmy Donnelly had told him. Detective Sergeant Cathy Mulgrew from Counter Terrorism Unit was working with that copper Miller. Now why, he asked himself, would the CTU be working with a divisional CID man?

What interest could she have in the death of his niece? According to Donnelly, Miller was a known drunkard, so it might be something as simple as an internal issue, the cops watching Miller prior to the police sacking him. The CTU, he knew, were capable of all sorts of devious work and that likely might include monitoring their own. His brow furrowed as he worried at the information, trying to determine what the CTU could possibly gain from the inquiry. Reluctantly, he concluded he neither knew nor could guess at any advantage the Brit bastards might obtain through Mary's death. Still, he decided, better let Liam know and instruct him to be on his guard, particularly if Miller brings the woman to Irene's flat, today. And why, he asked himself again, does Miller have to come to the flat when a phone call would suffice?

Suspicious by nature, Brogan wasn't a happy man. Not happy at all. Once again, he congratulated himself on his foresight in having Jimmy Donnelly ferret out what he could. Cathy Mulgrew? Brogan knew he would have to determine who she was, if only for his own peace of mind. And he knew the very man to ask.

*

Charlie arrived at his desk to find two small, yellow square post-it notes stuck to his desk lamp. The first from the uniformed assistant at the front office advised him that DS Mulgrew would be a little late, no reason given. The second note instructed Charlie, upon his arrival, to attend at DCI Rogers office. Charlie sighed and, crushing the note into his wastebasket, decided to get it over with right away.

DCI Nancy Rogers was tense as she awaited Charlie Miller, acutely conscious that the perspiration under her armpits threatened to declare that anxiety by staining her beige coloured blouse with damp patches. Fidgeting with her desk diary, she straightened the writing pad in preparation to taking notes. The knock on the door, though expected, still startled her and reaching for her coffee mug, she spilled some of the liquid onto the desktop.

"Come in!" she shouted, her annoyance directed at her own clumsiness.

Charlie entered as Rogers used a tissue to mop up the spilled coffee.

"Please take a seat, Sergeant Miller," she formally invited him, while deftly ignoring his guarded, but curious gaze.

Charlie sat down, surprised at the uncommon courtesy and slightly relieved that she was alone. He had half expected that sycophantic bastard John Brown to be present. He couldn't know that Rogers was equally pleased that he was also unaccompanied. Overcoming her fluster, Rogers raised her head to peer at Charlie through myopic eyes.

"So tell me. What progress have you made with the fire inquiry?"

"No arrest imminent," he admitted, "but I do have a couple of lines of inquiry."

Rogers picked up a pen and stared at him. "Go on," she instructed.

"There's no doubt in my mind that the deceased Mary Cavendish was in the wrong place at the wrong time. She wasn't the intended victim. I believe the fire was set to destroy documents that were stored in the law premises and that the person that set the fire was probably hired by a member of staff, or someone with access to the files, and instructed in what to torch."

Charlie hesitated, allowing Rogers to make her notes. She looked up and he continued.

"I've learned that a possible suspect might be one, Robert Turner."

"And he's suspected why?" she queried.

"Purely on his previous convictions, his modus operandi," Charlie admitted, "but at the moment he's all I've got," deliberately neglecting to mention the former PF Depute, Ronnie McPherson. After all, he privately thought, the link between McPherson and any wrongdoing in this case is tenuous, at best.

"Let's concentrate on this man Turner," Rogers said. What do you know about him?"

"I only learned of his previous fire raising conviction's last night," Charlie disclosed, choosing not to reveal from whom.

Rogers didn't press him any further, but changed tact, catching him by surprise.

"DS Mulgrew. How are you coping with her tagging your footsteps?"

"No problem, so far," he cautiously informed her, privately wondering where this was going.

"I've had dealings with her before," Rogers admitted, her lips tight and mean looking. "Were I you, I would be very careful what you say to her, particularly in private matters."

"Thank you ma'am, I'll bear that in mind," replied a puzzled Charlie, while not having a damn clue as to what Rogers was talking about.

"Anything else?" Rogers asked him.

"Only thing that might be of interest is that I've an appointment with the mother and her brother, today. I've the sad duty to beak the news the wee girl was pregnant. Early stages, by all account and still to be forensically confirmed, but I've no doubt that Professor Martin, who did the autopsy, will be proven to be correct."

"Will it benefit your inquiry revealing that information, I mean, won't it add to the mother's distress?" she asked in what Charlie perceived to be a rare show of compassion.

"Not really," he admitted, "but she was only fourteen and it might well shed some light on the reason she disappeared from her home. Also, I've managed to obtain some CCTV footage that seems to indicate she was in the company of a male, shortly before she returned to the cellar under the building. I don't believe that it will progress my inquiry, but I'd like to try and establish her movements prior to the incident."

"This male, do you have any idea who he might be?"

Charlie shuffled his feet and looked directly at Rogers.

"Of course, it's only supposition on my part, but I suspect that he was a punter. I've obtained a photographic print that I'll have copied and distributed and see if I can come up with a name. I believe that Mary Cavendish was prostituting herself for money to survive on the streets."

His voice softened as he spoke. "Sign of the times I know, but I believe Mary Cavendish was more than just a fire victim."

Her brow furrowed, Rogers flipped through her desk diary, then apparently finding the entry she was looking for, scribbled a name and phone number on the corner of a page that she tore off and handed to Charlie.

"That's Aileen Dee's number," Rogers explained. "Aileen runs a drop-in centre for the street girls, prostitutes that she counsels and helps with needle exchanges, that sort of thing. If your victim was on the game, Aileen or one of her girls will know about it. When you call her, mention my name."

Surprised, Charlie accepted the paper as Rogers asked him, "Anything else?"

He nodded his head. "I intend contacting the PF today and arranging to have the body released to the family, as soon as possible. Allow them to make their funeral arrangements. I see no point in retaining the wee girl's body, it'll only add to their distress."

"Leave that to me," offered Rogers, making copious notes in her pad. "I'll let you know what the PF decides, but I don't foresee it I'll be a problem. On that note, I'd like a preliminary report of your inquiries to date, submitted to the PF."

Charlie nodded again, aware that though neither liked each other, in the pecking order of things, decorum decreed the Detective Chief Inspector liaised with the PF in such matters. In that he couldn't fault Rogers, not for doing what was in essence, her duty. "And as we previously discussed, it would be helpful if this thing is wrapped up as quickly as possible."

Rising, he walked to the door and stopped. Turning, he took a deep breath and holding up the piece of paper Rogers had given him said, "Thank you for your assistance, ma'am," then closed the door behind him.

Rogers let out a relieved breath and licked her lips, her mouth unusually dry. It had gone better than she had hoped. Oddly, she suddenly realised, Miller had seemed more focused today. Reaching for her phone, she glanced again to confirm the number and then dialled Aileen Dee.

*

Cathy Mulgrew was sitting waiting for Charlie beside his desk, her red hair tied up in a bun, wearing a plain white blouse and a smart navy blue business suit, her slim, long and athletic legs showing beneath the knee length skirt. Next to her, he thought, I must look like a second prize drunk.

"Good morning, Sergeant Miller," she smiled at him, noting the clean pale blue shirt with dark blue tie and ironed, suit trousers, the faint scent of deodorant surprising her.

"Yes it is," he replied, returning her smile, "and so far so good."

Briefly, he recounted his meeting with Nancy Rogers, but omitted the warning that Rogers had issued him about Cathy, seeing little point in provoking further antipathy between the two women. Still, he wondered at the DCI's throwaway comment. Cathy interrupted his thoughts.

"So what's next?" she asked.

"We've a midday meeting with Mrs Cavendish. I've requested her brother be present, sort of suggested he might be a comfort in this time of need. Till then, though, I'd like to pull this guys previous convictions file," showing her the name

Robert Turner he'd written down, "and try to obtain a current address for him."

"What about Ronnie McPherson, our lawyer friend?"

Charlie shook his head. "I think I'd rather work round Mr McPherson for now. After all," he reminded her "we've nothing concrete on him, just a suggestion that he's dirty and works with the firm that got torched."

"I agree, boss," grinned Cathy.

"One other thing," his brow knitted as if not quite believing what had occurred, "Rogers provided me with a contact name, an Aileen Dee at this number," he said, producing for Cathy the scrap of paper. "She suggested Dee might be useful in tracing Mary Cavendish's final movements. You give her a phone and I'll go through and pull Turner's file off the computer. Okay?"

"Okay," Cathy grinned back at him.

*

The waste ground behind the derelict hotel on Castlemilk Road had in the recent past been used by the locals as a dump, lazily disposing of their unwanted garbage and household items there than travel the two miles to the council site. The ubiquitous black bin bag lay everywhere, most having been split open and their contents scattered, rotting food strewn about and seemingly confirmation of the presence of rats. Rusting washing machines and fridges, televisions with broken screens and other household debris abounded the rear car park where many of the paving slabs lay broken or torn from the ground.

Bobby Turner puffed nervously at the cigarette he held between his shaking fingers. He was indifferent to the chill in the shadowed doorway. It was the lateness of the man that caused Bobby to shake. Nervously, he again he glanced at his watch. Fourteen minutes past the appointed time. Bobby had decided to give him five minutes, which rolled into ten and now this.

Fourteen lengthy, nerve-wracking minutes.

He begun to think the man was working him over and was ignoring Bobby's threat. Angrily, he tossed the butt end of the fag down and viciously stamped it into the ground. The sound of a car engine surprised him and he stood still, slowly backing against the boarded up rear door of the building. A dark green coloured Volvo saloon car drove cautiously into the car park, the driver apparently concentrating on avoiding the scattered rubbish that lay about the ground. From his vantage point, Bobby could see the man was alone and he smiled to himself. The man stopped the car and switched off the engine. Bobby saw him look around, his head swivelling on his shoulders. Then he saw Bobby.

With a smile, the man opened the driver's door and stepped out of the car. Bobby walked towards him, his curiosity aroused by the man's wearing of a navy blue one-piece boiler suit and dark green Wellington boots of the type, Bobby saw, that the so-called gentry wore in the television programmes when they were showing Joe Public round their large, fancy country gardens. Bobby set his face grimly. He didn't want this prick to think he could intimidate Bobby.

"You're late. What kept you?" he accused the man.

The man smiled apologetically. "Sorry about that, my good fellow. Here now, though. That's what counts, eh?"

"You brought the money then?" asked Bobby, eager and anxious to get it over with and be finished with this smarmy bastard.

"It's in the boot. Didn't want to carry it in the car, dear chap, too risky with the number of you criminal types about, eh?"

Bobby stared at him, his eyes wide. My criminal types?

"Don't forget," he hissed in response, "it was you that wanted the fucking place torched. Now there's a dead girl and if I get caught, pal, you are going down with me. Don't forget it!"

"Steady on, old son. Didn't mean to offend you, eh? No harm done, eh?"

As Bobby moved to the rear of the vehicle, the man returned to the driver's door and, leaning inside, pulled a lever that released the catch on the boot. The lid of the boot sighed open and upward on its hydraulic pistons. Bobby leaned into the boot and stared curiously at the thick plastic sheeting that completely covered the carpeted flooring. A bulky plastic bag lay at the rear of the boot, just far enough inside to cause a now grinning Bobby to stretch, to reach it. His greed overcame his natural instinct for self-preservation and so intent was he on taking hold of the plastic bag, he didn't see the man retrieve something from the driver's side pocket. As Bobby pulled the now open plastic bag towards him, he peered inside and saw rolled up newspapers.

Turning, he began to protest and then anger turned to shock when he saw the man was holding a claw hammer, raised high above his head. The first downward strike hit Bobby a glancing blow on the right temple, but was powerful enough to cause him to spin backwards, splitting the skin on his forehead and causing his torso to topple into the boot. Instinctively, he reached with both hands to protect his head from a further strike, but the man then quickly crashed the hammer down onto Bobby's left knee cap that lay invitingly bent across the rim of the boot, shattering it beyond even surgical repair.

Bobby, his back arched and blood streaming from his head wound, tried to scream as he then forced his hands down to protect his splintered knee, but the scream turned to a strangled cry as the third, sideswipe blow viciously took him in the throat, breaking his larynx and causing blood to erupt into his windpipe. Now helpless, Bobby turned beseeching eyes towards his assailant, only to see the fourth blow smash into his unprotected face, breaking his nose and gouging at his left eye, splattering blood and mucous onto both he and his attacker. The final blow come crashing down onto his forehead with such force the hammer head buried itself almost an inch into Bobby's temple, driving the broken skull bone backwards into his brain.

With a final shudder, Bobby Turner, fire raiser and unintentional killer, died, his one remaining good eye looking his grim faced murderer in the face, ironically an opportunity the late Mary Cavendish was denied.

Chapter 8

Charlie Miller returned to the CID general office clutching a sheaf of paper in his hand and arriving as Cathy Mulgrew finished her phone call.

"How did you get on?" she asked.

Charlie waved the sheaf of paper at her. "This guy has accrued more convictions than Frank Sinatra had hit singles."

Cathy grimaced at Charlie's analogy, but worse still was his choice of music.

"Listen to this lot," he said, then related that Robert Turner began his criminal career at the tender age of nine years old, stealing lead from derelict buildings that he then sold on to a local scrap merchant.

"His recent antecedent history makes more interesting reading," he shook his head at the file. "Through the years our Mr Turner graduated to more serious crime that culminated in a lengthy sentence of three years for wilfully setting fire to a derelict warehouse in the dock area on the north side of the River Clyde. According to the report I dug out, the owner was trying to sell the place for private development, but the building was listed Category B by Historic Scotland and council planning permission had been denied. Simply put, the owner hired our Robert to raze the building, which he very ably did. The shell that was left was later bulldozed for safety reasons. As I said, Turner got three years, the owner five years. And," Charlie screwed his face in concentration, trying to work out what real period Turner would have served, "with time off for good behaviour, etcetera, Turner should have been released. ...what?" he looked at Cathy, his face comically contorted as he did his mental maths, "Two months ago?"

"I'm guessing he was indicted in the Sheriff Court, then?" asked Cathy.

Charlie checked the paperwork. "Correct. And," he looked up at her, a wily smile playing about his lips "prosecuting for the Crown was our very own Mr McPherson."

*

Liam McPhee's education at the Belfast primary and secondary schools he had been required to attend resulted in a basic understanding of the three R's: Robbing, rioting and republicanism. As for reading and writing, well, those particular subjects had never really interested McPhee. What he didn't understand, he ignored. When he couldn't add up, he simply used the services of someone who could. And not a lot of people refused Liam McPhee, at least not if they wanted to stay healthy. If McPhee wasn't capable of handling a situation alone, and those situations were rare indeed, he called upon the assistance of his fellow Volunteers in the unit of the Provisional IRA, to which he belonged. Fist or gun, McPhee always got his way. Well, nearly always, he recalled with a grimace, till that bastard Muldoon walked in and caught McPhee bending the little bleached-blonde haired and very naked Mrs Muldoon over the lounge sofa. McPhee sighed at the happy memory and fidgeted in his chair.

Watching Frank Brogan working at the collection cans and their contents bored the arse off him. Brogan's account ledger book lay open and the monies from each collection can laboriously entered in the relevant section. Or so it seemed. They had both long ago reached an agreement. Nobody other than they two knew how much money was deposited in each of the sealed cans. And nobody knew just what monies came out of the cans, what was posted to the Province or how much was diverted to Brogan and McPhee for personal expenses. Before he had been sent to Glasgow, the members of the fund raising Council had briefed McPhee that Brogan was trusted implicitly to carry out the all transactions on behalf of the Cause. Or as much as anyone could be trusted, they hastened to add and told him to keep his eyes peeled, anyway. Just in case, they had also added. So, as far as McPhee was concerned, they had no real suspicions or, more properly put, nothing concrete to go on. There was nothing to justify a summons for Brogan to travel over to the Province, where the Nutting Squad could have a wee chat with him. But bear it in mind they had smiled at him. And McPhee had agreed. Chauffeur Brogan… and watch him. Better that than Muldoon catching up with him one dark and lonely night.

He watched as Brogan separated the silver from the copper coins and the occasional currency note. The pile of small, empty plastic bank bags was soon filled. McPhee was impressed by the simplicity of Brogan's system. Once they were filled and contained their designated amount, the bags were recycled by McPhee back to the pubs and clubs and exchanged for currency notes of different denominations. The notes, less Brogan and McPhee's appropriation, were then sealed within registered envelopes and posted to safe addresses, either in the Free State or to the Province. Brogan never used the same addresses on a regular basis, but varied them according to instructions from the POW Council.

"The beauty of it," smirking Brogan had once explained to McPhee, "is we're using the Brit's own postal system to deliver cash to the Cause."

He glanced up as Brogan sighed heavily.

"Not great this week, just over thirteen hundred, Liam," Brogan announced with a shrug of his shoulders.

At Brogan's suggestion, both had agreed that greed might be their undoing so they'd take no more than fifteen per cent from the weeks taking, nine per cent to Brogan while McPhee was happy with his six per cent.

"After all," Brogan had said at the time, "your every need is catered for. Free bevy and free shags from whatever birds you fancy, eh?"

McPhee didn't argue. He was content to let Brogan take the lions share, figuring that if they were ever caught, he would simply put his hands up and declare his innocence, citing his ignorance of Brogan's system as his defence and arguing he thought he was receiving a wage. Yes, he figured, better to be prepared if things go apeshit.

"You'll want me to take the cans and coin now?" said McPhee, rising from his chair.

"Not right away, Liam. We've a small problem that might require your," he smiled at the analogy, "unique talents," then revealed the forthcoming meeting at his sisters house that would be attended by Sergeant Miller and his Counter Terrorism Unit tart, DS Cathy Mulgrew.

*

Charlie Miller again banged on the door, but received no response. Cathy Mulgrew and the young, uniformed officer that accompanied them stood behind him, one hand on his baton, keen to impress the detectives with his local knowledge.

"Sure this is the flat, son?" Charlie asked the officer.

The cop nodded his head to the rough looking detective, eyes wide and slightly overawed by the good-looking redhead.

"Aye, there's no doubt, sergeant. There was a serious assault in the ground floor flat last week and I did a door-to-door check for witnesses. Robert Turner lives alone at this address. He was very nervous when I spoke to him, but didn't have any information, so I'd no cause to speak to him about anything else."

Cathy caught Charlie's eye and pointed to the number of pinprick holes that were punched into the woodwork, around the doorframe.

"What are these?" the cop asked.

Cathy smiled. "Giro drop. When the occupant doesn't want the police or interested parties, such as debt collectors or dealers looking for their cash to know who lives at an address, they don't advertise by using a nameplate. But on DSS giro day, they usually pin their name written on a piece of paper to the door, so the postman doesn't forget to put their cheque through the letterbox."

The cop was impressed and shuffled his feet, keen to help but anxious to get back on patrol.

"Do you smell gas?" asked Charlie.

Cathy furrowed her eyebrows and wrinkled her nose, and then a glimmer of understanding sparkled in her eyes.

"Maybe, there's just a whiff? How about you?" she asked, turning to the young cop and with her feminine intuition, aware he fancied her and flashing him her best smile.

Unsure, the cop sniffed then shrugged his shoulders.

"Should I contact the gas board?" he asked.

Charlie shook his head.

"Might not be time. Contact your control room," he instructed the cop, "and let them know we're going to have to force the door. Safety first, eh?"

"Should I have the building evacuated and get the fire brigade, just in case…?" the cop suggested, pleased that this was turning out to be something more than a straight forward call to assist the CID.

"Eh, no need for that just now," Charlie interrupted, "let's see what were facing first, eh?"

Standing back, he raised his right foot and kicked hard at the flimsy lock. The wood splintered at the first strike and the door crashed open. Instructing the cop to remain at the door, Cathy rushed into the kitchen, while Charlie discreetly searched the flat and ensured it was indeed empty. With a straight face, Cathy poked her head out from the kitchen door and called out, "All switched off now, I've opened a window to clear the air."

The cop, relieved yet disappointed at the same time, radioed for his station to contact a council joiner to attend and repair the damaged door. That done, his next task was dealing with an elderly neighbour who had been disturbed from her daytime television soap and was complaining at the noise.

"Anything?" Cathy asked Charlie.

He shook his head. "The only thing that's of any interest is a holdall that's fully packed and the bathrooms empty. No toothbrush or shaving gear and probably in the holdall. I think our Mr Turner intends leaving. He's getting out of town, as Big John Wayne would say."

He glanced at his watch. "We could hang on, for a bit, in case Turner comes back, but we've also got that meeting with Mrs Cavendish," he reminded her, indecision on his face.

Cathy frowned at Charlie.

"I think we should go now," she whispered, "before that young cop finds out the cooker in the kitchen, like the rest of the flat, is all electric."

*

Barry Ashford had wrestled with the Irish problem for a long time, in fact, most of his working life. His service as a soldier with Military Intelligence and its obligatory then voluntary tours of the Province had introduced him to the spying game, a business even older than prostitution. It was a profession that he took to with enthusiasm. The fall of the Berlin Wall and the subsequent demise of the Soviet threat effectively cast a shadow over much of the Intelligence Corps work, ultimately bringing about his resignation of his commission and immediate recruitment by the Security Service. Having previously deployed their vast resources against communist insurgency in the United Kingdom, the Security Service Charter was re-written and their expertise recognised by the then Conservative Government who rightly, in his opinion, awarded them primacy in the terrorist war against the bog dwellers. As far as Ashford was concerned, it made for a very satisfactory transition. Simply put, he had traded khaki and camouflage for Saville Row silk, with the additional inducements of a more lucrative salary and better career prospects. Not many people, he admitted, were as satisfied with their position as he was. Career wise, things were rolling along nicely and his masters viewed his agent's reports as top quality stuff. But now this bloody business.

The short telephone call to his mobile phone had informed him the Glasgow police Counter Terrorism Unit weren't playing the game fairly. That he hadn't been as equally honest with the police neither occurred nor bothered him. They were, as far he was concerned, simply another tool with which to serve the national interest and not least, his own. And now the flatfoots were about to trample all over his operation, he snorted, putting at risk an agent whose recruitment and servicing could endanger not only the life of that agent, but Ashford's own career plans as well. And as far as he was concerned, that was a far more serious threat. Angrily, he punched in the telephone number of the secure, direct line to DCI Martin Cairney, and then took a deep breath to calm himself. At the second ring, Cairney answered.

"Martin? It's Barry Ashford here. So, my dear fellow, just who the fuck is DS Cathy Mulgrew?"

*

Irene Cavendish waited nervously for the arrival of Sergeant Miller. She fussed over the tea plates and cake she'd bought that rested on the tray in the kitchen and that left just the kettle to boil for the tea. She was all set. Hair pinned back, black blouse, buttoned to the throat, black skirt, black tights and plain, black shoes. Other than her cheap and tarnished wedding ring, the only jewellery she permitted herself was the tiny gold crucifix about her throat, suspended by the narrow gold chain. She glanced into the wall mirror, unconsciously nodding with approval at the refection, the epitome of the grief-stricken, widowed mother. She'd thought about the Sergeant's phone call, curious as to why he wanted to visit her again. No doubt this was procedure, keeping the family of the victim updated with any development. So, she wondered, did this mean there was a development?
Her thoughts turned to her brother Frank, sat reading his newspaper in the lounge. Liam McPhee, lovely man that he was, had asked to use her phone. Private call, he'd assured her, to his wife in Belfast. Would she mind if he took the call in her bedroom? Of course not, she'd told him. Probably things that a man would like to say to his wife, without having the embarrassment of someone else listening. Yes, she liked Liam. Nice man and always had kind things to say to her. She re-arranged the tray then stood back to critically examine it. There, hands clasped in front of her she nodded with satisfaction. Neat and tidy with paper doilies for each tea plate. Satisfied, she returned to the lounge to find both men sitting, talking quietly.
"Ah, Irene," Frank asked with a smile, "can you give us a minute?"
Again she nodded her head, knowing it must be republican business. She was so proud of her brother and his efforts to promote and keep alive the Irish heritage that her ancestors brought with them, to this Godless, Protestant land. With hardly a glance, she made her way into the kitchen.
When his sister was out of earshot, Brogan turned to McPhee. "So, what did Manus say?"
Manus Foley, Senior Intelligence Officer for the Belfast Brigade of the Provisional IRA had long been a thorn in the side of the security forces and was well respected, not least by the security forces themselves, for his intricate knowledge of the British opposition.
"He's made some inquiry and it seems that this Mulgrew isn't known to them over there. They've a right good index of all the CTU bastards that stop our boys at the Ports or have been involved in interviews when there has been a detention. But nothing that fits a red haired female called Mulgrew. Sure, though," he tapped a nicotine stained finger against the side of his nose, "that might not be her real name, Frank."
"According to Jimmy Donnelly, the wee janitor at the police station, she was introduced to a mate of his by that name. What reason would she have to use an alias?" Brogan spoke quietly, inwardly cursing that the idea hadn't struck him

earlier. Then, as if the thought had just struck McPhee, he asked, "Do you think she's out to have us?"

Brogan shook his head. "We're both well documented by the CTU and probably with Five as well," he grudgingly admitted. "But no, I don't think she'd be after us. Why would she be? I mean," he lowered his voice to a whisper, "there's nobody but you and I know we're creaming the money, so there's no leverage there against us."

His eyes narrowed in concentration. "I'm of the opinion it's to do with this guy Miller. Donnelly says he has a serious drink problem. No, Liam. I think it's an internal police matter. But it'll do no harm to be on our guard anyway, right?"

"Right Frank," replied McPhee and added with a grin, "Drunk or sober, I'm your man."

Brogan smiled at McPhee's humour. "Did Manus have anything else to say?"

McPhee shook his head, just as the doorbell sounded.

*

Charlie Miller was just applying the handbrake of the CID car at the bottom of the high-rise flats, when Cathy's mobile phone rang. Scrambling in her pocket she fetched it to her ear and answered, "Yes?"

Charlie sat waiting, casting a sideways glance at Cathy and seeing her face flush. Whoever was calling, he decided, wasn't imparting good news.

"Understood, boss," she replied then returned the phone to her pocket.

Charlie waited, aware that if he were to know, she'd tell him in her own good time. She turned to him, her face now pale.

"Shit! My boss has just learned that Frank Brogan knows I'm Counter Terrorism Unit. Now," she stared at Charlie, "as I've never met the man before, how could he possibly be aware that I'm CTU?"

Charlie was taken aback. "You can't think that I…" he began to protest.

"No, of course not! But how could he know? How many people are aware that you and I are working together?"

Charlie puckered his lips, deep in thought.

"I'd be guessing," he said slowly, "but anyone who saw us together at any time that knows where you work. And that probably includes the whole of my office, by now."

"Nothing else explains it, Charlie," Cathy stated with resignation. "We've got a mole. Someone, somewhere, somehow is providing Brogan with information."

A thought occurred to him. "But if your lot don't have a source within Brogan's organisation, how did your boss find out about Brogan being aware of your identity?"

A smile played round her lips. "Sorry, Charlie, need to know."

He shrugged his shoulders, accepting defeat.

"So, how do you want to play this?" he asked her.

Cathy sat silent for a moment, gathering her thoughts and working out her options.

"How about if," she began to suggest, "we carry on with the meeting, but watch their reactions and try to determine if they'll draw me out. They will be on guard, I suppose. But after all," she smiled at him, "we're the hunters, not the hunted."

"Okay then, Mata Hari, lets get this done."

*

The mood in Irene Cavendish's flat was sombre. After a polite but formal greeting at the door by Liam McPhee, Charlie introduced Cathy to Mrs Cavendish and her brother and felt churlish in refusing the offer of tea and cake, but hoped his brisk and officious manner soon made it clear this was not to be a social visit. Seated beside Cathy on the couch, he quickly noted that though Irene Cavendish sat opposite on one armchair, both her brother Frank and McPhee chose to stand either side of her in what he perceived to be a protective stance, though for the life of him he couldn't understand why. Cathy and him were hardly a threat, were they? Brogan in particular, he saw, could hardly take his eyes from Cathy, but whether through hate or lust, Charlie couldn't be sure. No matter, it wasn't social nicety and that was for certain.

"Mrs Cavendish," Charlie started, "I know this is a continuing sad time for you and I regret that I am the bearer of further bad news. However, it has come to light during the inquiry," tactfully he refrained from using the word autopsy, "that your daughter Mary was in the very early stages of pregnancy."

A strangled sob escaped Irene Cavendish's lips and her hand, holding the now crumpled white handkerchief, reached for her mouth, stifling any further cries. She swayed slightly and her brother reached down to steady her.

"Jesus Christ, man!" Brogan snapped at Charlie, "What kind of thing is that to tell a grieving mother!"

Charlie sat still, refusing to react to the provocation.

Cathy leaned forward, her face seemingly full of concern for Mrs Cavendish.

"Shall I fetch you a glass of water?" she offered.

"I'll get it," interrupted McPhee, his face suddenly pale and making towards the kitchen, only too pleased to be gone from the room following this startling news. Absently, Irene took the water from McPhee, the tears now streaming unchecked down her cheeks, but whether pity for her daughter or her own shame, Charlie couldn't decide.

"How can that be?" she eventually gasped.

Cathy didn't think this was the time for a birds and bees lecture and decided to intervene.

"Part of our inquiry has centred upon Mary's movements prior to her death. We know she'd been gone for just over a week. Can you recall how much money she'd take with her?"

"Why is that important and how does that fit in with her being pregnant?" asked Brogan.

Cathy looked at Charlie, who shrugged his shoulders and replied, "Frankly, we're still at an early stage, Mr Brogan. But we presume that Mary must have been shown or directed to her hiding place in the building beneath the office. That's a line of inquiry we're still pursuing. Besides somewhere to live, Mary would have needed money, for food and basic toiletries. So again, any idea how much she took with her?" he persisted.

Irene Cavendish shook her head, still shocked by this latest revelation.

"How far gone was she gone and," Irene hesitated, unwilling to accept the very idea, "do you know who the father was?"

"Tests are still being conducted, but I feel it's fairly sure to assume Mary must have been several week's expectant, certainly pregnant prior to leaving the house. As for the father, I rather hoped you might have an idea. Did she have any boyfriends, perhaps someone she was seeing regularly?"

"Will this make it any easier to catch her killer, putting my sister through this?" snapped Brogan, his voice angry and dripping with sarcasm.

"No, I admit it doesn't. But as I explained earlier, any background information might be useful. I don't want to miss anything. Perhaps, as her uncle, she confided in you Mr Brogan?"

Brogan's face turned bright red, but whether in anger or annoyance that Charlie should suggest he was anything less than a concerned uncle, he couldn't decide.

"If I thought for one minute my niece was sleeping around," then turning quickly to his sister, "begging your pardon, Irene; I would have instantly told her mother!"

"Mrs Cavendish," said Charlie, rising to his feet, "there's not much more I can tell you. The only piece of welcome news I have for you is that I'm making arrangements for Mary to be released to you to permit you to make your funeral arrangements. Again, I would like to offer my condolences on what must be a very difficult time."

Composed and again assuming the role of the grieving mother, Irene rose to her feet, dabbing at her eyes.

"Thank you, Sergeant. I take it this news of Mary's pregnancy won't be in the papers or anything like that?"

Charlie's face turned white with sudden understanding. Her daughter's death was a secondary issue compared to Irene Cavendish's good name in the parish. He struggled to keep his voice level and replied, "No, Mrs Cavendish. I believe this is a very private family issue. However, should you learn of anything that might identify the father, I will be grateful for a call," then pointedly staring at Brogan, added "there would be no reason for anyone to be chastised, over this matter. After all," his warning clear and unequivocal, "we wouldn't want this kind of information being public knowledge, would we?"

*

Frank Brogan stood behind the closed door and listened to the sound of the retreating footsteps in the corridor outside. He reflected on their visit and couldn't fathom out what the CTU bitch might have gained. Still, with her red hair in a French plait, she was a looker, he decided. Mulgrew, he chewed at his lower lip. Must have Irish blood somewhere in her, he guessed.

Returning to the lounge he saw his sister Irene watching McPhee, who was on his knees and running a hand underneath the couch where the couple had sat.

"What are you doing, Liam?"

"Can't be too careful now Frank. They bastards, pardon me Irene," he stammered, "might have left a wee present, know what I mean?"

Brogan lips quivered as he fought to stop from giggling and thought it highly unlikely the cops would have planted some kind of James Bond listening device to his sister's couch, but didn't think it wise to ridicule McPhee and accepted the big man had more experience in the ways of the Security Services than he did.

Irene continued to watch McPhee, quietly sobbing to herself.

Brogan placed his arm about her shoulders. "There, there, Irene. Calm yourself."

"The shame of it!" she cried, "What if people find out?"

He hugged her close, smiling in reassurance.

"Nobody will find out anything, don't you be worrying about that and even if they did," he nodded meaningfully towards McPhee. "Who in their right mind would speak ill of my family?"

*

Charlie and Cathy returned to their car in silence, both deep in thought about their encounter; Charlie with Irene Cavendish's reaction to his news and Cathy disappointed that the brief visit added nothing to her knowledge of either Brogan or McPhee, yet silently relieved that their knowledge of her being a CTU officer didn't lead to any kind of confrontation .

"So, what do you think?" she asked.

Charlie creased his brow and tapped his fingers on the steering wheel. "I don't believe the mother knew about her daughter's pregnancy. The news seemed to genuinely come as quite a shock. Took it well, though, didn't she?"

His voice dripped with sarcasm. Cathy glanced sharply at him.

"You don't like the mother, do you?" she shrewdly guessed.

"No, it's not that. I just don't believe the mother had such a great relationship with her daughter and likely drowned the wee lassie in religion and rules."

He shook his head, a brief flitting memory of a happy, laughing child running towards him with arms outstretched. He shrugged his shoulders, suddenly exhausted.

"Just feel the wee girl probably never had any chance at real life," he added lamely.

"So," he took a deep breath and sat upright in the driver's seat, "shall we visit Rogers pal, this Aileen Dee?

Cathy reached into her pocket and produced her phone.

"Promised I'd give her a ring before we arrived. Seems that some of her clients might have outstanding arrest warrants and they'll shit themselves if we turn up unannounced," she grinned.

"Well, then, we'd better go prepared, hadn't we?"

Chapter 9

The address Cathy directed Charlie to was situated at the shabby end of Argyle Street, to the west of the city centre and close by the M8 motorway that thundered high overhead on its concrete pillars. The streets that bordered the area was referred to locally as The Drag, an area roughly a mile square that became during twilight hours, the city's red light area, where prostitutes of both gender, nightly plied their trade to service the clients who came from near and far.

Aileen Dee's premises were located within a former shop, its street level windows and surrounding brickwork painted a gaudy pink colour. Stout security grills were welded over the windows, but had been unable to prevent neither a break in one corner of the glass nor the crude profanities scrawled across both it and the door. An A4 sheet of paper within a plastic sleeve hung limply, secured by sellotape to the door and indicated in hand-written, upper-case lettering that the drop-in centre was open.

Charlie banged on the door and a moment later, it opened a fraction. He realised the door had a stout chain preventing it being opened further. A young, pale face greeted him through the crack in the door.

"Mr Miller?" inquired the anxious voice.

Charlie nodded and practised his best, reassuring smile.

"That's right," he half turned to indicate Cathy, "and I have Miss Mulgrew with me."

The door closed and they heard the young girl wrestle with the chain. Cathy leaned forward, the smell of her perfume fragrant and catching Charlie unaware. "I forgot to say," she whispered softly in his ear, causing the bristle on the back of his neck to rise, "she asked that we've not to let on we're the police."

The door creaked open. The girl couldn't have been more than eighteen, he thought, yet had the lined and harrowed face of an older woman. Her make-up had been inexpertly applied and the bleached hair was drawn back in a severe ponytail, exposing the youthful acne of her forehead. The thin blouse and knee length denim skirt she wore were clean and ironed, but obviously had seen better days.

"Come in," she invited them with a nervous smile, "Aileen's through the back," and pointed towards the dimly lit hallway that led to the rear of the premises.

The front of the shop had been converted into a waiting room with old, battered couches and armchairs that formed a half circle in front of a scarred and file laden desk. The bright sunlight that fought to stream through the pink emulsion paint on the window created a faded cerise hue, but the room was sufficiently bright not to require extra lighting.

"I'm Angie," the girl smiled, her eagerness shining from her and raised her chin with pride in her responsibility. "I'm on reception duty today. Would you like a cup of tea?"

Charlie held up a brown paper bag containing the doughnuts he'd brought.

"Thought you'd never ask," he grinned at her, immediately earning his status as a good guy.

"I hope one of those is for me," boomed a voice from behind him.

He turned to be greeted by a powerfully built woman who stood almost an inch taller than himself, her hair cropped close to her head, her eyebrows pierced and adorned with silver and gold rings. Dressed in a loose working plaid shirt and jeans, Aileen Dee seemed to cultivate the look and mannerisms of a man and her homosexuality cried out in defiance of convention. Hand outstretched, she greeted the detectives warmly and shooed Angie out to the kitchen at the rear of the shop, to make the tea. Charlie realised that Dee wanted the girl gone, before she begun to speak. She raised the palms of her hands.

"I understand why you're here, Sergeant. Cathy Rogers filled me in with all I need to know."

Inviting them to sit, she turned and closed the inner door that led to the rear kitchen.

"I didn't know the wee girl that died," she began, "though I had heard a whisper that there was a young girl offering her services round the Drag. I'd put out feelers, hoping she might have called in, but," she sighed, "I can't force the girl and sometimes the boys," she pointedly remarked, "to come for help. I presume," she stared at them, "you know what we offer here?"

Charlie shook his head. "I'm sorry to say I don't, but I guess you're a voluntary service, counselling, that sort of thing?"

"That sort of thing," she repeated her voice full of resignation. "Yes, counselling is one of the services I try to offer. Well, that and pleading with the local social work, DSS, health services, council, housing department, church groups; basically any bugger that will listen. What I really offer my girls, and boys, of course," she smiled, "is the realisation that someone will listen, even if that someone can't do that much for them. I do have my little successes, now and again," she said without boast, "like Angie, back there. Thrown out of the house at fourteen, pregnant and aborted her first child at sixteen, another abortion a year later, but now?" She smiled softly, a smile that completely altered her facial features and hinted at the depth of compassion that lay beneath the stony expression she usually reserved for strangers.

"Well. Now Angie has her own flat, a little seedy, admittedly, but it's a start. And she starts college next term. For now, though, she's my little angel, doing the odd jobs around here and showing the rest of my young people that it is possible to achieve a life without selling your body."

A timid knock announced that Angie was back, bearing a tray with a slightly chipped teapot and three clean and scoured mugs. Milk and sugar bowls lay beside a plate that contained Charlie's doughnuts. He rose to help the girl and took the tray from her as Dee placed a small side table in the centre of the seating area.

"Fetch a mug for you Angie, there's a dear," instructed Dee. "They waited in silence till Angie returned, beaming with pleasure that she had been invited to join them.

Dee poured the tea into the mugs and then casually remarked, "I was telling Mr Miller and Miss Mulgrew that you're our first success story, Angie. How well you've done."

The girl flushed with embarrassment, twisting her hands together with obvious pleasure.

"I've had a lot of help."

Charlie saw the girl adored Dee and decided that though Dee was quite obviously lesbian her relationship with the girl was akin to mother and daughter. Surprised at himself, he realised he instinctively liked the big woman, but curiously wondered at her motivation.

Dee moved closer to Angie and took hold of her hand.

"Angie," she began, "do you remember telling me about the wee girl that died in the fire? How you knew her?

Angie nodded, surprise registering upon her face.

Dee spoke on, her voice soft and cajoling.

"Mr Miller and Miss Mulgrew are police officers Angie and there's no need to worry," her voice now firm and strong as she held Angie's hands tightly, but not so as to hurt her, "they're good people and they only want to find out who set fire to that place where the wee girl was found. You knew her," she coaxed, "didn't you?"

Charlie held his breath, aware that Cathy too had stopped stirring her tea, both content to let Dee take the lead and persuade the girl to speak.

"Yes," Angie replied, her response so quiet that they had to lean forward slightly and almost strain to hear her. "I met her at the puggies."

Charlie looked curiously at Dee.

"It's an amusement arcade just off Argyle Street," she explained, "where the school truants and runaways meet during the day. One-arm bandit machines and those type of things. The manager is a decent guy and lets me know if there's anyone I should be taking an interest in."

"I haven't done anything wrong, have I?" sobbed Angie, eyes widening and her voice breaking in fear.

"No, no, dear," Dee assured her, pulling her close and placing a protective arm around her shaking shoulders, gently pulling her head against Dee's immense chest. "The officers just want to know anything that might help them, that's all. Would I let anyone harm my wee angel," she smiled.

Privately, Charlie thought that anyone who tried to hurt this wee lassie would be a fucking idiot because Aileen Dee seemed more than capable of ripping an arm off and beating any aggressor across the head with the soggy end.

Angie took a deep breath and blew her nose on a small tissue she took from her pocket.

"Mary was a nice girl, not like me," she hesitated.

Charlie's throat tightened, a curious wave of sympathy for this wee girl sweeping through him.

"I tried to talk her into going home," Angie continued "because I knew that she just didn't have what it takes to survive on the street. She wasn't, what do you call it?" she looked at Dee.

"Streetwise?" suggested the big woman.

"Aye, streetwise. Anyway, we got to talking and she told me she was looking for somewhere to stay. I showed her the place…" her voice broke, unable to continue.

"Do you mean the place underneath the office, in the lane, Angie?" Cathy suggested, but gently.

Angie nodded. "I didn't know that anything would happen, I really didn't!" she cried out.

"There, there, there," Dee stroked the girls head, "the officers understand that," turning to them, "don't you?"

Charlie took that as a warning that he'd better understand or there would be no more interview.

"Of course," he replied on cue, "nobody could have known. You only did what you thought best, Angie. You tried to help someone who was in distress. You've nothing to feel bad about, okay?"

That earned him a smile from Dee, he was pleased to see.

Angie raised her head to look at him. "So I really won't get into trouble?"

Charlie shook his head. "Only if you make me eat any more sugary doughnuts and when I'm supposed to be on a diet," he smiled at her, easing the way forward for further information.

Angie relaxed and smiled back at him, then sat upright and took a deep breath. "I'm okay," she reassured Dee, took a deep breath then turned to Charlie. "What else do you want to know?"

Later, Charlie stood with Cathy and Aileen Dee outside the pink shop.

"That was very helpful, Ms Dee," he told her. "We can only guess Mary ran away from home, when she discovered she was pregnant and from what Angie has told us, it confirms our suspicions that Mary was about to or had resorted to prostitution in order to survive. It's definitely answered our question as to how Mary found herself in the cellar. I'll leave you my mobile number anyway, just in case anything else should turn up and, eh, if you need any kind of help or something…" his voice trailed away, slightly embarrassed and unsure just how he could help this kind but warrior woman.

Dee nodded in understanding.

"Are you any closer to solving your inquiry?"

"Not right now, though we do have a lead with a young guy that we're eager to speak with, but he seems to be on his toes." He shrugged and continued, "Truthfully? I don't know if I will solve this," he sighed, "but I can assure you, it won't be from the lack of trying."

"And you, Miss Mulgrew, do you see yourself passing this way again?"

Curiously, Charlie saw his partner blush as she shook her head, then she replied, "Maybe to drop in some of my old gear, clothes and stuff, if they'd be any use to you?" she asked.

Dee smiled warmly at Cathy. "Always welcome, as you will be yourself.

Dee turned to Charlie as she made to go back to her shop.

"Well, good luck anyway and oddly enough," she grinned at him, "you don't look like a useless drunken bastard."

Charlie and Cathy climbed into their car.

"I think she was making a pass at you," he teased her.

Cathy cocked her head at him. "Don't you think I'm worth making a pass at then?" she countered.

"Ah, yes, of course. Ahem."

He blustered as he cleared his throat, his joke backfiring on him.

"Right, then, what's next on the agenda," he asked quickly, to cover his self-inflicted confusion.

"Perhaps we might consider…" Cathy begun, but stopped when the police radio burst into life and calling out the vehicle call sign. Reaching down, she took hold of the handset and acknowledged the call that instructed Charlie to contact DCI Mitchell at Govan police office, as soon as possible.

Charlie looked at Cathy in puzzlement. Colin Mitchell was widely known and respected as a tenacious and dedicated detective, but why he was contacting Charlie confused him. His curiosity aroused, Charlie dialled Govan office on his mobile and, after being put through to the CID, received instructions from the CID clerk to meet with DCI Mitchell at Pollok House, the listed country mansion that was located in the vast expanse of Pollok Park in the south side of Glasgow.

Cathy made a face. "Do you think it's anything to do with crashing that door?" she asked.

"Unlikely," he shook his head, "Colin Mitchell's crashed a few doors himself in his time," he replied, "and I'm pleased to say I've been there with him, on a number of occasions."

She stared at him. "Old neighbours are you, then?"

Charlie smiled as he drove the car into the busy traffic trundling along Argyle Street.

"Less of the old, please, but yes, we were DC's together in the Serious Crime Squad, back in the early nineties. We worked on a few murder inquiries, in our time. Earned a few bob from the overtime, too," he grinned.

He thought fondly of those days, when life was so much easier. Or so it had seemed.

"Back then, there were two types of Squad detective, the shiny suit brigade that hit the dancing at the Savoy in Sauchiehall Street at night, then claimed expenses for meeting touts and then there was the 'every penny towards the mortgage types', like Colin and me. We were the needies and the others were the greedies. The needies and the greedies," he laughed.

Cathy sneaked a sidelong glance at Charlie and tried to imagine him as a young detective on the threshold of what must have seemed to be a promising career. What a waste, she sighed, the sudden insight causing her to think there was more to Charlie Miller than the eye immediately saw.

"So, what did you get up to last night?" he asked, abruptly changing the subject, yet curious to find out something about her personal life.

"Not much," she shrugged, "caught up with some ironing, we watched a documentary on the box, a glass of vino and then bed. And you?"

With a shake of his head, he decided to come clean, literally.

"Got stuck into some much needed housekeeping," he admitted. "The place was long overdue a spring clean, so got my apron and feather duster out and set about the flat. Didn't recognise it when I got up this morning," and that's closer to the truth than he dare reveal, he thought, then added, with a sudden admission, "Didn't even take a snifter when I got home last night either."

Now why did I admit to that, he thought to himself. Am I boasting? Do I need to tell her that to get her to like me? Shit! I'm acting like a fool he angrily reproached himself.

They sat in silence for a few minutes. The miles rolled by as they drove towards their rendeavous.

"Pollok Park," Cathy said brightly, keen to keep their bonhomie going, "that's where the Burrell Collection is housed, isn't it?"

"Yeah, it's in the middle of the parkland. I'm guessing you've never visited then?" She gave him a sideways grin. "If the road to hell is paved with good intentions, I'm looking at a three lane highway."

Charlie laughed out loud, acutely aware that he was becoming more relaxed having Cathy around.

"It's a stunning building, custom built to house the artefacts collected by Sir William Burrell that he accrued over eighty years of travelling throughout the world and gifted to the people of Glasgow. There's a few bobs worth in there, I can tell you and worth seeing if you and …I'm sorry, I don't know your partner's name?"

"It depends what mood I'm in," she replied sourly, taking him unawares and causing him to laugh.

"Well, if you get back on speaking terms, I'd take the opportunity to visit. There's even wild deer in the park," he continued, enjoying the role of narrator, "and a herd of shaggy Highland cattle. It's a big area and surrounded by housing estates, some council, but mostly private."

He sighed with pleasure, recalling impromptu picnics and afternoons chasing his squealing son round the trees. "Like a green jewel surrounded by modern suburbia."

"You're getting awful philosophical, Charlie Miller," she turned to him and grinned cheekily. "Do you think it's an age thing, then?"

He shook his head, a thin smile on his face and his thoughts elsewhere.

Cathy rightly guessed he liked her and fervently hoped that he wasn't planning to make a move on her. That would be a complete disaster. She had her partner and she wasn't looking for anyone else and definitely not someone like Charlie. She'd no illusions about her appeal to men and had many colleagues make an advance in the past, mistaking an open and working relationship for more than friendship, but she was by now adept at fobbing off the drunken fumble and straightforward line of patter. She considered telling him to avoid any embarrassment, head him off at the pass as it were. For hadn't she been walking that particular tightrope for a long time, now?

They arrived at the massive iron gates that led from the busy Dumbreck Road into the Pollok Park and were surprised to see a uniformed officer, dressed in a yellow fluorescent jacket and clipboard in hand, standing by the gate. Stopped by the cop's raised hand, Charlie produced his warrant card and was told he was expected and directed not to the road that led to Pollok House, but to a track that ran off the main road beside the imposing mansion. Blue and white-chequered police tape partitioned a narrow path through the trees."

"What's up, do you think?" asked Cathy.

"If you ask me, this has the feel of a murder," he replied as he negotiated the car through the thick woods, along the rutted and overgrown path, passing officers wearing navy blue coveralls, heads bent as they laboriously searched each side of the track. Again, they were stopped by another uniformed officer, who prevented them from driving any further and showed them where to park their vehicle alongside a half dozen others, marked and unmarked cars already abandoned. On foot now they followed the taped route and arrived at a scene of activity. A white igloo type tent surrounded by yet more tape sat in what they both knew to be a sterile area. Scenes of crime and Forensic personnel, distinguishable in their all in one white suit's, police photographers, uniformed and plain clothes officers moved silently about the area, engrossed in their tasks.

"Hi, Charlie, how's it hanging?" shouted a voice from the other side of the tent. When he'd joined the police some twenty-six years previously, Colin Mitchell had just made the minimum height, bestowing upon him at that time the dubious honour of being the smallest cop in Glasgow. His full head of hair now prematurely white was at odds with the neatly trimmed, jet-black moustache that adorned his upper lip. A compulsive nail biter, Mitchell had overcome the habit by replacing it with an addiction for chewing gum. With a huge grin on his face, he approached his former partner with obvious pleasure.

"Nice to see you again, old pal," he said, shaking Charlie's hand with a vice like grip.

"And you," he turned with hand outstretched to Cathy, "must be DS Mulgrew from the gas board?"

Cathy took Mitchell's hand and responded with a tight smile, deciding any reply might be presumed flippant and cheeky.

"You're looking for me, Colin?"

Mitchell indicated the tent and drew a fresh gum stick from his coat pocket. He didn't bother offering any to either Charlie or Cathy. To her disgust, he rolled his used gum into the foil from the wrapper and put it in his coat pocket.

"Heard you were looking for a Robert Turner from Castlemilk earlier this morning. That right?"

Charlie nodded, guessing that Mitchell would already know the answer.

"He turned up as an MO suspect in a fire that I'm investigating in the city centre. You might have heard about it. Young girl died."

"Yeah, it was in the Chief's report," Mitchell replied, referring to the twenty-four hour summary of serious crime that was published daily for the attention of all senior detective personnel and anyone else who had the good sense to read it.

"So," Charlie queried, waving a hand about him, "I presume you've got something that brings me into this, then?"

"Police dog handlers, as you know, have their premises about half a mile over there," replied Mitchell, pointing towards the edge of the park, "and often use this wooded area to train the dogs in search procedures. Pure luck they were out this morning and turned up the body of a male, otherwise he could have lain undiscovered for God knows how long."

"And that body, I'm guessing, would be Robert Turner?"

"Tentative identification from a DSS signing on card in his rear pocket, but he's got some distinctive tattoos on both arms. You know the type, ACAB, that sort of thing, a load of amateur Indian ink jobs that was likely done in the nick. I'm just waiting on the Records department getting back to me. I'm sure the tattoos will be recorded in his antecedent description forms, so that should probably confirm the identification."

"ACAB?" asked a puzzled Cathy.

"All Cops Are Bastards," smiled Mitchell.

Charlie stared at the DCI, already suspecting the reply. "I take it that nobody can conduct a facial ID?"

Mitchell grimaced.

"Not much of his face or his head left, I'm afraid. Whoever did this used some sort of a heavy weapon, possibly a hammer of some type according to the casualty surgeon's preliminary examination."

"If the killer left the card in his pocket, he wasn't too bothered about Turner being identified, then why destroy the face?" asked Cathy.

"Who knows what goes through these peoples minds," shrugged Mitchell, "but it seems to me at this stage that the assault was vicious and quick. There doesn't seem to be any defence wounds, though of course the post mortem examination will probably reveal more, so I'm of the opinion that Turner knew his killer and didn't believe him to be a threat or to expect any attack."

"From what you've told us," Charlie said, "you're of the opinion the body has been dumped here. Do you have any idea of the locus for the murder?"

"None whatsoever," he shook his head. "Now, what can you offer me in the way of assistance?"

Charlie looked at Cathy and in turn, shook his head. "I'm sorry, Colin, nothing much. Our opinion is that Turner, if indeed it was him that set the fire, was acting on behalf of a third party, but I have to stress that is only conjecture. There was nothing to suggest the motive was theft, but there is every inference the culprit brought the gear for a professional torching. Regretfully, the wee girl, Mary Cavendish, was simply in the wrong place at the wrong time. A runaway," he explained. "It's our assessment the contractor for the fire hired Turner to torch the place. I haven't turned up any suspects, but," he hated admitting it, "the senior partner, Steven Taylor has provided us with a staff list and there is an employee of the firm that I will be looking at."

Mitchell raised his eyebrows in anticipation at the mention of the unnamed employee, but Charlie quickly added, "However, any connection between the employee and your body is very, very tenuous at best and at this stage of my inquiry and without having interviewed the employee, I'd rather play down the possibility of a definite lead. And besides, I'm sure there's a likelihood your team will have enough to go on without my inquiry getting in your way. I promise you though, if I do prove or even suspect any collusion between your murder and my fire suspect, you're my first phone call."

*

Back at their car, Charlie was aware of Cathy staring at him.

"Okay, out with it, what's on your mind?"

"How did you manage to flimflam him?" she began. "I mean, if I'd been Senior Investigating Officer in a murder inquiry, I couldn't see me letting anyone walk off with what might prove to be a significant lead in the case. You, Charlie Miller, must either be extremely highly thought of or have balls of steel!"

He winced at her crudity and then smiled at his own audacity, the presumption that Colin Mitchell wouldn't object to Charlie keeping him informed of the fire inquiry.

"You're right. It was bloody cheeky of me, but Colin's a good man. He knows I won't let him down, that anything I… sorry, anything *we* turn up that infers a connection with his case, will go straight to him."

He half turned to face her, the smile now widening to a grin.

"I might be a drunk, Cathy but I'm an honest drunk."

Chapter 10

Constable Sadie Forrest always enjoyed her days off, particularly when she could spend them having lunch with Geraldine, her lively six-year-old daughter, but right now the break was over and it was back to school for the little scamp. The child was a miniature version of her mother, both having wavy, shoulder length fair hair, piercing light blue eyes and a ready smile and drew more than one admiring glance from passers-by. Hand in hand, they slowly walked the short distance from the park to the primary school; Sadie trailing her daughters back-pack in her free hand to allow Geraldine to clutch the tattered Cracker, her one-eyed teddy bear from whom she was usually inseparable. But not if her pal's were watching, Sadie observed with a wry grin. At the gate, her daughter's friends run to meet Geraldine as Sadie discreetly took the teddy and placed him in her shoulder bag. Then she bent down to wipe the crumbs from the freckled cheeks, doing as mothers have done since time immemorial, licking her handkerchief and wiping it across her daughters face.

"Mum, my pals are watching," she protested, pulling away like the big girl she now believed she was.

But not too big, Sadie smiled, to hurriedly turn and give one final hug before running to join her classmates. The bell signalled the return to class and Sadie strolled towards the church across the road. Her watch reminded her that the meeting for the parents of the primary three First Communion pupils was due to begin in a few minutes. She was pleased to see old Father Flynn standing at the open door, greeting the mothers and a few fathers, patting the heads of the noisy pre-school toddlers that accompanied them.

"Aye, it's yourself, Sadie," he smiled at her, then reached for her elbow and gently drew her to one side. "I haven't seen you for some months, Sadie Forrest. Have you turned into a Protestant or something?" he chided her, his brogue soft and gentle and a smile on his weathered face.

"It's the shifts, Father," she replied, knowing the fib would lie on her conscience till her next confession.

The old priest recognised her embarrassment and decided not to press the issue. "I was speaking with your mammy, the other day. She tells me that since you and that rogue of a husband divorced, you've hardly been out of the house, other than to work or take the wee girl out. Now, what kind of life is that for such a pretty young woman like you? If I wasn't a holy man of God I might even pursue you myself," he mischievously grinned at her."

Sadie returned his grin and swallowed hard. This wasn't the time to discuss her personal life, not with half of the parish passing her by, wondering what sin she'd committed that caused old Father Flynn to speak in low whispers.

"Do you think that we might have a wee chat, once the meeting is over, Father?" she begged, her eyes alerting him to the curious stares of the local gossips.

The old priest startled. Bloody hellfire, he thought to himself, suddenly aware of the furtive glances directed at them. As if this young woman hasn't enough trouble in her life and me, who should know better. Old fool that I am!

"Of course, me darling, of course," he hurriedly replied. "Stay behind after the meeting and we'll have a wee cup of tea. Okay?"

She nodded her head in quick agreement and made her escape into the cold chill of the cavernous chapel, her heels clicking on the stone floor and announcing to everyone that Sadie Forrest's gentle reproach from Father Flynn was, for the time being, over.

*

The Paisley office of Taylor, Taylor, Frobisher and Partners was not, as Charlie thought, located in Paisley, but just across the burgh boundary in the smaller, neighbouring town of Renfrew. Postcode snobbery, he fancied. The office took in the ground and first floor of a grimy tenement building with its entrance located in the common close and through what had at one time been the front door of a flatted dwelling house. It didn't help that the adjoining property was a rough, working mans pub and the stink of urine that pervaded the common close testified to the out of hours use as a public lavatory. Wrinkling her nose against the smell, Cathy led the way into the dismal and dimly lit passageway and tried the door with the faded brass nameplate.

"It's locked," she announced, and then rattled her knuckles against the stout, wooden door that bore the scars of neglect and graffiti.

"Hi tech stuff," she quipped, pointing to the bare wires that protruded from a hole in the wall that had seemingly at one time been connected to an electric push button.

The door creaked open at Cathy's second attempt to attract attention. A woman of indeterminate age appeared, her grey hair tied severely in a bun. Thick-rimmed spectacles perched on the end of her nose, secured by a gold chain suspended from the legs and hanging about the shapeless grey cardigan that stretched across her broad shoulders. She stood warily, holding the door slightly ajar and in a high pitched and pretentious voice, snootily asked them their business. Cathy's warrant card produced a barely audible sigh of impatience and they were reluctantly invited into a small hallway with doors leading to front and rear offices. The clatter of manual typewriters could be clearly heard.

Seems technology hasn't quite reached this dump yet, Cathy thought.

A third, closed door led to what Charlie guessed must be a toilet. A set of narrow wooden stairs, not much more than a ladder, rose from the hallway and, he guessed rightly, up through a professional conversion in the ceiling to the flat above and what he later saw to be two further offices. The alteration from flats to office had clearly been completed several years previously for peeling paint declared the decor was long overdue a makeover.

"Is it Mr McPherson you've come to see?" asked the secretary with forced politeness, her voice almost a hush.

Presumably, Cathy thought, from working too many years within cloistered law offices.

Her beady eyes betrayed her apparent contempt for the police.

"Yes please," replied Charlie loudly, with a broad, friendly smile, adding to the woman's discomfort.

Instructing rather than inviting them to wait, the secretary regally climbed the steep stairway, her large backside wobbling in the too tight, tweed skirt as she negotiated the narrow confines of the entrance to the upper floor. Charlie smiled at Cathy's deadpan expression, wisely refraining from commenting in case he provoked laughter from his neighbour at the secretary's vain attempt to maintain a dignified modesty.

"Mr McPherson will see you now," her disembodied voice called down from above.

With a grin, Charlie invited Cathy to lead the way, but eyebrows raised, she politely refused.

Staring him in the eye, she warned him, "You're not getting a look at *my* knickers, Sergeant Miller."

Ronnie McPherson stood up and walked round from behind the large, mahogany desk that lay piled with papers and files. It seemed he had sole use of the former lounge where the fading floral wallpaper, heavy wooden furniture, cast iron fireplace and threadbare carpet belonged to a different era. The damp patches around the window added to the general decay of the room and was a sure sign that dry rot had come calling. Charlie judged McPherson to be in his late thirties and just short of medium height. His fashionably cut, slicked back, dark hair and round, clean-shaven features suited the condescending look he wore upon his face. His portly appearance identified him in Charlie's mind as a shiny butt, or politely put, a man whose occupation caused him to polish the arse of his trousers. Curiously, Cathy thought his white shirt, broad red braces and garish silk tie were at odds with the rundown appearance of his surroundings. The old Glasgow put-down leapt to mind, 'fur coat, nae knickers'.

Pulling forward a second chair to join that already facing his desk, McPherson invited them both to sit down.

"To what do I owe the pleasure?" he smilingly asked while returning to his large, swivel seat.

"We're investigating the fire that occurred at your Glasgow office, Mr McPherson…."

"Please, Ronnie, and you are?"

"Detective Sergeant Miller and this is my colleague, Detective Sergeant Mulgrew."

The smile remained fixed on McPherson's face. A clear and definite line had been drawn. No forenames. Formality was the order of the day.

"May I offer you a cup of tea, coffee perhaps?" then without awaiting a reply, called out, "Jean, some refreshment for our guests."

The angry rattle of china and low muttering could be heard through the half open door.

"Now, then…officers, again, what can I do for you?"

"I understand you are a former Depute Procurator Fiscal, is that correct?"

There was a definite pause before he replied and the smile remained fixed, but Cathy watched his hands tighten and his knuckles turn white as the fingers intertwined on top of his leather desk-writing pad.

"That's correct," he eventually admitted, "but what exactly has that to do with the fire?"

Cathy realised right away the defensive action McPherson was adopting. Answer a question with a question. She hoped Miller was up to this. McPherson didn't strike her as a fool and his response to the fraud allegation against him proved he was capable of taking the initiative.

"I'll come to that, but you did serve with the PF's department in Glasgow, is that right, sir?" Charlie persisted.

McPherson stared at him, taking a few seconds to answer.

"Yes, but you obviously know I did," he answered, tight lipped.

"As a Depute Fiscal, you will have prosecuted quite a number of cases I presume?"

McPherson stared and again did not immediately answer. His mind was working overtime. This can't be about the fraud, he decided.

"Prosecute cases? Yes, that's also correct. Do you have any particular cases in mind?"

Charlie reached into the inside pocket of his jacket and withdrew the folded computer printout that listed Robert Turner's convictions. The squeak of the door announced the frosty secretary carrying a wooden tray with cups, saucers and a teapot that she noisily banged down on the edge of McPherson's desk, causing him to wince.

"I assume you will manage to pour for yourselves," she growled, and then haughtily stamped from the room, firmly conveying the message that tea duty was unworthy of her.

Resisting the urge to giggle, Cathy stood and, with open palm, conveyed her offer to pour the tea.

McPherson nodded with a forced smile on his lips as he turned to Charlie.

"As I was saying, Mr McPherson, do you recall prosecuting a case of wilful fire raising, roughly speaking about three years ago? One of the accused had been contracted by the owner of the property to burn down a building that had been listed by the Historic Scotland Society?"

He did remember the case. So that's what this is about, he thought? Fuck all to do with the fraud. Almost sighing with relief, he smiled and accepted the cup from Cathy, his smile now relaxed and confident, eyes greedily appraising her slim figure and settling upon her chest. He turned again to face Charlie.

"Yes, I do as a matter of fact. Greasy little tyke, one of those immigrant persons who thought they'd come over and make a fast fortune by burning down an old property, then selling the land to a developer for a greatly inflated price. He got his comeuppance at the court, as I recall."

Cathy knew he had sneaked a look at her tit's and, her legs crossed at the knee, guessed he was now trying not to get caught looking up her skirt. And that'll be why he's such a wee fat shite, she thought as she watched McPherson carelessly spoon three heaped sugars into his cup, then choose three chocolate digestive biscuit's from the open packet.

Charlie oblivious to Cathy's observations, made a notation upon the paper file he held.

"Might I ask if you have ever discussed the case with anyone, since that time, sir?"

McPherson was taken aback. Discussed the case? Rapidly, his mind tried to recall the rules of evidence, but he couldn't think of any reason why such a discussion, subsequent to a trial, might be unlawful.

"The matter was judicially dealt with, Sergeant," he slowly replied, while wondering if this smart arse cop was trying to catch him out, "and was no longer Subjudice so, in answer to your question yes, I suppose I may have mentioned it to colleagues or at a party or something. I really can't recall. But you are aware that the case was widely reported in the press?"

Charlie hadn't been aware, but decided not to admit to that fact and was annoyed for not thinking of it sooner. He wouldn't pursue that line, he decided, and pressed on.

"Our interest lies in the co-accused, a Robert Turner. It was he who acted on the owner's instruction and set the fire. Do you recall him at all, sir?"

McPherson slowly shook his head. "Can't honestly say that I do," he replied slowly. "Too many faces over too many years, I'm afraid. Much the same as your own job, I expect, eh?"

Cathy had watched McPherson throughout the interview and now thought he was becoming too comfortable, like a man who had nothing to fear. And that's just it, as realisation set in. He has nothing to fear. He doesn't know anything.

Unbeknown to her, Charlie had reached a similar conclusion, deciding he was getting nowhere with McPherson, who was becoming increasingly pompous as the interview progressed. Setting his untouched cup and saucer down on the desktop, he replaced Turner's conviction sheet inside his pocket and stood to leave.

"Thank you for your co-operation, Mr McPherson," he stiffly acknowledged and nodded to the lawyer who had risen to see them out his door and lead them into the small hallway.

"And will you be interviewing everyone in the firm or just ex-Deputes?" the accusation came, biting and sarcastic, satisfied now that he was no longer under any suspicion.

Realising this could erupt into a confrontation Cathy sought to defuse the situation and smiled benignly at the portly little man.

"I believe we'll try to get round all your colleagues, Mr McPherson. With whom do you think we should begin?"

Startled, he retorted, "Why, with his defence lawyer, I would have thought."

Charlie and Cathy both stopped, hardly daring to breathe.

Slowly, the big detective turned to McPherson and flashed his best smile.

"So you do remember Robert Turner, sir, and you're saying Turner's defence lawyer works in this firm, with you?"

"Of course I don't remember Turner," he scoffed, the sneer evident and supercilious, "I told you that. But his legal defence? Well. That's quite another matter. Before I joined the firm of course, but we're colleagues now," he added. "Mr Taylor, John Taylor, the firm's senior partner."

*

The removal of the murdered man from Pollok Park to Glasgow mortuary was efficiently accomplished by the firm of undertakers contracted by the police for such duties. To DCI Mitchell's disappointment, no further evidence was discovered nor anything to indicate how the body had been transported to the locus. Frustrated by this news, he arranged for the post mortem examination to be carried out for the following morning and was pleased to learn it was to be performed by Professor Henry Martin. In due course, Mitchell assembled his investigation team at the major incident room within Govan police office, welcoming the additional support of the remaining few detectives from the Major Crime Unit not employed on Euro protection duties and thereafter begun his short, concise briefing. His opening statement confirmed that the deceased was now officially identified as Robert Turner. A potted history of the little known life of the deceased included his recorded convictions, known associates and a slim profile of his life style that was sadly out of date as, Mitchell wryly observed, Turner hadn't come to the attention of the police in the recent past.

The briefing culminated with a short DVD film shot by the Scenes of Crime photographer, of the locus where the body was found. The graphic horror of Turner's injuries was immortalised in full colour film. A headshot photograph of the deceased, taken at the time of his last known conviction for fire-raising, was issued to each inquiry team of two detectives and each team then actioned to make a specific investigation.

*

Detective Sergeant 'Peasy' Byrne and his partner, DC Emma Ferguson of the Serious Crime Squad, drew the onerous task of trawling the area where the deceased had lived, speaking to neighbours, friends and generally glean what information they could to add to the skeletal profile that currently existed. Jokingly referred to by their SCS colleagues as Pa and daughter, the duo nevertheless was an accomplished double act and had, in their two-year partnership, accrued a significant number of arrests. Climbing into the passenger seat of their squad car, Byrne checked his watch and estimated how many hours of their regular shift remained before the overtime kicked in. He smiled in anticipation at the possibility of a lengthy and lucrative murder inquiry.

"But first," the grizzled detective winked at his younger colleague, "the South Side cafe for a couple of bacon rolls and a cuppa, eh lass?"

*

The parents meeting concluded, Sadie Forrest dipped the fingers of her right hand in the small bowl of holy water, made the sign of the cross on her forehead and screwed her eyes against the glare as she stepped from the dimly lit church porch into the brightness of the November day. Father Flynn, she saw, was making his farewells to some of the parents, then turned and spied Sadie and nodded towards the kitchen door of the small chapel house, situated in the well maintained grounds of the church. Taking her coat from her, he ushered Sadie into the front room and sat her down in one of the large, comfortable armchairs, then turned and spoke briefly to his housekeeper and asked her to bring a pot of tea. As she left, he made a face at Sadie, put a finger to his lips and listened for a few seconds at the closed door. Satisfied the housekeeper had indeed gone, the priest bent down and switched on the two bars of the electric fire to drive the chill from the room, then sat down facing her.

"She's a good and pious woman," he explained, then to Sadie's amusement added, "but it's amazing how many confidences become local news in this parish. Well, my girl, how are you really faring these days?"

"I'm fine, Father. Honestly."

Sitting with her priest invoked a sudden memory of childhood, of Sunday mass with her parents, wearing her best dress and her catechism book clutched in her hand. Her two brothers, bored and fidgeting, scolded for their lack of attention in God's house. Their protestations falling on deaf ears that it was quiet, mouse like little Sadie who had pinched them and now sat in innocence, devoutly awaiting communion, the Body of Christ. She almost blushed to, at the memory of her whispered confessions before this elderly man, the childish misdemeanours and transgression that, at the time, had promised eternal purgatory or hell.

"Your mammy was telling me that you and wee Geraldine are in a flat in the Merchant City area in the town, these days?"

"That's right. When my husband and I first separated, I couldn't afford the mortgage on one salary, so I'd no option but to move. Of course, I miss the garden, but a plus factor is that I'm close to work and my mother minds the wee one, when I'm on shift. Oh, and of course Jellybean… sorry," she smiled, "my pet name. Geraldine gets to attend my old school, across the road."

"Jellybean suits the wee imp," he smiled at Sadie, then his face clouded over as he asked, "So there's no hope of any reconciliation then?"

Sadie gave a wry grin and without thinking, lightly touched the fading one inch scar beside her left eye."

"I'm thirty-six this year, Father. You might not have noticed, but there's a wee touch of grey through this," she smiled, flicking her hair back from her face. "And I'm no match against a twenty-three year old student who lap dances in her spare time. Besides," she shrugged her shoulders, "I don't really want him back."

A sudden need to confess overwhelmed her. "I haven't told anyone this, but just before we broke up, he blackened my eye. Came in one night with a drink in him and tried to wake our daughter up from her bed. Of course I argued with him and he lashed out, caught me right across the side of the face."

The old priest again saw her unconsciously touch the scar by her left eye.

"Jellybean woke up and it was a right carry on, I can tell you, with her screaming and him giving me dogs abuse."

She involuntarily shuddered at the memory.

"I keep my police baton at work, but I have to admit if I'd had it in the house that night, he was getting it right across the head and to hell with the consequence. Hitting me is one thing, but terrorising my child, that's a step too far."

The old priest smiled with sadness, his own bitter memories rising at the prompting of this young woman's tale.

"Me daddy was a drunkard," he began, "spending what little money there was on the porter, the Guinness, you know," he explained. "Used to hit me mammy something terrible, he did."

With a sudden snort, he clapped both hands together. "Well, Sadie me girl," and to her surprise exclaimed, "You're well rid of the bastard."

Flynn grinned at his own profanity. "I know that as your priest I'm supposed to encourage you to make the best of your marriage, but if that's how that man would treat you, then the devil take him, that's what I say."

Sadie tightly smiled and nodded her head, too choked to reply at the unexpected support. They sat in companionable silence, till a moment later a timid knock at the door brought the housekeeper with a tray of tea.

Thanking her, Flynn poured two cups and asked, "And your job? Still enjoying it?"

"It's a living, Father. Pays the mortgage and I'm working with a decent group of people. The hours can be long and I miss the wee one, but my mother's been great and the two of them get along fine."

"No social life though, eh Sadie? You're still a young woman and," he smiled, "I've noticed a few heads turn when you pass by. You really should be thinking about yourself a wee bit more. Get out. Meet a few men. Life's too short to spend all your time working and caring for a child that will grow up and make her own way in life."

Sadie blushed at the complement, suspecting her mothers influence was partially responsible for prompting the priest's kind opinion, but however well intentioned the his advice was, she didn't have to accept it and the last thing she needed in her life, right now, was another man.

"Tell me, Sadic, if I were to broach a subject with you, you might be able to keep it to yourself? Like the confessional thing, you understand?"

"Of course, Father. Anything you tell me would be between us, but," she warned him, "If it was to do with anything illegal, then I would be obliged to report it. But you know that, don't you?"

"I'm ashamed to have even doubted you, my dear," he smiled at her, "please accept my apology."

She became suddenly aware the old priest's attitude had changed. Was he nervous and uncertain? Her heart beat a little faster, certain now that his summons to this room hadn't been totally centred upon her domestic circumstances or spiritual well being.

"I suppose," he began, falteringly, "that as a police officer you would have some knowledge or even experience of sex crime, I mean, like against young people?"

She appreciated he was embarrassed, not used to having to discuss such intimate matters with a woman, indeed, if at all with anyone. Unconsciously, she slipped into her professional mode and recognised that to elicit whatever tale he had to tell her, she first had to put him at ease and thought she'd explain her experience, let him decide if she was capable of dealing with his problem.

"I spent almost three years working with a Female and Child Unit, the FACU we call it, Father. My job was mainly dealing with women and children who have been subjected to abuse of some sort, either physical or sexual so trust me, there's nothing that you can say that would shock me."

A heart stopping chill run down her spine as if for first time she realised she was looking at a lonely, old celibate man. The temptations that came with his calling were well known amongst both the clergy and lay people and one unfortunate incident was currently being widely reported in the press. But she'd gone this far and assumed he needed her counsel. With a dry mouth she added, "Some of the cases I dealt with involved young boys."

Completely unaware of Sadie's misgiving, the old priest lowered his head, wondering how far he could take this without breaking the solemn vow of the confessional, a vow he had maintained for almost fifty years.

"There was a death, recently," he began, "a young girl who had come to me in the confessional, just before she ran…" when a timid knock interrupted him.

It wasn't about him. Sadie involuntarily sighed with relief, her face reddening, ashamed of her inner doubt.

"Yes!" he irritably called out and far more sharply than he intended.

The housekeeper poked her head around the door, smiling in apology.

"Frank Brogan is here to see you, Father. It's about his niece's funeral arrangements."

Sadie saw the old priests face turn a ghastly pale and his breathing rapidly increased. He's about to hyperventilate, she thought anxiously and reached to steady him as he rose from his seat.

"I'll be all right, my dear," he told her quickly, avoiding her eye. "Look, can we maybe curtail this for the moment? But I'd still like that advice, if you don't mind?"

She stood, realising she was being dismissed, though ever so politely.

"Of course I don't mind, Father. Look, I'll leave my mobile number with your housekeeper. Just give me a call when you're free, okay?"

He smiled in appreciation and, taking her by the elbow, steered her towards the front door.

Frank Brogan sat stiffly on a straight-backed, old-fashioned wooden chair. He rose to greet the priest and nodded courteously to Sadie.

Pretty, he thought as he cast a smile towards her, and her face was vaguely familiar too. But it was this old fart he'd come to see, to warn.

"Thanks again, my dear. I'll give you a call when I can, bye now," he called after her, unaccountably apprehensive as he hurried her through the door.

*

DCI Nancy Rogers and Acting DI John Brown stared at each other across the top of the heap of statements that lay between them, their cardboard files scattered upon her desk. Her brief perusal of the contents had disappointed her. Nervously, he licked his lips and drummed his fingers on his knee, waiting for the expected explosion.

"So, what you're telling me John is that after almost, what is in now? About eight weeks?"

He nodded his reluctant agreement.

"Eight weeks of intensive inquiry, the diversion of resources from other investigations, the inordinate amount of divisional overtime that your inquiry has incurred…."

Swallowing hard, he noticed the emphasis on 'your inquiry', realising that Rogers had him figured for a scapegoat if… no… not if …but when the thing went arse end up.

She stopped speaking and stared at him, determined not to reach for the small blue cylinder in her handbag the doctor had prescribed and had assured her would both alleviate her recent breathlessness and the sharp, stabbing pain in her enormous chest.

"Ma'am…" Brown began.

She held up a hand, palm outwards, shutting off his whining voice from further grating on her already taut nerves and giving her the opportunity to catch her breath, to inhale slowly and decrease her racing pulse to at least a fast gallop. She had known it was a mistake, appointing him to the acting rank, but there had been little choice. Her senior DI was now assisting the PF to wind up the recent and protracted city centre murder inquiry while her second Detective Inspector was off long-term sick with his bad back and Miller? Well, he was a complete non-starter. That really only left Brown so, admittedly, the choice had been made for her. And yet, she had to confess, Miller's recent attitude was remarkable. He had obviously got the bit between his teeth for this one. Her friend, Aileen Dee seemed impressed, but wryly recalled Aileen had said the same thing about that cow Mulgrew.

She turned her attention back to Brown, who cowered in his chair, still desperately keen to impress, but fearing the permanence of the post was slipping from his grasp.

"Let me get this right. Your collation of all these reports," she said slowly, waving a podgy hand at her laden desk, "has concluded that the culprit for the attacks over the last two years has been variously described as five feet five to six feet two inches tall, of skinny to heavy build, short dark or long fair hair, clean shaven with a beard and more colours to his eyes than the fucking rainbow!"

She sighed heavily.

"Small consolation, I suppose is that you've decided he's male. Or is that open to dispute?"

Brown swallowed hard and rightly guessed now wouldn't be the best time to argue for more men.

She shook her head. "Tell me, John. How did you arrive at the decision to construct this description of him yourself? Did it ever occur to you to bring in a professional profiler?"

Rogers sat back in her seat and shuffled some papers, not bothering to wait for his half-hearted excuse as she continued speaking. "I presume that the DNA inquiry has not yet been resulted?"

"The results should be with me by next month," he tersely replied.

She leaned forward and rested her large frame on her elbows, hands clasped together as though in supplication. With an effort, she brought her irregular breathing under control.

"Next month? And how many more women will be victimised by this bastard through the month we're waiting?"

She rubbed a hand across her warm brow, aware that perspiration was beginning to form.

"Facing facts as they stand John, we're no further forward, are we?"

He shook his head in defeat, his silence deafening as it drummed his career towards his return to Sergeant rank, with little hope of promotion and a snowball's chance in hell of any kind of recommendation from this bitch bastard!"

"Right," she decided, straightening her blouse and reaching for the telephone. "Let me think this through and I'll inform you later what I decide. Thank you John," she dismissed him without further ado.

Miserably, he stood and left the room without a backward glance. As the door closed behind him, her eyes tightened and she hastily reached down and fumbled in her handbag, groping for the inhaler that brought a sudden burst of relief. At her last consultation, the doctor's usual weight warning once again fell on deaf ears. If it was that fucking easy, she had growled at him, do you think I'd be the size I am? His harsh response had worried her since. Uneasily, she glanced at the large wall clock, mounted above the filing cabinet. With a sigh she accepted she was caught between a rock and a hard place. Quit the job, lose weight and increase her chance of a full life or continue as she was and count the months, perhaps even weeks, till the grim reaper come calling.

The trill of the phone interrupted her thoughts. The officer in the control room informed her that DCI Colin Mitchell was keen to have Charlie Miller contact him, ASAP and did she know of his current whereabouts?

With a blast at the constable that she was not a fucking answering service, the man sheep-facedly hung up. Her brow wrinkled in curiosity as she wondered why her opposite number in the Govan division would be urgently seeking Miller's whereabouts?

Chapter 11

At the stroke of three o'clock, a tide of midget human beings poured out from the narrow double doors and ran full pelt at the open, metal gates. Sadie Forrest, standing patiently with the other parents waiting to collect their offspring, wisely stood to one side to allow the flow of children to pass by as the disorganised mass squeezed through the ten foot gap, miraculously without harm, the clamour of noise deafening yet cheerful. Geraldine, arms linked with three friends, waved to her mum then detached herself and run full speed for the customary hug. Hand in hand, they walked to the parked car then, when the friends had disappeared from sight, Cracker the teddy was discreetly fetched from Sadie's bag and joyfully hugged by her daughter.

On the drive home, Sadie reflected on her conversation with Father Flynn and his near panic at the arrival of Frank Brogan. Of course, she knew who Frank Brogan was, both through parish gossip and the Divisional Intelligence Bulletins that hinted at his involvement with a proscribed terrorist organisation, but never really told much more than that, simply a general request asking for any information that the beat cops might acquire during their shift in the Gallowgate area.

She'd already guessed to whom the old priest was referring when he'd mentioned the young girl that had died. It had to be Mary Cavendish, the poor soul with the mother from hell. Guiltily, she reproached herself for her unkind thoughts. After all, the woman had lost her daughter so Sadie had no rights to judge her. Still, she remembered her curiosity at the IRA poster on the wall. Strange to see something like that being displayed, for she knew that no decent, practising Catholic would consider supporting such an organisation.

She glanced in the rear-view mirror and smiled. Cracker was getting a rundown on the day's activities in the classroom.

Her thoughts again turned to Flynn and his reference to abuse. Damn. If only the housekeeper hadn't come in, she was sure that he was about to disclose something about Mary Cavendish; some secret that was so dreadful that he would contemplate breaking his confessional vow of silence. It was her guess that Brogans sudden presence had stifled the priest from continuing. Maybe she was making a leap, but did Brogan have anything to do with the secret Flynn was about to impart, she wondered? But how would she handle this? She might give the priest advice that would at best be trite and useless or at worst, send him down a path where it might interfere with the Central Divisions ongoing inquiry. She knew that if she did nothing the incident would annoy her, worry at her through the night. Restlessly, she pondered her next move, and then came to a sharp decision.

"Jellybean," she called over her shoulder, "mind if mummy makes a wee call before we go home, pet? I've a man to see."

*

DS 'Peasy' Byrne had climbed more stairs than he reckoned was healthy for a man his age and girth. Yet, for all their effort and door knocking, it seemed the late Bobby Turner had either been a recluse or of little interest to his neighbours. "Emma, my girl, I think we'll call it a day for the door to door and get back to the office and write up what we've got, so far," he wheezed, thinking to himself that the reports would take less than ten minutes and maybe allow them a decent knocking off time, for a change. "No point in hammering overtime if there's nothing to show for it, eh?"

Wearily, Ferguson nodded her head and indicated the shop on the corner.

"That's obviously the local newsagents. Maybe try there, Pa just before we go, eh?"

Mr Singh had adopted his customary stance behind the counter and greeted the detectives with wary courtesy, recognising that these two well-dressed individuals weren't locals, but definitely held some kind of official status. He stifled a laugh as he recalled a recent description of his local male customers, that the only time they'd be seen wearing a suit was if they were the accused.

Producing his warrant card, Byrne explained that he and his colleague were making inquiry into the sudden death of one, Robert Turner, known to his few acquaintances as Bobby.

Mr Singh passed a hand across his face and under his breath, quietly uttered a few words in Punjabi, a prayer for the soul of Turner, guessed Byrne.

"So, you did know him then, Mr Singh?"

"Young Bobby was good customer mine," he replied, his accented English clear and polite, if a little broken. "Such a nice boy, never make trouble. Always have a smile."

Emma Ferguson listened to this exchange, but kept her eye on the young girl behind the counter. Her eyes had fluttered at Byrne's news, her mouth opening slightly and her pretty, light brown face had gone a ghastly shade of pale. Ferguson suspected a teenage crush there, for the late Bobby Turner.

"Did you know anything of his family perhaps, maybe friends?" Byrne persisted. Mr Singh slowly shook his head. "I know Bobby since small boy," he reached down with his hand, indicating waist height, "a nice boy."

His brow furrowed in contemplation. "No brothers or sisters, just Bobby. Mum and dad both died few years ago. Dad liked the bevy, good customer also," he raised then shook his hand at his mouth, as though drinking from a bottle, then continued. "But mum, she work hard. School cleaner I think. Yes, sure. She was school cleaner. Forty cigarettes a day, Marlboro," he said with a sad smile, forever the attentive shopkeeper. "Poor woman," he shook in head in sadness, "died shortly after dad died. Bobby, he kept flat going. Not know address but could show you the close?" he offered.

Byrne shook his head. "No need, sir. We've been there. What about friends?"

"Ah," he sighed, "that I'm not sure about. Bobby keeps himself to himself. Very private man is Bobby."

Ferguson saw the girls head lower, her eyes downcast and lips now tight together. An elderly woman, dowdy green coat and headscarf tied under her chin, entered the shop and stopped dead, her eyes immediately taking in the two detectives.

"Fucking polis," she grunted, and then left, slamming the door behind her.

Singh grimaced and shaking his head said, "Sorry, the police not popular in this area."

Ferguson caught Byrne's eye. The rapport between them had been built through two years of serious inquiry and was almost telepathic. With a vague nod at the young girl, she conveyed her intentions to him.

"On second thought, perhaps you maybe just confirm the entrance to the flats for me, sir? Show me where you believe it is? Just to confirm the address is the one we have, you understand."

With a smile, eager to be helpful, Singh walked from behind the counter and led Byrne through the door to the street outside.

"You liked Bobby, didn't you?" Ferguson asked the young girl, smiling broadly and eager to dispel any apprehension the youngster might have about speaking to the police.

Nervously, the girl glanced at the closed door. Her grandfather stood with his back to her, pointing down the street.

"He was always nice," she whispered in a strong Glasgow accent. "Never took the piss like some of they smart arses with their fucking comments about my sari, know what I mean?"

Ferguson, bemused at the unexpected earthiness, pushed on.

"Anything that you can tell us that might help us find out who hurt him?"

"He asked me out once, when my Granddad wasn't looking, but you know how it is?"

Her face revealed an obvious disappointment that the tryst hadn't occurred.

"When did you last see him?"

The girl sighed heavily. "Yesterday, he came in for the papers and change. Change for the telephone."

Ferguson looked around the shop, puzzled. "So where is the phone?"

"It's the public phone, just down the street. That's if the thing is working," she added, lamely.

"Can you recall what time of the day, this was?"

The girl shut her eyes tight, concentrating on establishing a time from the long hours that was no different to every other boring day in this place.

"Early, I'm sure. It was early morning. Yes," she confirmed with a smile, "the daily papers hadn't all been separated into their racks so I'm guessing it was about half past eight?"

Ferguson made a note in her book and turned as Mr Singh and Byrne came back through the door.

"Thanks," she smiled at the Singh's, "if there's anything else, we'll be in touch."

As they walked to their squad car, Ferguson related her conversation with the girl and added her opinion that Turner had used the public phone rather than risk a trace from the called number back to his own phone.

"And you checked the phone in the flat, Pa and it was working, yeah?"

He nodded, then added, "I've arranged a subscriber check for the line in the flat, see what that turns up. But if what you think is right enough, I'm not too hopeful we'll get anything from the landline."

A short walk later, they arrived at the scarred, windowless and battered telephone kiosk, a tribute to the manufactured endurance of the once vivid red, cast iron box. With old-fashioned courtesy, Byrne elected to enter the urine smelling health risk and gingerly lifted the receiver between forefinger and thumb, then distastefully placed it close to, but not at his ear. The dialling tone echoed loud and clear. Taking a note of the faded number he smiled at Ferguson.

"About half past eight, yesterday morning, you say? Let's do an hour each way and see what a subscriber check turns up. And that, my wee pal, is us through for the day."

*

The disclosure by Ronnie McPherson that his colleague, Steven Taylor had been the defence counsel for the now deceased Bobby Turner had come as a total surprise, but they refused to get over excited, knowing that it wasn't so much a breakthrough as an avenue for further inquiry. All the same, Charlie's mind was in deep thought. The inquiry wasn't dead yet. Returning to the CID general office at the Central police station, they discussed the development and argued their options for following it through.

"I'm telling you, Charlie, if we bring him in we can have a good go at him. From your description, he doesn't seem to be your average, standard 'fuck the polis' type of criminal. He sounds like a wimp. A bit of pressure and he'll fold."

She sat down heavily at his desk as he walked to the table and boiled the kettle.

"What have we got?" he began. "We know his company seems to be having financial problems. Christ, the state of the Renfrew office bears that out. We have McPherson's word that he was tied into Turner through a three-year-old case. Still to be confirmed, and remember," he stared at her, conveying his unease that she didn't go overboard with this, "we can only surmise that the Hope Street office was torched to hide some, and I stress this is just a guess, some financial irregularity, albeit it was a professional job. And that brings us nicely to Turner. As yet we have no conclusive proof that Turner…"

"But…" she began to interrupt.

"…that Turner," he continued, ignoring her outburst, "did the torching. Have we?" Hands outstretched, he faced her, daring her to contradict what they both knew to be fact.

Cathy sighed heavily and sat back, her hands at her brow, rubbing hard.

"You're right," she admitted, "I got carried away when I heard Taylor's name. It just sounded too good to be true."

"We've still a long way to go," he reminded her as he carried the two mugs across to the desk.

"So, *mon capitaine*," she grinned at him, both now at ease with each other, "what's our next move?"

"I'll have one of those, please," Nancy Rogers strode heavily into the room, then noisily scraped a chair across to Charlie's desk and settled her huge bulk.

Surprised, Charlie stood and walked back to the tea table, unsure if his astonishment was due to Rogers sudden presence or her unnatural courtesy in saying please.

"Sugar, milk?" he called over his shoulder.

"No sugar and I don't take vicious, horrible cow milk," she told him, pokerfaced. Bugger, he thought spooning the coffee from the jar, glad his back was towards her and she couldn't see his face flushed and that he was too embarrassed to turn round. Some twat has told her. Taking a deep breath, he brought her coffee and sat down.

"What can I do for you, ma'am?" his voice steady and even.

"You had a phone call today. DCI Mitchell from Govan was trying to contact you, urgently, apparently."

Charlie glanced at his mobile, recalling he had set it on silent when in the Renfrew law office. Shit. Right enough, there was a message waiting.

Cathy sat silently bristling, wondering how this as going to turn out.

"Are there any developments in your fire?" Rogers asked him.

Charlie decided that to keep Rogers out of the loop could spell trouble.

Cathy interrupted his thoughts. "While you're bringing the DCI up to speed," she coldly announced, "perhaps I should do a check on our man Taylor?" and left the room without even a glance at Rogers.

Inwardly, Charlie sighed. He had enough problems without trying to referee these two.

"Right," he sat down and began. "We've had limited success," and proceeded to recount the developments that had occurred since his last interview with Rogers. "So you think Taylor might possibly be involved in the fire and, by implication, Mary Cavendish's death?"

He hesitated before replying. "I wouldn't want to be cross examined on that, based on the little we have. However, my gut feeling is that having seen the state of the Renfrew premises, old typewriters, lack of modern technology, that sort of thing, I suspect the firm probably has a financial problem that might easily be solved by diverting clients funds. We both know it's not unheard of and hard to prove if both the client and the firm are unwilling to make any complaint. Particularly if the client is keen to avoid tax queries, death duties and so on. Chances are that any paper trail has been destroyed in the fire." He shrugged his shoulders, almost as if in resignation. "To be frank, I'm stymied unless one of the firm's clients comes forward and makes a complaint that there is some sort of irregularity in their account, so where do I begin? No, I think my best move is to try to establish some sort of link between DCI Mitchell's body, the late Robert Turner and my suspect, Steven Taylor, and take it from there. Whether I will be able to prove my case, I don't know. At best I might be able to throw some light on Mitchell's inquiry, so if I don't get a result for the fire, Govan may well get a result for their murder."

He looked her in the eye and his brow narrowed, giving her the opportunity to contribute with her own take on the inquiry and said, "Unless you have any ideas, ma'am?"

Rogers didn't, but was impressed by the clarity of Charlie's thinking. Her mouth twisted and she bit at her lower lip. "Do you intend formally interviewing Taylor?"

"No," he shook his head, and then added "at least not immediately. From the brief meeting I had with him at the locus of the fire, he doesn't strike me as the shrewdest of lawyers, but still waters run deep and all that. Besides, other than an inference I've no real evidence that he is implicated. For the time being, I'd rather work round him and see what I can dig up. I've a friend in the Fraud Squad that I could ask to have a quiet look at the firm's finances, check if anything leaps out. Debts, overdue bank loans, that sort of thing. I'll also have to confirm McPherson's statement, that Taylor was indeed Turner's defence counsel. That shouldn't be a problem though, there's bound to be a court record of the trial."

Her mouth twisted again and her eyebrows knitted together, considering his information.

"Right, contact DCI Mitchell," she instructed "and fill him in with what you have."

She shifted her bulk and decided to ask the question he had known was coming. "How is it working out with Cathy Mulgrew?" she inquired.

"Fine and I've no complaint," he shook his head. "Initial teething problems perhaps, but we've laid ground rules and our separate agenda's don't interfere. The question of Mary Cavendish's pregnancy isn't really an issue, as far as the inquiry goes, but it has provided Cathy with the opportunity to get a close look at her man. What she makes of that is anyone's guess. I don't really see it adding anything her knowledge of the guy, but you know the spooky mob," he half grinned. "Look, listen and reveal nothing. I can truthfully say that her agenda doesn't interfere with my ongoing inquiry. However, if she's available, I'd like her to continue working with me, for the moment anyway. We haven't wound up the inquiry and it might still involve further contact with her target and it is useful having a corroborating officer in attendance, just in case something should break." Rogers nodded her head. "I don't see a problem there. Is there anything else that you need?"

Charlie hesitated, but only briefly and then reached into his desk drawer for the large, brown envelope. "This may be nothing, but you recall me telling you I suspect the wee girl was prostituting herself?"

Again, Rogers nodded.

Charlie drew the photograph, captured by the CCTV camera, from the envelope. "Mary ran from this lane a few seconds before the photograph was taken. I viewed the tape several times and in my opinion, she was running in fear of her life. We'll never know what caused her to take off, but I'm as sure as I can be that this guy was with her. You can clearly see that he's holding his balls and unless I'm way out, that's not a smile on his face. When she was discovered, she was clutching two ten pounds notes. Okay," he sat back, palms outstretched, "I'm only guessing it might have been payment for sex, but nevertheless, what ever caused her to run scared the shit out of her. I know that John Brown is running the sexual assault inquiry. Perhaps this photo might help. What do you think?"

As Rogers scanned the photograph, a curious excitement shivered down her spine. Call it detective instinct, female intuition, but whatever it was, this was a lead and, she almost grinned at the irony of it, from Charlie Miller of all people. Who would have believed it? She stared at him, concealing her emotions.

"Thanks, I'll see that Brown gets this," while thinking, like fuck he will. I'll personally have this run through the database, rather than have that useless moron balls it up. With a parting, "Keep me informed," she turned on her heel and left Charlie wondering what had come over her.

*

Cathy Mulgrew entered the uniform control room and immediately realised that something was going on. Standing with paper in hand, she listened as the uniformed and civilian staff operated the radio and CCTV monitors to coordinate a foot chase through the busy town centre. Patiently, she waited and smiled when a few moments later, a breathless but triumphant message was broadcast from the loudspeaker that the pursuing officers had cornered then arrested their suspect. A lanky civilian detached himself from the CCTV console and approached her, a ready grin on his face.

"Cathy Mulgrew, isn't it?"

His face was familiar, but she couldn't place from where. Seeing her indecision, he introduced himself.

"I'm John Fields. Well, Gracie to this mob in here," he beamed, with a backward nod at his colleagues.

Cathy flushed and swallowed hard.

"What can I do for you, Cathy?"

Handing Gracie the paper containing Taylor's personal details, she asked for a background check. Gracie settled himself down at the monitor that linked with the Police National Computer.

"I'll need your registered number," he asked her, "for Data Protection."

Deftly, he typed in the digits Cathy gave him and then tabbed through the boxes, inserting Taylor's personal details as required.

"Bad guy, is he?"

"Not at the moment, he isn't. Simply a suspect in the fire that the wee girl died in," she replied, her face screwed up and eyes fixed on the screen, willing it to turn up something against the man she was sure was somehow implicated.

Had she known at that time, Cathy might not have been so forthcoming with her response. But then again, who would have suspected that the station janitor, idly emptying the nearby waste paper basket, would have been at all interested in the name and address of the man whose details Gracie had typed into the machine and were now lying in full view, on the computer screen.

*

Sadie Forrest squeezed the rusting Metro into a narrow parking bay and undid her seatbelt.

"Now, Jellybean, when we're in here," she indicated the building, "I do the talking. Okay?"

Her daughter smiled broadly and vigorously nodded her head. Clutching her teddy bear Cracker, she slid from the restraining belt and climbed from the car, taking her mums hand and stared curiously at the glass-fronted entrance to the Central Division police station.

"Is this where you work?"

"No, but it's like this building, only newer and with lots more windows. Right, remember. I'm the boss so," and with her hand, made a zipping noise across her lips.

Her daughter giggled at her mother's funny impression and imitated the gesture before both strode slowly towards the doors. The little girls face full of curiosity while Sadie earnestly hoped she wasn't about to waste the Detective Sergeant's time with nonsense. Other than flashing him a grateful smile, neither took much notice of the elderly man who with courtesy and trembling hands, held the front door open and quickly passed them by on his way out of the station.

*

His fingers fumbling, the old janitor dialled the number that Frank Brogan had given him and half hoped there would be no reply. At the second ring, a strong Belfast accent answered, "Yes?"

"It's me, Jimmy."

A slight pause, then Brogan's cheerful voice, greeted him with, "Jimmy, me old lad. How the devil are you?"

He winced and closed his eyes tight, ashamed for what he was about to do.

"I have a name and address. A suspect, I think."

*

"So, what did she want?"

Charlie blew through pursed lips and ran his fingers through his hair. Suddenly, he felt tired, his mouth dry and throat parched and knew that right now he badly wanted, no, needed a drink. But not yet, he inwardly decided. Maybe this evening, but then again, maybe just a quick half, on his way home.

Quietly and without preamble, he recounted his conversation with Rogers, and then admitted he had given her the photograph of the man exiting the lane after Mary Cavendish. He knew Cathy wouldn't be pleased. She stood over him with her arms folded across her chest and shook her head.

"That was a bad move, Charlie," she began softly, "if that photograph should prove to be of value to the sex attack's inquiry team and," she paused for effect, "let's just suppose it's the man they're after, you and I both know that she'll take the credit for any capture that might arise from the use of photo. For fucks sake," she burst out suddenly, throwing her arms wide, "don't you think that with your recent history, you need all the kudos you can muster? What were you thinking?"

Had Cathy known Charlie longer, she might have recognised the flaring of his nostrils and the short, rapid breath. Quick of thought, but slow to be provoked, Charlie Miller had a low temper threshold, but today he was tired and would brook no argument. Gently, he placed both hands, palms down, on the desk before him and took a deep breath.

"Right, for one, the sex attack inquiry isn't ours. I made the decision and if you recall, the fire raising is still my inquiry," he replied, his voice steady, but the anger now evident in his tone. "For two, I don't give a rats curse about credit. I really don't care who arrests this nutcase. If we obtain spin-off information from our inquiry and can render assistance to the sex attack inquiry, we'll do it. Just so long as the bastard gets taken off the street and no other women get hurt," his voice began to rise. "And as for three," he loudly repeated, now standing and facing her, their noses inches apart and just close enough for him to smell the scent lightly dabbed on her graceful neck, a fragrant smell that threw his anger and train of thought into complete and utter disarray. "Aw, fuck, I forget what three was," he muttered, embarrassed now and anxious to end this confrontation. He sat down heavily and took a deep breath.

"The decision's been made, Cathy so it's academic what you think. Now," he looked up at her, "what did you turn up on Taylor?

She knew she'd been petulant, that the arrest of a sexual predator was the main priority, regardless of who was awarded the credit, but her dislike of Rogers made it difficult for her to admit he was right. Her rage had consumed her and she smarted from his reminder that he had primacy in their inquiry and that he was in charge, that it was his case. She tossed the blank sheet of paper on his desk.

"Nothing," she hissed at him, still unable to contain her anger, "not even a parking ticket. Taylor's not recorded on the PNC under the details we have that I presume will be correct?"

He nodded his head. "The staff list provides us with full names, addresses and dates of birth. There's no reason for him to falsify his own staff list. So, because he isn't known to the police won't mean he's off the hook. Also, we only have the tenuous link from McPherson that Taylor defended Robert Turner during the fire raising case. Beside," he reminded her, "we haven't conclusive proof that Turner is the fire raiser. That's still speculation on our part."

They sat in silence, each lost in their own thought, sipping at their coffee. Cathy continued to fume and rage at what she perceived to be Rogers getting one over on them both.

Charlie couldn't make up his mind whether to purchase a bottle of Whyte and McKay for home consumption, or call in at his local and find a quiet corner where he could sink a few in peace and quiet and gather his thoughts.

The phone on his desk rang. She heard him first acknowledge then suggest the visitor be brought through.

"There's a constable Sadie Forrest to see me. No idea what it's about," he told her and added, "you can hang about or we can call it a day?"

Still annoyed at their row, she stood and lifted her coat.

"I'll see you tomorrow, then," her voice curt and officious, then turned to hurry past the fair-haired woman and child who were being ushered into the CID office by a smiling Gracie Fields.

*

Flaherty's bar was usually quiet in the later afternoon, early evening. Normally Jimmy Donnelly liked this time of the day, an opportunity to enjoy his Guinness in peace and while away the half hour or so, listening to the scratchy stereo belting out tunes to honour the heroic deeds of the men of the Provisional IRA. But not today, for today, Jimmy had assumed the role of informant, a spy in the camp of those who liked and trusted him. The thought of what he had and was about to do brought a foul taste to his mouth, a taste that wouldn't wash away even with the sharp tang of his beloved Guinness. He took a cursory sip of his pint and placed the glass down as a shadow stood over him. Liam McPhee clapped him on the shoulder like some long lost friend.

"How's about you, Jimmy me boy?" he greeted the older man, the smile set on his face, but the eyes devoid of humour. "You'll have something for me, then?"

With a furtive glance about him and in a low whispered voice, Jimmy repeated the information he had stolen with a glance from the computer monitor. McPhee took no notes. He had experienced such assignations when active with the 'Ra and besides, it wasn't too hard to remember a name and address.

"So, just how strong a suspect is this Taylor?" he asked.

Out of sight under the table, Jimmy unconsciously wrung his hands. He'd thought long and hard about what he had to do. Too vague and Brogan would continue to use him till he came up with something more concrete. Too specific and he could be sentencing a total stranger to assault or worse. But the vision of his granddaughters face floated before his eyes. Young and innocent, she'd be helpless if this bastard got his hands on her. And he knew he'd nowhere to turn to. The police, now that he had betrayed them, would be of little use and he'd known other grasses who had suffered in the fullness of time, for the 'Ra had long memories.

"Strong," he replied, the word almost choking him.

McPhee clapped him cheerfully on the back again, to any casual observer, two old pals having a pint together.

"Drink up, old yin. Frank will be pleased and you'll have another glass of the porter on me," he laughed, winking to the barmaid to attend at the table.

*

Sadie Forrest sat down as Charlie made them a cup of tea. Of course, now he remembered who she was, the cop who had broken the news to Irene Cavendish, about the death of her daughter, Mary. He was conscious of the little girl silently watching him as she stood beside her mother, one hand reassuringly on her mum's knee and the other clutching a tattered and bedraggled teddy bear. Charlie wasn't sure, but he thought the bear was missing an eye.

"So," he returned with two steaming mugs, adopting a puzzled look, "first things first. What's the teddy's name?"

The little girl smiled shyly "Cracker," she mumbled.

"And," he addressed the teddy, "what's your owner's name?"

Sadie smiled at his attempt to charm her daughter. The little girl lifted the teddy and whispered in its scruffy ear, then mimicked a squeaky voice from the teddy. "Geraldine."

With a glance at Sadie, Charlie reached into his desk drawer and drew out a large writing pad and pencil. Again he addressed the teddy.

"Do you think Geraldine could draw me a picture of you for my desk," he solemnly asked.

The small girl nodded the teddy's head then followed Charlie to a nearby desk where he helped her kneel on the seat of a swivel chair and set the pad and pencil down in from of her. With a backward glance to reassure her that her mum wasn't leaving without her, the little girl earnestly set to her task.

"You must have children of your own," Sadie smiled at him.

He nodded in return, thinking it wasn't worth going into details. He'd noticed the absence of a wedding ring.

"So, Ms Forrest, what can I do for you?"

"It's probably nothing, Sergeant," she began, inwardly cursing the slight flush she knew was rising from her neck to her face, "but it's about the death of Mary Cavendish."

As they sat drinking their tea and her daughter scribbled a drawing for the nice man, Sadie Forrest slowly and concisely recounted her conversation with her parish priest, Father Flynn.

*

Night fell quickly that November evening and Father Jim Flynn, completely unaware that he was the subject of discussion taking place a few miles away at the Central Division police station, shouted through to the kitchen of the parish house to let his elderly housekeeper know he was off to open the church for evening devotions. The old priest hadn't reached the front door, but she was out after him, berating and chastising him for even considering making the short walk without his heavy coat "and for a man your age," she primly reminded him.

Shrugging his way into his sombre black coat, the old priest muttered in frustration, yet secretly pleased at the widowed woman's thoughtfulness. Opening the front door, he glanced upwards at the clouded sky and resigned himself to another heavy fall of rain, silently praying that the diocese would soon forward the cash to replace the missing slates from the church roof before the under felt became completely soaked and crashed down onto his alter. With a sigh, he pulled the coat tighter and stepped out into the cold.

*

"So you think that Father Flynn might have some relevant information, but he's bound by his vow of silence and is therefore prevented from directly reveal this information?"

"I know it's just my opinion, Sergeant…"

"Please," he raised his hand and smiled at her, "Charlie."

As she blushed, she thought for a big, rough guy, he had a pleasant charm about him.

A cute blush, he observed.

"As I say, it's just my opinion and I feel sure that he would have said more in a kind of roundabout way, you know, using a third party example. Does this make sense?" she asked, acutely aware she might be talking drivel.

Charlie's brow furrowed as he nodded his head, his thoughts dancing back and forth.

"Let's summarise so far. You believe the priest wanted your professional advice on a matter relating to the possible sexual exploitation of a young woman? So far correct? And you believe this young woman to be, or had been," he corrected himself, "Mary Cavendish. Yes?"

To each comment, Sadie nodded her head in agreement.

He leaned forward, his voice low and conspiratorial. "Well, Sadie, for your information only and I must stress this is in confidence, Mary Cavendish was pregnant."

She sat back, surprised to discover she wasn't as shocked as she should be. She looked at Charlie and read in his eyes what she herself believed. She decided to press on with her suspicion.

"I'm speculating that Mary has made her confession to Father Flynn, who probably knows the name of the father of her child and wants him taken to task for having sex with an underage girl. A girl," she concluded, "who although dead, he still feels obliged to protect. Would that be your guess, Charlie?"

His name sounded strange on her lips. God! What was she thinking! He was obviously married; the ring on his left hand indicated that fact. And he has already told her he has children!

"Finished!" called the squeaky voice behind them.

They both turned and smiled at the tousled haired Geraldine, proudly displaying her artwork between her two small hands.

*

The old priest wearily climbed the short flight of broad, sandstone steps to the massive oak doors with their iron hinges and ornate glass windows, now protected by steel mesh wire grills, a token gesture against the vandalism that scarred the area. Fingers stiff with arthritis, he scrambled in the long coat pockets for the heavy door keys. At first, he couldn't understand why it seemed so dark then with a sigh, realised that once again the overhead bulb had failed and needed replaced. Hearing a crunch underfoot, he gingerly stepped back and was puzzled to see small, shrapnel like pieces of white glass on the worn step. Looking upwards, he was startled to find the light wasn't just out, but smashed beyond repair. Bloody kids, he thought ungraciously.

*

"Thanks for coming in, Sadie. Needless to say, I'd be grateful if you could re-establish contact with Father Flynn and follow up on your conversation. It might be that he won't reveal too much and there's little likelihood that identifying the father of Mary Cavendish's baby will further my fire-raising inquiry, but anything that throws light on why she ran from home would have to be included in my report to the Fiscal. To be honest, it won't do any real good and certainly not help the mother any, but if I thought that the sod that got her pregnant had put undue pressure on that wee girl to have sex or to skip from home. Well," he faltered, "I'd probably make it my business to go after him for something."

Charlie shrugged his shoulders and smiled lamely.

"Don't get me wrong," he hastily added, "I'm no knight in shining armour, but I've never liked people and kids in particular, being taken advantage of."

Sadie smiled at him. He really was a nice guy, she decided, even if he didn't realise it. Some woman was obviously very lucky. Turning, she reached for her daughter's hand.

"Come on, Jellybean, time for our dinner. Say goodbye to Mr Miller."

The girl shyly smiled and waved at Charlie, then skipped lightly after her mother.

*

The old housekeeper shook the excess flour from her hands and rubbed them on her apron. She glanced at the clock and was puzzled. Father Flynn was usually back by now, she knew, moaning at her and pestering her for his evening meal. She walked to the front door and pulled it open, peered through the fading light towards the church doors. Funny, she thought, still closed and the porch light was off too. With a sudden apprehension and no thought for the cold, she began to walk the short distance to the doors.

*

Charlie had made up his mind. He'd buy a bottle from the local off-licence, fish supper from Mario's then some mind numbing television. He pulled on his coat then turned to say goodnight to the arriving late shift detectives, wishing them a quiet evening.

"You'll be taking your Picasso home, Charlie?" inquired the older of the two with a grin.

Charlie stared in curiosity and then a half smile of understanding settled on his lips. He strolled to the desk the wee girl had sat at, stopped short and grimaced.

"Bugger!" he said out loud.

There, propped lazily against a thick file, Cracker the teddy sat staring forlornly at Charlie with his single brown, glass eye.

*

The housekeeper's sight had been failing for years, but stubbornly she'd resisted the need for glasses. Now, she wished she hadn't and approached the huddled heap with foreboding.

"Dear God," she cried out loudly, one hand to her throat while the other hand reached for the prone figure. Then common sense prevailed and she hurried back to the parish house to summon an ambulance.

Chapter 12

The non-descript saloon car parked by the telephone kiosk in the twilight hours of the quiet street in the town of Dumbarton drew little attention from passers-by. The driver, his window opened slightly to allow the release of the pungent cigarette smoke stared through the passenger window to the Clyde River, where the water lapped gently against the shoreline. A tramp steamer, bright green light illuminated and pointing towards shore, lazily made its way down river from one of the few docks still operated by the Glasgow City Mercantile Company, its hold packed with hard goods and likely bound for the Orkney Isles.

Barry Ashford drew deeply on his unfiltered French cigarette and glanced in the rear-view mirror. The unlit, dark blue van, parked fifty yards to the rear and on the opposite side of the road, contained the two, armed Security Service minders for insurance only. He wasn't expecting trouble but, reminded himself, when dealing with the Provo's, always expect the unexpected. The clock on the dashboard told him the call was late by nearly five minutes. He would give it five more, then abandon and move to the next rendeavous point. The trill of the phone interrupted his thoughts. Without undue haste, he climbed from the seat and sneaked a furtive glance about. The phone stopped ringing. He stood by the open door kiosk and silently counted to twenty then as if on cue, the phone rang again. He was pleased the caller had remembered his tradecraft. Reaching for the receiver he threw his cigarette butt to the ground and trod on it.

"Hello chum," he greeted the caller cheerfully, "what's new with you, then?"

For the next few minutes, he listened intently and closed his eyes. His voice turned harsh with annoyance.

"Listen, you fucking halfwit," he roared at the handset, "I don't give a shit about any vendetta you might involve yourself with. The well being of a Glasgow lawyer has nothing and I repeat, absolutely nothing to do with the success of your mission. Must I remind you," his voice now dripping with sarcasm, "that your primary function is to secure information, information that you will in turn provide to me, not to get yourself side tracked by this ridiculous revenge plot!" He took a deep breath. "If, and I repeat if, the police should make inquiry into your proposed assault against this Taylor character and if the police identify you as the assailant, then I am in no position to bail you out! Got that? You're on your own. I'm already out on a limb for you, my fine fellow. Word is that your little shenanigans with the funds is becoming of interest to your colleagues in Belfast, so your shelf life might now be drawing to a close."

Ashford turned to discover two teenage girls, dressed in the fashionable Goth style, staring open-mouthed at him from outside the kiosk.

"Hold on dear," he smiled at the receiver, opened the door and growled, "Fuck off!"

The girls startled and stepped back, but not before one decided to respond with the middle finger of her right hand. He watched them saunter down the road and smiled at their petulant arrogance.

"As I was saying, dear boy, we can't go around doing damage to the local populace just because we suspect them of arson and murder now, can we? I'm sure you'll agree that last thing we need is to bring attention to ourselves." He paused, an idea framing itself in his mind. "However, not withstanding the suspicions raised by your colleagues in the Province regarding your monetary appropriations, this may very well present us with an excellent opportunity. Now listen carefully, here's what I propose."

*

The ambulance, blue lights flashing, siren wailing and coincidentally driven by one of Father Flynn's parishioners, roared into the reserved bay at the casualty ward of the Glasgow Royal Infirmary and was immediately greeted by the on duty consultant. As he stepped through the rear doors of the ambulance, he stopped the two paramedics from stretchering the old priest from the vehicle.

"Hold on guys, let's have a wee look before we go anywhere here."

Deftly, the consultant ran his hands lightly round the back of the unconscious priest's skull, now encased in a sturdy neck brace, and gently withdrew them, his protective gloves stained with blood that seeped through the temporary bandaged head. A stethoscope check revealed faint and erratic breathing. Prising open his eyelids, the consultant shone a pencil torch into Flynn's pupils. He shook his head slowly.

"Look," he addressed the two men, "I'm not happy with having the old guy in here. I'd prefer to get him straight down to the Neurological Department at the Southern General. There's a standby surgeon there at the moment. When I got your radio message I phoned him and his advice is, if it's safe, to transport the patient there right away. You game for it?"

The two men looked at each other and nodded.

"Can we assist?"

The doctor turned to find a uniformed traffic policewoman stood at the open doors.

"Got the call about a possible assault and came straight here," she added, "but if you're taking him to the Southern, I'll get the road cleared."

The consultant grimly smiled.

"Right then, the decision is made. I'm with you," he added to the paramedics, "so close those doors and let's get going."

*

Charlie Miller decided to walk the short distance from the Central Division station to Sadie Forrest's address in the Merchant City. The plastic carrier bag containing the teddy bear swung lightly against his leg. The early evening revellers and late shift office staff were few, though the area was renowned for its pubs and restaurants. Resigning himself to the task, Charlie remembered what a favourite toy meant to a child and the heartbreak it caused if the toy wasn't there at night to be cuddled. With a smile he remembered a forty-minute round trip he'd made to recover a bright red plastic racing car, missing one wheel he vaguely recalled, that his son had left after a visit to his in-laws. His return had been greeted with hugs and kisses and not only from the child. With a sigh, he knew he was long overdue phoning his in-laws and resolved to make the call. Maybe tomorrow, he thought.

"Have you got a couple of bob for a cup of tea, mister?" said the voice, startling him from his thoughts.

The shabby figure with the hung drawn look that emerged from the lane shuffled towards Charlie.

Christ, he thought to himself. The boy can't be anymore than sixteen.

"You not got a home to go to, son?"

The youth, his face wan and haggard, stared at Charlie.

"No, mister, I'm on the street. Any chance of the price of a cuppa?" he repeated, his thin hand extended in hopeful anticipation.

The smell of body odour bore out the teenager's tale of rough living. Something in Charlie snapped. Much later, when he recounted the story, he couldn't for the life of him explain what came over him. Taking the youth by the elbow he steered the startled and unresisting teenager towards a nearby take away fish and chip shop. The half dozen customers awaiting their orders were surprised to see the slightly dishevelled, but burly man lead the shabbily dressed teenager into the shop.

"One fish and chips please," Charlie called to the man behind the counter, ignoring the queue.

The assistant, stocky and round faced, both ears pierced and sporting gold studs, his gelled hair tied back in a pony tail and wearing a grease stained apron, stared at the poker-faced Charlie.

"We don't serve his likes in here," he replied, using a spatula to point at the teenager.

The customers waited edgily, their curiosity peaked as they stood watching Charlie for his response. Charlie released his grip on the youths elbow and smiled at him.

"Just wait there, son," he told him reassuringly, then turned back to face the assistant.

"His likes, you said. That right?"

Reaching into his jacket pocket, he drew out his warrant card and slapped it down on the counter with the crested badge facing upwards.

"Do see that badge there, pal?" he spoke through clenched teeth. "Well, that badge authorises me to do my civic duty and my nose tells me that there is a nasty smell coming from your shop and that likely means a severe lack of hygiene. My civic duty tells me that I will be phoning the environmental people tomorrow morning first thing and have them get their arses round here to give this place the once over! Then, of course, if I have any information that you might be dealing drugs from here, I'll have to sit a few cops outside turning over every customer that dare venture into this pigsty! Not to mention giving the place the once over now and again for stolen property! Understand me so far, pal?"

The assistant, pale faced and now goggle eyed, stared at the red faced and enraged Charlie. Swallowing hard, he nodded his head.

"So, like I said, one… fucking… fish… and… chips, if you please!"

"Will you be wanting salt and vinegar on that?" the humbled assistant mumbled in reply.

Outside the shop, the youth clutched the newspaper wrapped supper and stared at Charlie, a little fearful and unsure whether the big guy was a real cop or a nutter pretending to be one.

"What's your name son?"

"Andy. Andrew, I mean. Andrew McEwan, sir."

"Well, Andrew McEwan, here's what your going to do. You're going to eat your supper while you're walking and you're going to walk to Argyle Street. Know where that is?"

The youth, a little uncertainly, nodded his head.

"Walk down towards Anderston and you'll come across a shop. It's painted pink and a bit shabby, but don't worry about that. There's a woman there called Aileen Dee. If it's closed get yourself in there first thing tomorrow morning, understand? Tell her Charlie Miller sent you. Will you remember that?"

The wide-eyed youth nodded again, anxious to be both eating his supper and away from this big, mad mental bastard.

With a nod and a grin, Charlie turned and headed off. In the distance, the sound of emergency vehicle sirens echoed between the tall, graceful buildings of the old Merchant City neighbourhood.

*

Cathy Mulgrew sank slowly into the foaming bubble bath and soaked the tension of the day from her body. She had been more than a little upset at her argument with Charlie. Despite her initial misgivings, she liked him and for all his faults that included his dreadful taste in clothes, thought him a more capable police officer than she had been led to believe. She still had her doubts about his decision to provide Nancy Rogers with the photograph of the unidentified male, but grudgingly admitted it was the correct thing to do. The graceful voice of Adele's latest chart song drifted through to the bathroom. She smiled as she listened to her partner dueting with the London singer and grimaced at the slightly off key accompaniment. Reaching for a glass of wine, Cathy reflected on her last conversation with her boss, Martin Cairney. The relationship of Barry Ashford and the Security Service with Frank Brogan had cast a completely different light on the inquiry. Reluctantly, she knew that her involvement was now low key and she'd have to tread warily. Still, something had been niggling at her and she couldn't quite put her finger on it. Something at the back of her mind about the dead girl. She pursed her lips and blew bubbles from her nose. A shout from the lounge warned her she had ten minutes to dry off before dinner. Cathy stepped from the bath and wrapped the snow-white towel about her, then opened it to stare at herself in the full-length mirror. She critically examined her body, turning back and forth, the better to see from different angles. Mmm, not too bad, she decided. A second holler warned her she now had just five minutes. Briskly, she rubbed at her legs then between her legs. She stopped and stared at the hair about her Venus mound. A sudden realisation hit her. That's what had been niggling at her. She grabbed at her watch from the vanity bureau. If she was quick, she still had time to phone the late shift at the laboratory.

*

Charlie arrived at close number eighteen and scanned the tenant's names beside the doorbell buttons, then selected 'S Forrest' and pushed twice. A disembodied tinny voice asked who was there?
"It's Charlie Miller," he replied. "From the…"
The door buzzed open before he could finish as the voice instructed him to take the stairs to the third floor. Unaccountably feeling rather foolish, he wearily climbed the stairs and was met by Sadie Forrest, who stood holding her front door ajar, a sky blue sweat shirt over the top of dark coloured baggy tracksuit pants, her hair loose, falling around her shoulders and a quizzical look on her face. As he climbed the last few stairs, he held the plastic bag aloft.
"Thought you might need this," he said as he drew out the battered teddy bear.
A flash of pink pyjamas bolted from the door and snatched the teddy from his hand.
"Cracker!" screamed the little girl as she hugged the bear close to her.
"Geraldine!" her mother called, but the chastisement faded on her breath as Charlie waved away the apology.
"No need," he grinned at Sadie. "The main thing is that Cracker is home, safe and well."
Sadie smiled at him. "How did you get our address?"
"Called your office and eventually persuaded your indoor Inspector it was an

urgent operational matter," he grinned at her. "So, if you're asked…."
She nodded, smiling at him. "Cup of tea or are you expected home?"
Charlie hesitated, but the decision was suddenly taken from him when a small
hand reached into his and a pleading voice said, "Please come in."
He stared at the little girl. It had been a long time since he had been near a child.
With a strange lump in his throat, he nodded and followed Sadie and her daughter
into the flat.

*

Irene Cavendish set the coffee table with cups and saucers and arranged the
biscuit's in soldierly fashion about the tea plates. Frank had said he'd be there
before Coronation Street began, so that would be any time now, she reckoned.
The doorbell rung and the voice called out reassuringly that it was "Just me!"
followed almost immediately with the entrance of Frank Brogan and Liam
McPhee. Irene ushered the two men to their seats on the couch and fetched the
teapot from the kitchen.
"You have some news?" she asked.
Brogan nodded his head. "Irene," he began, "before we go any further I have to
tell you I don't think this is a very good idea. I mean, if anything happens to the
guy the police are looking at, there's a good chance they'll think we're somehow
connected and they're going to be all over us like a bad rash. It won't take much to
work out that we are someway involved. Christ…"
"Do not take the Lords name in vain in my house!" she hissed at him.
"I'm sorry, Irene. No offence. But what I'm trying to tell you is that…"
Irene poured the tea carefully into the three cups and as she did so, interrupted
without looking at him.
"When our mother and father died, Francis," she began, "wasn't it me that took
care of you? Didn't I go out and work all hours to keep you fed and clothed?"
"I know all that Irene…"
"Don't interrupt me," she spat, her lips trembling and her face chalk white.
Brogan flushed as McPhee looked down, embarrassed and confused, wishing he
was at the pub and not party to this domestic scene.
She slammed the teapot down hard on the coffee table, the shock causing the
china cups to bounce and spill some liquid onto the varnished wooden surface.
McPhee reached for a napkin.
"Leave it!" she snapped at him, and then turned to her brother. "And didn't I put
up with that husband of mine all those years, through his drinking and yes, his
womanising. I knew all about it, may God forgive him and may he rot in hell for
eternity! And during those early years, wasn't I keeping you in money for your
drink and football matches till you could support yourself?"
She paused for breath as Brogan looked away, unable to maintain her unwavering
gaze.
"And like the bible says, an eye for an eye and a tooth for a tooth. And I want that
man, whose name you have, I want the account squared! I want him dead!"

*

The old housekeeper sat wringing her hands as the detectives supped their tea, patiently waiting on her regaining her composure. "No," she told them, "I didn't see anyone out there with Father Flynn. No," she repeated, "I don't know when the light was broken and didn't know it had been. No," she shook her head, "I can't think of anyone who would hurt him nor would want to for wasn't he the kindest of men? No, I don't know what he would have in his pockets nor if he carried cash or a wallet with him."

Then finally, with weariness, "No, there are no next of kin that I'm aware of, just his parishioners. We're his family."

*

Charlie sat in the comfortable chair in the small lounge, the walls painted a pastel colour and hung with inexpensive but tasteful prints. The neat and functional furniture served to enhance rather than dominate the room. Displayed on the main wall was a recently taken, professionally shot black and white photograph of Sadie and Geraldine. Charlie was quick to notice there didn't seem to be any pictures of Sadie's husband or partner, but thought it prudent not to bring the subject up.

"Tea or coffee?" she called from the adjoining small, but compact kitchen.

"Coffee will be fine, thanks. White, no sugar," he added.

Geraldine sat at his feet, playing with Cracker and whispering in the teddy's ear.

"Right, young madam, bed," ordered her mother, entering with a mug in each hand. Charlie leaned forward and spread two coasters on the low coffee table.

"Night," called the girl, shyly waving a small hand at Charlie then, to his surprise, she rushed back to plant a sloppy wet kiss on his cheek and whispered a breathless, "Thank you."

He smiled in response as her mother ushered her through the door, calling to her she would be in to tuck her into bed in five minutes. Sadie sat in the opposite chair, one leg neatly tucked beneath the other.

"That was very kind of you, bringing Cracker back."

He smiled tolerantly. "I know that kids can get very attached to certain toys, dolls, that sort of thing."

"Yes, you mentioned you had children. Boy or girl or both?" she smiled at him. He stared briefly at his coffee, sensing that no matter what he said or how he said it, he was about to involuntarily embarrass this young woman. With a sigh he replied, "Boy. Charles. After me," he added unnecessarily. Then almost apologetically, "Please don't get upset when I tell you this, but my son died. Along with his mother," he added. "A road traffic accident, eh, almost three years ago, now."

Sadie stared at him, aghast. His half smiling attempt to make her feel at ease with his dreadful revelation astounded her. The seconds passed and seemed eternal. My God, she thought. How does he cope? A sudden rush of sympathy swept through her for this big, untidy man. But nothing she could say would possibly be appropriate. Nothing could alleviate the shock of his short statement. She placed her mug down softly on the table and stared at him and fought hard against an irresistible urge to hold him close.

Then suddenly, as if it was expected of him, he sat back in the chair and slowly began to recount the details of the incident, the shock and horror of the crash; the feelings of rage and guilt that fought within him to surmount all other emotion. Without realising it, he unburdened his soul. After three, heart searching, lengthy and seemingly timeless years, Charlie Miller finally revealed his pain. And to a stranger, yet he felt no discomfort at the telling.

"Are you lonely?"

The question took him by surprise.

"Lonely?" he repeated. Of the numerous sympathetic and even countless platitudes offered at the time, he had never been asked that question. He thought about it and decided she was a smart and perceptive woman.

"Yes, I suppose I am," he confessed, shrugging his shoulders. "I'm not proud to admit I took refuge in the bottle. In fact," he raised his eyebrows at the memory, "I seem to have been on one lengthy binge. Events and occasions over the last nearly three years just seemed to merge into one hellish long day and endless night of avoiding work and friends, family; anyone or anything that reminded me of Ali. Alison," he explained, though Sadie had guessed that.

"Our son Charles or wee Chic, as I called him. She hated that," he smiled.

"Geraldine, Jellybean. It's a parent's prerogative," she joked, "pet names for our kids."

"And you, single parent?"

She exhaled noisily though her pursed lips.

"I wasn't always. My ex-husband found a younger, sexier woman and that was that. It's my daughter I feel for. I don't miss him, but she sometimes asks after him, though she hasn't done for a while," she thought with some surprise, her brow creasing at the realisation.

"No chance of any reconciliation?"

She smiled, thinking what the odds were she would be asked that very question twice in one day and shaking her head, replied, "Absolutely none."

Charlie was taken aback by her determined reply and decided not to push the issue. They sat in comfortable silence, sipping at their coffee. The ringing of the phone startled them both. With an apologetic smile, Sadie stood and took the call on the wall phone in the kitchen. From the sound of her greeting, he presumed she was speaking with her mother. Charlie settled comfortably in his chair, surprised to realise he was enjoying the cosiness of their chat, the familiar feeling of the company of a woman and being in a family atmosphere He raised his eyebrows and decided he had better push off before Sadie got the wrong idea. Now why did I think that, he wondered? Sadie stood in the doorway of the kitchen, her eyes wide and her face drawn and pale. He knew immediately something was wrong.

"It's Father Flynn. It's all over the parish. He's been attacked."

*

Liam McPhee inserted the key in the ignition, but didn't turn it. Staring through the windscreen, he asked the question that had to be asked, "When?"

Frank Brogan stroked his hand across his face.

"Soon," he softly exhaled. "Better getting it done and over with. A straight hit. Nothing too fancy, mind. Do him and get to hell out of it."

In the darkness of the car, McPhee sneered. What the fuck did Brogan know about straight hits? How many hits has he been on? How would he know what it's like, lying in ambush in some darkened street or sodden field, waiting for a Brit patrol to pass by, praying to Christ that it wasn't a set-up, that the fucking SAS weren't drawing a bead on your head as you lay there, with your guts in turmoil, hoping to God you wouldn't shit your pants. The memories came flooding back. Stark memories of the boys who had boasted of their prowess with a AK47 and were now dead. Of the boys who were wanted and had to flee and were now, what the Brit's called OTR - on the run.

So, Frank fucking Brogan. What do you know about hits?

Calmly, he drew breath and decided to goad him.

"You'll need to be there, Frank."

He sensed, rather than saw, Brogan startle.

"I thought…, what I mean…. I was thinking, maybe we could call upon your experience. You know, from your combat skills against the Brit's." He licked his lips. This didn't feel right, capitulating to McPhee. He was the boss, not this illiterate bog dwelling reject from the Ardoyne. However, needs must and no way was Frank Brogan going to be placed in a position where the police could get their grubby paws on him, no way at all.

"I'm open to suggestions, Liam. How would you play it?" he asked, hoping it didn't sound like a whine.

McPhee smirked once again. A rush of adrenalin coursed through him as the old feeling of impending action seized him.

"Leave it to me, Frankie boy," knowing Brogan hated being addressed like that, "there's a man across the water that I'll need to speak with."

*

The nightshift staff nurse glanced at the chart, then at the bloodless face of the old priest who lay hooked up to the monitors. Poor old soul, she thought. Without thinking, she made the Sign of the Cross as her Irish grandmother had taught, God rest her. The scribbled notes of the Neuro surgeon seemed to indicate twelve hours at most. But he's one of our own the nurse silently reminded God, so see what You can do, eh?

*

Sadie held the door as Charlie shuffled into his overcoat. The news imparted by her mother about Father Flynn had been grim and a subsequent call by Sadie to her nightshift station Inspector had produced little further information, other than the old priest had been found unconscious with a wound to the back of the head. At this time, he had told her, local CID was treating the incident as suspicious. Both Charlie and Sadie knew that statement covered any eventuality, but with no witnesses and no apparent forensic evidence, the CID inquiry was an uphill climb from the outset. They had discussed the unfortunate timing of the incident and considered a connection with Flynn's partial disclosure to Sadie, but with the little they knew, were forced to agree they were grasping at straws; adding two and two and coming up with five, as Charlie said. Awkwardly, they stood, unsure how to say goodbye and oddly reluctant to do so. On a sudden impulse, Sadie leaned forward and kissed Charlie on his right cheek. He smiled with surprise and, he had to admit, a little pleasure.

She rubbed gently at his face where her lipstick had stained his cheek.

"What did I do to deserve that?"

She blushed at her recklessness. "That," she said, "was for returning Cracker. And this," she leaned close to him and lightly kissed him on the opposite cheek, "is from me."

Charlie's smile turned into a huge grin. "Sadie Forrest, I could get to like you, so keep your eye on that teddy because I'm considering bear-napping him to bring him back again."

Sadie watched Charlie walk down the stairs and waved him goodbye. She felt a curious tightness in her chest. Not a pain, but a feeling of well being that she hadn't experienced for a long, long time. Her fingers strayed to her lips and she blushed again. God, what was I thinking! But then she smiled, a tight little smile and the blush still upon her cheeks, gently closed the door and she leaned against it. Charlie had admitted he was lonely. Curiously, he hadn't asked her.

*

Liam McPhee drove Frank Brogan's Vauxhall Vectra to the outskirts of Coatbridge, the town to the east of Glasgow where the Catholic population's fiercely Irish republican supporters frequently demonstrated their loyalty to the Cause with fund-raising functions and flute band parades. He drove about the streets at random, stopping and starting and frequently changing direction. Satisfied at last, or as best he could be that there was no following vehicle, he stopped at a telephone kiosk and alighted from the car. Checking his watch, he waited till the minute hand struck the half hour then dialled the secure number he had been instructed to commit to memory. At the second ring, the call was answered by the gruffly familiar voice of his old acquaintance, Manus Foley. McPhee smiled in anticipation.

"Hello, Foley you old rogue, so how's about you? I've a wee problem that might require a decision from the Army Council and, if they agree, I'll then need some technical assistance."

Having peaked Foley's interest, McPhee then proceeded to explain at length his predicament and what resources he would require to sort out his dilemma.

Chapter 13 – Wednesday morning

DCI Colin Mitchell arrived early at the Murder Incident room within Govan police office and stood nursing his freshly brewed coffee, staring at the large white melamine board that displayed a montage of photographs of the deceased and the scene of the murder, post-it notes with messages, handwritten comments in chino graph pen and lines drawn between the various inquiries. None of it yet made any sense, he knew. Nothing so far, despite all the footslogging and door to door inquires, had turned up a shred of evidence that indicted the identity, much less the guilt of the perpetrator. A polite cough interrupted his thoughts. DS 'Peasy' Byrne of the Serious Crime team stood behind him.

"Good morning, boss. You've got a cup then?"

Mitchell smiled and held up his mug. "You're in early, 'Peasy'. Wet the bed again?" he joked.

Byrne laughed and move to the kettle, his own mug in hand.

"I've got a wee line of inquiry, this morning boss. Young Emma and I did a subscriber check on Turner's phone and the public telephone kiosk, just down the road from his flat. I'm expecting an early result from the BT night staff. Thought it would be here by now," he sighed.

Mitchell creased his brow. He'd lifted the mail from the front desk and was sure there had been a large brown manila envelope addressed to Byrne.

"Hang on," he told him, then scrambled through the correspondence lying in the administration 'In' tray. "Here we go," he handed him the large envelope, "letter for DS Byrne."

Byrne took the envelope from him and tore open the flap, then extracted three sheets of closely typed figures and data.

"Bloody hell, boss, I'd need to be a Philadelphia lawyer to understand this lot."

"Let me see that," smiled Mitchell. With a grin he scanned the first sheet, then the second. With a start, he checked again. A thoughtful smile slowly spread across his face. Sure enough, there was a name he recognised and the mobile phone number against the name had been called from the public telephone kiosk.

"Peasy," he stared at Byrne with a new sense of urgency, "get a hold of Charlie Miller, he's a DS in the CID at the Central Division. I don't care where he is or what he's doing. Have him attend here right now!"

*

As Mitchell was issuing his instruction, the subject of that instruction was in his underwear, standing upright in front of his mirrored wardrobe, pulling in his belly and wryly accepting that his waistline would never recover from the onslaught of age. "Charlie, my boy," he spoke out loud, "you've failed your MoT." With a shake of his head and scornful frown at the mirror, he run a hand through his tangled hair and made his way into the kitchen. Since he had blitzed and spring-cleaned the house, it had regained a sense of normalcy and the cupboards now stocked food items, basic though they may be. He leaned over the open door of the fridge and fetched the carton of milk. Tipping his head back, he made to drink from the spout and stopped. With a grin, he remembered his wife's admonishment when he did that and reached into the cupboard for a glass. Pouring the milk he thought about her and realised that he hadn't smiled about her for a very long time. Nor his son, wee Chic. The milk tasted cool and pleasant to his lips and the chill of it took his breath away as it streamed down his throat. The off-licence, he suddenly remembered. He had jumped a taxi and come straight home. He hadn't stopped off for a bottle. Well, bugger me he thought, oddly pleased at his oversight and bringing a grin to his face. The ringing of his mobile phone interrupted his thoughts.

*

Cathy Mulgrew re-read Charlie's text message and wondered at his change of plan to meet him at Govan office. Must be a meeting with DCI Mitchell, she assumed. Grabbing her coat and handbag, she blew a kiss towards the noise of a saucepan banging in kitchen, called out goodbye and closed the front door behind her.

*

DCI Nancy Rogers and acting Detective Inspector, John Brown sat closeted in her room, the CCTV photograph of Charlie's unknown male now copied and piled in bundles on the desk in front of them.

"Now, you're quite clear about that? Copies to all headquarters intelligence departments, Serious Crime Squad, Scottish Crime and Drug Enforcement Agency and all Force divisional intelligence collators?"

"Yes ma'am, quite clear," he agreed, seething that she was treating him like a fucking postman.

"I've a feeling in my water this is our guy."

"Can I ask where you obtained this?"

She stared blankly at him, guessing it was driving him crazy how she had come by the photograph.

"Let's just say it's perhaps something you should have considered, John. But of course, you didn't. Will that suffice for now?"

His face turned red, the open hostility revealing itself in his silence. Without a word, he collected the bundles in his arms and left the room.

*

The detached Victorian sandstone built house located in the elegant, tree-lined avenue in the affluent suburb of Newton Mearns had seen better days. The large garden to the front urgently needed the services of a lawnmower, while the driveway required both weeding and several broken slabs, replaced. In contrast to the house, the two-tone Bentley saloon car that was parked in the driveway stood like shining like a jewel in the November sunlight, its polished chrome and bodywork gleaming and its immaculate appearance at odds with its surroundings. Charlie Miller and Cathy Mulgrew walked slowly through the rusting gates at the entrance to the driveway and heatedly debated their assignment. "I think this is a bad idea," he hissed, noticing the grime that would obscure any quick look into the house through the heavy curtained windows.

She shook her head in disbelief at his reticence.

"This is the best opportunity we have to get Steven Taylor into the office under formal interview conditions. Mitchell's team has established a link with the dead guy Turner, through the subscriber check," she reminded him. "The mobile phone's number subscribes to Steven Taylor. For Christ sake, Charlie, what more do you want?"

"It's too tenuous a link," he argued, "I'd rather have made further enquiry before we approached him. We don't have sufficient evidence to arrest, charge or even detain Taylor under the six hour rule. And the phone number doesn't even subscribe to this address, but to his company address in Hope Street."

"I don't see how that makes a difference and also, don't forget he was Turner's defence counsel years ago, admittedly not recently," she hissed back at him, "but that's why Mitchell wants us to persuade him into the office under the guise of your inquiry, see if we can rattle him while we take a formal statement about the fire.

He sensed she was exasperated that he was unhappy with Colin Mitchell's decision of what Mitchell regarded as a significant break.

He stared at her, bewildered. Didn't she get it? There was no evidence to prove that Turner set the fire. And he wasn't slow in picking up on her comment when she referred to the investigation as your inquiry, not our inquiry. Presumably she was still angry about their argument, the previous evening. He shook his head at what he was about to do. Jesus, he thought. Am I the only one in both these investigations thinking straight? But Mitchell had insisted, had beaten down Charlie's protestations and ordered him to fetch Taylor in for interview.

"But make it look as if it's regarding your fire," he had instructed.

The brass fittings on the heavy oak door had almost turned green with *Verdi Gris*. Gingerly, Cathy pulled firmly at the old fashioned lever and from within the house heard a bell tinkle. She looked at Charlie, an expectant smile on her face, but his head was turned away. She was annoyed that he wasn't committed to this course of action, but to hell with him. If he wanted to act like a child, so be it. This capture was going down, whether he believed in it or not.

The door squeaked open on hinges thirsting for a trickle of oil. Steven Taylor, hair uncombed, face unshaven and wearing a shapeless grey cardigan over a dark coloured polo shirt, old cavalry twill trousers and plaid slippers, stood peering at them through rheumy eyes.

"Mister Taylor," Cathy began, "CID from Central Division in the city. You'll remember DS Miller," and indicated Charlie standing glumly behind her.

"Oh yes. The officer who attended the fire I believe?"

Charlie nodded and gave a tight smile in recognition as Cathy continued.

"Wonder if we might come in and have a quick word, sir?"

"Where are my manners? Yes, yes of course, please do," he shuffled to one side to permit them to enter.

The entrance hall was dark and gloomy and led to a formal lounge at the front of the house. Even in the half-light that penetrated the dirty windows, Charlie could see evidence of neglect. Cobwebs hung from the high light fixture and newspapers lay strewn about the old fashioned settees and the floor. Two lighter square patches on the ornate wallpaper indicated where pictures had apparently been removed. Sold, he surmised if the state of this place is anything to go by. A smell of mould and rotten food permeated the air.

"Sorry about the condition of the place," began Taylor, "Cleaning ladies day off," he guffawed.

'Day off' thought Charlie. More like complete desertion as far as he could tell. Cathy unobtrusively wrinkled her nose in repugnance at the odour and glanced around. She had already decided that Charlie wanted no part of this and she would take control. Drawing herself to her full height, she faced Taylor.

"It would be helpful Mr Taylor if you could accompany us to the police office where we will be able to obtain a statement from you, regarding the recent fire that occurred at your office."

"Why would we have to travel to your station? Couldn't you note my statement here?"

Cathy saw him swallow hard, his Adams apple bouncing around in his throat like a cheerleader's tit. He was clearly nervous. She pressed on.

"I'd rather note it under formal conditions, particularly as that the fire resulted in the death of a young woman. I'm sure that given the circumstances you will be rather keen to assist us, particularly when your insurance company approach us for any information or suspicions that we might have. I don't profess to be any kind of expert in insurance matters," she gushed, smiling broadly and pretending inexperience, "but it's obviously in your own interest to assist the police to identify the culprit as quickly as possible and thereby enable your insurance company to settle the claim and get your firm back into business. That would be correct, sir, yes?"

The challenge was set. Cathy and Charlie waited with bated breath for his response, but weren't prepared for what came next. Taylor slowly sat down on a couch, disturbing the floral throw over and revealing the threadbare material underneath. He lowered his head into his hands.

"There is no insurance," he finally admitted, his voice soft and anguished.

"I'm sorry to hear that, Mr Taylor. Can you explain why not?"

He lifted his head and stared at her, his face grey and suddenly ten years older.

"It may have escaped your attention, young woman, but my financial position has been somewhat erratic these last few years. Look about you. Do you imagine I enjoy residing in this deplorable circumstance? Can you honestly believe if my business was successful, I would greet guests in these conditions," as he threw his arms about him to press home his point.

With a sigh he stood up. "While I may not be the sharpest lawyer in town," he quipped, "it occurs to me, officers, that perhaps you suspect my involvement in the fire that gutted my firm's office, yes?'"

He smiled as he saw his statement had struck a nerve.

"Well, frankly, I'm glad the place burned down. It was dragging me to ruin and destitution. Nay, it has dragged me to ruin and destitution," he corrected himself, "but did I have the foresight or even the courage to commit the act? Alas, no. Though the fire has destroyed more than just my firm, as you so succinctly put it," he turned to Cathy, his voice growing stronger, "it has taken the life of a young woman and that, dear lady, is more than even I am capable of. No. I'm afraid you will have to seek elsewhere to find your culprit, because it certainly is not I."

He shook his head, weary of this interview and crossed to the stained window where he rubbed at the dust, then wiped his hand on his trouser leg. Cathy caught Charlie's eye. His glance was enough. Let Taylor go on speaking.

"The firm my father began and that I inherited was a well-respected and viable concern. In father's day," he said wistfully, "the client's were plentiful for Glasgow then was a vibrant city, full of enterprise. Not for nothing was it the second city of the Empire, the Merchant City. I continued with the tried and tested methodical system my father had begun, believing that the clients respected integrity and solicitude with their accounts."

The bitterness rose like bile in his throat.

"Unfortunately I ignored, or rather paid no heed to the march of time and, to my everlasting regret, completely discounted these Johnny Come Lately companies and financial institutions with their advertisements and inducements and who were able to provide my clients with a far better return on their investments. In truth, things never recovered. My wife left with our young son and she's since remarried." He glanced at Cathy, a thoughtful look upon his face. "My son will be man now. And as for the company, well, I've been trying to hold things together for almost a decade, but it's a fight that I can't win. I have neither the resources nor the energy left."

Deflated, his shoulders slumped and again he sank back down on the settee. He turned to face Charlie.

"You seem to be a fair man, yet you say nothing, Detective Sergeant Miller. Criminal law is not my discipline, but I suspect that you have reservations about my involvement?"

Charlie looked squarely at Taylor and realised that his initial assessment was wrong. Shabby and worn out, he certainly seemed, but Taylor was no fool. He half smiled at the bedraggled lawyer. He indicated an armchair and Taylor waved for him to sit down.

"Suppose we put some questions to you here, sir, think you could assist us with a few answers?"

"What do you have in mind? Charlie," Cathy interrupted, "DCI Mitchell clearly stated…"

She got no further. Charlie raised his hand to silence her. The rebuke was plain to see.

"He's not here and I am, Cathy. Just bear with me for a few minutes, you can do that can't you?"

Her face flushed in anger and her lips tightened. She could feel this was getting away from her. No way was Taylor about to voluntarily accompany them now. Silently she nodded, but vowed to vent her fury on Charlie when they got outside.

"As I was saying, Mr Taylor, I know that you previously told me you don't do criminal work. Is that true?"

"Yes and no. There was a time, some years ago though I can't recall exactly, when the prospect of earning extra income by volunteering to take on some clientele accused of crimes was appealing, certainly when I heard of the money to be earned through the Legal Aid system."

He smiled self-consciously. "Regretfully, I didn't last very long, no more than a few months, in fact. I'm sorry to say that regardless of my best efforts, all my clients were duly convicted." His smile turned to a self-deprecating grin. "I wasn't a popular choice at the detention cells for the custody prisoners that later appeared before the Sheriff Court."

Charlie nodded in understanding. There was fierce competition between the lawyers who attended the early morning court sessions, touting amongst themselves for the juiciest cases.

"Can you recall defending a man by the name of Robert Turner? A fire raising case," he added.

Behind him, Cathy winced, certain that Charlie was revealing too much information and allowing Taylor to prepare himself for a future defence.

Taylor rubbed a hand across his forehead. "Robert Turner," he slowly repeated, then as if the rubbing action had worked, cried, "Yes! I do remember him. A rather shallow young man as I recall and quite prepared to offer up his accomplice as a sacrifice to lessen his own sentence."

"Have you had any contact with him since that time?"

Taylor's eyes widened with surprise. "Of course not," he declared, "Why would I?"

Then, as if the connection dawned on him, "Is he the person you suspect might have burned down my office?"

Charlie stared at him. Either he was as slow as Charlie had first suspected or his surprise was total innocence. But which was it? He decided on a different tract. "Do you own a mobile phone, sir?"

Taylor hesitated, a hesitation that wasn't lost on either detective.

"Eh, yes, I suppose I do."

"And where is that phone now?"

Taylor looked baffled. Why on earth would he ask that he wondered?

"Here, in the house, I think. Yes, yes. I'm sure I brought the ghastly thing home." He stood and appeared to be trying to collect his thoughts, then made his way to a dark brown drawer unit, placed against the far wall. Charlie and Cathy watched as he rummaged in a low drawer.

"Yes I was right," then drew a box from the drawer. "Here you go," and handed the box to Charlie.

The box was brightly coloured with the depiction of the phone inside and featured the manufacturers name and description of the contents. Charlie prised off the lid and as Cathy leaned over, both saw the phone nestled in its polystyrene packaging. The phone charger remained sealed in its polythene bag and the wire was tied with a small metal clip. The mobile phone number was attached to the inside of the lid by an adhesive label and matched the number he'd noted from 'Peasy' Byrnes list. It seemed obvious to both detectives the phone had never been used.

Charlie saw that Taylor was confused and then recalled when they had first met

Taylor had told him that he was not at all technical minded.

He asked the obvious. "I presume you don't use this phone, sir?"

Taylor blushed. "I know I should, constant contact with the office and all that, because Tom - Tom Frobisher my partner," he reminded Charlie, "keeps nagging me. But frankly, I don't know how and was too embarrassed to ask. And as for the instruction manual, well, I mean, they might make sense to a ten year old, but I couldn't make hide nor hair of it," he sheepishly admitted.

"The phone SIM card, Charlie, check the SIM card," Cathy suggested, her curiosity aroused by the discovery of the phone.

Charlie removed the phone from its packaging and levered off the rear panel. The SIM card was missing.

"Might I ask what a SIM card is?" inquired Taylor.

"In layman terms, it's a miniature electronic square that fit's in here," he pointed with his forefinger, "that contains the phones memory and is in fact the heart of the phone. It stores not only the phone number, but also all data that is typed into the phone via this," as he tapped the phones keypad. "As you can see, the SIM card for this item has been removed, making this phone virtually useless."

"So this SIM card can't be used without the phone?"

"Not strictly true. This phone is useless without the SIM card, but the SIM card can be inserted into another phone, providing that other phone is connected to the same telephone service provider and,'" he turned to look at Cathy, "if I'm not mistaken, that's likely what has happened. The question now is, Mr Taylor, who else has had access to this boxed phone?"

Taylor rubbed his chin between his forefinger and thumb.

"Why, anyone who was in the office when the damned things were delivered. Pardon me, Sergeant," he smiled at Cathy.

"And how many were delivered? Can you recall?"

"One for each of the partners and associates, so, I would guess about ten. Oh and the senior secretaries were also provided with phones so perhaps twelve, maybe thirteen?"

"I assume these phones weren't your idea, Mr Taylor?" interjected Cathy, her anger at Charlie now forgotten with this new information.

"Indeed they were not," he forcibly replied. "Mr Frobisher's idea, Tom, my partner," he added unnecessarily.

A sudden thought occurred to Charlie.

"Was the upgrading from paper to computer filing also Mr Frobisher's idea?"

"Why yes, it was. Admittedly, it had been long overdue, but Tom decided that if we were to rescue the firm, we had to delve deep into what little funds remained. Speculate to accumulate, as it were."

"But you weren't entirely convinced?"

Taylor took a deep breath. "No, I wasn't. But he is quite a forceful man is Tom, but I believe he has the best interest of the firm at heart."

I bet he has, thought Charlie, a suspicion forming in his head. He cast a sideways glance at Cathy. Her eyes betrayed her thoughts and he recognised she was on the same wavelength.

Nice man that Steven Taylor was turning out to be, he had soared from strong suspect to bottom rung, naive patsy.

"I'd like to bring you back to your brief criminal court experience. Who would be aware of your clients, at that time?"

Taylor looked puzzled. "Why, I couldn't really say. No doubt their details will be recorded on a paper file somewhere in the office, or," realisation dawned on him, "they would have been prior to the fire. But I'm sure I probably mentioned their names to several people, probably over lunch as an anecdote. I'm sure you know what I mean," he smiled.

Charlie guessed that Taylor would have retold the stores with himself as the butt of the joke.

"And would these people have included Mr Frobisher?"

"I suppose so. Why?"

Charlie ignored the question.

"Just one final question, if you please Mr Taylor. The client's funds that your firm manages, what records of these funds remain and have any of the clients recently contacted you regarding any dubiety as to their accounts?"

Taylor stared at him. "I can see where you are going with this, Mr Miller. You suspect that the fire was deliberately started to cover up a wrongdoing in the accounts. And you probably believe that this wrongdoing is attributed to one of my staff."

He sat forward and once again dropped his head into his hands. The three of them sat for several minutes in silence while Taylor absorbed this dreadful suspicion. With a deep sigh, he shook his head and looked at Charlie.

"Let me start by responding to the first part of your question. Though the firm's record of the individual clients assets have been totally destroyed, each client has their own record of their assets and I have already set in motion a contact procedure to obtain a copy of the client's assets so that the firm might prepare copies for our own records. The clients copies will, naturally, have been endorsed by the company's signatories, such as one of the partners or a senior secretary, so we will be able to validate the authenticity of the account, does that make that clear?"

Both Charlie and Cathy nodded in understanding.

"As for the second part of your question, that I'm afraid is a little harder to explain. A few months prior to the fire, I independently received confidential letters from the executors of three estates where the clients had died within the preceding twelve months. Such was the volume and wealth of each estate that the executors had spent some considerable time tying up the assets and those assets included some that our firm handled, though they are in reality a minor though still significant part of each estate. The letters indicated that in each case, the executors were unable to account for large sums of money that had been handled by my firm. As you might imagine, had word of this problem got out, it would have devastated our good name and caused the loss of clients en masse, not to mention an investigation by the governing body, the Banking Ombudsman."

"What would be, say, a total ball park figure of the sum involve in these three estates?"

Taylor, his eyes closed, took a few seconds to mentally calculate and then replied, "This only a guess mind, but I would say in the region of one hundred and sixty thousand pounds."

Charlie made a brief notation in his pocketbook then asked him, "Who else knew of these complaints?"

"Why no one else," his hesitation was apparent when at last he added, "Except of course Tom Frobisher."

*

As they returned to their vehicle, the previous acrimony that existed between Charlie and Cathy had all but disappeared, their attention now focused on the information they had received.

"Do you suppose he's telling the truth?" she asked him, knowing that she had already made her own mind up.

"What is it the yanks say? I'd bet my bottom dollar on it? Yes, think he's telling the truth and I can understand why he didn't volunteer the information in the first place. He's at the shitty end of a greasy pole and nowhere to go but down. I'm no whiz kid when it comes to my own accounts," he confessed, and with his thumb, indicated over his shoulder as he continued, "but that pile that Taylor's sitting in is probably his only asset right now. Property round here soaring as it is, he'd do better to sell it and start anew. God only knows how he's going to break the news to his staff. According to the list I received, there are bound to be a few out on their ear. And as for those dodgy accounts that he's had letters about? I think those will be the tip of the iceberg and Mr Taylor should consider finding himself a good lawyer."

He gave her a sideways grin and then said, "And as for Mr Thomas Frobisher? Now isn't that an interesting development? So," he continued, "do you want to phone Mitchell with the news or shall I?"

*

As they returned to the unmarked CID car, then pulled away with Miller driving and Mulgrew using her mobile phone, neither detective saw the dark blue coloured Vauxhall Vectra further down the road with the two men within observing them. Frank Brogan, his ban expired and his newly returned driving licence nestling in his jacket pocket, sat behind the driving wheel, fat cigar stuck between the fingers of his podgy right hand. Liam McPhee raised the bottle of fruit juice to his lips and watched the police car approach the brow of the hill.

"It seems that old Jimmy Donnelly got it right, then. The address certainly checks out and those two," McPhee pointed towards the disappearing car, "are old pals of ours, aren't they?" he grinned at Brogan, then added, "Give it five minutes, Frank, just in case this guy Taylor decides to pop his head out to make sure the coppers have driven off."

Brogan wasn't happy acceding to McPhee's instructions, but reluctantly accepted that he knew more about this kind of thing than Brogan did, whose total knowledge of surveillance was watching television.

The minutes passed slowly in silence, each man lost in his own thoughts. Brogan anxiously checked his rear view mirrors, obsessed that some nosey-parker would have called the cops about two suspicious men loitering in the street in a strange car. McPhee recalling with animalistic satisfaction the previous nights sexual encounter with the barmaid from Flaherty's and her reluctance to participate in his one-sided gratification. He hadn't meant to slap her so hard, but she had to learn that when it came to his enjoyment, her pleasure was secondary to his for as far as he was concerned, she was solely there to be used. He checked his watch.

"Right Frank let's take a wee turn by. Slowly now," he cautioned Brogan, "give me the opportunity to see what kind of car he has and which way it faces. If it's garaged at night, it could present a problem."

Brogan started the engine and slipped the gear. Almost immediately, the car stalled with a jerk, causing McPhee to lose his grip on the open bottle and spilling juice on his trousers.

"Sorry," Brogan began, and then stopped. What the fuck am I apologising to him for, I'm the boss here he wordlessly rebuked himself, placing the car in neutral and re-starting the engine.

"Slowly Frank, slowly," said McPhee, dabbing with a tissue at his damp trousers, his voice patronisingly low. He placed a reassuring hand on Brogan's arm, "after all, it's been a full year since you've been driving. Take your time, son."

The car lurched forward, then quickly picked up speed, passing Taylor's gate at fourteen miles per hour.

"Jesus," said McPhee, turning and straightening in the seat, "I haven't seen one of those auld bangers in years and it looked in fine condition to." He grinned at Brogan. "Shame to see it turned to scrap, eh Frank?"

*

Manus Foley perfumed a perfunctory check underneath his car and then delicately run his hand under the wheel arches. Satisfied, he looked up and down the street before finally climbing into the driving seat. The peace process might be on track, but he wasn't a man to take chances. Not after all these years that included two, failed assassination attempts by the Ulster Loyalist hit squads. Turning onto the Falls Road, he marvelled at the changes in Belfast since the British army retreated into its fortress like bases and began the withdrawal of its Emergency Order troops, an Order first introduced into the Province over thirty years previously. He laughed at the irony of it, to protect the Catholic populace against the wave of Unionist violence. Since that time the words Belfast, Londonderry and Northern Ireland had been synonymous with violence and atrocity. But now he mused, a fragile normalcy was slowly returning to the city.

The police officer on point's duty at the junction waved Foley through, recognising the IRA man but pointedly ignoring him as he turned to face the on coming traffic. Foley smiled. The movements of the Senior Intelligence Officer of the provisional IRA would, a short year before, had the copper reaching for his radio to broadcast Foley's position and have him stopped and turned over by one of the Brit's fast reaction mobile patrols. He sighed, a half smile playing on his lips. How times have changed. Still, didn't do any harm to check the rear view mirror now and again for after all, old habits die hard. He checked the dashboard clock. One hour forty minutes should see him safely across the unmanned border crossing into the Free State and then ten minutes to the meeting place. Whistling softly, he changed lanes and pressed lightly down on the accelerator.

*

Sadie Forrest collected her utility belt and cap from her locker and made her way into the muster room. Most of her shift was already seated, awaiting the Sergeant issuing beat duties and allocating the paperwork that is the bane of all police officers lives.

"Sadie," the sergeant called to her, "the control room are stuck for an extra hand on the telephones and radio. One of the civvies called in sick. Couldn't pop through and give them a hand, eh?"

Sadie nodded, pleased to be indoors and assured an early finish if the night shift were on time. She thought about her late night visitor and blushed. Charlie Miller will be thinking I'm a right forward tart, she mused. But knew in her heart that wasn't the case. He seemed a really nice guy. Her only concern now was would he contact her and if he didn't, did she have the bottle to phone him? God! She thought. One chat and I'm acting like a teenager. Seating herself at the control room console, she signed on to the different computer systems and prepared herself for a typically busy night. The Celtic were playing at home at Parkhead football ground and though their opposition reputedly didn't pose much of a challenge, the associated disorder that accompanied such events usually made for a busy old night at the Eastern Divisional police station. Settling down to catch up on outstanding incidents, she flicked through the file that included a brief summary of the finding of Father Flynn and the subsequent inquiry, to date. The detective in charge had written that while there was nothing to suggest an assault had occurred, the matter was subject to investigation and the CID patiently awaited developments from the Neuro Ward at the Southern General Hospital. Flynn's condition was described as serious, but stable. Sadie thought back to the brief conversation she had earlier that day, with her mother who revealed that the housekeeper, known locally as a pious but gossiping busybody, was not pointing fingers but telling everyone who cared to listen that Father Flynn was in a state of agitation shortly before his injury occurred and this state of agitation was caused by a tremendous shouting match with non other than Frank Brogan. Her mother had added that the housekeeper would not be pressed on why both Flynn and Brogan argued. She remembered her mothers sarcasm when describing the housekeeper, who had apparently inferred she knew why the two men had argued, but was bound to secrecy. Sadie's mother had remarked that the housekeeper couldn't hold her breath, let alone a bloody secret. They had agreed the housekeeper likely hadn't known what the argument was about, but where was the prestige in admitting that? Still, she pondered, it might be the sort of thing that

Charlie would be interested in knowing. Wouldn't do any harm to phone and let him know, she convinced herself.

*

The Incident Room at Govan police office was empty, save for the few staff engaged in laboriously filing reports and answering the odd telephone call. DCI Colin Mitchell was at the kettle when Charlie and Cathy arrived. With a nod of his head, he indicated the screened off area where his desk and files were located and dragged and extra chair with him. Once seated, he sat back in his chair, hands behind his head and stared coldly at Charlie.

"Well?"

Charlie had expected Mitchell to be annoyed, but he wasn't prepared to roll over and take flak.

"Before you start," he began, "I'm fully aware what your instruction had been and what I did… "

"What we did, sir."

Charlie turned, surprised at the unexpected support from Cathy. He nodded slightly at her, and then faced Mitchell again.

"What we did was in the best interest of both investigations. I know I didn't agree with your original instruction…"

"You made that fucking clear!" Mitchell interrupted.

"…but the circumstances of the interview with Steven Taylor revealed some interesting facts. Besides," he half turned towards Cathy, "we don't believe he's responsible for either your murder or my fire raising. Do we?"

Cathy shook her head and took up the story. "Charlie and I have discussed the details that Taylor provided and then there's the mobile phone."

She spoke at length, describing in fine detail the interview and discovery of the missing SIM card, the three letters of complaint to Taylor's firm and rounding up with their suspicion regarding Thomas Frobisher. Charlie was impressed by her recall and sat, watching the DCI's expression change from anger to keen interest. Mitchell leaned forward, his elbows resting on the desktop. Curiously, Cathy saw he wasn't chewing gum, but his fingernails were now down to the quick.

"Right," he began, let's suppose this guy Frobisher is your man. How do you suggest we tackle him?"

Charlie stared at Mitchell. Again, the question haunted him and he felt obliged to speak out. He held out his right hand and used his fingers to count off.

"Let's not forget, there is still no evidence to connect Robert Turner to the fire. If I'm right, you have neither a suspect nor anything to connect any suspect with the murder scene. There is nothing to connect Turner with either Taylor or Frobisher. There is at this time no evidence to prove theft of the client's monies from Taylor's firm." His voice rose in frustration as he accentuated his words. "Am I making any sense here?"

Cathy and Mitchell stared at him in silence.

Resignedly, Mitchell nodded his head.

"Sorry, Charlie," he grinned at him, "Trust you to take the feet away from me.

You always were the most tenacious, level headed bastard. You're right, of course. I got carried away with the belief that this murder, a real who dunnit, could be solved by tying up both our enquiries." He took a deep breath. "I appreciate what you've said and again, you're correct. The evidence, if we call even call it that," he shook his head, "is purely circumstantial. But here's a hypothetical scenario for you to chew over. Let's suppose it was Turner that set your fire and that he was contracted to do so to hide the theft of client's money. You have to admit, it fits in nicely."

"Too nicely," Charlie agreed, "for the problem is Colin, that even though I've just berated you two with my sense of black and white evidence," he flashed a quick grin, "I actually agree that they are linked. I believe someone hired Turner to set the fire, as you've said and that my victim Mary Cavendish was a sad and tragic result. And further to what Cathy and I have discussed on our way back here, our man Frobisher is now increasingly looking favourite as the front runner." Mitchell stared at him.

"I've known you a long time, Charlie Miller. Not much that you can hide from an old sweat like me and I can hear the wheels in your brain going round. So, what have you got in mind?"

*

Manus Foley parked in the tourist's car park adjacent to the wild and seething water of the Atlantic Ocean. The view was spectacular, not least because it afforded a clear and unobstructed sight along both approaches to the car park and there was little chance of anyone approaching without being observed. The noise of a straining diesel engine attracted his attention. The small green postal van chugged dutifully towards him, its sole occupant waving in greeting as he arrived. "How's about you, Manus," the little man grinned, his uniform cap set at a jaunty angle, not at all resembling the feared bomb-maker whose terror campaign was the scourge of the security forces during the early 1980s and whose home made devices resulted in the death and maiming of many unsuspecting soldiers and police officers.

"Eamon, you old rascal, are you well?"

The men shook hands, and then embraced. Embarrassed, they parted, but still smiling, happy and comfortable together as old friends and comrades in arms should be.

"So," began Eamon, "the war's finally over then?"

"Aye, it is. But the peace is as hard a fight. The politicians," Foley spat on the ground, "are giving too much away, Eamon. When I think of the boys we lost to those Brit and Loyalist bastards, a whole generation of fine young men. Still, they won't be forgotten."

"So, there must be a reason you've called me from retirement?"

Foley smiled. The auld bastard was as sharp as ever.

"A colleague has a wee problem across the water, a subject that has come to our attention. The subject has become a thorn and has to be blunted. Unfortunately, there is a time limit before the police become involved. Our man is asking for something simple, something that he's used before like an under car bomb, what the Brit's I think call an IDE."

Eamon laughed. "You mean an IED, an Improvised Explosive Device," he explained. Then more thoughtfully, "I haven't made up one of those for a very long time, not since before I was OTR and the Movement provided me with my new name and this job."

They both stood for a moment in silence. Foley knew what the little man had given up when he had gone on the run. Family, friends and a way of life in the massive housing estate where his feats were local legend, where the cops still hunted him and to where he could never return, no matter what amnesty was agreed, for the charge of murder never went away. He placed an arm about Eamon's shoulder.

"Do you still have the makings? And there's the added problem that it has to appear to be a local matter and must under no circumstances be traced back to the 'Ra."

Eamon rubbed his chin in thought.

"The equipment isn't a problem. I brought me tools and some plastic with me and they're well hidden, safe, sound and dry. And you're definite your man has knowledge of how to place and arm the device?"

"Oh aye," Foley smiled at him, "and more than a few times."

Eamon twisted in his mouth and narrowed his eyes in concentration. "The explosive could present a difficulty. Would it matter if the Prods get the blame?"

Foley stared at him. "How would you manage that?" he asked, his puzzlement clear on his face.

"Do you recall that last time the Prods stuck a wee present underneath your own car, all those years ago?"

Foley nodded, bewildered but clearly remembering his shock and horror when he found the bomb attached to his exhaust pipe.

"Well, when I disarmed and recovered their worthless piece of crap, the Proddy's very kindly provided me with a slab of their new and expensive Czechoslovakian made Semtex. Now, forensic science has moved on and contrary to what most people believe, when the stuff blows, it doesn't all go bang and disappear. Follow me?"

The excitement was evident in his voice. Foley nodded again, amused more by his friends passion for his subject than his interest in Eamon's description.

"So, when the police recover the remnants of a device, they can usually count on at least a sample sliver of the type of explosive used. With sufficient samples they will be able to determine the origin of the explosive and if the Brit's have done their homework, they will already have the Proddy's Semtex documented and should be able to work out that the origin of the explosive in my device has a Proddy signature. Do you understand?"

"And by this you mean that any subsequent investigation will bring the blame for the bomb back to the Proddy's?"

"Correct!" beamed the small postman and then added, "Provided, of course, your man on the mainland doesn't get himself captured.

Foley was impressed and pleased that this operation was getting better, by the minute.

"So, it only remains for me to ask how long it will take to construct and make the arrangements for uplifting it."

Eamon laughed out loud. "You're not hanging about Manus, are you? When exactly are we talking about here?"

Foley clapped the small man on the shoulder.

"Eamon, it's a time critical issue we have here. I need the bomb to be ready for uplifting by the early hours of tomorrow morning."

Chapter 14

Charlie Miller and Cathy Mulgrew had just left DCI Colin Mitchell to make his arrangements when the ring tone of Charlie's phone activated. With an apologetic glance at Cathy, he answered and was pleased to find Sadie on the other end.

"I was just about to call you," he cheerfully told her.

"Sure you were," she chided him with a laugh.

He could hear the sounds of a radio message being broadcast in her background.

"Free to speak?" she asked.

"Of course, shoot."

"I'm at the control room in the office, but before I came in this afternoon I heard that Father Flynn's housekeeper is putting it about that Frank Brogan was arguing with him, just before the Father was found injured."

"Frank Brogan, eh? That's very interesting," he replied and waved a hand at Cathy whose curiosity at the mention of Brogan's name caused her eyebrows to rise. "Is there any news on the priest's condition?"

"I'd a look at the CID summary and as of a couple of hours ago he's still serious but stable, at the SGH."

"What about the inquiry? Have CID decided if it is an assault or an accidental injury?"

"Nothing on that yet, but I hear they're keeping their options open and I know they had scenes of crime examine the locus. Only thing that is of interest is that when he was discovered, an overhead light was broken and the entrance to the church would have been in darkness, so if anyone had been loitering about...." she left the rest unsaid. "According to the housekeeper, that light hasn't been a problem before."

"So Frank Brogan is being fired in by the housekeeper as a possible suspect, eh?"

His mention of Brogan caused Cathy, her arms folded across her breasts, to impatiently tap her right hand fingers against her shoulder. Charlie raised a forefinger, indicating she should wait a moment.

"Yes, but only amongst the parishioners. No way would she have the nerve to mention his name to us, so officially you haven't heard that. Okay?"

"Look, Sadie, need to go right now," he turned away slightly, and lowered his voice. "What time you get off?"

She smiled at the handset in her hand. "If the nightshift are on time, I should be home for about ten-fifteen. "My mother will have Jellybean in bed by then."

"Why don't I bring you in some chips?"

"Why Charlie Miller!" she laughed delightedly. "You really know how to win a girls heart, don't you?"

As Charlie folded his phone into his pocket, Cathy could hardly contain her curiosity.

"So, what was that about Frank Brogan and chips?"

Briefly, Charlie recounted Sadie's information, emphasising that Brogan was not officially a suspect.

"And the chips," she asked with a twinkle in her eye.

"Ahem," he coughed to hide his embarrassment, "that was just a promise to a friend.

Cathy guessed the friend was a newly acquired female one, but whom? Then she recalled the fair-haired woman and child.

"My God, Charlie Miller," she exclaimed with surprise, "You really are a fast worker, aren't you?"

Charlie smiled with pleasure, but wondered why he felt like a schoolboy caught with his fingers in the sweetie jar.

"So Frank Brogan, what d you think?"

"On that subject," she began, "I have a small confession to make."

"Am I going to get really angry here?" he teased her.

"On the contrary, I hope you'll congratulate me on my brilliant detective foresight," she replied good-humouredly. "Do you recall that Brogan is or was till yesterday, a disqualified driver?"

He nodded, wondering where this was going. "As you know, when any arrested person is brought into a police station, we have the lawful right to examine and search them, etcetera. And that lawful right includes, wait for it," she teased him, anticipating his surprise, "a mouth swab for DNA." Charlie stopped walking and stared at her. "Oh, God," his eyes opened wide with a sudden comprehension, the disgust evident on his face, "The dirty bastard! And the funeral is tomorrow."

"Whoa, there Charlie. Don't jump the gun. All I've done is authorise a comparative examination between the swab taken from Brogan at his time of arrest and the foetus carried by Mary Cavendish. The result should arrive some time this afternoon, or early evening at the latest. Remember, it's just an idea. It's not positive yet."

To her astonishment, Charlie grabbed her and, pinning her by the arms, kissed her on the cheek.

"You absolute beauty Cathy Mulgrew," he cried, a huge cheeky grin on his face. "When you need to, you really do come through."

He didn't need to say it. She knew he was referring to her support for him, with Colin Mitchell.

"I hope this doesn't mean that were going steady," she laughed at his delight.

"Nah, I'm too ugly for a raving beauty like you," he teased her, "and besides, things are already looking up for me."

She watched him walk towards the lift, uncommonly moved by his show of affection.

I hope so Charlie, she thought to herself. I really do hope so.

*

The staff nurse looked up from her station and glanced down the ward to where the small group of people knelt by the old priests bed. She didn't really understand what a rosary was and the rules did state two visitors per bed, but under the circumstances, she felt she could make an exception just this once. The steady hum of the lifesaving equipment hooked up to her unconscious charges acted as a harmonious backdrop to the whispered prayers that travelled the length of the ward. The nurse thought the solemn ceremony somehow appropriate to the subdued lighting and calm ambience of the ward. A shadow stood over her. She raised her head and saw a large, rather dishevelled man standing patiently waiting on her attention.

"May I help you," she softly asked.

"Father Flynn," Charlie replied, "but I'm not a relative. I just met him recently actually. Wondered how he was doing," he faltered, clearly ill at ease and feeling like an intruder.

The nurse smiled and pointed down the ward. "The prayer group have just begun, if you would care to join them," she offered.

Charlie was aghast. He hadn't considered that the old priest would have visitors. "No, that's very kind of you, but I just wondered…."

She understood. "He's doing as well as can be expected. He's in Gods hands now. The surgeons have examined him earlier today and to be honest, there's not much more they can do for him. When," she said, rather than admit if, "he wakens, it will be the first step to recovery. We can only hope and pray."

The sound of a dozen voices, softly chanting in unison caused her to turn and stare down the ward. When she turned back, Charlie was walking towards the exit.

*

The small bachelor flat above the hardware store in the Donegal village had been Eamon the postman's home since fleeing across the border from the north, several years before. Its compact interior served his basic needs for he didn't truly consider it home and still harboured an ambition to return to his life in Belfast. One day, please God. Nothing in the flat indicated his past service with or any affiliation to the Provo's, for though he confidently believed himself safe from raids by the Brit's and their police, he had no such regard for An Garda Siochana, the Irish police whom he suspected were in league with their northern counterparts.

Wearing thin, surgical gloves, he sat at the folding bureau that also doubled as his dinner table. A strong desk lamp was clamped to the edge of the table and shone brightly onto the surface. The tools of his trade were laid upon their protective cloth tool bag, as sharp and clean as the day he had assembled them. The desk magnifying glass he used wasn't really essential, but he was never one to take unnecessary risks. That was why he was still alive when so many of his cohorts had died making silly and basic mistakes. Slowly he used the junior hacksaw blade to cut a small V shaped hole in the side of the black, hard plastic videocassette case. That done he filed away the ragged edge till the hole was smooth to touch. Next he squeezed a smear of strong, fast acting adhesive onto the rear of a thin, but powerful magnet and attached the magnet to the flat outside of the video case. The bomb container was now ready.

From a hessian sack that lay on the floor beside him, he withdrew a small, thirty-second timer unit whose legitimate purpose had been to activate the shutter lens of an old fashioned Japanese manufactured camera. This item would ensure that in the event of a premature activation, the bomber would have at least thirty seconds to escape before the electrical circuit completed and the detonation of the explosive occurred. With a soldering iron, he attached two pins to opposite ends of the timer and gently hand wound the mechanism. Releasing the small switch, he watched fascinated as it completed its thirty-second cycle, but instead of clicking the camera button as it had been designed, the small needle turned and rubbed both pins together. Satisfied that a contact would be made, he turned his attention to the initiation device. To one end of a six-inch clear, plastic tube, he glued an end piece with two nails piercing the end piece and separately protruding through to the inside the tube. Carefully, he inserted a metal ball bearing that was just small enough to run freely through the tube. He then sealed the other end of the tube with a similar end piece. With a sharpened nail, he pierced a small hole halfway down the tube. Eamon then glued the tube to the inside of the video case with the two pins protruding. To these pins he soldered a thin red and a thin black wire. Tilting the case, he watched as the metal ball bearing rolled up and down the tube, making contact with the two pins at one end. Lastly, he inserted a wooden matchstick into the hole in the tube, ensuring the ball bearing was at the end of the tube opposite to the two pinheads and now unable to pass by the obstructing matchstick. A strong, threadlike piece of nylon string was glued to the protruding end of the matchstick and the thread curled, ready for its next attachment.

Reaching again into the hessian sack, he withdrew a slab of putty like material. Semtex had always fascinated him. Unlike the early days when he and his colleagues had to rely on the unstable home made explosive, Semtex was easier to use, more reliable and far, far more deadly. Painstakingly, he moulded the Semtex to the inside of the case and then used a piece of wooden doweling to pierce a hole in the moulded explosive. His throat had become suddenly dry. He was nearing the dangerous part of the construction. A brand new nine-volt battery was likewise glued to the inside of the case and the black wire soldered to the negative terminal. The electrical power unit for the detonator was now in place. The timer was next. Carefully he secured it by glue to the side of the video case and soldered the red wire to one of the pinheads. A second piece of red wire was soldered to the other pinhead and the timer wound back. The strong thread attached to the matchstick was likewise glued to the timer release switch and now fed through the V shaped hole that he had earlier made in the side of the videocassette case. Eamon closed the case and, with a sharp tug, pulled the thread. The whirring noise from inside the box brought a smile to his face. He opened the box and replaced the pulled matchstick and as before, taking great care the ball bearing was at the non-pin end of the tube and again reset the timer mechanism. He stared at the sack. And now, my beauties, it's time.

The sack revealed an old cigar box, bound with a thick rubber band. With infinite care, he opened the box and removed the top layer of cotton wool. Half a dozen metal tubes, each with red and black wires protruding from one end, lay within. The electric detonators, stolen from a blasting company in the south of England a number of years previously, were as dangerous as the day they had been manufactured. He smiled at them. Without the services of one of the cigarette like tubes, his assembly so far was as much use as a tit on a bull and far less dangerous, for though the detonating power of the Semtex was awesome, it could not be ignited without the services of an initiator. The initiator would be one of the electric detonators that he held so warily in his hand.

Gently, he removed one of the detonators and returned the others to the sack. Placing the detonator within the hole he had poked in the Semtex, Eamon licked his parched lips and ensured the ball bearing was back behind the matchstick and the timer mechanism was set for use. He then soldered the black wire from the detonator to the positive terminal of the battery. Finally, the detonators red wire was twisted to the red wire that he'd earlier soldered onto the second pin on the timer mechanism. The circuit was complete, but inoperative due to his primitive but effective safety devices. The internal assembly completed, he closed the lid and drew a fine film of glue round the case to seal it tight, then encased the whole item in a thick layer of bubble wrapping. Lastly, he placed the bomb in a plastic shopping bag with the logo of a popular British food giant on the front. Snapping off the gloves, he threw them into the sack and exhaled loudly.

Pleased with his labour, he fetched a cold bottle of Guinness from the fridge and uncorked it, then silently toasted his unknown victim.

*

Steven Taylor had watched the detectives drive off. Miller's advice not to speak to anyone about their visit had been courteous, but edged with a sharp warning. It occurred to him that perhaps he should give Thomas a phone call, but a nagging doubt had crept in. The detectives hadn't exactly accused Frobisher of anything, but still, the seed had been sown. What to do, what to do. Life was so difficult these days. Perhaps, a drink before dinner will provide me with the opportunity to mull it over, he thought, as he shuffled off towards the kitchen and whatever food he could find there.

*

Acting Detective Inspector John Brown drummed his fingers against the desktop, a nervous habit that he had recently acquired, since taking on this fucking acting rank he grimly recalled. The knock at his door interrupted him.

"What?" he called out irritably.

Mickey Hughes, the CCTV supervisor limped into the office.

"Morning John, how's it hanging?" he cheerfully inquired.

"Detective Inspector to you, Hughes," growled Brown in an attempt to intimidate the gimpy bastard, "so, what do you want?"

Mickey's smile froze on his face. Brown he decided, was one, mean and torn faced shit. However, he'd committed himself now and had no option but to pass the report.

"You put out a request for information about a CCTV photograph?"

Immediately, Browns attitude changed. His demeanour became more solicitous and he jumped to his feet.

"Sorry, Mickey," he began, "bad day and all that. You know what I mean. And yes, I did put out a request. Why? Heard anything?"

"Just that because it was a CCTV photograph, it's obviously provoked interest because I got a phone call from the Motherwell CCTV supervisor who thought he recognised the guy from footage that he watched recently. Run the tape several times apparently and is almost certain it's the same man. Seems your suspect works in a butchers shop that sits in a row of shops covered by one of his fixed cameras."

Brown held his breath, his excitement causing a sharp stabbing pain in his chest. He could almost taste the arrest.

"Didn't give you a name, did he?"

"What, the name of the shop?"

"The suspect Mickey, the name of the suspect!" hissed Brown.

"Oh, I'm sorry. No. He doesn't have that information, but the shop is McGlone's on Merry Street in Motherwell, just off the town centre. Do you want the supervisor's name?"

Brown's mind was racing. He licked his lips in nervous anticipation. Already he had decided what officers he would have accompany him to make the arrest.

Mickey stood impatiently, peeved that Brown was now ignoring him.

"Anything else?" Brown asked sharply.

"What? Oh, no. Nothing else" replied Mickey.

"Thanks and," Brown hesitated, his eyes betraying his cunning, but fuck it, why not. "You'll keep this to yourself for now?"

Mickey stared at him with a sudden awareness. He's cutting Nancy Rogers out of the picture. None of my business, he decided. I've done my bit and passed the information along. How Brown wants to handle it is up to him.

"Right, my lips are sealed," he promised, silently vowing that if asked, he'd say he was ordered not to speak to anyone by Brown.

*

Night had fallen and a slight drizzle of rain trickled from the cloudy skies. Charlie stood outside Sadie's apartment block with a plastic carrier bag containing two fish suppers. He reached forward to press her doorbell and stopped, his finger poised in midair. What am I doing here, he asked himself. He lowered his hand to his side and glanced up at the lit window. The raindrops dribbled their way down his open and rugged face. It wouldn't be fair on her, he thought. He carried to much pain, too many memories. He couldn't be close to someone again. Better just to let it be, phone her tomorrow and make some excuse. After all, they'd only spoken over a cup of coffee, it's not as if they were courting or anything, or really scrious with each other. He sighed heavily and, decision made, turned to leave.

"Not standing me up are you, Charlie boy, and after you promised me chips, too." She stood there in the shadows; her fawn coloured raincoat over her uniform and belted at her slim waist, fair hair tied up and covered with a pale blue headscarf. Her arms folded with her handbag slung across her shoulder. He blinked rapidly as the drizzle coursed down his face, but he didn't notice it as he stared and thought she looked beautiful, standing there in the falling rain.

The explanation caught in his throat as she slowly walked towards him and reached forward, holding his face in both her hands and reaching up to kiss him on the lips, a full and passionate kiss.

"And that's from me," she smiled at him.

*

Cathy was disappointed the laboratory hadn't been able to provide her with the DNA result, that day. Technical difficulties they had told her, but assured Cathy that either tomorrow afternoon or early evening, they'd be in touch.

"Pity," Charlie had consoled her, "it would have been nice to challenge Brogan at his niece's funeral, if the match proved to be positive."

Stick it to the bastard, was what he had really meant.

She sipped at her wine then diallcd DCI Martin Cairney's home number.

"Sorry it's so late, boss," she began, "but I thought I'd check in with you; let you know how things are going."

She recounted the details of the investigation and how she and Charlie Miller had liaised with DCI Mitchell and his murder and now both inquiries were tied in together. No, she hadn't made any progress on the Brogan inquiry yet, but hoped to find out more at the funeral, tomorrow morning. Yes, smiling to herself at his concern, she'd be careful of that thug McPhee. No, she'd no problem with DS Miller. Quite the contrary, he was everything that DCI Nancy Rogers had said he wasn't. No, she couldn't be definite about how long her secondment would last. And finally yes, with a smile, she'd make sure she got a good night sleep.

Replacing the handset, she reached down and, deep in thought, gently stroked the naked leg that sat across her thigh.

*

John Brown had worked himself into a furious rage by the time he got home. His wife waited with trepidation. Cowed and submissive by years of haranguing abuse, she knew better than to speak to him when he was in one of his moods. He poured a whisky then run his finger along the front of the display cabinet. "When did you last dust in here?" he quizzed her, his voice low and menacing. She swallowed hard, her reply choked back by fear. Her timidity further infuriated him. He reached out and grabbed her by the collar of her dress and pulled her head down to the level of the shelf on the cabinet. She braced herself, knowing what was about to happen.

"You're a slovenly bitch. I don't know why I married you, you dirty cow," he screamed at her, throwing her against the cabinet. She fell heavily, but he had turned away, his interest in her lost the moment she gave in. She wasn't worth him, he knew. He should have married someone more his equal. But now he was stuck with the stupid bitch. He sat in his favourite armchair and thought about the Motherwell visit. It hadn't occurred to him that the shop might be shut, that it was their half-day closing. The three detective constables who had accompanied him were sniggering behind his back. He'd heard one whisper that he should have phoned the local station, made sure the shop was open. Have the CCTV supervisor view the premises and ensure the suspect was there. Smart bastards they are, talking behind his back. He'd show them, sort them out. When it came to their annual appraisal, he'd make sure that it was he who completed their reports. See if they'd laugh then.

He took a large mouthful of his drink. The scene outside the shop preoccupied him. The four of them had floundered about. He couldn't even ask at the local police station, worried he'd tip his hand and someone else would make the arrest before him. But it would happen tomorrow morning. He'd ordered the other three to be at the office by six am. They'd stake out the shop, await the arrival of their suspect then nab him. Yes, he unconsciously nodded his head in agreement to his train of thought. It would work. Let's see them laugh at me after I jail the bastard. Me. Let them try and stop my promotion then.

*

The driver negotiated the articulated lorry along the dark, winding country road with care. His headlights cut a deep ribbon of light through the darkness and warned the few approaching vehicles of his presence, but the bloody sheep he snorted. They sods had no sense at all. The phone call had come just as he had completed loading the long container with its bags of animal grain onto his tractor unit. The instruction had been short, but clear. A pick-up to be made at the usual place and warning him to take the usual precautions. He turned on the radio and smiled as his favourite Country and Western station belted out a number by the great Jim Reeves. Tunelessly, he whistled an accompaniment and turned onto the side road that run parallel with his route to the seaport. Three kilometres further down the road he glanced in his mirror. The chances of meeting another vehicle in the wild hills of Donegal at this time of night were unlikely, but it didn't hurt to be careful. He slowed the truck to twenty kilometres an hour, his eyes probing the nearside verge for the sign. Sure enough, there it lay; the marker post that indicated all clear. A further kilometre down the road, he stopped the truck and took a final glance about him and in his mirrors, then jumped down from the cab.

A shiver coursed its way down his spine, but whether from exiting the warm cab to the cold or in the expectation of a police ambush, he wasn't sure. Fiddling with the zipper of his trousers, he pretended to take out his dick in preparation for peeing and disappeared into the ditch beside the road. With a quick glance about him, he retrieved the plastic carrier bag and stuffed it clumsily into his quilted jacket. Returning to his cab, he drove off. He began to breathe easier and hadn't been aware he'd been holding his breath. The plastic carrier bag he would later secrete in the hidden compartment, when he was further down the road and away from any prying eyes. The dashboard clock told him he had plenty of time to catch the ferry that would convey him overnight to the Scottish port of Stranraer. With a sigh of relief that the first part of his mission was successful, he turned the radio up louder and joined Tammy Wynette as she stood by her man.

In the darkness, Eamon the postman observed the successful pick-up and began to make his way to a secure payphone.

Chapter 15- Thursday morning

Charlie Miller woke confused. Where the hell was he? The pastel coloured walls seemed strangely familiar. Sadie's couch, that's where he was and that's why his large frame wouldn't stretch fully, he realised. He made to turn his head and immediately the pain from a crick in his neck introduced itself, but no sore head. For that he was at least grateful, though his throat felt as though he'd consumed half a dozen packets of salted crisps. He breathed onto his hand and smelled the sour breath. Whoa, he thought, time for some Colgate. His watch told him it was almost five thirty. Quietly, his bladder bursting from too much coffee the night before, he threw back the cover and turned to place his feet down, wincing at the cold of the fashionable laminated flooring. With an effort he stood up, conscious that his slacks lay folded on the arm of a nearby chair. In shirt and underpants, he reached for his trousers as a voice whispered behind him, "Now there's a sight to behold first thing in the morning."

Sadie, a white cotton robe wrapped loosely round bright yellow pyjamas, leaned against the doorframe of the small hallway, her fair hair tumbled about her shoulders. Her face clear of make-up, the faint scar above her left eye was a vivid white against her fair skin. Caught in mid-step, Charlie asked, "Did I wake you?"

"No, I was lying thinking about you. I couldn't make up my mind last night whether to be pleased that you didn't make a move on me or annoyed that you didn't find me attractive."

Charlie hesitated. How the hell do I answer that one? He decided discretion was the best option.

"If I manage to get my trousers on without falling over, do you think you could rattle up a cup of tea, gorgeous?"

She beamed at him. Anyone who called her gorgeous first thing in the morning was worthy of a cuppa.

"I'll get the kettle going. You know where the bathroom is," she replied as she glided past him towards the kitchen, "and you'll find a spare toothbrush in the cabinet," she whispered over her shoulder.

Grateful for the interruption, Charlie fumbled his way into trousers and shirt and carried his shoes through with him. Five minutes later, washed, combed and a mouth no longer capable of combustion, he joined Sadie who had tea and toast waiting for him.

"I have to admit," he told her warmly, "breakfast hasn't been a regular occurrence these last few years, but this is great."

They ignored the stools at the small breakfast bar and stood facing each other, he sipping tea from the pink floral mug and she with her arms folded.

"So tell me, Charlie, why didn't you make a move last night?"

He sipped at the scalding tea and hesitated again. The truth could be embarrassing, but if he wanted to see more of Sadie, he'd be as well to get it right from the start. His face screwed as he finally admitted, "I didn't know how."

Her puzzled expression caused him to continue. "When my wife and son died, I lost it big time. She'd meant everything to me. Well, they both did of course. But she had been my whole life. I could never have imagined life without her. She was there when I awoke and when I went to sleep. Without her presence, I felt nothing. Physically, we had a great relationship, probably better than most. When she was killed the physical attraction for women died within me." He glanced down at the mug. "But then I met you," an embarrassed half smile played about his lips. "I'm so attracted to you that it hurts. Last night I thought about walking away because I feared that if anything came of our…friendship, and anything happened to you. Where would I be then?" Again he smiled at her, an open heartfelt smile. "But there you stood, Sadie Forrest, in all your loveliness and I knew then that I was being selfish, thinking only of my own painful experience." He put down his mug and moved close to her. "Heck, I can't believe that I hardly know you. This is crazy. It's only been a few short days and yet, I've got this unbelievable feeling, a strong feeling that I don't want to lose you…. or that wee tearaway Jellybean," he smilingly added, not knowing that simple statement was to her surprise and tremendous relief.

"As for last night? Yes, I wanted nothing more than to be with you, but I'm scared of making a move that might ruin my chance." He reached forward to take her by the hand. "So Sadie Forrest, I need a bit of cooperation here. I need you to hint or tell me that you don't feel sorry for me, that you like me because I'm Charlie Miller the man, not Charlie Miller the widower, the old sad drunk with the hangdog stare. So, what do you say?"

He waited for her response, the muscles in his body tense with anxiety, a sense of shock overtaking him that he had exposed his feelings so openly like this.

Sadie didn't say anything, simply threw her arms round his neck and kissed him long and hard, then held him tightly, so that he thought his chest would cave in with the pressure. She bit her lip as the tears flowed unchecked down her cheeks.

"Whoa," he softly laughed at her, "I won't be going anywhere. Well, apart from home for a change of clothes, then work. What I mean is…"

"You won't be going anywhere out of my life?" she finished for him.

He nodded, as they stood clasped together, enjoying the comfort of their presence. Charlie indicated with his eyes at the wall clock.

"I'd better jump a taxi and get home for a change."

"Finish your tea," she instructed him, "I'll phone for a taxi and Charlie," she stroked his face with her hand, her eyes full of promise, "I should be finished by eleven tonight. Bring a change of clothing with you and I'll have my mother take Jellybean for a sleepover."

*

Acting Detective Inspector John Brown paced the floor of the CID general office at the Central Division. The two detective constables who lounged at their desks watched him through sleep ridden eyes.

"I told him to be here by six am!" he thundered to no one in particular.

"It's not yet six, boss," ventured one of the detectives.

Brown turned on his heel. "Don't come the mickey with me, son," he threatened, "keep your smart arse comments to…"

The door opened to admit the fourth member of their party. Tensely, the seated detectives waited for Brown's outbursts, keen to see how he handled the grin on their colleagues face.

"Problem boss?" the latecomer innocently asked.

Brown seethed, but didn't respond. "Right," he snapped, "let's get this show on the road," and stormed through the rear door towards the car park.

The seated detectives slowly rose to their feet and looked at each other, broad grins on their faces.

"Chickenshit," one commented, nodding towards the open door and the retreating figure of Brown.

*

The phone call had come at 2am, that morning and merely said the plan had been approved and the Council had agreed executive action. The package was en route and due for delivery at the usual place at seven am, that morning.

Liam McPhee waited patiently within Brogan's Vauxhall Vectra in the near empty service station car park, adjacent to the A77, the principal two lane highway for travellers and haulage that connected the City of Glasgow with the Port of Stranraer on the Ayrshire coast. He was early by almost thirty minutes, but he hadn't wasted that time. His hands in his pockets, his breath misting in the chilly air, a short brisk walk with his eyes sharp and alert, had taken him around the perimeter and the roads entering and exiting the car park. The walk had been crucial. There did not seem to be any indication of surveillance vehicles, but McPhee took no chances. Hadn't a number of the boys been arrested or worse for the lack of simple precaution? He lit a cigarette as he waited, watching the smoke curl into the air. He thought about Brogan's sister, Irene and her mad demand for revenge. Shit! She'd be telling Frank how to collect funds, next. For all his bluster, he really was a bag of shite! Still, the wee girl Mary had been a looker with those tight little tit's of hers just forming up nicely. He would have given her one himself, had the opportunity arisen. His eyes narrowed in puzzlement. Strange she got herself pregnant, what with her mammy never off her back and dogging her every movement. He couldn't for the life of him ever recall seeing her with a boyfriend.

A sudden thought crossed his mind that brought a smile to his face, but no, he decided. Even Frank wasn't that crass. Or could he have been? The roar of a diesel engine caused McPhee to snap his head up. Instantly, his training took over and he became vigilant. He watched as the large articulated lorry, its wheels churning, sped into the gravel surfaced car park and executed a full circle of the area before coming to a halt beside the neon lit cafe. He recognised the actions of a man prepared to make a run for it at the sight of strange and suspicious vehicles. With a final look about him, McPhee got out of the Vectra and walked towards the lorry. The driver saw him coming and climbed from the cab then took McPhee in a bear hug and greeted him like a long lost friend.

"So, how's about you, Liam?"

"I'm fine. You've got something for me?" he responded with a wide grin, but anxious to have the business conducted and out of this place.

The driver glanced about him and reached up through the door to the floor of the cab from where he fetched the shopping bag containing the bubble wrapped parcel.

"And may God guide your arm, Liam."

McPhee took the wrapped parcel and grinning his thanks, shook the driver's hand. He stowed the parcel inside his jacket, clapped the driver fondly on the shoulder then turned to walk away.

"Slainte," he called out over his shoulder, wishing his old friend good health.

"Tiochfaidh ar la," (our day I'll come) the driver called after him.

*

The car containing John Brown and his three detectives sped east on the M8 motorway towards Motherwell. Sitting in the front passenger seat, Brown nervously drummed his fingers on his knee as his mind raced, trying to work out a justification as to why he had not informed his DCI about this significant development, why he had taken it upon himself to execute the arrest and also why he hadn't informed the local division of his intention to make a major arrest in their area. He decided to deal with these questions when he had the bastard under lock and key, when he was fireproof for having locked up the notorious sex attacker. His breath grew rapid as he imagined the glory that would result and the promotion that had eluded him all those years.

*

The bright fluorescent lights in the Incident Room at Govan identified more than a few late night revellers as tea and coffee was passed out to the assembled throng of detectives and their civilian colleagues, who made up the Robert Turner murder inquiry team.

DCI Colin Mitchell, jaws chomping the usual slab of chewing gum, rattled his knuckles on the desk and called for attention, then to muttered greetings and smiles introduced Charlie Miller and Cathy Mulgrew. That done, he commenced his briefing.

"Right then, settle down folks and listen in," he began. "Charlie and Cathy here will make the arrest. The fire at the law firm offices is their inquiry and I think it only right they have primacy in laying hands on our suspect. The rest of us, including scenes of crime," he indicated the small team of specialists, "will be on standby and scattered in our vehicles in the streets nearby, ready to move in. Charlie and Cathy will be in possession of a Sheriff's search warrant that has been granted in respect of evidence that is suspected to be located at the target address. I can reveal that the warrant encompasses anything, and I mean anything," he stressed, "of further evidential value and by that I mean anything that we can associate or suspect to be associated with the murder inquiry. At this juncture I would remind you we still have not discovered the murder weapon. Everyone clear on that?"

The throng nodded their heads in understanding. Mitchell stifled a smile when he saw a few hung over heads wincing at the jerky movements.

"During the course of the last twelve hours, one of the Force Surveillance Teams has been monitoring the target house and," he glanced at his watch, "as of the last update twenty minutes ago, I can confirm the suspect is at home. Seems he had a party last night so," he smiled at Charlie and Cathy, "better take some aspirin with you for his head."

Mitchell paused for a gulp of his coffee. Cathy was bemused to see he didn't remove his chewing gum as he did so.

"The suspect will thereafter be conveyed to Govan where the formal interrogation regarding the murder of Bobby Turner will be conducted under tape-recorded conditions by 'Peasy' Byrne and Emma Ferguson of the Serious team," he indicated the two officers, then asked the gathering, "Any questions?"

A hand was raised at the back. "Why aren't Charlie and Cathy doing the interview, Boss? Surely for continuity purpose, it would be better for them to continue dealing with the suspect?"

"Agreed," replied Mitchell, "but the reason for that," he turned and indicated with his thumb at Charlie and Cathy, "is that our colleagues here will be leaving immediately after they detain the suspect for the funeral of Mary Cavendish, the girl that died in the fire."

"If I might," interrupted Charlie, then gaining Mitchell's nod, began speaking. "Mary Cavendish, as you will know from your briefing packs, was an innocent in this affair. I don't wish to distract you from your designated tasks, but suffice to say that Cathy and I are still investigating some unresolved issues regarding Mary's presence at the fire scene. I can tell you that these issues will not interfere with your murder inquiry, but will assist Cathy and me in the preparation of our report to the PF." Charlie saw a hand start to rise and waved it down. "I know what you're thinking. The inquiries have overlapped and should be conducted as one. However, DCI Mitchell has kindly agreed that Cathy and I will continue to pursue our own investigation and we will subsequently submit our separate reports that the PF will no doubt unite as one prosecution. But, notwithstanding what I have just said, we are agreed that the suspect will be handed over to you lot," he grinned, then to laughter, "for interrogation, torture, hanging and sundry drawn and quartering."

Mitchell waved the grinning assembly back to order. "Right, folks, grab a last cuppa then were on our way… and good luck."

*

Irene Cavendish set up the board and plugged in the old steam iron. As she waited on the element heating, she reflected on what the day was to bring. The last funeral she had attended for a family member had been her husband all those years before. Her lips set in a grim smile as she recalled the pleasure she had experienced watching the cheap wooden coffin sink slowly into the rain soaked earth. Those about her had presumed her shivers had been pain and sorrow. How little they knew. She couldn't wait for the bastard to be covered up, couldn't wait for the day to be over when she would regain control of her own life. And with a tight smile she thought of the lair where he lay with no headstone to mark the spot, her private act of revenge. The meagre insurance policy had barely covered the expense of the service and the undertaker's fee. But she knew that even if he had left her a wealthy woman, she would still have purchased the cheapest coffin and service that was available, for in her mind he wasn't worth the effort. Irene considered on reflection that if she had the foresight, she would have had him cremated for there would be no life after death, no resurrection for him. Hell was where he was bound and rightly so.

The iron hissed its warning and she reached for the plain, black dress. She had decided that a nice face veil would be suitable, just enough to demonstrate to all those attending the service the grief she was enduring. And, of course, allow her the privacy to observe exactly who took the time to come to her daughter's funeral. For she was keen to see who were willing to pay their respects, guessing that among the genuinely pious, there would be the nosey-parkers and those who wished to be seen and associated with attending the funeral of Frank Brogan's niece. Particularly, her mouth turned down, since those vile stories began flying about regarding his supposed argument with Father Flynn, just before the old priest was discovered injured.

Irene had a shrewd guess how the rumours had started. She'd never liked or trusted that old witch of a housekeeper, spouting her stories about Father Flynn and how she cared for his every need. She was a wicked old bugger, she was. Well, the stories couldn't possibly be true, for after all, wasn't Frank the very man advocating peace in the Old Country? And a gentler and most generous man would not be found in this part of Glasgow.

Carefully, she spat at the underside of the iron and watched as the small ball of spittle fried on the hotplate. Satisfied that it was at the correct temperature, she began ironing the cotton material of the dress and hummed the tune of a popular hymn. As she did so, so engrossed was she in her task that sadly, not once did she give any thought to the true purpose of the day.

The funeral ceremony for her young, teenage daughter.

*

The owner of McGlone's Butchers in Merry Street, Motherwell parked his car at the rear of the shop and fumbled in his pocket for the key for the roller shutters that covered the front window. Greeting his fellow retailers as they passed by, the man pushed upwards and watched as the heavy steel shutters rolled back into their case. Humming softly, he opened the door and, as he always did, smiled at the tinkling of the old fashioned bell above the door. Had he been more observant, he might have noticed the car across the street with the two men sitting watching him. Or the third man, who lounged against the metal railing slightly up the road, reading a morning newspaper. Or the fourth man, who waited in the bus shelter across the road, but ignored the passing buses. But why should he notice these men, for they paid little interest in him, for he did not resemble the man in the photograph that Acting Detective Inspector John Brown had spread across the steering wheel of the car.

*

The convoy of unmarked police vehicles moved out from the secure yard at Govan police office and made its way across the city through the rush hour traffic towards the prosperous and growing suburb of Bearsden, where the old money and Nuevo rich of the city built their affluent abodes, surrounding them with trimmed, high hedgerows and protected them with state of the art alarm systems. Not for these citizens the streets where nightly, the drunken louts shouted, bawled and puked their guts after a heavy night on the bevy, but a quiet residential hamlet with tree lined avenues and driveways that boasted top of the range cars.

Once clear of the Clyde Tunnel congestion, the traffic eased, most of it travelling towards the city centre offices and flowing against the route of the convoy.

Charlie and Cathy, together in the lead vehicle, observed that most of the passing vehicles contained the driver only.

"No wonder there's a hole in the ozone layer," she wryly commented.

The plan called for them to sop a few streets from their target address, establish radio contact with the surveillance vehicles and confirm their suspect was still at home. The bad news, the surveillance commander reported, was the heavy metal electric gates were shut, having been closed since the last partygoer had departed in the early hours.

Charlie glanced at Cathy, a grin on his face. "I might get a look at those long pins of yours if we've got to climb the gate," he softly laughed, looking down at her knee length skirt.

"Don't kid yourself, big boy," she retorted, grinning, "You've already got yourself a woman, so stay away from me. But, if I'd known I was going to be climbing gates, I might have worn the sussies and really raised your blood pressure."

He laughed again, pleased at the comfortable ease of their partnership.

"Ready?"

She nodded, the tense excitement reminding her of her divisional CID days, early morning raids, chasing the bad guys and, sometimes, putting in the front door with the use of the heavy steel boom that did so much damage. She adjusted the radio concealed under her loose fitting suit jacket and carefully inserted the covert satellite earpiece. Finally she smoothed back her long, red hair to screen any trace of the earpiece.

"Yeah, let's go."

Charlie parked their vehicle on the roadway outside and they walked the short distance to the eight-foot gates that ran between the equally high, brick walls. A metal box on the wall invited callers to press the button and speak into the mouthpiece. With a grimace at Cathy, Charlie followed the instruction. Several minutes passed before he was greeted by a harsh, tinny bellow.

"Who is it and what the fuck do you want at this time of the morning?"

He smiled tolerantly, recognising the plummy English voice of Thomas Frobisher.

"Morning Mr Frobisher, it's Detective Sergeant Miller, Central Division CID. Regarding the fire," he added, tongue in cheek and knowing full well there would be no other reason for calling, "looking for a wee word with you, please."

A lengthy pause followed, but then Frobisher replied, "Can't this wait till the office? I'm far too busy to speak with you now."

They had agreed that any mention of the warrant could cause problems; particularly if Frobisher decided not to open the gates, so would not produce it unless no other option existed.

Charlie pressed on. "It's about an interview I've had with your partner, Steven Taylor. To be frank there's a couple of things he told me I think I'd rather discuss with you."

He realised what he had done. By inferring he was unhappy with Taylor's statement, he had cast a shadow of doubt upon him. He guessed Frobisher's curiosity would be working overtime and he'd be eager to know what information the detective intended imparting. Charlie and Cathy waited with bated breath. A loud metallic click indicated the gates unlocking as Frobisher's voice rang through the tin box.

"Come on up. The front door will be open."

The walk along the lengthy monoblock driveway gave them both the opportunity to take in the detached property. Charlie guessed that Frobisher wouldn't get much change from half a million for the house and the off the road silver coloured BMW and dark green Volvo saloon cars in the driveway, both with private plates, suggested that the owners weren't short of a bob or two.

"So, how do you think he manages this on his salary from Taylor, Taylor, Frobisher and Partners if the firm is going bust?" she whispered at his side.

"According to Fraser McManus at the Fraud Squad, his discreet check at the Inland Revenue revealed from Frobisher's tax returns that his wife doesn't hold down a job and his only declared income is his salary. And you're right, I don't think his earnings would pay for all this," he replied.

Frobisher stood at the door in a bright red, three-quarter length silk dressing gown, waiting to greet them. The scowl on his face betrayed his irritation at being disturbed. His eyes betrayed his previous night's alcohol intake and, according to Cathy's crude description, resembled two piss holes in the snow.

"You didn't tell me you were accompanied," he growled at Charlie.

Charlie smiled hugely in response. "Let me introduce Detective Sergeant Mulgrew, sir," he replied, edging unobtrusively forward and forcing Frobisher to step back.

"Well," he mumbled ungraciously, "suppose you'd better come in then."

He led the detectives through the brightly lit hallway to a large sitting room whose panoramic window gave a view across the well-tended lawn. Charlie could see the sitting room was tastefully and expensively furnished and the pictures that adorned the walls looked pricey originals, rather than prints. The rugs on the floor were either costly imitation or genuine Chinese. The furniture was heavy and smelled of deep-waxed leather, but the whole scene was spoiled by evidence of the previous night's party. Discarded glasses lay about the furniture and both wine and beer bottle were liberally distributed throughout the room, most of them empty but some retaining a residue of their contents. The atmosphere smelled of cigar smoke and booze. An expensive gentleman's jacket, the yellow silk lining exposed, lay carelessly thrown across the back of a chair.

Cathy wrinkled her nose and thought she detected the faint sickly sweet smell of cannabis. One to remember, she thought.

"Good night last night, sir?" Charlie asked in a genial voice.

Frobisher merely grunted in response and indicated they should sit down.

"Now," he asked, sprawling himself across what was apparently the master chair, "what's all this about Steven? You have some evidence to link him to the fire?" Whether accidentally or by design, his dressing gown had fallen open and to her amazement, Cathy saw he was wearing cerise coloured boxer shorts. He cast a lecherous glance in her direction and she knew the act was deliberate. She turned her head away in disgust, as Charlie continued.

"We interviewed him yesterday, yes, and indeed were puzzled by some of the answers he provided us with. For example, I believe you are aware that Mr Taylor was in receipt of a number of letters expressing concern about the administration of certain funds that were managed by your firm?"

Charlie's brief previous contact with him wasn't enough to form an estimation of his ability as a lawyer, but he thought Frobisher's obvious arrogance and apparent disregard for the police might be of use against him. These factors and his hangover condition from his previous night's excesses might make him susceptible to what Charlie had in mind.

Frobisher's eyes narrowed. "I am aware of the letters, but what exactly would those have to do with the fire?"

"To your knowledge, did Mr Taylor reveal the existence of the letters to anyone else?"

He shook his head. "I don't know, I can't really say. Look! I'm asking you again, what connection would the letters have with the fire?"

Charlie paused. The fine sheen of sweat reflected by the light from Frobisher's forehead was an indication of one of two things; either he was suffering from alcohol dehydration and didn't Charlie have enough experience of that? Or simply, he was nervous and had something to hide."

"It's our opinion Mr Frobisher, that the fire was set by a third party to conceal the theft of funds from the accounts of at least three of the firm's clients. We are further of the opinion the third party was contracted by the thief to carry out this act. Mr Taylor, as you will probably be aware, has instigated contact with all the firms clients to establish what funds they believe are being managed by the firm and thereafter, to contact the various banks used by the firm to substantiate those funds still exist."

Charlie stood up and, as though stretching himself, slowly walked about the room. Frobisher's eyes never left him.

"It is also our belief that the culprit who carried out the fire-raising was a man called Robert Turner."

He suddenly turned to face an open-mouthed Frobisher.

"Know the name, do you sir?"

Frobisher gasped and shook his head.

"I…...I've... I've never heard that name," he stuttered in response and then trying to regain his composure, continued, "No, I don't know the name. No."

Charlie smiled at him, a humourless smile. "Mr Taylor seems to recall telling a few anecdotes about his brief career as a criminal lawyer and swears he mentioned the story to you. Recall the story, do you sir?"

Frobisher dabbed at his sweaty forehead with a handkerchief.

"Really, Sergeant Miller, I can't be expected to remember all of Steven's tales and after all, he has been under some pressure in the recent past. You will no doubt be aware of his recent ah, how shall I put this, his financial difficulties?"

Cathy sat silently, watching the oral swordplay and knew Frobisher was rattled. His feeble attempt to cast doubt on Taylor's integrity due to his monetary problems wasn't cutting any ice with Charlie, she saw. Keenly, she waited on her cue.

"And these financial difficulties you speak of," responded Charlie, "are directly attributed to the present difficulties being experienced by the firm. Is that a fair comment, sir?"

"I would agree..." Frobisher began, then stopped, as if suddenly aware that the firm also provided him with his well-heeled existence that was so obviously displayed about him. "That is to say," he blustered, "how Steven manages his personal affairs is really none of my business and you can't hold this," he expansively swept his arms, "against me simply because I'm a far more astute business manager than my colleague!"

"Thomas! What on earth is going on?"

The platinum blonde with the model looks who stood in the doorway wearing the black silk Japanese Kimono could easily have passed for Frobisher's daughter, however, neither Charlie nor Cathy had any doubt that the woman was not. The Kimono was loosely worn and with the belt trailing on the floor, had slipped just enough to reveal a milky white shoulder and the top of her left breast. To Cathy, the woman seemed either drugged or drunk. Charlie however, saw this as the perfect opportunity and, as Frobisher angrily shouted and ordered the now disappearing woman to get her arse back to bed, he gave a discreet nod to Cathy.

"So tell me, Mr Frobisher," interrupted Cathy, flashing him her best smile and attracting his attention, "just how long have you worked as a partner at the firm?" He glared at her, unaware that behind his back Charlie had inconspicuously removed his mobile phone from his coat pocket.

"I'm sure Sergeant Mulgrew," he leered at her, his confidence returning by the minute, "that you will no doubt already be in possession of that information." Charlie pressed a preset button on the phones keypad.

"Yes of course, Mr Frobisher and your service with the company also encompasses the period that is referred to in the letters of complaint to Mr Taylor," she replied sweetly, resisting the strongest of urges to boot this sarcastic shit in the goolies.

"And just to confirm your reply to my colleague's earlier question," she stared at him, maintaining eye contact and silently praying that Charlie's idea works, "you have neither met nor to your recollection have any knowledge of the deceased suspect for the fire raising, Robert Turner?"

"None whatsoever," he responded with a smirk, "and I can categorically state…" The ringing of a mobile phone from the pocket of the jacket, carelessly slung across the chair, interrupted him. He reached over and withdrew the phone. "Hello," he answered, "Hello…?"

A sudden chill run down his spine as Frobisher realised his voice was echoing behind him. With a sense of dread he turned to see Charlie holding a mobile phone out in front of him, facing it towards Frobisher.

"If that is the case, then sir," said Charlie ever so politely, "perhaps you might be able to explain why the murdered man Robert Turner has your phone number?"

*

The two female staff that arrived for work at McGlone's Butchers in Motherwell paid no attention to the four watching men. Anxiously, John Brown checked his watch. The drumming of his fingers on the dashboard was now seriously getting on the detective constables nerves. Ten more minutes of this, he vowed and I'll be having words with the bastard.

*

The now weeping and snivelling Frobisher, his collapse complete and in a vain attempt at remorse, tried to explain that the whole thing was a mistake, that he was the victim of a blackmail plot and had merely attempted to defend himself against the cunning and vicious Turner.

Oh, and the hammer, he added in a half-hearted attempt at cooperation with the detectives, was stowed in the boot of his Volvo.

Regretfully for Frobisher, his pleas fell on deaf ears. Nor did his situation improve the throbbing in his head from his hangover. The arrival of DCI Colin Mitchell and his team, summoned by Cathy via her covert radio, instigated an almost immediate search of Frobisher's house and surrounding grounds. Charlie was a little surprised that Frobisher hadn't concocted a better alibi and rightly presumed the arrogant bastard didn't expected a knock from the CID, later learning he was unable or unwilling to believe any connection could possibly be made between him and Turner and that if by the slightest chance there had been, then his colleague Steven Taylor would make a suitable fall guy and fool the local plod. In a low voice Charlie apprised 'Peasy' Byrne and his colleague, Emma Ferguson, of Frobisher's confessional admissions that was, in effect, their starter for ten for the formal taped interview that was to occur later.

The blonde discovered dozing in the large and ornate bed was hustled protesting and half naked by a uniformed woman constable, to the obvious delight of her male colleagues, into a marked police vehicle for later interview regarding her possession of the several cannabis joints that were found partially concealed in her handbag.

The offending hammer, washed and scrubbed, was exactly where Frobisher had said it was. Later examination would reveal the presence of minute traces of blood and hair adhering to the wooden shaft, all subsequently proven to be from the head of the late and unlamented Robert Turner.

*

Charlie and Cathy handed over primacy of the locus to a jubilant Colin Mitchell then departed in time to make their way to the funeral service for Mary Cavendish that was being held at St Michael's Church in the Gallowgate.

"Relieved it worked?" asked Cathy.

Charlie pursed his lips before replying. "I'm relieved that he didn't ditch the phone, though for the life of me I can't think why not. On the face of it, I suppose he thought he was fool proof and after all," he smiled, "we still haven't any real hard and solid evidence that Robert Turner set the fire, only Frobisher's confession. However, I'm relieved that he burst to the crime so easily. My first meeting with him confirmed what I suspected, that he was a pompous bag of shite, too much mouth and very little bottle. Oh, I know," he cut off her laughing protest, "that Frobisher's verbal admissions have confirmed our suspicions, but it's unlikely that he'll be convicted of colluding with Turner and orchestrating the fire. A smart defence lawyer will deal that one out of the charge sheet in favour of accepting a guilty plea to the murder charge alone. So I suppose Cathy that you and I," he glanced at her as she drove, "will have to satisfy ourselves that yes, we've done our job. We've proven who committed the crime and caused Mary's death. As for a conviction," he sighed heavily, "well, I think we'll have to be content with the knowledge that the culprit's have got their comeuppance, one dead and the other likely to do life for murder. Then there is the theft of the funds from his firm's clients. I don't honestly know how that will pan out, but its Colin Mitchell's baby now. There's still a fair bit of inquiry to be made, but we've done out part, Cathy."

He leaned over slightly and patted her shoulder. "Well done, partner. I'm pleased we worked together. All in all," he grinned happily, "a good result."

A dribble of rain splattered the windscreen as Cathy drove through the city centre to the Gallowgate.

*

The young staff nurse at the Neuro ward made a notation on Father Flynn's medical clipboard and wished him good morning. Her training had stressed that unconscious patients sometimes heard what was going on about them, even though the patient's brain could neither assimilate nor instruct the body to respond to such noises. Quietly, she hummed to herself her dear departed mammy's favourite tune, 'Danny Boy' and leaned over to tuck the old priests head round slightly and ease the uncomfortable position he had shrugged into.
"Sure now Father, should you not be wakening up and giving me a big smile?" she whispered to him, her Cork brogue thick enough to cut with a knife. She stopped suddenly, unsure of what she had seen. Patiently, she waited and watched his eyes. A minute, then two, passed. Yes, a definite flicker. With growing excitement, she waited yet again; waited to confirm her suspicion. Yes, he did it again. A tear escaped her eye. Get a grip, she roughly told herself. Yet the excitement of the moment overcame her, the miracle it seemed was possible. Quickly she made her way to the nurse's station and with trembling fingers dialled the attending surgeon's extension.

*

Frank Brogan tied the knot of his black tie for the third time, not quite satisfied with his efforts. He wanted to impress today, for he had little doubt that the Gallowgate would turn out en masse for Mary's funeral. Like Irene his sister, he knew that amongst the congregation would be the genuinely grieved, but the majority would be there simply to show Catholic solidarity because one of their own had been taken. And of course there would be those whose curiosity had been aroused, wondering and guessing how the niece of Frank Brogan would be revenged and wholly expecting that he would not rest till the bastard that killed her was himself killed. Whether he wanted it or not, he had a reputation to maintain and as the local representative of the Provisional IRA, he could not be seen to allow such a dastardly deed to go unpunished. But plans for that were, he smiled wickedly to himself, already underway.
He thought of the service and was pleased that old bastard Flynn was not conducting the mass. He had also heard the rumours of his supposed involvement in Flynn's assault. There would be those pointing fingers, but not openly, for hadn't he Liam McPhee to discourage and deal with any dissenters? Confident in his reputation and association with the Provo's, Brogan knew he was fireproof. They could whisper and scheme all they wanted, but he, Frank Brogan, feared nobody.
His knot tied, he turned from the wardrobe mirror and sat heavily on the bed. But that wasn't quite true, was it? Another knew of his scam with the funds he raised on behalf of the organisation. Liam McPhee. Granted, the big Belfast man had never alluded to any complaint or annoyance at the division of the money they scammed and seemed grateful for the use of the car during Frank's ban, but the

ban was by and other than the odd task he was sent, that left McPhee effectively grounded. With a sigh, he realised he might have to up the big mans share. Maybe buy him a cheap run-around. But there still existed the danger that McPhee knew of his pilfering and that, he thought, can't go on forever. The clock chimed the hour. He looked out from his window. The official car sat in the roadway outside his close, awaiting his attendance to convey him the short distance to uplift up his sister Irene. With a final glance in the mirror, he squared his shoulders. Yes, he looked the part. For today was not just a funeral, today was Frank Brogan's day.

*

Due to the large number of vehicles that were carrying mourners, Cathy was obliged to park the car over a hundred yards from the church. They watched as two lengthy black coloured undertaker vehicles passed by, presuming they conveyed Mary's mother, Frank Brogan and other close relatives. They turned up their collars to prepare themselves to face the drizzling rain and were about to leave the car when Cathy scrambled in her shoulder bag to answer the insistent ring of her mobile phone.

"It's the lab," she told Charlie. "Yes, yes," he heard her reply then saw her face fall. "Well, I suppose I'll just have to wait, won't I?" she angrily snapped at the caller, slamming the phone back down into her shoulder bag. "Total incompetents," she moaned, "promise one thing and tell you another. Seems they've had a rush job on and we won't get the result till lunchtime tomorrow, now."

"No worries," he smiled at her then pointed to the church entrance where the bulky figure of Brogan was clearly visible as he and a black suited driver assisted Irene Cavendish alight from the huge sedan. "He won't be going anywhere I can't find him."

Cathy cast a sideways look at Charlie. His previous good humour had deserted him. There was something odd about that simple comment, something she just couldn't put her finger on, something that caused a chill to run down her spine. "Right," he said grimly, "let's pay our respects to that wee soul."

*

Steven Taylor sat glumly in his favourite armchair, the daily newspaper lying unread and discarded on the floor beside him. The torn envelope that lay upon his lap and its contents had not brought good news. It was, as he feared, far worse than even he suspected. The theft of client's funds had reached a staggering amount, much more than he was capable of paying back. He ran a bony hand across his face. How he come to find himself in such an impossible situation, he wondered for the thousandth time. Added to his problems, the visit the previous day from the police compounded his difficulties. He sat for what seemed an age, his mind unable to grasp the complexity of his dilemma. Then an almost childish smile settled upon his face. My car, he spoke softly to himself, my beautiful Bentley. Time it was polished. That'll cheer me up no end, he firmly decided and with a happy grin, his troubles temporarily forgotten, went and sought out his bag of chamois dusters and tins of wax.

Chapter 16

Irene Cavendish sat with her chin up and tilted forward, her body stiffly straight and pushed back against the hard wood of the front pew that pressed firmly against her spine. She knew all eyes would be on her, could almost feel the attention focused on the widowed mother of the dear little girl, so cruelly taken from life by the act of a madman. And so dignified, they would say. "Look how composed she is in the face of such adversity and tragedy", they'd say. How they'll admire her serenity, her self control. She had thought about a few tears perhaps, maybe dab at her face with the crisp white cotton handkerchief she had purchased, just for today.

She glanced at the plain, wooden coffin that rested on the trestles to her right with the wreath of flowers adorning the lid that had cost as much as a full week's groceries. Can't have anyone say I didn't do right by my daughter, can I?

Her thoughts turned to Mary and the anger that still consumed her. Rage that her sluttish child should conduct herself so, without dignity and with bestial lust. Horror that Mary should become pregnant and others might discover her mother's shame.

Her hand rolled the handkerchief into a tight little ball of white. Her body tensed with continuing fury as she awaited the start of the service and the appearance of the locum priest, who had temporarily replaced dear Father Flynn. Beside her, Frank Brogan perspired in the tight collar, his vanity discouraging him from purchasing a larger size, fuming at the delay. The church continued to fill up behind him.

He glanced back and saw Liam McPhee, sitting on the other side and a few rows behind, who winked at him and subtly gave a thumb up sign. Brogan smiled softly, acknowledging the signal. The package had arrived. And in the manner of the much-stereotyped Glasgow thug, Frank Brogan silently promised that, tonight, Mister Steven fucking Taylor, you are getting it!

*

The consultant surgeon bent over the bed and shone his pencil torch into Father Flynn's eyes, while uttering the time honoured phrase, 'Hmmm' that the nurse privately interpreted as quite literally he didn't have a bloody clue what he was looking at and further, didn't have the balls to admit it.

"I think a further CAT scan is called for, Staff," he decided after a moments thought.

The staff nurse glowered behind his back, knowing full well there could be no other decision at this time and aware the moment's hesitation had been taken up by the surgeon silently costing the expensive procedure against the time honoured, 'Let's give it another day and see,' that is so favoured by hospital administrators upon whose desk the bill would finally fall.

"But you see a definite improvement?" she persisted.

"Ah, now there is as you so rightly discovered some indication that," he glanced at the name above the bed, "Mr Flynn..."

"Mr Flynn is Father Flynn," she corrected him with a scowl, her brogue more pronounced with her annoyance.

"Yes, of course. Father Flynn. As I was saying, there is more evidence that he is recoiling at light. So, let's get that scan organised and we'll see, eh?" as he smiled in an attempt at joviality to placate this fiery, Irish redhead.

"And I can alert the police that there has been a development in his condition?"

He hesitated before replying. "Let's wait for now, see how things progress," he cautioned.

*

The young priest chosen to conduct Mary Cavendish's funeral service was but a few weeks released from the seminary and panic stricken at the thought of performing this, his first official engagement, alone. Standing in the vestry, he was almost hyperventilating and his body shook with trepidation. Please God, he prayed, don't let me balls up...sorry, make a mess of this. With a deep breath, he collected the senior citizens who performed duty as altar servers and strode dry-mouthed, towards his fate.

At the rear of the church, Charlie Miller was impressed by the large turnout and noted a couple of local journalists, no doubt following up the story of the victim of the fire. One spotted him and nodded in recognition, before sidling up to squeeze into the pew against him.

"Long time no see, Charlie boy. Heard you are the investigating officer, anything yet on the guy that did it?"

He smiled at the hack. "You're chancing your arm, old son. Don't you know we've a press office to answer your questions? Give them a bell, see if they've got anything for you," he whispered with a tight grin.

"Who's your lady friend?" inquired the reporter, ignoring the good-natured jibe.

"She's no lady, she's a Sergeant," replied Charlie with tongue in cheek, aware that Cathy was listening to every word and who indicated with a frown for the reporter to shut up, that the priest was taking to the altar.

Though not a particularly religious man, Charlie thought that the service that followed was a stilted affair, not least because the young priest who performed the ceremony seemed unsure of what was going on and stuttered his way through most of the proceedings. The saving grace was the choral music, sung by a predominantly senior group of parishioner's, whose elucidate recital brought a dignity and solemnity that more than made up for the young priest's disastrous performance. Unable to clearly see the distant Irene Cavendish, he heard the whispered comments from those around him and was unusually touched by the kindness of the speaker's sentiments towards her. However, he found that he was unable to share those opinions, that there was something about the woman that repulsed him, an emotion he found difficult to ignore.

The service progressed and, in due course, the coffin bearing Mary Cavendish passed down the centre aisle through the standing congregation and towards the front doors. Frank Brogan, staring straight ahead, was one of the six pallbearers.

An overwhelming rage swept through Charlie and his body tensed. Beside him, Cathy realised that he was angry and gently placed a restraining hand on his arm. The soft touch helped dispel his anger and he relaxed, feeling drained and helpless, but whether his anger was because he strongly suspected Brogan of impregnating his innocent niece or of assaulting the old priest, Charlie didn't know. In truth he didn't care. Brogan was scum and Charlie Miller intended to have him.

The rain was stopped and the sun peeked from behind watery clouds as the funeral cortege slowly made its way east along the famous London Road, past the mourners who lined the street corners and onwards through the Springfield Road junction, scene of the many pitched gang fights during the troubled first half of the twentieth century, when Glasgow had earned the dubious title of Razor City. Cathy drove in silence, sensing that Charlie was troubled.

"Do you want to talk about it?"

Charlie smiled; a tight little smile and replied, "Nothing to say, really. A few, short days ago I was thinking about my next drink. My life was a real mess. Trusted to do nothing that might involve more than an hours thought, not caring what I was doing or who I might have been hurting," his brow furrowed as he suddenly thought again of his concerned in-laws, "and just being a real asshole, basically," he finished lamely.

"And what about now?"

He softly exhaled, breathing through pursed lips.

"When I was handed this inquiry, I made a promise to myself," he hesitated, "to the wee girl, really. I promised that I'd find out who did this to her and make them pay." He gave a short, humourless laugh. "Don't ask me why, of all the murders and serious crime investigation's I have ever been involved with, that this one should be any different, but it is. I felt different. I felt as though there was a purpose to what I was doing. Well, you me, I should say. And we did it. Between us we found out why she died and we caught the bastards that did it. But that's not enough, Cathy," he stared at her as she drove, "we might have accomplished something, but not everything. Mary Cavendish shouldn't have had to run away from home and hide down that fucking dark hole."

The vehemence in his voice was evident. Cathy decided to let him talk on, without comment. She guessed Charlie needed to get this off his chest.

"I'm usually the one that needs facts, solid facts," he continued, "and I know at the moment this is pure speculation, but I've a strong feeling she ran because between them, her mother and her uncle drove her from the safety of her home, a place where she should have felt… No, not felt, should have *been* safe and protected. Christ!" he burst out, his voice now breaking, "and she was only fourteen… and I'm attending the funeral of another child."

A sob escaped his lips and he began to breathe deeply.

She knew he was at the point of breaking and pulled the car over to the side of the road. She stared straight ahead, afraid to look at him. Charlie, his head down, dragged a hankie from his coat pocket and loudly blew his nose. He's needed this, she instinctively knew. He's upset, but not just for Mary Cavendish; he's weeping for his wife, child and all the things that have gone wrong in his life. Poor sod. The minutes passed and he sat upright, blinking rapidly as he stared through the windscreen as the last of the vehicles bearing mourners to the graveside, passed by.

"Sorry," he apologised shamefacedly, "I didn't mean for that to happen."

"Nothing to apologise for," she awkwardly replied. "You've bottled things up far too long, Charlie Miller. It'll do you good to re-join the human race."

He turned to face her, his eyes bright and a slow smile creeping upon his face. "Then you think I'm curable, Cathy Mulgrew?"

"Your nose is running again," she replied, returning his smile. "So, are you ready to say goodbye to this wee lassie?"

*

John Brown and his team of three detectives had waited all morning for their suspect, but still nobody even remotely resembling him had appeared at McGlone's the Butchers.

"Boss," ventured the detective in the car with him, "do you not think we should call in at Motherwell and speak with this CCTV guy? Besides," he complained through gritted teeth, "I need to pee."

Brown was incandescent with rage. So much so the detective constable thought his face was about to explode.

"Don't fucking question me and my decisions," he raged, "I'm in charge here!"

"Nobody's saying otherwise and I'm not arguing with you," the detective calmly replied, "but unless you want me to pee all over this fucking car, I have to go to the fucking toilet," he responded, with some emphasis.

Brown stared at detective, inwardly believing him to be an insolent prick. "Right," he snapped back, "decision made. Get out there and pull in those other two dimwit's and if any of you have missed the suspect and he is in that shop, there'll be hell to pay!"

Resignedly, the detective left the car and fetched his colleagues, confiding that Adolf was on the warpath and best keep their gobs shut. Once back in the vehicle, Brown instructed the detective to drive towards Motherwell police office. His mobile phone bleeped and alerted him to a call.

"Yes!" he snapped.

"Just where the fuck are you?" inquired the gritty and sarcastic voice of DCI Nancy Rogers.

*

The short burial service at the Catholic cemetery in London Road seemed to Charlie and Cathy to be an edited version of the church service. Standing a short distance from the grave and the blanket of umbrellas that surrounded it, they watched as the coffin was gently lowered into the ground. The attending throng consoled the small detached group that consisted of Irene Cavendish and her brother and what appeared to be family members. As the larger group dispersed, the detectives saw Irene and her brother and other relatives being gently, but firmly escorted by the undertaking staff to their cortege vehicles for the short trip to the local church hall, where beverage and supper was being served by the famous Cooperative, who had succoured and buried Glasgow's citizenry for a century or more.

Charlie smiled grimly as he saw one of the undertakers discreetly check his watch. Time is money and even the bereaved is on a schedule. As the cars drove towards them, Irene Cavendish looked from the window and visibly startled, obviously surprised to see the two detectives. A short distance further on the car carrying her stopped suddenly and she hastily dismounted from the rear door. The driver was perplexed. He had never in all his time as a funeral driver been told to slam on his brakes and "Fucking stop this motor now!"

As Irene approached him, Charlie could see Frank Brogan scrambling out after her and prepared himself for a confrontation.

"Why are you here!" she demanded of him, the veil now thrown back across her small, black hat and her face flushed with anger. "This is a private service. I don't want your type of people at my daughter's funeral," she bitterly screamed at him, her eyes flashing and the intensity of her anger taking him aback.

Completely oblivious to the stares of the mourners, some of whom she had so recently courted with her demure performance, she stood before him her arms slightly raised and her hands drawn back like claws.

"I've come to pay my respects," he added calmly, feeling the mounting anger that threatened to engulf him once again rising to the fore.

"Call yourself detectives," she spat at them both, drawing the words out loudly and slowly in exaggerated sarcasm, "well, detectives, I know who killed my child. I know and I will have my revenge," she screamed, ignoring the restraining hands that Brogan placed about her as he fought to pull her back, fearing that in her impulsive madness, she might attack the two officers.

Charlie and Cathy stood saying nothing, uneasy and aware that any comment they made could provoke a volatile situation and conscious that the now watching and unpredictable crowd might perceive them to be a threat to a distraught woman who had just buried her daughter.

Liam McPhee appeared. Ignoring the detectives, he assisted Brogan in pulling Irene back to the car where without further ado they unceremoniously pushed the struggling and voluble woman into the rear, her screamed threats echoing towards the detectives.

The crowd, seeing the excitement was over, cast curious glances at Charlie and Cathy as they began to disperse, some eager to get home to discuss and phone their friends with the circumstances of the unexpected drama that had unfolded within the cemetery.

"So," said Charlie, his face impassive, but swallowing hard, "I think that went well, don't you?"

Back in their car, Cathy asked him, "What do you think she meant, she knows who killed Mary?"

"Haven't a clue," he admitted, "but I can only guess that she's either gone completely off her head or somehow she's learned about the arrest of Thomas Frobisher and maybe even his connection with Robert Turner. Then again," he added, his mind wandering back to the earlier church service, "there was a couple of reporters at the funeral, today. You know how it is; there's always a cop prepared to give the local tabloids a phone tip if it means a few quid in his pocket. Chances are that someone has tipped off the media about the police operation this morning and Irene's been contacted earlier by one of the reporters. You know how it goes, 'How do you feel about the arrest of so and so', that kind of thing."

Cathy nodded her head in understanding. "Seems likely you're right. So Charlie, where to now?"

"Now?" he repeated thoughtfully, "now we head back to the office. Cathy my girl, I think we deserve a wee flyer today, so that we're nice and refreshed for the lab result tomorrow morning. I've got a feeling in my bones that we'll be rattling your Frank Brogan's door. Good and, pardon my French, very fucking hard!"

*

The detective constable drove the CID car into Motherwell office's back yard and had hardly brought the vehicle to a halt before John Brown was out and racing to find a phone.

"Poor sod," he shook his head in mock sympathy at the running figure, "but that's what he gets for trying to deceive Nancy Rogers."

"Poor sod, my arse," his colleague disagreed from the rear seat. "Brown's out for himself and by trying to pull a flanker on Rogers, he thinks he's ruined his chances for this promotion he's been brown nosing after for the last couple of years. That bastard," he reminded the other two, "has grassed more people to the bosses than women I've had my leg over," he cheekily boasted. "Right," he grinned as he swung open his door, "you two lazy farts find us a kettle and a brew. I'm away for a pee."

Brown, sat at the clerk's desk in the Motherwell CID general office, took a deep breath and dialled the internal number that would directly connect him with Nancy Rogers.

"Yes?"

"It's me, ma'am John Brown."

"Just what are you up to," she demanded.

"I had a tip off about our suspect…."

You mean the guy in the photograph?"

"Aye, that's right and I…"

"So, have you got him?"

"Eh, no, but..."

"So, where is he then?"

"I'm currently pursuing inquiries and…"

"Don't give me that old crap! Who is he and were is he now?"

He swallowed hard as his mind cried Bitch! Bitch! Bitch!

"I'm at Motherwell just now, intending to interview a CCTV operator who has information…"

"Well, when you've done that, get your arse back here and be prepared to provide me with a full report. I'm keen to know why it takes four of you to interview a CCTV operator," she added, her voice dripping with sarcasm, "particularly as I'm short staffed as it is. And another thing," she growled, her voice barbed and cynical, "you might be interested to know I've just had a phone call from the Assistant Chief Constable (crime). It seems that Charlie Miller is to be congratulated. Not only has he apparently solved the wee girl's death in the fire, but he has also significantly contributed to solving the Govan murder and according to the grapevine, it was a real whodunit. Could be, John," she allowed herself a little intimacy to cruelly drive home the taunt, "that Miller might be a candidate for the next DI's position here at the Central Division. See you when you return," then hung up before he could respond, chuckling at her duplicity and guessing that Brown would be choking with rage.

As indeed he was. The information imparted by Rogers not only took him by surprise, but almost to the point of collapse. His head reeled and his breath grew quicker. A tightening in his chest preceded blurred vision and he grasped the desk for support. The elderly uniformed officer, who performed the duties of clerk, reached out a hand of concern, only to be told to "Fuck off!" by the irate Brown. Shrugging his shoulders, the officer move away, clearly heard muttering "Wanker" under his breath.

Brown slowly regained control and staggered to his feet. With a visible effort, he made his way to the refreshment room where having recovered his breath, he ordered his sullen detective constables back to the car to await his return. Then, like a man possessed, he sought out the CCTV supervisor who had unwittingly led him into this problem and caused him so much grief.

*

Sadie Forrest, hat in hand, sported her most beguiling smile to persuade her Sergeant that tonight was an important event and, despite his best efforts, resisted the urge to reveal why she wanted an early finish to her shift. An older man in the twilight of his career, he liked Sadie and knew her to be a woman who respected her privacy, suspecting that she was lonely with too little social life. Certainly, he had no complaint about her work ethos and indeed considered her one of his best tutor cops.

"Is it a date you have tonight, lass?" he teased her and opened his eyes wide in surprise when she blushed. "My God," he laughed, "the iron maiden has a heart after all!"

"I'd be grateful if you didn't put it about, you old sod," she told him, wagging a finger in warning.

"You're looking awfully pale," he teased her with a cheeky grin, "I think you'd better get yourself away home and into bed," then rubbed his chin in mock innuendo, "or would that involve too much hard work, do you think?"

*

The few family members that remained in the parish hall surrounded the seated Irene Cavendish to bid their farewells. Solemnly, she accepted their sympathetic condolence and cast a thoughtful eye to where her brother Frank and Liam McPhee were deep in conversation.

"I'll not need your help, Frank," McPhee insisted, taking care to support Brogan with one hand while trying to avoid spilling the drink in his other hand.

Brogan, apparently worse the wear for drink, insisted that he'd be of use.

"I could be your lookout," he slurred, "in case the police arrive. You need me Liam," he insisted.

McPhee sighed. The last thing he needed was a drunken hero for the Cause trying to prove his manhood and making an arse of himself. McPhee neither saw nor heard the soft-footed approach of Irene.

"Will it be tonight then, Liam?" she asked, her eyes bright with a fervour that scared him shitless.

Dear God, he thought, if half the Provo's were as committed as this woman, there'd be a united Ireland within weeks.

"There, there now, Irene," he tried to console her, "don't you be worrying about anything now, love. Sure, you've got your grief to attend to."

"Don't fob me off like one of your floosies, Liam McPhee!" she hissed at him. "It was my daughter the man murdered, so I'm entitled to know what is about to happen, aren't I Frank?" she looked to her brother for support.

Brogan, his head spinning from the whisky and porter, nodded a sickly grin then vomited across the hall's wooden floor. Her eyes rose to heaven and shaking her head, Irene grasped her brother by his arm and steered him towards the vacant toilet where she began to wipe him off. Crying now, he begged her forgiveness.

"For what?" presuming he was apologising for the mess.

"For Mary," he sobbed.

"Mary?" she repeated, puzzled, "because she's dead, you mean?"

"For the baby," he wailed, his head reeling and oblivious to his admission, "it wasn't my fault. She was teasing me the way she dressed, with her short school skirt and her blouse and that. You know how they are at that age."

His head hung low. He needed sleep. Just let me sleep. That's what I need, he thought.

She stood horrified, unable to comprehend what she was hearing. For the baby? Mary? Frank?'

"Frank! What are you telling me," she slapped him hard on the side of the head, causing his head to jerk upright. A bob of spittle rolled down from the corner of his mouth.

"What?"

"Tell me again, Frank. What do you mean about you and Mary?" But Irene didn't need her brother to reply. The full horror of his statement had already sunk home, the treachery of her wee brother Frank and that of her slut of a daughter. Cold shivers run through her at the thought that this might get out. She'd never be able to hold her head up again. She'd be the talk of the neighbourhood. She could never attend Mass again. Her life would be finished. She glanced furtively about her as an idea formed in her mind. Nobody need know. Then dreadful thought struck her - the police. Well, if she and Frank kept their mouths shut, they need never know either. Why should they, she reasoned? Her good name would be protected. She stared down at her now unconscious brother. She knew enough about drunks and their weaknesses. Enough to know that, come the morning, he'd never remember what he had confessed. And she'd never tell.

On the other side of the doorway, Liam McPhee shook his head and smirked. Why you old bugger, Frank. Never thought you had it in you, he leered and quickly downed his whisky.

*

"But why'd I have to go to Grannies tonight?" moaned Sadie's daughter, Geraldine. "Charlie's my friend too," she added, the hurt in her face breaking Sadie's heart, but not enough to persuade her from sending Jellybean to her Gran. "Listen," she told her, using the age old tactic that has been tried and tested by countless parents, "be a good girl, do as you're told and you and I are going for a McDonald's tomorrow," she beamed, trying hard to ignore the sorrow in those beautiful, blue eyes. The petted lip and tears might have worked at any other time, but not tonight Sadie grimly decided, definitely not tonight.

*

John Brown returned home, seething and humiliated after his interview with Nancy Rogers. His wife, sitting fretfully in the lounge, her knees together and her hands clasped tightly in her lap, gave a last glance around the room to ensure everything was in order. That nothing was out of place. She heard then saw him race the car into the secluded driveway, a sure sign he'd had a bad day. Her hand reached for her throat and her eyes opened wide with foreboding as she fearfully tiptoed to the kitchen to prepare herself for the worse. God, she implored, closing her eyes tightly, please stop him hurting me. Please, please!

The car door slammed, then bad temperedly slammed again. With bated breath she waited for the sound of his heavy footsteps on the gravel stoned driveway, of his key in the door, the shouted demand for a drink and then she knew it would begin. The verbal abuse and, if she was lucky, a few hard slaps before he tired of hitting her unresisting face and head. Still, she waited. The seconds rolled into one, then two minutes.

Cautiously, she sneaked a glance through the net curtained window and saw him lying on the ground, face down and his head at an odd angle, one hand beneath his body and the other clawing at the gravelled driveway. She thought she saw white saliva coming from his mouth as his body jerked in rhythmic motion. He gave one lengthy shudder and then ceased moving. She made to rush from the kitchen to help him, find out what was wrong then stopped at the kitchen door. She backed away from the door and turned her head to stare at her reflection in the mirror on the wall. The face that stared back at her was that of a sad woman in her late forties, a once pretty and independent woman. Now a haggard shell of her former self, reduced to begging for mercy, afraid to open her mouth unless spoken to.

Reduced to this, she saw; a cheerless, timid and terrified woman. Again she looked through the window. He hadn't moved. I should really call for help, she thought.

But first, a slow and hesitant smile began to spread across her face, a cup of tea. She swallowed hard. Just to settle my nerves.

*

Liam McPhee, keeping a weather eye open for the cops and their breathalysers, drove Brogan home and carefully parked the Vectra in its dedicated parking bay. Assisting the stumbling and incoherent Brogan to get upstairs, he managed to manoeuvre him into the bedroom and deposited him fully clothed onto his bed. With an effort, he turned Brogan onto his side to prevent him choking to death, smiling as he did so. As an afterthought, he threw a quilted cover across the prone body. He thought about what he had heard Brogan confess to his sister Irene. Shaking his head he grinned down at the snoring figure. It's none of my business he decided, if the arse wants to shag his niece. Keeping it in the family, he chuckled to himself.

He stood above the bed, staring at Brogan and a thought occurred to him that brought a slow smile to his pockmarked face. In the lounge, he found a pencil and paper and laboriously scribbled a note that he left on the dining table with Brogan's car keys, where he could not fail to spot them. After a final look around, he quietly closed and locked the door behind him and posted the key through the letterbox.

*

Barry Ashford lay fully dressed upon the large bed in his hotel suite while his two Security Service minders played cards in the adjoining room. The smoke from his French cigarette curled to the ceiling, a half eaten meal slowly congealing on the wheeled trolley and an empty bottle of expensive white wine sat upturned in the chill bucket. His patience was wearing thin. The expected phone call was now over an hour late. A thought occurred to him and he checked the battery level of the mobile phone upon the bedside cabinet. The green light indicated plenty of life yet, he saw. Wearily, he sucked another lungful of smoke into his thin frame and sighed deeply as the tobacco narcotic worked its magic. The phone bleeped. Instantly he was alert and swung his legs over the side of the bed. He allowed the phone to bleep twice more, before replying to its urgent summons.

"Yes?" It sounded to an irate Ashford as though the caller had heavily imbibed and was immediately annoyed at the heavy slur to his voice and his noticeable effort at pronunciation. "So, it will go ahead tonight as planned?" enquired Ashford. The answer satisfied, yet worried him also. "Will there be any risk of civilian casualties?" Again, the response seemed to satisfy Ashford's inane fear of police reprisal; however, he insisted that the caller took pains to ensure the minimum risk to civilians. "Don't call me a fucking old woman!" he literally screamed down the line, "Just remember, laddie, that I hold your reproductive organs in my delicate little hands!" He took a deep breath and rose to his feet. "If this works out," he said, forcing his voice to be calm, "and you avoid arrest, then we could eventually be looking at complete control of the Scottish operation and access to the Army Council with all that entails and beyond our expectation." He listened intently as the caller revealed the proposed time and tactics for deploying the device. Ashford smiled in anticipation of the prestige that the success of the operation would bring him. "'Good luck then, chummy and don't forget our meeting at the windy place, when this is all over."

Chapter 17

DCI Nancy Rogers had decided to stay late at the office to review the statements and intelligence reports in John Brown's files. The additional information he had gleaned from the Motherwell CCTV operator had proven to be of little value, after all. The supervisor, though keen to assist, had not been able to recall exactly when he had last seen the male whose likeness to the suspect had initiated his phone call. A wasted day, she had rebuked Brown, then instructed that tomorrow he call upon the butcher and establish both the identity and when the suspect had last worked at the shop. Something, Brown should have done in the first instance, she scathingly reminded him.

Of course she knew why he had avoided telling her about his plan, knew that he was seeking to impress with an arrest that would raise his profile with the CID management. She was puzzled by his reaction. He hadn't replied, hadn't argued, which she found odd. But of course that was John Brown. The barb about Charlie Miller's success had struck home. At one point she thought him close to collapse, but with an effort he had raised himself to his feet then stormed from her office. It was common knowledge the man was a coward and a bully and, if the rumours were true, she suspected it likely his wife would bear the brunt of Brown's failure. Idly, she cross referenced the latest statements and perused their contents, taking in very little. Her breathing was becoming more laboured and she reached into her handbag for the inhaler. The phone rang. The duty Inspector at the Maryhill police station regretted disturbing her, but thought she ought to know immediately, rather than learn tomorrow from the personnel department. She wasn't prepared for what he told her. Stunned, she replaced the receiver and sat back. Her first thought was who to appoint as acting Sergeant till John Brown was replaced?

*

Charlie dragged the overnight bag from the top of his cupboard and used a wet cloth to dust it off, trying to recall the last time he had used it. Satisfied, or as best he could be with its condition he carried it through to the bedroom and rummaged in his drawer for spare underclothes and socks. A shirt was next, wrinkled but clean. He reached for his spare, serviceable suit and paused. What the hell am I doing, he wondered and not for the first time. He'd known Sadie for a few short days. Yes, they had seemed to hit it off and yes, he was a lucky man that she had taken an interest in him. But was he being fair to her? He sat down on the edge of the bed and looked at himself in the mirror. Just what can she possibly see in me?

Self-doubt pounded at his recently discovered confidence. But he knew he wouldn't let her down, no… he couldn't let her down. Rising to his feet he thought, thank God one of us is off her head, sighed with anticipated pleasure and finished packing the bag.

*

The consultant surgeon examined the CAT scan results and chewed the end of his pencil, worrying at it and conscious that the Irish nurse's critical eyes were upon him.

"So?" she finally asked, prompting him for a decision.

He turned slowly, peeked at her over the top of his designer specs that he liked to think made him look more professional and smiled slowly. "I think you've got your miracle, Staff."

*

Steven Taylor finished his meagre meal and started on his nightly tour of the ground floor, pulling curtains over and locking the front and rear doors. The light from the lounge window illuminated the gleaming Bentley that was now locked and secured. He stared at the stately old lady, with pride. His afternoon's exertions had been worth it for its chrome shone and sparkled and the deep red hue reflected warmly in the moonlight. And the task had, at least for a brief time, removed all thought of the disaster that was about to befall him. With a final nod of satisfaction for a job well done, he pulled the curtain closed, leaving the vehicle to the cloaking darkness of the driveway.

*

Sadie Forrest sprinkled cologne into the running water of her bath and set unlit candles about the flat, fussing whether to light them now or wait till Charlie arrived. In the bedroom, she changed the sheets and bit her lip to stop giggling as she turned the quilt back, ready. Loosening the belt around her robe, she critically examined her body in the full-length bedroom mirror. Turning to and fro, she decided that for her age, she wasn't doing too badly, but smilingly pledged she'd need to keep an eye on her waistline. Moving closer to the mirror, she run a finger gently down the small scar at her left eye, a constant and visible reminder that taking a relationship for granted could prove to be a big mistake. Funny, she thought, that Charlie hadn't asked how she had come by it. The thought of him brought back the niggling doubt. She sat down heavily on the bed, pulling her robe about her. Was she taking this too fast? What exactly did she feel for the big guy? And would he be frightened off at the thought of becoming involved with a recently divorced woman who had a child?

Her ex-husband came to mind and the years she had been with him, but she'd never really known him at all, never been able to judge his moods or his thoughts. Somehow, it seemed different with Charlie whom she'd intuitively decided was a good man. Quiet and reserved yet, she suspected, with an untapped sense of humour. She'd had no need to use birth control for some time now, and recalled with embarrassment calling into the chemist shop on her way home, hovering about the condom display like a pubescent schoolgirl. For some unaccountable reason, she instinctively knew that Charlie wouldn't think about protection. She smiled again self-consciously at her reflection. "Sadie Forrest," she spoke out loud, "you might just have turned a big, big corner."

*

Liam McPhee drank his second pint of water prior to forcing the fingers of his right hand down his throat. The sudden surge of cold water in his stomach met the alcohol he had earlier consumed and caused a nauseous reaction. Kneeling down, he held both sides of the toilet bowl and prepared himself. The projectile vomit careered into the bowl with such force it rebounded against the enamelled side and splashed back against his face and neck. As the foul smell assailed his nostrils, his body heaved and again the bile rose in his throat. The second discharge was less forceful and he knew from long experience that his stomach contents were almost gone. Once more, he dispelled vomit then shook himself, sweating at his exertions. With a sudden shudder, he climbed to his feet, flushed the toilet then dunked his head in the cold water of the washbasin. That done he stared at his dripping face in the mirror and smiled at his reflection. Drunk or sober, I'm your man.

*

Aileen Dee tugged on then laced up the scuffed working boots and donned the heavy, moleskin jacket. A grey coloured cloth cap on her cropped, stubble of hair completed the outfit, her only display of femininity being the large hooped earrings and a slash of bright red lipstick. Switching off the lights in the drop-in centre, she locked the front door and easily lifted the heavy, rusting metal grills into place before shackling them with the stout padlocks. Dusting off her hands, she glanced at the dark clouds hovering above and hesitated, unsure whether or not to take her nightly walk through the unlit lanes and gloomy streets nearby and speak with some of the working girls plying their trade, before making her way to the flat. Turning up her collar, she determined that if the rain held off by the time she reached Blythswood Square, she would take the opportunity to pass out some of the free NHS condoms she habitually carried in her pockets. But if the rain began to fall, as it seemed more likely, she'd be taking a night off and heading home for a bath.

*

Charlie took one last look around his flat and shrugged into his overcoat. A sudden memory caused him to reach in and remove the folded photograph from the pocket. He looked at the image and choked back an emotion. "I'm doing my best, Mary," he whispered softly, "but it's not ended yet. I've your uncle Frank to speak with tomorrow. And if he did to you what I think he did, well then my poor wee soul, I'll make sure he pays for it."

*

The widow of John Brown, a polystyrene beaker of weak tea cupped in her hands, sat numbly on the hard, plastic chair in the soulless casualty ward of the Victoria Infirmary and hardly heard her sister and brother-in-law's words of condolence. The sister was concerned, for she didn't seem to realise what had happened and the smile on her face, the staff nurse had told her, must be the result of deep shock. Had they but known, the recently widowed woman felt none of the expected emotions. No pain, no grief and no heartache, just a wonderful sense of relief.

*

Barry Ashford paced up and down his room, drawing deeply at his cigarette, painfully aware that the undertaking was now out of his hands and silently praying to whatever God would listen that his agent had got this right. If anything should go wrong….

No, he decided, the consequence of a balls-up was too horrific to contemplate. All the same, he couldn't stop thinking about what was to occur. The success of the operation depended upon the Provo, Liam McPhee placing the device without being caught by some nosey patrolling cop. Christ! The consequences would be calamitous and certainly the end of his career and how the fuck he would explain to his masters at the Security Service that he condoned a venture like this!

A sudden, very nasty thought occurred to him. Jesus! I could end up in prison! But the reward for success was incalculable. For the first time that evening he smiled. Success could mean unprecedented access to the inner sanctum of the IRA's Army Council and all that implied. Have faith, he persuaded himself. Have faith.

But fucking faith didn't win any medals did it? A sudden thought occurred to him. He reached for the telephone by the bed and dialled an extension number.

"You two get yourselves in here, I've a little job needs done."

*

Cathy Mulgrew was on a high. The success of the morning raid and arrest of Thomas Frobisher for the murder and collusion in the fire raising had reminded her that she was an operational police officer and not just a desk bound warrior. She unlocked the front door and shouted, "I'm home." Her nostrils were immediately assailed by the smell from the kitchen, of Chinese food and the crackling sound of vegetables being stir fried in the wok. "Hi, honey," her partner greeted her, wrapped in a Homer Simpson apron, holding two glasses of white wine and smiling at her from the doorway. "Hungry?"

"Starving," agreed Cathy, sipping her wine and planting a full kiss on the waiting lips. "And an early night is called for too," she reached up and tousled the fair hair with affection, her eyes conveying an unsaid promise, then teasingly added, "Charlie Miller and I might be arresting a very, very bad man tomorrow morning."

*

Liam McPhee, three cups of strong coffee later and now dressed in a navy sweater, black jeans, short dark jacket, woollen hat and training shoes, softly closed the door of the flat behind him. He stood silently for a few seconds then, satisfied he was alone in the stairway, quietly but quickly made his way downstairs and out to the darkness of the courtyard at the rear of the tenement building. The communal bins stood racked together in their brick store. Gently, he opened the wooden gate and selected the third bin, from which he removed the plastic bag he'd secreted earlier that morning. The weight felt the same. His constant fear was that he was under surveillance and his movements noted. If he was, he knew the device would likely have been 'jacked' by the police, who would have introduced some sort of chemical into the explosive to render it incapable of detonating. Then, as had happened to so many of his associates, he'd be caught planting the device by the police or security forces, safe in the knowledge the device would be incapable of exploding. He knew he was being paranoid, that there was no surveillance. But the feeling persisted. He desperately wanted to look inside the bag, but reckoned that if he shone a light it might be seen from any of the rear tenement windows that overlooked the courtyard. And that could result in a prowler phone call to the police. Making his way through the darkened courtyard, he emerged with the carrier bag in a parallel street and flagged down a passing private hire taxi.

*

Charlie's taxi dropped him in the Merchant City near to Sadie's flat. He'd convinced himself he wanted to stop off at a licensed grocer and buy a bottle of good wine, but the truth was that he was nervous and needed the fresh air to prepare himself. The rain had begun to drizzle yet again, forcing him to take shelter in a doorway. He looked up to where the lights in her building beckoned. I'm being stupid he scolded himself and, with a deep breath, made his way to the front door of the flats.

*

Aileen Dee had spoken with some of the regular girls and listened patiently to their moans and whines about their customers, the 'Toms', whose expectations of the services they desired far exceeded that of the money they were prepared to pay. Gratefully, they accepted the condoms that she provided and promised faithfully to attend the health course she was setting up at her centre. As usual, she knew that with most, she was wasting her breath, but if the message got through to at least one girl, then it was worth it. The drizzle of rain forced the girls to scatter and take shelter under the nearby building overhangs, while the more robust raised their umbrella's and stood at the corners, their inviting smiles and short skirts displaying their readiness to service the kerb crawling men with money in their hands. With a final and pointless caution about using the darkened lanes, Dee decided enough was enough and began the long walk back to her flat. A sudden howl interrupted her thoughts.

*

Sadie pressed the button that operated the front door and, with a last glance in the mirror, hurriedly lit the candles. God, I feel like a teenager on my first date, she thought as her stomach muscles again tightened in anxiety. Though she was expecting it, the knock on the door made her jump. Charlie stood there, his hair ruffled and his coat damp from the sudden downpour. She reached for the bag in his hand.

"Hi," he smiled at her.

"Hi, yourself," she replied, her mouth suddenly dry, but then tilted her head to allow him to kiss her. The kiss continued and she dropped the bag, throwing her arms around his neck and pulling him down towards her.

"Can I come in then?" he grinned at her.

*

A few streets from where the target vehicle lay, McPhee got out of the taxi, tipping the driver and adopting what he believed to be his best Scottish accent to thank him. The quick glance about him revealed the road to be deserted. The rain helped, keeping people indoors. The lights from nearby houses twinkled in the darkness as the street lamps fought in vain to brighten the roadway. He began to make his way to where the vehicle lay. An approaching van caused him to step aside into a doorway, but the teenage driver seemed too preoccupied to notice McPhee. He breathed a sigh of relief, suddenly conscious that he was tense and began to hum a quiet tune, to calm his nerves. A few minutes walk brought him within view of his target. The vehicle lay isolated and vulnerable in the darkness, its sleek lines unprepared for the destruction that he intended to visit upon it. He stood for a moment in the darkness of a high hedgerow, just long enough to satisfy himself as best he could that there was no ambushing police and to pull on a pair of plastic surgical gloves. Quickly, he approached the vehicle and hesitated briefly, suddenly aware of the enormity of his actions. A last look round, a deep breath, then he bent down, removed the device from its protective bubble wrap and lay flat on the ground parallel to the driver's side of the car. Expertly, he placed the device on the palm of his large hand and stretched his arm out underneath the vehicle where, with a soft thud, he heard the magnet click to the metal underside. The device was in position. He reached for the twine that hung limply from the video cassette case and with a sharp tug, pulled hard as he had been taught, all those years ago. The timer began its rotation to unite the two small metal connections. If there was a problem with the device, he now had thirty seconds to get clear before it detonated. Rolling over he glanced about him before rising to his feet. He crumpled the carrier bag, stuffed it into his jacket then quickly strode away into the night. The whole operation had taken less than fourteen seconds. A minute passed and nothing happened. No explosion. McPhee exhaled nosily, aware he had unconsciously been holding his breath.

With a grin, he began walking, keen to be gone from the area before he sought a taxi and leaving behind him underneath the vehicle, the armed and deadly explosive device.

*

Aileen Dee heard the noise again, a gasp and what sounded like a strangled cry. Warily, she entered the darkened lane, her mouth half-open and listening intently. For all her size and strength, she had a childish phobia about the dark and shuddered at the thought she might become trapped without light in this sinister, dirty and narrow lane. But the sound persisted. She looked behind her, but the working girls had all fled to shelter from the rain and the street, usually bustling with traffic, was unaccountably deserted. Her mouth dry and heart thumping, she tiptoed into the darkness making hardly a sound and, as she was later to recount, "For a bird my size, that was some fucking doing!"

*

Charlie set out his shaving gear and toothbrush in the bathroom, when it hit him. Shit! I've no condoms! He placed his hands on the washbasin and shook his head, cursing inwardly at his lack of forethought. With a sigh, he realised the best course of action was to confess and take the flak. Yet he knew she wouldn't mind his forgetfulness. Somehow, he just knew Sadie Forrest would forgive him anything.

*

McPhee decided to walk a little further before hailing a taxi. The rain beat down on the darkened streets, soaking through the woollen hat and running in rivulets down his face, but he paid no attention. His thoughts were of the device and its consequence. If it goes well and according to plan, Liam McPhee could be exonerated for past offences and look forward to a return to Belfast. Then watch me, he smirked.

*

Sadie grinned at him, standing there blushing, his eyes begging forgiveness, then jokingly adopted a petted lip.
"Does this mean you don't find me attractive and would rather not sleep with me?"
Charlie swallowed hard and stuttered in reply, his palms outstretched and probably looking like the prat he felt. She stood before him, the shapely curve of her breasts pushing at the flimsy material of the silky slip, her hair falling loosely about her shoulders. Her perfume intoxicated him and his breathing grew rapid with his sudden desire for her.
"I figured you'd have other things on your mind, Charlie Miller," she moved closer as she teased him, "So I bought these," and produced a packet from behind her.
With a sigh of relief he reached out and took her in his arms. She laughed with sudden surprise.
"Why, Charlie is that a baton in your pocket? And now," she looked up at him coyly, her blue eyes sparkling, "What …exactly…can I do for you?"

*

Steven Taylor awoke with a start. He thought he'd heard something outside and stumbled, half dazed from his bed towards the window that overlooked the driveway. Pulling aside the heavy curtain, he rubbed at the condensation and peered out through the smeared glass, but the darkness of the night revealed nothing. His car sat immobile, gleaming in the partial moonlight. Probably those damned foxes again, he muttered, recalling the spilled dustbin of a few days previously and the debris scattered throughout his garden, before dazedly returning to his bed.

*

Irene Cavendish sat motionless in the armchair in the lounge of her high rise flat, still wearing her mourning clothes, her hands laid flat on the heavy bible in her lap, a cup of tea on the side table, cold and ignored. The evening's revelation from her brother Frank that he had sired her daughter's child weighed heavily on her mind and robbed her of the desire to sleep. Though Frank was drunk when he had confessed, it all depended now on just how drunken he had been, for she knew in her heart that he was a weak man without the strength of character that his sister had inherited from their mother. She knew that if he recalled what he had told Irene, he would not let the matter rest. He would first deny the incident, weep and claim he was drunk then seek forgiveness and that, she knew, is where the danger lay, for Irene needed the matter to be forgotten and dismissed from his mind, as if the whole, shoddy episode had never occurred.

She shivered with fear that if the shameful secret should become widely known its disclosure would make her life in the parish intolerable. She would never mention it again, she vowed, and she would pray, pray and pray again, for Mary. She clutched the bible and squeezed it tightly to her bosom, determined to appeal for the Lord's forgiveness for her daughter's mortal sin.

*

Liam McPhee arrived at his tenement building without incident. He hadn't even seen a cop on the journey back. The task completed, he was feeling good and with his hangover now dispelled, promised himself a shot of whisky from the bottle in his flat, a curer. Such was his sense of security he failed to pay attention to the parked cars in the street and didn't spot the two Security Service minders who observed him from their darkened vehicle. With a 'Thank fuck' that the duty was now over, the driver used his mobile phone to inform a relieved Barry Ashford that the Provo McPhee had arrived home safely.

*

The girl was seventeen and had celebrated her birthday in the pub a few weeks previously, where her friend had told her that the money was easily earned. "Always make sure the punters use a condom and you'll be all right," her friend had warned her. "Some just want hand jobs," the friend had added, providing an intimation of experience. At just one year older, her face caked in cheap make-up and dressed in a short skirt that exposed the uncomfortable stocking tops the punters always seem to find exciting, the younger girl's friend was already a veteran in the ways of men.

"Stick to the drag area and you'll be okay. Look at me. I've been doing it for months now and it's easy money, I'm telling you," she bragged in an attempt to reassure the timid teenager.

And sure enough and just as the friend had promised, the first week was money easy earned, but now this.

The man had seemed nice enough and his offer of four tenner's for a quick shag was tempting. But in the darkness of the lane his charm had quickly evaporated. "You're a fucking slut!" he had hissed at her, dragging her deeper into the lane and making her tearfully repeat the words back to him. Then had come the blow to her face and his rough seizure of a handful of her hair, pushing at her and forcing her to squat on the wet, cobbled ground. "Get down, you bitch," he had threatened her, "on your knees, slut!"

Her terror of him had choked back her scream and then the breath was knocked from her by a vicious kick to her stomach. With a twist of his hand that held her hair, he compelled her to turn her head round to face his crotch and with his other hand, undid his belted trousers and allowed them to fall down around his knees. The girl was nauseous and tried to push away from him, shoving at his naked thighs, but his free hand came down heavily on the side of her face. The sudden, fierce slap dazed her and she imagined she saw stars. Still gripping her hair, he forced her head backwards and the rain splashed down onto her bruised face. She could see he had become excited and that his exposed penis was now erect. His breathing became more laboured and his free hand savagely grabbed at the back of her neck, ordering her to open her mouth. She knew she was going to die. The man gritted his teeth in anticipation of his pleasure and then stopped. He listened intently, trying to control his breathing and whispered through gritted teeth for the sobbing girl to "Shut the fuck up!"

The hairs on the back of his neck had risen and a sudden chill ran down his spine. From the darkness behind him had come a low and menacing snarl.

Chapter 18 – Friday morning

The digital alarm clock broke through Charlie's dreamless sleep and announced the six o'clock news bulletin. He stared at the brilliant white ceiling as a glow of the November sun peeped through the crack in the dark blue curtains. For the first time since the accident, he was not alone. The fair hair that tumbled across his left shoulder stirred and a bleary-eyed Sadie greeted him with a tired smile.

"Morning," she whispered, her voice soft and gentle.

A feeling of immense happiness rushed through him and he rolled over to envelop her in his arms.

"And good morning to you, gorgeous," he replied.

She snuggled into his arms, enjoying the moment and closed her eyes again.

"I like it when you call me gorgeous. Do you have to get up right away?"

He sighed, happy and comfortable lying there with Sadie, but acutely aware he had an early rendeavous with Cathy Mulgrew at the Central Division CID office. "I'm expecting some information to come through early, today," he told her, "so, if it pans out, I might be arresting an old friend of ours this morning."

Her fingers marched under the cover and along his thigh and her hand reached down and curled into his groin. He stiffened and blinked rapidly.

"But another ten minutes or so won't make that much difference," he said with a grin.

*

Cathy Mulgrew reached over and stopped the alarm activating before it awoke her partner, snoring softly beside her. Bending over, she kissed the fair head and slipped from between the covers, tiptoeing into the bathroom for her shower. Standing under the running water, she realised she had a good feeling about today. If the lab report phoned the result as they had promised and Charlie's hunch was correct, Frank Brogan's days as the co-ordinator for the IRA's fundraising in the West of Scotland were about to come to a sudden end. She knew from her experience at the CTU that the Provo's were forever boasting to their supporters of their unity in standing by their prisoners, aiding their families when they were arrested and loudly proclaiming their innocence to the world in an ongoing anti-British campaign. The Yanks and the Aussies in particular loved it and happily contributed funds to help. But that was for terrorist activities, not shagging children. Not incestuously impregnating their nieces. Lets see how loud they shout for Frank Brogan, when he gets the jail, she smirked.

*

As Cathy showered, across the city Nancy Rogers was driving to work and considering whom she would appoint to replace John Brown. She assessed the names running through her head not for their ability, but on whom she could rely to keep their ears and eyes open and report back to her anything that she needed to know. In short, who among her detective constables could she tempt with an acting Sergeant rank, to tout for her amongst their colleagues?

*

Slowly, Frank Brogan came to. The slightest movement of his head brought about a horrific pain and his throat felt like it had been scraped with a rusty razor blade. He opened his eyes to a shaft of light penetrating through the closed curtains. Very slowly, he slid his legs over the edge of the bed and placed his feet, still in his shoes, onto the floor and sat up, cradling his head in his hands. His bladder reminded him that unless he got to the toilet immediately, he'd be peeing the bed again. Staggering towards the bathroom, one hand on the wall for support, his stomach retched and his arse exploded with a foul smelling flatulence that caused him to retch and race for the toilet bowl. With barely a second to spare, he heaved into the bowl and stood clutching the cistern. Gasping for air, the warm trickle down his leg revealed his bladder had had enough of waiting around for him to empty it. He shook his head in disgust and self-loathing. His brow knitted as a sudden memory flashed into his mind and his eyes stared sightlessly in shock. Oh, no! Oh my God! Oh no!

*

Several miles away in the darkened flat, Liam McPhee slept soundly, neither dream nor nightmare disturbing him, his conscience untroubled.

*

It was a cheerful Charlie Miller who arrived in the general office that morning, greeting his sombre colleagues with a smile as he made his way to the kettle. "You haven't heard then?" inquired DC Carol McFarlane, her face pale and drawn.
Charlie stared around him at the watching faces, seeing for the first time their sober faces.

"Heard what?"

"It's John Brown. He died last night. Heart attack, we heard, on his way into the house. Seems he collapsed in the driveway. His wife got an ambulance, but it was too late," she finished lamely.

Charlie turned away. John Brown died? He shook his head as he tried to take in the news. He didn't like Brown. Hell, nobody liked Brown, but he hadn't wished the man dead. His poor wife. He stared blankly at the wall, trying unaccountably and in vain to recall the last thing he had said to Brown, worrying now that he was dead, that he'd upset him, caused him any grief.

Cathy strode in through the double doors and called to him.

"One of those for me?" she asked smiling, indicating the mugs on the table. She saw the grim faces about her. Her eyes narrowed in curiosity. "What?"

*

Jimmy Donnelly the janitor hadn't been his usual self these last few days, thought Mickey Hughes. He caught sight of the old man as he passed by Mickey's CCTV room.

"Time for a cuppa?" he called out cheerfully.

With a sigh, the janitor nodded and sat down heavily in the one spare chair the small room allowed, his shoulders rounded and looking like he was carrying the weight of the world.

"You got something on your mind, Jimmy?"

The weary eyes stared at Hughes. "I'm thinking of retiring," he hesitantly confessed, "the jobs getting too much for me. I can't handle these new rules they've got. Don't say this and don't say that in case you offend somebody or other. I'm just finding it too difficult to change at my age."

Hughes limped over, handed him the mug and clapped a hand on his shoulder. "Look, why don't you think about that, you've been here longer than most of the cops, Jimmy. Don't worry too much about these new rules and regulations," he scoffed, "things are always changing, but good jannies are hard to find." Donnelly smiled at the compliment and, for a heartbeat almost got the whole thing off his chest. But his silence betrayed his fear. Dear God, he thought. If anything happens to that man Taylor, then I'm as guilty as that bastard Frank Brogan.

*

Irene Cavendish awoke with a start, a cramp in her neck resulting from having fallen asleep in the old fashioned winged armchair. With a shock she realised that today was the day. The bible lay heavily in her lap. She stroked the fake leather cover and placed in gently down on the side table beside the stone cold tea. Painfully, she pushed herself up onto her feet and shuffled over to the cheap-framed print of Jesus Christ, displaying His perfectly formed heart in His open chest, the light radiating from it and His benevolent smile indicating His willingness to forgive any wrongdoing. His hands were splayed wide open and exhibiting the raw wounds caused by the nails driven into His flesh. With a cheap plastic lighter, she lit the red candle on the bracket attached to the frame and painfully lowered herself to her knees, before the picture.

"Dear Lord," she earnestly began, "I don't know what my Frank has told Liam McPhee to do, but keep him safe and guide his hand in revenging my daughter Mary," then, almost as an afterthought, "and please forgive her for tempting poor Frank and making him do….that thing."

*

Those detectives who naively thought that DCI Nancy Rogers might be mourning the death of her acting Detective Inspector were rudely disappointed when she threw open the doors of the general office and strode in, her face flushed and a broad smile revealing her yellowing teeth.

"They caught the sex attacker last night," she announced.

The assembled detectives were stunned, amazed at her callousness. Any other time the news would have been greeted with a deep satisfaction, a relief that the culprit had been arrested and no other women would be victimised by him, but not today.

Today was reserved for John Brown. Granted, it was common knowledge that Brown had been a horrible bastard, but any expectation they had of a show of sorrow or grief were quickly dispelled by the huge grin of success on Rogers face.

"Where's Miller and Mulgrew?" she asked.

"Gone, ma'am," replied Carol McFarlane hesitantly, unsure if Charlie and Cathy's hurried rush from the office was anything to do with this fat cows presence.

Rogers' mood changed and she scowled at the younger woman. "Gone where?"

"No idea, ma'am," McFarlane shook her head. "Sergeant Mulgrew received a call on her mobile phone and they both hurried out. I did hear Charlie…Sergeant Miller I mean, say something about "Got the bastard," but I don't know what he meant."

*

Frank Brogan, showered, wearing clean clothes and seated at his dining table, rubbed hard at his forehead hard with the heels of his hands, but the nightmare persisted. He had stupidly told Irene last night, what he had done and it had returned to haunt him. No matter how he tried to justify it, he had shagged his niece. Shagged her? Christ, he'd got her pregnant!

He remembered the day it had happened, when he'd called to visit Irene and found Mary alone in the flat, home from school for lunch.

"She's at church, again," Mary had said, rolling her eyes to heaven. He'd watched her in the kitchen making him tea, complimented her on her looks, her nice legs; told her she was getting big and that he just wanted a wee cuddle. At least, to begin with. She'd pushed away from him when he'd tried to embrace her, running from him into the hallway, slamming her bedroom door in his face and trying to hold it closed. But he knew she wanted it. It was obvious, the way she dressed, tarting herself up with the short school skirt and tight blouse that showed her tit's off. He had to hold her down on her bed as she fought him and been surprised and taken aback by the strength of her resistance when he'd tore her clothes off. He hadn't expected her to cry and sob like a wee girl. When it was over, she had threatened to tell Irene. He'd offered her the money, all of fifty quid, but she'd thrown it back at him. But he told her that Irene would believe him… and Mary had believed that, known it to be true, for wasn't he the golden boy, his sisters favourite?

Her death in the fire had been a relief, the knowledge that his secret would be safe. No one would ever know. The detective's news about the pregnancy had been as much a shock to him as to Irene. He knew now in his heart that was why Mary had run, to get away from him and because of the pregnancy. Christ, what a mess. But they couldn't prove anything. Or could they, he wondered? He sipped at the strong coffee, spilling some over his shoes as his hand shook slightly.

Irene! I have to speak to Irene before I do anything else, he decided and find out exactly what I said. A faint glimmer of hope arose within him. Maybe I just rambled, he thought. Perhaps she couldn't make sense of what I told her. He decided he'd bluff her, tell her she was talking nonsense for, after all, didn't she always believe him?

He finished his coffee and for the first time, saw the Vectra car keys and Liam McPhee's note. With shaking hands he held the scrap of paper to the light and screwed his eyes, trying to bring the childish scrawl into focus. The words dispelled any doubt or misgivings he had.

Irene knew.

He crumpled the note in his fist, a wave of nausea once more sweeping through him.

And so did McPhee.

*

Charlie drove fast and with purpose. Today he would end it, make the bastard Brogan pay for the death of Mary Cavendish. Cathy cast a sideways glance at him and not without some admiration. What a difference there was in him compared to a short few days previously. And if her suspicions were correct, last night had definitely been a turning point in his life. Yes, she decided, there was definitely someone in his life, but figured that she'd wait till he told her, rather be nosey.

"Slow down there, cowboy," she chided, "Brogan won't be going anywhere. We've got him, Charlie. He can't deny the DNA evidence. He's the father of Mary's baby and we can prove from her birth certificate that she was only fourteen, so there will be a conviction. And he'll be placed on the Sex Offenders register, so it's a double whammy. You have him for the Sexual Offences Act and my lot can keep track of his whereabouts for the foreseeable future. We both win in this case."

"I know that Cathy, and you're right," he eased off on the accelerator, "don't want to get a speeding ticket do I? I'm too eager to get my hands on him and with a bit of luck, maybe he'll resist arrest," he wryly grinned.

The mood he's in, Brogan would be as well to come mousy quiet, Cathy thought with a sideways glance at the determined face of Charlie.

His mood became more sombre.

"Wonder how the mother will take the news," he turned to glance at her, then added spitefully, "Though, to be absolutely honest, I really don't care."

Barry Ashford drove the van with care along the rutted track and stopped at the appointed rendeavous. He was, as usual, early for the meeting. The radio scanner lying on the passenger seat and tuned to the police emergency channel stuttered into life, a distant voice deploying a unit to attend a road traffic accident in Duke Street in Glasgow city centre, but nothing yet regarding an explosion. The two minders, lying miserably in a gully thirty yards away and shivering in their Gortex camouflage suits, mutually cursed the snobby bastard in the van who had instructed they take yet more photographs.

*

The red haired Irish nurse bent over Father Flynn's bed and fluffed the pillows, while gently raising the old priest's head to make him more comfortable. "There now father," she spoke softly, "isn't that better?"
To her delighted surprise, the old man slowly opened his eyes and whispered, "And what's the chance of a wee cup of tea round here then, me dear?"

*

Sadie Forrest phoned to check on her daughter Geraldine and remind her mother to pack a lunch for the little girl. "Yes," said her mother, "she's fine and yes," she gently chastised Sadie, "even an old codger like me remembers that children have to eat. Would like a wee word with her, before I take her to school?"
To Sadie's surprise, the first thing Geraldine asked was is Charlie there and will she be seeing him today?
"Jellybean, he's left for work but I think that we might be seeing Charlie later. Maybe even every day, if we're very lucky," she smiled happily.

*

Frank Brogan had made a decision. He grabbed his car keys and headed downstairs towards his Vectra. He guessed that following his drinking the previous evening at the wake, he'd likely be over the limit, but he had to see Irene and the quicker he got it over with, the better he'd feel. Locking his front door, he noticed his hands still shook.

*

Across the city, the lawyer Steven Taylor decided that today he'd pay a visit to the Renfrew office, show face and begin to sow the seed of redundancy. Redundancy, he shook his head. My goodness, I'll be doing well if I manage this months salaries, he thought. He opened the front door and patted his jacket pocket, then remembered his Bentley keys were lying on the kitchen table beside the cleaning materials.

*

Barry Ashford spotted the hired car as it approached along the track towards him and gave a discreet nod to the hidden and prostrate minders. The radio scanner beside him continued with its calls, but not what he expected to hear. The car stopped abreast of his van and the driver rolled down the window.
"Good morning chum," he humourlessly greeted the driver.

"And how's about you, Barry," replied Liam McPhee with a broad smile on his face.

*

Just after nine o'clock, Charlie drove the CID car into the deserted street and parked the CID car in the only available spot, some thirty yards from the entrance to Brogan's tenement building. As he locked the car, he looked up and saw Brogan walking unsteadily towards a dark coloured Vectra.
"Mr Brogan!" he called out sharply, seeing him turn and hesitate at Charlie's shout, surprise and confusion fixed upon his drawn, pale face.

*

Steven Taylor locked his front door and, car keys in hand, walked to the Bentley then stopped. With a smile, he admired the graceful lines and sleek beauty. If only life was as straightforward and pleasurable, he sighed.

*

Frank Brogan was flabbergasted, instinctively aware that the bastard Miller knew! He knew about Mary! He panicked and ran for the car.
Charlie, with Cathy following some way behind, broke into a run, determined not to let him get away and covered the short distance in record time, his chest heaving with exertion and his legs aching from the uncommon exercise. He reached the Vectra just as Brogan, his eyes wide in shock, slammed and locked the driver's door, grinning inanely at the big man who pounded helplessly on the window.
"Get back to the car, Cathy!" he instructed, throwing her the keys, "the bastard's making a run for it!" as he frustratingly hammered at the window.

*

Steven Taylor unlocked the driver's door and stood for a few seconds, eyes half closed, as he took time to smell the polish that emanated from the leather seats, evoking memories of better days.

*

His hands shaking and trying to ignore the angry, distorted face and clenched fists of the madman pounding at his window, Brogan forcefully inserted the key into the ignition and turned it sharply, pressing down on the accelerator and hearing the cold engine burst into life with a loud roar. Charlie, knowing that he couldn't prevent Brogan from driving off, turned and ran for the CID car, seeing Cathy already seated behind the wheel and slamming the driver's door shut.

*

Steven Taylor inserted the key into the ignition and smoothly pulled at the old-fashioned ignition switch, gently probing with his foot at the accelerator and hearing with satisfaction the car purr into life.

*

Brogan watched as the big detective run down the street towards the CID car and anxiously revved the Vectra engine. Letting out the clutch too quickly, the car started forward with a lurch then stalled, causing Brogan to jerk forward, his chest banging against the unforgiving steering wheel.

Charlie, just five yards from the CID car, turned when he heard the roaring engine noise of the Vectra quit.

Underneath Frank Brogan's vehicle and attached to the metal undercarriage by the thin but powerful magnet, was the device contained within the video cassette case that had been painstakingly constructed by Eamon the postman and in the early hours of that morning attached to the Vectra by Liam McPhee. When he had placed and armed the device, McPhee had planned that Brogan would follow up on the note he had deviously left with the car keys and use the car to travel to meet with Irene. With luck, he figured the device would not detonate till Brogan hit the first of the many speed bumps that abounded the child safe area, but either forgot or didn't foresee that Brogan's one-year ban had created a lack of driving practice and that this unwittingly would assist McPhee in his plan.

When the Vectra jerked to a shuddering halt as it stalled, the small ball bearing in the plastic tube, the matchstick now removed, rolled smoothly forward and simultaneously struck both metal pinheads, causing a circuit to exist between them. The circuit complete, the electric charge from the small, nine-volt battery instantly travelled from the positive terminal, along the thin wiring, through the timer whose terminals had already touched and onwards into the detonator. Travelling through the detonator, the electric charge continued its route in an instant back to the negative terminal of the battery and thus, the sequence was complete. The electric cycle having occurred, the effect was deadly and almost instantaneous.

The detonation wave from the electrical detonator that ignited and exploded the Semtex created a rapid shock wave, travelling at almost 13,000 miles per hour. This shock wave travelling upwards pulverised the metal underside of the Vectra and caused the flooring under Brogan to buckle and contort. Simultaneously, as the shock wave travelled downwards it met the resisting tarmac of the road, creating a bounce effect that repelled the wave back into the flooring and substantially increased its magnitude against the metal underside of the car. The blast-wave that immediately follows the shock wave, however, travels much slower at some 600 miles per hour, and it is this that causes the structural and bone crushing damage. The blast-wave turned the already vulnerable metal flooring into fragmentation type shards of metal and lifted the vehicle some fourteen feet into the air, turning it onto its drivers side as it did so and depositing it some twenty feet from it's original parking space where it eventually came to rest against the wall of a nearby tenement building. Following on the heels of the blast wave is the fireball, which admittedly lasts just a micro second, but consumes anything combustible and is normally viewed as a blinding white or yellow flash.

And as for Frank Brogan, sitting unrestrained within the Vectra? At the point of detonation, Brogan had no time to consider what was happening, nor any time to request forgiveness from his God, for he was lifted bodily from his seat by the shock wave and violently crushed against the car roof where the top of his skull cracked open. Though still clinically alive at this point, the subsequent and instantaneous blast wave tore the metal flooring to hundreds of jagged shreds, which then cleaved through his body, ripping his legs from his torso, his right arm from it's socket and inflicting multiple wounds that the pathologist later decided were far too numerous to count. The vehicles handbrake was torn from its mounting and blown upwards. This item, the pathologist later contended, was responsible for severing Brogan's right arm just below the elbow and later discovered on the grassy knoll nearby, where it accompanied the arm as they flew through the car roof that had itself been torn asunder. The fireball, not to be outdone by its explosive cohorts, completed the damage to Brogan's flesh by burning off his body hair and charring his skin. The only positive aspect to this combination was that the fireball cauterised the gaping wounds where his legs once where. Regretfully, this primitive but savage first aid was of little use to a man already dead from shock and multiple injury.

*

Cathy was preparing to drive off in pursuit of Brogan and waving for Charlie to hurry and get his arse into the car, when the Vectra exploded. Her first awareness was that an invisible giant hand had suddenly scooped the car from the road and lifted it high into the air. The blinding flash beneath the vehicle seemed to occur as the Vectra windows exploded outwards and she watched in dumb fascination as the car was thrown against the building. In what she later described as almost slow motion, she observed with horror as the shock wave continued towards her and bodily lifted Charlie, throwing him into the air and across the bonnet of the CID car, crashing him against the windscreen and over the roof.
The windscreen cracked, but fortunately held together as her car buckled and writhed in the aftermath of the blast wave. Numbly gripping the steering wheel, she could only stare in fascination, as the Vectra's petrol tank decided enough was enough and exploded.
Spellbound, Cathy looked upwards as a huge and secondary fireball mushroomed into the air.

*

"So, Liam," began Barry Ashford, "you're quite certain that when you informed Manus Foley about Brogan's theft of the funds, he didn't suspect that you might be implicated in the theft nor of your," he hesitated to use the word collusion, "…association with us?"
McPhee stared hard at Ashford. Did the man think he was daft?
"I've already told you, Barry," he knew it annoyed the prick, using his Christian name, "Foley doesn't suspect a thing. As far as the Provo's is concerned, I've been doing a good job over here, for them. They sent me here to get me away from that dickhead that wanted to pop one into me head and also to keep an eye on Frank. They suspected he was pilfering the money, but they didn't know how to go about proving it. Sure, I took a cut, but I had me living expenses, didn't I? The paltry allowance they gave me for being over here," he spat in disgust, again knowing it would annoy the fastidious Ashford, "was of no use to man or beast. But that," he craftily added, "will now all be down to our Frank, for I took the liberty of

blagging his ledger when I dropped him off, last night. If they need written proof, I've got his book."

"And how difficult was it to persuade Foley to represent your request to the Army Council for executive action against Brogan?"

McPhee sighed. Hadn't they already been through all this on the phone?

"When I informed on Frank, Foley confided that with the peace initiative getting under way, the funds were starting to dry up from all over the place; London, Manchester, Liverpool, Birmingham and even the United States." He shook his head as though irritated at having to explain again what Ashford understood anyway. "Everyone knew the money that was raised was being used to re-arm the Provo's and according to Foley, nobody was that keen to fund another war." He paused, recalling the bitter conversation with the Provo's senior intelligence officer. "There was also a deep underlying suspicion that some of the fund-raisers were lining their own pockets, but it's not like a fucking bank account. The Council couldn't be asking for receipts, you know what I mean? Anyway, using the evidence that I provided him with, Foley was able to persuade the Council that an example should be made to keep the rest in line. When it goes off, the bomb will be headline news throughout the mainland. The rest of those fuckers will know why Frank copped it. Only the Prods will get the blame, so it won't affect the ongoing discussions with the Brit's. But the message will be clear to those who need reminding." He sniggered. "So there'll be no need for a warning letter for those boys, is there?"

"What about Brogan's sister, the one that wanted revenge?"

"That's the beauty of it," McPhee replied. "Frank thought the bomb that I had smuggled over was for some fucking lawyer that he'd discovered might be involved with his niece's death and ordered me to deal with it. Deal with it?" he snarled, "The bastard was good at ordering other men's death's, just wouldn't get his own dirty hands bloodied."

"Well," smiled Ashford at last, impatient to be gone from this wet and windy moor, "I think that's a job well done. I see no reason for you not to be accepted back into the fold, as it were and our continuous," he smiled again, "association, will reap rewards for us both. If my assessment should prove to be correct then your standing within the Provo's will be greatly enhanced by this action and you will be both invited to continue the fundraising here in Glasgow and welcomed back into the higher echelon meetings of the Council. All in all, my dear chap, an excellent result."

"And what about that little indiscretion back in Belfast?" McPhee reminded him, eager to have the underage sex offence purged for all time.

"All in good time, Liam, all in good time," while shrewdly aware that McPhee's indiscretion was now a side issue, no longer significant now that he had the photographic evidence of the big Belfast man collaborating with the Security Service.

"One final question, if you please. You don't think Brogan's sister might be a problem?"

"She lives high up in one of them multi storey flats in the Gallowgate," McPhee replied, "so if she does prove to be a problem," his voice now harsh and sinister, "then she'd better learn how to fucking fly."

The radio scanner beside Ashford burst into life, requesting all available units attend the report of a bomb blast in the Gallowgate area of Glasgow, adding the instruction that the first unit's in attendance update the control room immediately.

*

Charlie lay on his back, wondering how he had got there, his breathing laboured and rasping. Cathy's face appeared directly above him, her eyes tearstained and dabbing at his forehead with a bright, red handkerchief. But the hankie wasn't red. It was covered in blood, he saw. But who's bleeding? She was kneeling and speaking to him he knew, for he could see her lips moving, but there was no sound. He tried to sit up, but his body wouldn't respond. That's strange, he thought, and then slowly become aware he was seeing Cathy through only one eye. He tried to raise his arm, but that didn't seem to be working either. His head hurt and it was difficult to breathe.

A uniformed cop stood behind Cathy, bending over and staring down at him. Funny, his lips were moving too, but he wasn't saying anything. Or maybe, Charlie thought, I can't hear them. But why not and why is the cop looking at Charlie and shaking his head?

His body ached and he could smell smoke and it was getting dark. Very dark. "*Charlie!*" screamed Cathy. "*Hang on Charlie!*" she screamed again. "*Please hang on!*" she cried, tears running unchecked down her face, sobbing and oblivious to the two cops, who attempted to pull her upright and away from the bleeding mess that was Detective Sergeant Charlie Miller.

*

Sadie Forrest was running a bath and listening to the Radio Clyde morning show when the programme was interrupted by the report of a bomb blast in the Gallowgate area of Glasgow. She stood still, a hollow feeling in the pit of her stomach as the broadcaster excitedly relayed the information, scant though it was. Though she'd never seen nor heard one before, Cathy figured a bomb blast must make an incredible noise and decided to phone her mother, ask if she'd heard been able to hear anything from where she lived? As she dialled the number, her hand shook slightly. Charlie was going after Frank Brogan today, but surely that couldn't be connected. A sudden apprehensive fear seized her. With a start she remembered what Brogan did, who he was connected with. Or could it?

Dear God, she prayed, please let Charlie be safe.

*

The noise of the bomb had reverberated around the Gallowgate area. The pall of smoke that resulted from the explosion climbed lazily into the air and billowed wide, spreading like some giant black balloon and filling the surrounding streets with the acrid smell of burning rubber from the petrol fuelled flaming tyres. From her balcony, Irene Cavendish looked down onto the rooftops of the tenement buildings, seeing the flash of blue lights in the murky gloom and hearing the faint urgency of two-tone sirens. She smiled. Her Frank and Liam McPhee hadn't let her down. The man that had killed her daughter was taken care of. Funny though, that he should live so close to where Frank had his flat.

*

Cathy Mulgrew, wrapped in a pale blue blanket, sat on the bench seat in the rear of an ambulance and watched detachedly through the open doors as the two fire crews fought and slowly overcome the petrol inferno blazing from the twisted metal wreck which had been Frank Brogan's Vauxhall Vectra. The twenty or so police officers engaged in evacuating the tenement buildings adjacent to the scene, once assured she was uninjured, had decided to leave her alone and in the care of the ambulance crew standing close by, who kept a discreet watch over the shocked detective, ready to render assistance and grateful they weren't being called upon to provide first aid to the poor bastard in the car. Or what was left of him. And as for the detective taken away in the other ambulance? Well, that was anyone's guess, but some had seen the ambulance men shaking their heads.

Chapter 19 – Sunday morning

The closed door meeting that was formally convened in the fifth floor conference suite at Police Headquarters, two days after the bomb blast in the Gallowgate area of the City of Glasgow was attended by the Chief Constable, his Assistant Chief Constable in charge of crime, the Fire and Rescue Brigade Fire Master, the Senior Forensic Scientist who functioned for both the police and the brigade, DCI Martin Cairney of the Counter Terrorism Unit and Mister Barry Ashford of the Security Service, whom Cairney had previously informed his Chief was fortuitously in the City on an unrelated matter. No minutes were taken at the meeting. As an unprecedented favour, the Chief graciously extended Ashford the privilege of smoking, but immediately regretted that decision when he produced his foul smelling French cigarettes.

"To business, gentlemen," the Chief began. "You have before you a summary of the incident that occurred," he indicated the buff coloured folders on the massive polished desk, "and that includes some photographs taken at the aftermath of the scene, spread out here," indicating a montage of coloured prints, lying loosely on the table top. "Perhaps you'd like to start, Jim?" he turned to the Fire Master.

"Thanks. Yes, well, as you'll be aware my boys attended the call that what was initially described as a bomb blast, though invariably these things usually turn out to be petrol tanks going up, igniting through some shoddy sort of DIY, that kind of thing," he explained. "Upon their arrival, they discovered the vehicle had apparently been subjected to some sort of massive explosion and the occupant," he indicated the photograph in front of him, his revulsion of the injuries evident, "did not survive."

Not surprised Brogan didn't survive, thought the Chief privately, grimacing at the memory of what he had viewed in the city mortuary. The Fire Master continued.

"Some minor blast and fire damage was also dealt with and I understand Glasgow

District Council is currently assessing the structural damage to the nearby buildings. We were lucky, damned lucky in my opinion, that the timing was such it was just after the schools were in and there was no school kids out and about on the streets." He shook his head and added, "And as for the police officer? Well, that was unfortunate. My Fire Investigation Team," reported the Fire Master, "made a preliminary analysis of the wreckage and have tentatively concluded, subject to your findings," he nodded to the scientist, "that the vehicle had been either conveying or fitted with some sort of improvised explosive device. To the underside," he added unnecessarily, sitting back and reluctant to say more and wondering what the fuck the MI5 guy with the foul smelling tobacco was doing at the meeting.

"Sandy?" said the Chief Constable to his scientist.

The tall, grey haired man with the bi-focal specs perched on the tip of his sharp nose shuffled some papers he had brought and noisily cleared his throat, noticeably unused to this type of high-level meeting and obviously ill at ease. "Ahem, Mr Ashford here," using the papers to point to the smoke engulfed agent, "was kind enough to arrange some data that has been sent from his office in London. Comparison with that data and evidential samples discovered at the scene indicate the explosive used in the construction of the…" he hesitated, glancing at the Security Service man who gave the slightest of nods, but not so discreet as failed to be noticed by Cairney, "ahem… of the bomb seem to indicate a match with a batch of Czechoslovakian manufactured Semtex that was earlier used by the Loyalist terrorist group, the Ulster Volunteer Force back in the late-eighties. My team have assessed the device was contained within a rectangular plastic box; probably a video cassette case it seems and calculated it contained approximately half a kilo of Semtex. It seems, therefore, there is little doubt that the Semtex and the manner of the construction of the IED are consistent with that used by the UVF."

He sat back, relieved his contribution to the proceedings was over and pleased that he had related the information exactly as Ashford had instructed.

"So there's no dubiety about the manufacture?" asked Cairney, whose question took him by surprise.

"Ahem, no, none at all," he stuttered, "at least, not according to the information I have." He swallowed hard, anxious not to look at the Security Service agent.

Cairney suspected a fit up, but how to go about proving it? No doubt in my mind, he sighed to himself, the Prof's been got at.

"And the deceased, Martin?" the Chief turned to his CTU officer, "what can you tell us about him. Without revealing too many secrets, of course," he smiled at his little joke, but Cairney detected a subtle warning in the invite.

"Recorded by us as an Irish republican supporter and actively engaged locally in raising funds. No known history of violence and nothing to previously suggest he was the target for an assassination plot. But we're working on our sources and still have several people to speak with." He didn't add that the CTU had thoroughly penetrated the local Loyalist organisations and though of course they had known

Frank Brogan as a leading republican, nobody had a fucking clue who topped him nor who locally had the technical wizardry to construct such a device. "In short, we're still making inquiry," he finished lamely, cursing at the presence of Ashford who seemed to be smirking behind his cloud of smoke.

"Mister Ashford, do you wish to make any comment?" inquired the Chief.

Lazily and for effect, he ground his fag end into the glass ashtray and reached into the packet for a replacement.

"I'm sure it's not necessary, but I am obliged to remind you gentlemen that we are all," he waved his hand at the others, "bound by the restrictions imposed upon us by the Official Secrets Act?" He paused to wait for the nodding of heads acknowledging his statement.

The Chief bristled. He also had spotted the cautious signal between Ashford and the scientist and recalled Cairney's hasty warning prior to the meeting. The little shit was contriving to cover up something. But not in his Force, he vowed, Official bloody Secrets or not!

"Please continue, Mister Ashford," his voice calm, but the warning clear and unmistaken.

"Yes quite, Chief Constable. As you gentlemen are so obviously aware, the current peace talks in the Province and London are progressing as expected and Her Majesty's Government, whom of course we all serve," he guffawed at his own humour, though the joke was lost on the rest, "have decided that this unpleasant incident should perhaps be accredited to an electrical fault and subsequent detonation of the vehicles petrol tank, which was of course full at the material time. I am assured by our experts that such an amount of petrol, ignited in a confined space such as the metal tank, would result in a similar type of damage as that experienced by the vehicle and the unfortunate Mister Brogan."

He sat back, a half smile on his face as a stunned silence descended on the group. The Chief stared at him with an incredulous expression upon his face.

"Are you suggesting that we cover up a fucking bomb blast in the middle of my city?"

"Balls to that," interrupted the Fire Master, as he began to rise to his feet, "I'm having no part of this."

"Please sit down, sir," demanded Ashford firmly, his eyes levelled at the Fire Master and the instruction evident in his hissing voice. He turned to the Chief Constable, his hand raised to cut off any indignant protest. "I'm sorry," he began, "but the matter is not open to negotiation. If you should require clarification," he raised his hand again to prevent any interruption and repeated, "if you should require clarification on this issue, then allow me to provide you with the phone number of a highly placed and very senior Government Minister who will indubitably confirm the….request."

His voice mellowed, as he light his cigarette and allowed the warning to sink in. "Gentlemen, gentlemen," he continued "it's not for me to instruct you in your chosen disciplines and I appreciate you will have misgivings about the," he hesitated, searching for the word that wouldn't commence an argument, "proposal, but my masters at Whitehall have viewed this carefully and decided that for the overall good, the peace talks must have primacy. Therefore, any suggestion that the republican's are being targeted by Loyalist's might in turn lead to questions of Government complicity with the Prods and could jeopardise the success of the negotiations. I'm sure you can see that, can't you? And besides," he added, "we don't want any backlash amongst the local tribes, do we?"

He sat back, pleased that his inference of an escalation in the religiously divided city had prompted a sharp glance between the Chief Constable and the CTU man, Martin bloody Cairney.

"So, Mister Ashford," questioned the Chief, his eyes narrowing as he stared with open hostility at the cunning bastard, "'how do you propose we satisfy an enraged, frightened public and a curious media that it was a petrol tank and not a bomb?"

"Why Chief Constable," he smiled wickedly, "you have a very adept and professional Press Office, don't you?"

*

The Chief Constable shook hands with the Fire Master, as he departed through the main door of Headquarters and turned to his ACC in charge of crime, shaking his head slowly as they walked back to his office.

"What a piece of work that Ashford is," he said, the bitterness evident in his voice.

"Your hands are tied boss," replied the ACC, "there's not much we can do if Whitehall are for this nonsense. Not if we're going to get the extra funding in this years budget," he added. "You know how these things work. Toe the line, or else."

The Chief rubbed a hand through his wiry hair, knowing his younger colleague was right but still hating the Machiavellian politics that came with the job.

"Sometimes," he said bitterly, "I wish I was still a copper and not a bloody politician."

They stood together at the entrance to the command suite corridor, both raging at the complicity in which they were bound to collude.

"You asked about DS Miller?" the ACC reminded him, keen to get his Chief out of this morose mood he'd settled into.

"Oh, yeah, of course. I popped by the hospital yesterday evening on my way home, but no change. He was still unconscious and hooked up to those infernal machines. So, what's the latest?"

"Unfortunately still no change. I spoke with the Neuro surgeon attending him. Seems like a good bloke. Told me that the physical injuries will heal in time and he'll get along fine without his spleen. The cuts and bruises from the bits of the vehicle that tore into him can be treated, though he'll be left with a few nasty scars on his body and that includes a three inch one on his left cheek and I'm not talking about his arse," he said humourlessly, then added seriously, "apparently he was lucky. The tear in his cheek stopped just short of his eye. No, the main concern is the blow to the head that he received when he landed on the ground, after he got blown over the top of the CID car. The doc told me that apart from a superficial wound to the scalp, their CAT scan shows no apparent damage to the brain, but he did land on the back of his head which they tell me is the most vulnerable place to damage. Let me check this," he pulled out a small pocket notebook and began to quote the doctor, "Miller's eyes responded to light, the pupils were not fixed or dilated, which seems to indicate no pressure on the brain." He looked up at the Chief. "And that's a good thing, they tell me. "Really," he added as he shrugged his shoulders, "it's a waiting game now."

"Remind me, what's the situation regarding family?"

"Miller's a widower, wife and young son tragically killed a few years ago, but there was a young policewoman visiting when I called by. She seemed quite upset, so I didn't get much out of her. Oh, and his partner at the time DS Cathy Mulgrew. She's been off the last couple of days with shock, but due back to work tomorrow. Martin Cairney's her boss, so he'll be keeping his eye on her."

The Chief stared at his ACC, puzzled. "So DS Mulgrew, she's CTU?"

"Aye sir, it seems they were working together from the start of Miller's fire inquiry and stuck together to arrest Brogan. You might also be interested to know that they two are the pair that was instrumental in solving DCI Mitchell's murder, over in Govan. Turns out the there was a tenuous link between the two cases. Colin Mitchell was raving about them, seems they made quite a team."

"Is that right? So, they got two results did they?"

"Two and a half, actually," replied the ACC, a slow grin on his face. "I got a phone call from an old pal of mine from our time on the beat as probationary cops. Guy called Mickey Hughes who ended up as a traffic motorcyclist before he came a cropper and lost a bit of his leg. Mickey works at the Central Division now as a civilian CCTV supervisor. According to Mickey, he thought I should know that Charlie Miller got him to run through some DVD footage and pulled a picture from it that he had photographed. Guess who featured in the photo?"

The Chief stared in surprise, then a dawning realisation. "Not that bastard they've locked up for the sex attacks!"

"The very one," grinned the ACC.

"But I thought Nancy Rogers was claiming credit for that arrest?"

"Yeah," the ACC smirked, his mouth twisted in obvious anger. "I'd been told that as well. Seems that all we're hearing isn't quite the truth, is it?"

"Well, well, well. So this DS Miller has turned out to be a bit of a dark horse, hasn't he?" The Chief rubbed his chin reflectively, impressed by what he was hearing. "Get on to personnel. Pull Miller's personal file," then almost as an afterthought, "DS Mulgrew's as well. Could be we've found the first pair of our Detective Inspectors we're short of."

Aye, thought the ACC, but maybe just one though, depending if Miller lives.

*

DCI Martin Cairney invited Barry Ashford to take a seat.

"Coffee?"

"White, two sugar please," Ashford nodded, outwardly calm but tensely awaiting the indignant outburst that he knew was boiling within Cairney, waiting to explode. He watched him fill the two mugs from the cheap, stained kettle.

"Okay, now that there is just the two of us here Barry. Anything you'd like to tell me?"

Ashford sipped at his coffee, wondering how much the big guy suspected.

"Nothing that is going to be of any use to you locally Martin," he shook his head. "To our regret, the death of our agent Frank Brogan will cause us immeasurable difficulty both here and in the Province. Alas," he attempted some brevity, eager to be done with this conversation, "the well has now dried up."

Cairney stared at him, not sure if he believed all he was hearing. "So in short terms you are telling me, admitting at last that in my area and without my knowledge, the Security Service was running Frank Brogan as a bona fide agent against the Provo's?"

"Now that he's dead, there's little point in concealing the issue, Martin. Is there?" Cairney sighed with resignation. He just couldn't believe anything this prick told him.

"You knew I'd an officer in the field, working against him, didn't you?"

Careful, thought Ashford. "Yes. He told me that your officer, Miss Mulgrew and her colleague had visited him and his sister after the death of his niece. But of course, he was hardly likely to admit he was working for us, was he now?"

"Something stinks here Barry and I don't quite believe you're telling me the whole truth now, are you?"

Ashford carefully placed the half full mug on the desk in front of him and stood in preparation to leave this smutty little place and its small-minded people. His mouth smiled while his eyes remained fixed and staring, the smile of the assassin. "That's the name of the game, old boy. Need to know. Isn't it, now?"

Chapter 20

Everything is white. Well, not quite all the same colour of white, if indeed white has a colour, but different shades of whiteness. There's a round white object, well not quite round but near enough round, bobbing about disturbing the background of brilliant whiteness. Not quite white, but slightly darker than the whiteness surrounding it. The object, can't quite make it out, it has a bleached whiteness on top of it. It won't stay still, keeps coming forwards, then backwards, then forwards, then…. Bloody stay still, won't you?

The object has returned to annoy me. I'm sure it is the same object as before, with the same whiter top. Funny, this time it seems to have something in the round object, something that breaks up its smoothness. I can't quite make it out. Ah well. Who really cares anyway? What the fuck have I done to deserve this thing coming again to annoy me? Wait! It seems to be a bit clearer, this time. Yes! its definitely a bit….

"Charlie? Charlie? Can you hear me son?"

The object's dancing in front of me again and it knows my name. How does it know my name?

"Are you there, Charlie Miller?"

The voice, I know that voice. Where have I heard that voice before? It's hard to open my eyes, I can't stop them flickering. There's a sudden stabbing pain from the brightness, some kind of light above me, shining brightly at me. Please, please, turn the light down.

Wait, I see it now. The object is a face, pale and framed by a bandage wrapped about its head with a tuft of grey hair peeking out from under it. I'm sure I know that voice!

"Thanks be to God!" says Father Jim Flynn, his voice breaking with a sob. "You've come back to us, son. Thank God!"

*

"Fifteen days?" Charlie gasped, "I've been out for fifteen whole days?"

Cathy Mulgrew smiled at him as she popped another of his grapes into her mouth. Dressed in an emerald green frock with her red hair tied back, Charlie thought she looked stunning, like a young Hollywood starlet.

"The doctor told me that aside from your injuries, you needed the rest. Seems your system was badly run down and your tolerance was at an all time low. Now," she asked, her eyes twinkling, "how could that have happened?"

Her friend stood at the foot of the bed, nervously twiddling with the row of pearls about her neck.

"This is Jo," Cathy introduced her, then with a little hesitation, "my partner."

Charlie stared at Jo who was a Wow! Factor of ten, he thought with her fair hair fashionably cut in a modern choppy bob and similarly dressed in a pale blue two-piece top and skirt.

"Partner as in…?"

Cathy stared at him, her eyes piercingly green and daring him to be homophobic. "Partner as in…together," she announced, her head tilting slightly as she carefully watched for his reaction. With a start, though she didn't know why, she suddenly realised it was important to her that she had his approval.

A slow smile spread across his face. "Well, I'm very pleased to meet you Jo," he told the now smiling young woman, "and I know now why Cathy didn't fancy me," he pulled a face or as much as the bandages allowed, "you're far prettier than me. Though," he added with a grin, "it's obviously a close run thing."

Cathy, her throat swelling with emotion, reached out and gently took his hand. "You don't need me," she mocked, "you've already got two women in your life, Charlie Miller."

She nodded towards his bedside unit.

"What?" he asked, his one unbandaged eye quizzing her.

She reached out and fetched down Cracker the bear, a plaster stuck to the left side of its face as it stared forlornly at Charlie from its one remaining eye.

"Snap," she grinned at him. "Jellybean and I have become good friends, since you decided to come in here for a break," she told him. "Jo and I have eaten more McDonalds than is good for our figures, these last few days, haven't we sweetheart?"

Jo nodded then replied in a soft, almost whispered voice, "I'll just pop out for a cuppa, let you two catch up," and quietly closed the door to the private room behind her.

"You've met Sadie?"

Cathy nodded. "She seems very nice. We, that is Jo, Sadie and I, have been for a drink and Jo and I have looked after Jellybean the odd night, when Sadie's been manning your bedside, listening to you grunting, farting and snoring, though not always in that order."

He grinned at her, wincing slightly as the bandage around his face and head tightened. Cathy looked at him with concern.

"You okay?"

"I will be when I get this lot off. The doctor was in earlier, gave me a run down on what my injuries were. Said I was damned lucky not to lose my eye, amongst other things. Didn't mention though, how long I'd been comatose. Bloody hell, fifteen days, eh?" he repeated.

Charlie sighed in wonder. Why then, after all that sleep, did he feel knackered?

"The doc told me that there had been some concern about brain damage, but then realised they were looking in the wrong place. It was in my arse," he grinned at her.

"You have had quite a few visitors," she reminded him. "The old priest, Father Flynn, he's along the ward in another room, but I understand he's due to be discharged, soon. Bullied some young Irish nurse to wheel him along here morning and afternoon to visit with you. Apparently he spent most of the time talking to you, though you were unconscious. Something about hearing being the last thing to go. Never gave up on you, just like Sadie."

Then, almost as an afterthought, "Oh and he slipped and fell. That's how he cracked his head. Nothing to do with Brogan after all, his injury was a simple accident."

She paused and stared at him, her eyes moist and gripped his hand tight. "You gave us an awful fright, Charlie. I…we I mean, we…anyway. You're getting better and that's the main thing."

He was touched by her kindness and kept hold of her hand, squeezing it gently. Cathy Mulgrew had proven to be a real friend, one he was determined to keep.

"So, tell me what's been happening?"

She took a deep breath to recover her composure. God, this man had some effect on people, she thought. She bit her lip, wondering how he would react to this.

"First thing is that the bomb wasn't a bomb."

He stared at her in some confusion.

"I can't go into details here," she interrupted his protest, "but when you get out, we'll sit down and I'll tell you the whole story. The *real* story," she emphasised.

"Anyway, as you'll have guessed, Brogan didn't survive, so the inquiry regarding him being Mary's father is academic, though I understand the word got round your office. Seems the paperwork followed the phone call and, with you being off, it was opened and read by quite a few so it's in the public domain now." She paused for breath, letting the information sweep across him. "And as for Brogan? Well, they found most of him in the car, a leg in the Gallowgate, a couple of bits in London Road, a bit in..." she watched his face.

He smiled, realising she was pulling his leg.

"Anyway," she finished, "he was buried a couple of days ago, but word got round about his shenanigans with his niece, so the funeral was poorly attended."

She didn't add that according to reports, Irene Cavendish, some ghoulish parishioners and the media were the only mourners. He lay back, staring at the ceiling. He couldn't fully remember the explosion, it wasn't totally clear yet, but in good time, he thought, in good time.

"Moving on," Cathy continued, "Thomas Frobisher has been fully committed for trial. Seems he gave an excellent account on tape of the murder, hoping for a plea bargain by cooperating with us. The bosses are pleased it was quickly solved. Saved a few bob on overtime," she cynically added. "Oh and there is some good news for his former partner, Steven Taylor, on that front. Seems Frobisher banked most of the money he stole and again in the spirit of cooperation, he's offered restitution, so his partner might have a good opportunity to have it seized by the court and returned to the firm, but that could be a long process so it's anyone's guess if his firm will survive the scandal anyway." She paused while Charlie absorbed this information and saw him nod to go on. "Nancy Rogers has retired."

He turned slightly to stare at her, flinching at some discomfort, his good eye opening wide with astonishment.

"The official line is that her doctor has recommended early retirement due to a severe asthmatic problem, but the word is that she set herself up for taking the credit for the capture of the sex attacker, the guy that you…okay, we," she blushed, "tentatively identified from the photograph in the lane. Seems she's pissed off more people that even we had given her credit for and that," her voice dropped to a whisper, "included the Chief." She raised her voice to its normal pitch and added, "Anyway, she's gone. So that's that," she declared with some finality.

"So who caught the sex attacker?"

Cathy smiled, clearly enjoying the role of narrator. "Therein lies a story. You remember our old friend Aileen Dee?"

Charlie nodded, eager to hear the story.

"Appears she almost nightly tours the drag area, speaking to the younger girls, counselling them and giving out free condoms, that sort of thing. Well, turns out she was passing a lane and caught the guy attacking a slip of a girl that he'd force to the ground. He'd belted her one and had his trousers down round his knees, just about to…"

"I can guess," interrupted Charlie, "go on."

"Anyway, he was so intent on what he was doing he didn't realise that Dee was behind him. You recall of course how big she is?"

Charlie nodded again.

"Suffice to say he didn't get the opportunity to run anywhere with his trousers and underpants round his ankles, so when the cops arrived he was on the ground, broken nose," she shut her eyes, trying to recall exactly what injuries the attacker suffered, "Severely, and I mean severely," she emphasised with a grin, "swollen testicles and penis, no teeth left to speak of, bald patches, crushed fingers and various bite and scratch marks," she beamed at him.

Charlie gave an involuntarily shudder, imagining what it must be like to have someone the size of Aileen Dee dance about on your willie.

"And the girl he was assaulting?"

"Banged about, but okay and now being taught the errors of her way by big Aileen. The media latched onto it and she's being hailed a hero. Women's aid groups are flocking to support her drop-in centre and she's getting a lot of financial backing now, I hear. Thought Jo and I might drop by, some time," she added, slightly embarrassed and not knowing why. "The guy, it turns out, was a butcher to trade and used to work in Motherwell somewhere. I heard that John Brown had got that information and had been out there looking for him. Last thing he'd done, apparently. One other thing, Charlie," she stared at him. "They found a photograph in your coat pocket, a picture of Mary Cavendish. They gave it to me, thought it might be relevant, part of the inquiry like."

She hesitated, unsure if she'd done the right thing.

"I burned it. I didn't think you needed it anymore."

He squeezed her hand and simply replied, "Thanks."

The door knocked softly and opened. An anxious face peeked round.

"Sadie!" Charlie called.

She pushed open the door and strolled in. She had obviously come straight from work, a light blue jacket on top of her uniform shirt and trousers; her fair hair tied in a ponytail and held by a checked black and white bobble. She'd been determined to be casual, be cheerful and not to cry, but her emotions let her down and the tears flowed when she saw him awake. Her lips trembled and she put a hand to her mouth, stifling the sobs.

"Right," said Cathy, "I'll let you two have some time together. See you later, Detective Inspector," she grinned at him.

He tore his gaze from Sadie and looked curiously at Cathy.

"But that's not for me to disclose," she winked at Sadie, gave her a brief hug and left the room.

Sadie stood looking at him for a few seconds, weeping freely, then gave in and threw herself on him, kissing his face, bandage and all.

Charlie was in pain and it didn't help having Sadie lying across the top of him, but it was worth it to hold her, feel her against him, knowing she loved him and that he loved her. He closed his eyes as she lay against him and he knew that things could only get better.

*

Irene Cavendish stood motionless in the cold, windy balcony of her high rise flat, her hands gripping the railing and leaning hard on the metal bar that pressed against her flat bosom, her cup of tea, now frozen and lying untouched on the cheap plastic garden table beside the heavy bible. She stared down at the destruction far below that was the empty car park. The wind tore at her hair and loosened it from its restraining clips, but she didn't notice, didn't care. She couldn't understand why her world had come crashing down about her. As for the death of Mary, well, she could cope with that. She'd even enjoyed the solicitudes of her fellow parishioners, piously tell them her wee girl was now an angel in heaven and was Irene's contribution to our Father's house. But poor Frank, she would even manage to get over that, for hadn't she always? But the horrible things they were saying about him, the vicious gossip about what he was supposed to have done to Mary. How did these rumours get around? Who would say such things about a kind and decent man who only wanted to help people and stand up for the Cause, for the Movement?

"Why would these people," she snarled aloud, "tell such lies about Frank?"

She knew she couldn't return to church, wouldn't return. No more cleaning and flower arranging as she had always done. That would teach them! They'd stared at her, whispered behind her back. Sneered and told their lies. Her anger overcame her grief. And where were his so called friends when she was burying poor Frank, she spat? Where was Liam McPhee? Her mouth turned down in disgust. This is all Mary's fault, with her cheap makeup and high and mighty ideas. If only she'd listened to me, her mother. If only she'd paid more attention to the holy book. If only…her shoulders stooped.

A tear escaped her eye. She dragged the plastic chair over to her. Tugging at her skirt, she lifted her right leg and stepped onto the chair.

7121441R00118

Printed in Great Britain
by Amazon.co.uk, Ltd.,
Marston Gate.